TRIPLE
JEOPARDY

TRIPLE JEOPARDY

CHRISTOPHER LOWERY

Urbane
PUBLICATIONS

urbanepublications.com

First published in Great Britain in 2021 by Urbane Publications Ltd
Unit E3 The Premier Centre Abbey Park Romsey SO51 9DG
Copyright © Christopher Lowery, 2021

A CIP catalogue record for this book is available from the British Library.

ISBN 978-1-912666-95-9
MOBI 978-1-912666-96-6

Design and Typeset by Michelle Morgan

Cover by Michelle Morgan

Printed and bound by 4edge UK

URBANE
urbanepublications.com

To my amazing, long-suffering wife, Marjorie,
still at my side after all these years.

Revenge is a dish best served cold.

Old proverb.

PREFACE

Santa Monica, California

May, 2019

Ricardo Menendez's iPhone alarm awakened him at 6:30 am. In fact, he'd been unable to sleep for most of the night and only fallen into a light doze around 4:00. By 7:30 he had shaved and showered, dressing in his dark blue suit with a red tie. Despite his Spanish origins, Ricardo was a conservative dresser, like everything else he did in life, he didn't like taking risks, not usually anyway. That was why he wasn't married. He had gone out with some good-looking girls in college and afterwards, but the consensus seemed to be that he was an unadventurous bore and no girl in her right mind wanted to spend her life being bored.

He looked around the apartment then picked up a letter from the table, folded it and placed it in an envelope, torn open along the top, that already contained several other items of correspondence. He'd re-read the letter a couple of times while he was getting ready and it was now covered with notes in his untidy scrawl. He put the envelope into the inside pocket of his jacket. Menendez took his wallet, driver's licence and car keys from the bureau in the hall then opened the bottom drawer, took an item out and shoved it into the other inside jacket pocket. In the mirror he saw the bulge and transferred it to the side pocket. Lastly, he picked up a stamped, addressed envelope, keeping it safe in his hand, and walked out through the office.

He locked the door behind him, ensuring that the 'CLOSED' sign was visible behind the glass panel. His Ford was in front of the building and at 8:00 he parked it at the diner on the corner of Overland and Regent Street. He checked the address and the stamps on the envelope, kissed the seal and pushed it into the nearby post box, then entered the café. The teenage waitress dumped a mug of coffee in front of him and went to the kitchen with his order. Menendez glanced around at the other customers in the café; they were all eating, reading newspapers or looking at phones and he gazed out the window at the park on the other side of the street.

It was a bright, clear morning, already warm, and several dog owners were walking their pets around the park. He regretted that he'd never owned a pet. Not a cat, they were far too independent and sure of themselves. A small to medium sized dog would have been good company for him and he would have enjoyed looking after it. He was a very tidy and well organised man and apart from this last experience his life had been without any major disruptions. A dog would probably have enjoyed the stability and routine he'd established.

The girl came back with his eggs, bacon and pancakes and he poured a generous dose of syrup over the meal then devoured it greedily, feeling hungrier than he had for some time. He pushed the empty plate aside and put his glasses on, sitting with another mug of coffee, checking the items in the envelope and reading the letter one more time. He could have recited the contents from memory, so many times had he gone through it word for word, looking for some meaning that might have escaped him, but there was none and even if there had been he knew it would make no difference in the end.

At eight-forty Ricardo climbed back into his car and drove the ten-minute trip along the Santa Monica Freeway to downtown LA and parked under the bank building. It was a huge skyscraper, thirty stories or more, and the Small & Medium Business Department was on the twelfth to fifteenth floors. The woman at the reception desk looked at his driver's licence and called up to confirm his appointment with Joe Cunningham, the Department Head. He received a name tag to clip on the lapel of his jacket then went through the security gate and rode the elevator up to the fifteenth floor, walked along to the door marked, *Joseph Cunningham, S&M Managing Director, SouthWest.*

'Good morning, Joe. Thanks for seeing me.' He shook hands with the tall black man and sat opposite him in an uncomfortable metal chair with a lattice back. There was a dossier in front of the banker, but it was upside down and he couldn't read the title on it without his glasses. He'd met Cunningham on a number of occasions over the last several years, but this was the first time since he'd returned from his trip. The previous discussions had been by telephone and email until he'd received the letter two days ago and called to make this appointment.

'So, what's this all about, Ricky?' The man looked at his watch as if he didn't have much time to spare. Although there was a coffee mug in front of him, he didn't offer any.

He didn't much like people shortening his name like that, but decided to ignore it, in the circumstances. 'Well,

I figured you'd guess. It's about this letter of course.' He took the envelope from his jacket pocket and laid the open letter and a bank statement on the desk.

'I already explained on the telephone, Ricky. I thought you'd be really happy that we're refunding the entire amount, but you don't look too happy. What's the problem?'

'No, I mean, yes, thanks, that's very correct of you and I appreciate it, but it's not as simple as that.'

'I'm not sure I understand. What more can we do than that?'

Ricardo placed his spectacles on his nose and looked down at his scribbled notes. He cleared his throat and picked up the statement. 'There was a hundred fifty-seven thousand dollars in my company account when I left for my hiking trip five weeks ago. Last week when I got back I checked my account and it was almost empty. There was only twelve hundred forty dollars left in it. In the meantime, while I was away there was another hundred thousand or so that came in from clients. So, some scam artist has siphoned off almost two hundred fifty thousand of my hard-earned business cash while nobody in your bank was paying attention.'

The banker moved uncomfortably in his chair. 'We're all aware of the problem. There was a security breach in our Internet Banking Network and somebody hacked into about a hundred thousand of the business accounts at this branch. That's public knowledge. We announced the breach as soon as it was discovered, we fixed it and it won't happen again. What's just as important is that we've got insurance cover for this kind of sting. We're reimbursing every single dime of the money that was stolen from about twelve thousand customers. No questions asked, we just check the claims and the insurance pays out. There's not many banks would have acted so transparently and quickly, and we've had a lot of customers calling to thank us for being so upfront and proactive.'

Ignoring the comment, Ricardo said, 'Look at these transactions, Joe.' Then, reading from the statement, 'A week after I left, a first payment of five thousand dollars to *High Income Mortgage Fund of Chile*, followed by another seventy-five grand. Then *First Buenos Aires Real Estate Partners*, same procedure, one small payment then a bigger one, eighty thousand. The third rip-off was the same, *Mexican Growth Ventures*, exactly eighty-five thousand dollars. Sum total, two hundred and forty-five grand, stolen from my account under your noses, all by some scam artist touting non-existent Latino investments. Wait!' He interrupted the banker as he started to respond. 'Do you really think I would invest almost a quarter of a million dollars into three crap funds in South America, or anywhere else for that matter? You've known me for over fifteen years. You know I don't take chances like that with my money. What in hell where you thinking?'

'Ricky, I never even saw those transactions. Everything's automated now, you know that. An order comes in and it gets processed by the system and the system broke. Even if I'd seen them, I would probably have thought you were making plans for your retirement, maybe going down to Mexico or somewhere, know what I mean?'

There was no response from Menendez, just a blank stare, and he went on, 'I'm sorry that it happened but you'll be fully reimbursed within the month, so there's no harm done. What more can I do?'

'I already told you Joe. It's not as simple as that.' He picked up the letter and consulted the notes he'd written on it, the other man waiting silently.

'Before I left for Europe, I mailed about twenty cheques to be presented for payment on different dates during the month while I was away. All together about two hundred grand, including three big payments. I'm a one-man business, nobody to look after the shop while I'm away, so I do this every year and it's always worked out fine. But not this last time. Apart from a couple of small items all of the cheques were returned unpaid, which of course I didn't find out about until I got back last weekend and collected my mail.'

He took the remaining documents from the envelope and put them on the desk. 'There was this other mail as well. Mail that came after some of those cheques bounced. Cheques that bounced even though I made sure the funds would be there to cover them. Now do you see what I mean?'

'Ricky, you can't blame all this on the bank. You've got to take your own responsibility in business, you know that better than me. All of this information was available to you online, that's what's great about Internet banking. Don't tell me you didn't keep up to date through our online banking service?'

'Joe, I told you before I left I was going on a pilgrimage, remember? I walked the *Camino de Santiago*, from St. Jean Pied de Port in France to Santiago de Compostela in Spain. It took me 35 days, staying in hostels and most of the time there was no signal. In any case, I didn't want to spoil the experience, it was way too special.'

'OK, sorry, I forgot, it sounds like it was a terrific trip.

But it actually makes no difference whether you checked or not.' Cunningham leaned forward, hands on the desk, straining to get his message across. 'Ricky, all of those payments can be made again in a week or so and there will be no harm done. I still don't see the problem.'

Menendez ignored him and picked up the remaining papers. He read from them in turn. 'Item one. This is from my supplier in Seattle advising me that under the terms of our contract, they're revoking my distributorship agreement for attempting to make a payment with insufficient funds.

'Item two. This is from my car rental company. Two monthly payments have been missed so they're repossessing the car on Monday.

'Item three. This is from the owners of my office and apartment. They've been trying to get rid of me for years and now they've succeeded; four weeks of unpaid rent. I've got to get out by the end of the month.

'Item four. A letter from one of my biggest customers. They sent in a payment of sixty thousand dollars and an order for two month's supply of merchandise. My supplier has refused to fulfil the order and the customer is threatening to sue me for non-performance and consequential damages to his business.'

Ricardo's voice was rising and becoming shrill. Cunningham squirmed in his chair. 'What exactly do you expect the bank to do?'

'Hang on, Joe. I'm not through yet.' He shook his head, as if in disbelief. 'When I got back and saw what had happened, I figured I could still sort things out with some ready cash, 'cos I knew it would take you guys a while to cut through the crap and make the reimbursement. You remember that security company you recommended to me couple years ago?'

The banker thought for a moment, searching his memory. 'You mean for the safety deposit box? Sure I do, *RH Security International*, in Santa Monica. Did you use them?'

'I rented a box there, a small one, put some cash in. You know, for emergencies. Like this one.' He paused, staring at Cunningham, who said nothing and looked down at his desk, wondering what was coming next.

'I went down there as soon as I got back from Spain, that cash could maybe have sorted things out. Have you been down there recently, Joe?'

He shook his head and Ricky went on, 'It's gone. They closed the branch.'

'I didn't know that. Where have they moved to?'

'When I called their number, I got a recorded message that said the business was sold and moved to San Diego. So, I called the new number they gave me and spoke to someone down there. The woman said they'd written to me about it last year, but I never received anything about it, never heard from them at all since I rented the box.'

Again, the banker remained silent and he continued. 'Crappy old office they got there, I drove down the next day. Changed the name to 'West Coast Security Central' or some such. The lady told me they'd bought the RH business, closed it down and moved everything to San Diego.'

'You didn't know about the move?'

'Not a thing. She told me how they'd contacted everyone to get them to claim their possessions and deposit them in a new box in San Diego. Anyone who didn't reply, well they moved the original boxes down from LA themselves. Funny how I never got that letter.'

'And did you find your box?'

'Yep. They had a locked room in back, with a few hundred boxes, no real security, far as I could see. Just the boxes on shelves around the walls. Anyway, my key still worked, so I opened the box up.'

'And you found the cash you'd deposited?'

Menendez's laugh was humourless, as was his face. 'It wasn't quite like I remembered.'

'The cash didn't help, is that what you're saying?'

'Five grand doesn't fill too much of a quarter million dollar hole.'

'Oh, I see. I thought there might have been more, from what you said.'

'Funny, so did I.'

Cunningham shifted nervously in his seat. 'What do you mean?'

'I put a hundred fifty grand in that box two years ago and somehow it'd shrunk down to five. That's what you guys call devaluation, right? But like I said, I never got that letter. Kinda convenient, don't you think?'

'You're saying ....'

'I'm saying that between them moving that box from LA and setting it up in San Diego, they lost most of my money. Matter of fact, almost all my money, outside the business.'

'But you've made a claim, surely you have the original receipt or an insurance policy or something of the sort?'

'Joe, we both know the only reason people put cash in safety deposit boxes is because it's not declared. Same with me. There's no proof it ever existed, so they're saying it didn't. I've got five grand and no claim.'

Both men sat silent, Cunningham looking down at his desk again, Menendez looking at him expectantly. After a long moment, he picked up the letter and the other documents, placed them carefully into the envelope and put it back into his inside jacket pocket.

He heaved a deep sigh. 'The thing is, Joe, I'm tired. I'm sixty-three years old and I've had enough of working my ass off to make a hundred grand a year. And for once in my life I got lucky. One of my customers, young guy, under forty, really smart, came to see me about buying me out. With what he makes from his own franchise plus my main distributorship, he can clear almost two hundred grand a year and he's young enough to build it up. He just came into some money and he got a loan from his bank. He offered me a cool five hundred grand to take it over. Half a million bucks, cash.'

He gazed at the ceiling, a dreamy look in his eyes. 'Next year my pension kicks in. With that much in the bank I could live a decent life. Some of the guys I've met on the hiking trips do that. They have a little nest egg and they live pretty good, dipping into the cash to top up their pension. Twenty-five grand a year pays for a lot of extras and half a million would spin out for twenty years. You were right about me leaving, wrong about Mexico. I want to go live in Spain, it's a lot less expensive than LA and I've still got family back there to visit with. I always wanted to travel around Europe, you know, see some new places before I get too old.' He looked expectantly at the other man.

Cunningham brightened up. 'That's terrific, Ricky. I'm really happy for you. When will the deal get done?'

'Joe, you're not listening.' His voice became shriller and his eyes seemed to stare through the banker. 'There's no business left to sell. I've lost my supplier, my office, my best customer and I'm probably about to get sued into the bargain. That dream is over. Even if you reimburse me the quarter million, after sorting all that shit out, if I'm lucky I might get a hundred grand out of what's left of the business and then I'd have to disappear, so the fucking lawyers couldn't find me. A hundred grand wouldn't get me far, Joe, in Spain or any other place.'

The two men sat looking at each other in silence, each consumed by his own thoughts. Menendez waiting to hear how the banker would respond, Cunningham unable to tell him anything more than he already had.

After a minute or two, he finally said, 'Well, Joe. Now you know why it's not that simple. What you got to say?'

Cunningham spread his hands in front of him. 'I'm sorry, Ricky, that's really bad luck. You don't deserve it. But apart from that I don't know what more you expect me to say.'

'What I need you to say is that the bank will give me, or even just lend me a few hundred grand to compensate me for this situation and then we'll be even. I'll then be able to get on with my retirement, just like I planned.'

'You know that's not going to happen, Ricky. Banks don't accept responsibility for consequential damages. They never have and they never will, whatever the circumstances. We're reimbursing your business funds as promised by month's end, but that's the limit of our liability. It's in black and white in the online banking agreements that we signed together and there are no exceptions. I'm sorry about what happened with the security box, but it has nothing to do with us. The business problem was caused by our system and we're paying for that, but there's nothing I or anyone else can do to change whatever else happened.'

'I figured that would be your answer. There's also nothing I can do about the fucking Internet banking system. So that leaves me just one choice.' Ricardo reached into his side pocket and pulled out the pistol he'd taken from the bureau in the hall. He pointed it at the banker's head.

'What the fuck?' Cunningham put his hands out as if to protect himself from the gun. 'Don't do anything stupid Ricky, please!' Too late he remembered the emergency button under his desktop and started reaching towards it.

'I'm sorry, Joe. Really sorry.' The pistol was a lightweight Ruger 3260 that he'd bought for personal protection when there'd been some drug-related violence near his home a few years before. He'd never fired it and had to practice the previous day taking off the safety catch and firing it empty. It held 7 plus 1 shells and it was fully loaded now.

Before Cunningham could find the button, he pulled the trigger and the wall behind the desk was covered in tissue, blood and brains.

'Stupid shit. What's a few hundred grand to a bank this size? Not enough to get shot for.'

He turned to leave when the door burst open. A young man in shirtsleeves was standing there. He quickly took in the scene. 'What in Christ's name?' Ricardo shot him in the chest and his body was thrown into the corridor by the blast.

Now he could hear shouting. A woman was screaming and an alarm bell started ringing. He stepped over the man's body and watched people running towards the elevators and stairs. He went back into Cunningham's office and shut the door. Sat on the metal chair with the lattice back and put the pistol into his mouth. Pulled the trigger.

ONE
Seven Months Earlier

Rolle, Suisse Romande, Switzerland
October, 2018

The majestic old bateau was a 68m paddle steamer built in 1904, the oldest, and considered by many to be the most beautiful, of the fleet of passenger steamers operated by the CGN, the Geneva Navigation Company. Named *Le Montreux*, the ship was still plying its trade after more than a century, carrying up to 560 passengers across the *Lac Léman* between the Haute-Savoie of France and the Swiss cantons of Geneva and Vaud. It was coming up to 2pm on a sunny, but cool autumn day, the sunlight illuminating the infinite shades of greens and reds amongst the countless vineyards planted neatly along the hillsides below the Jura mountains. The passengers standing outside on the upper deck, gazed in admiration at the 13th century *Chateau de Rolle* and the tiny, forested *Ile de la Harpe*, as the old ship cruised slowly past, towards the jetty of the pretty little Swiss town.

On the upper deck, on a bench at the stern of the vessel, a skinny man, with long hair, in a duffel coat and tight jeans, was sitting with an attractive woman in a camel-hair coat. They were deep in conversation, speaking French, ignoring the tranquil beauty that surrounded them. He sipped the last of his coffee. 'Between Berne, Basel, Zurich and Geneva there were over a million boxes. Half of them in Geneva, where I was manager,' he added proudly. 'Throughout Europe, another five million more; it was a big business. I don't know about the other countries, but most of the Swiss clients have claimed and recovered their valuables, and there's only about a couple of thousand left unclaimed, so we did a decent job.'

'What about those unclaimed ones, have you sent out any reminders?'

'We're doing it one by one, but it's slow work. The original letters were sent by registered mail in January last year, but a lot of addresses were probably wrong. Some clients had paid up to 5 or 10 years of fees and the others paid mostly by bank transfer or cheque and never bothered to come back to update their details. We're still receiving payments, but I just return them and send a copy of the letter and eventually they might turn up to claim their stuff. Then there's the out of contract boxes, of course.'

'Out of contract, what does that mean?'

'The fees haven't been paid for a while, sometimes a long time. It's usually because the owner passed away and nobody knew about the security box, so it just sits there with whatever's inside.'

'I see.' She licked her lips, thinking back to her employment many years ago with Klein, Fellay, the private bank in Geneva. 'Just like the millions of dormant accounts at banks where the accountholder died, and nobody has claimed the balance. Do you know how many billions are sitting on their books that they just confiscate quietly when the time-limit runs out?'

'Sorry, I don't get the point.'

'Wait. What was the policy on those boxes?'

'There wasn't really a policy, everything got moved to

the Geneva building. All the Swiss unclaimed boxes are there now, it's easier to administer. We've got so much space there we just keep them, hoping the customers will turn up to pay the back fees and claim the merchandise, but not many have.'

'How many of them are out of contract?'

'Maybe 1,000, I don't have the exact number.'

'That's half of them. How many of the rest have prepaid for several more years?'

'You mean those that haven't contacted us already? Most of them, that's why they're still unclaimed.'

'So, that's about 1,000 owners who you'll never find unless they contact you and pay their outstanding fees, plus another 1,000 who probably won't contact you until their fees become due. That could be for a year or two, unless they learn the business is closed. Any other way they'd know about it?'

'Not by word of mouth, it's not the kind of thing you tell your friends about, it's a very confidential business. We posted a message on the website, but hardly anybody bothers to look at it. It's not the most exciting piece of work and now it's defunct anyway.'

'I looked at the website actually, that's why I contacted you. You're going to open the unclaimed boxes in June next year, right?'

'That's probably right, but what's this about? I don't see the point of all these questions.'

'Wait, Claude. When is the building due to be demolished?'

'Not before the end of next year. Edificio 2000, that's the development company, the new owners, submitted the plans for the new apartment project last year and they don't expect the approval for another year. It would be after that.'

'Not before the end of next year,' she repeated, pulling her coat collar tighter against the cold and forcing herself to speak calmly, hardly able to contain her excitement. This was far bigger than she'd expected or even imagined. 'And including the prepaid and out of contract ones there could be up to 2,000 unclaimed boxes left that you have to open. What happens to them?'

He shrugged, 'It won't be as many as that, because it's going down all the time, but there'll be quite a lot. Anyway, they'll be removed and emptied before the building's demolished. Then the goods will be stored somewhere, maybe in Zurich. We'll need to compile a complete list of contents for future claims and I suppose I'll have to continue to try to find the clients one by one, if they don't contact us or renew their prepayments. That's if I'm still in the job, of course. Why are you so interested in this?'

She looked around, the boat had now docked and there was no one nearby. 'Does Edificio 2000 know how many boxes are still unclaimed?'

'They get a report at the end of each quarter, so the last one was end of September. It hasn't changed much since then, but I've had no further contact about it from them, it's just a nuisance as far as they're concerned.'

'Do they inspect the building regularly?'

'They never go there. Their offices are in the *Tessin*; Locarno, near the Italian border. That's over 200km away, so they won't be coming here very often until they get the permits to demolish the building and commence construction. They're much more interested in what they'll build, not what they'll knock down.'

'What's the procedure to open the unclaimed boxes?'

'We drill through the three keyholes in the safe doors, take out the boxes and inventory the contents. It's not difficult. The security system itself is complicated and secure, but we just switch it off, then taking the boxes out is a no-brainer.'

'Then you send everything to a storage facility somewhere? Why did you mention Zurich, I thought you said it was closed?'

Now he showed more interest, looking keenly at the woman as he tried to follow her thoughts. 'It was closed down a couple of years ago and we moved it to a smaller office, without security facilities. It was never a big operation, about 200,000 or so boxes and they were mostly claimed.' He laughed, 'Maybe the manager there was more efficient than me. Anyway, we brought the rest to Geneva, with the others. I mentioned it because I'm still officially the *administrateur*, the CEO of the Zurich company, but I hardly ever go there anymore. That's the address we gave on the letter we sent, but there's only a secretary there, explaining the situation to customers, or asking us to track down their valuables in Geneva. She's just a kid, does what she's told and doesn't ask questions, sends me the queries she receives then forgets them until the next time. She's got very little to do. Like I said, most of the owners who could be traced have already claimed their possessions.'

'Do you know why the company went bust? And how come the Zurich subsidiary is still in existence?'

'It's a long story. I was hired in 2007, when it was the oldest and most successful security company in Geneva. It was set up after the war by Dr Dietrich Haldeman, apparently a brilliant man. I never met him, he died before I joined, but he had quite a reputation. The company had expanded here and outside Switzerland, but when his son, Patrick, took over after his death, he mortgaged everything and made all kinds of crazy investments. After the 2008 financial crash, he ended up with enormous liabilities and the companies went bankrupt, one after the other; total catastrophe. We struggled on in Geneva for a few more years, but it finally went bust in 2016 and the building was sold to *Edificio*. The Zurich subsidiary was smaller and had very little debt, so we paid it off and kept the company to administer the fallout from Geneva.'

'So, now you work for the Zurich office?'

'Yes and no. Since 2017 I've been officially employed by the Zurich company, but I get paid by Edificio 2000.'

Trying to control her excitement, she said, 'So, Geneva and the other companies are down the drain, but Zurich is still legally alive and the developers will have to pay you and a secretary every month to manage future claims from customers. It could take years, and they're in Locarno and you might be in Zurich. They can't be very happy about that?'

He shook his head. 'They hate it. They're very uncomfortable with the whole situation, sitting with valuables belonging to people all over the world. As far as the Zurich idea is concerned, I don't want to end up in such a dead-end job, but I'd be surprised if they could find anyone else with the right knowledge and experience to do it.'

'Are you sure they'll send everything there?'

'No, but we've been talking about it for a while now. It would be sensible and economical, since it's already set up and it's still a clean company. What do you have in mind?' he asked quietly, pushing aside his too-long greasy hair.

She paused, gathering her thoughts. 'What if you tell them it would make more sense to start emptying the unclaimed boxes sooner rather than later, so they can be ready when they get the planning approval. It must be a complicated project, demolishing a building and replacing it. If the boxes were all emptied and the goods shipped to Zurich ahead of time, it would be one less headache for them to worry about.'

'That would probably help them, but how does it help us? I'm assuming you didn't arrange to meet me to enquire after my health?'

Her answer came like a bombshell. 'What if we could acquire the company, to take over the problem from them. Do you think they'd buy the idea?'

His eyes narrowed as he digested the suggestion. 'Now I get it. You mean we try to pick up the Zurich company for peanuts, drill the boxes, then get the transfer of property signed off by them and I move with the goods to Zurich to administer whatever claims might come later?'

'You've been the trusted director of the company now for ten years, right?' He nodded. 'So who could be better to hand over the problem to than you? You just said it would be difficult for them to find someone for the job, you can save them all that trouble. What do you think?'

'I think they'd be pretty pleased if it was all wrapped up and they didn't have to bother about it. It's just another box to be ticked, *Ensure all unclaimed valuables are inventoried and stored and owners contacted again. Problem solved.*' He laughed quietly, 'As a matter of fact, they'd probably pay me to take the stuff off their hands.

I could ask for a few years' salary and expenses to make sure I got the job finished, keep their conscience clean. It's a huge company, they can afford it.'

'Even better, but there must be a lot of value in 2,000 security boxes. We could make sure it didn't get wasted. You'd be in a good position to make sure that any further claims were, let's say, poorly handled. I mean, no proof, no claim. Very hard to recuperate property in those circumstances.'

Jolidon now understood the reason for the meeting she'd initiated, it was a clever idea, but he was still sceptical. He searched his memory for their last encounter, bringing it back to mind. *It was in 2010, at the time of the drug deal with that Moroccan, Prince Bensouda. That was the last time I made any real money. Maybe this is the next time.* He remembered something else, *She was very interested in Mrs Jenny Bishop and asked me about her last visit to the vault. What was that about?* Attempting subtlety, he asked, 'You're living in London now?'

She told him as little as possible. Like him, she was French, known to him only by her maiden name of Esther Bonnard, not her married name, Esther Rousseau, which had been circulated by Interpol since 2008, nor the many other aliases she'd used in her career. The man who'd fallen for her this time, Harry Fern-Chapman, was a successful London-based fund manager with a flat in Chelsea. She'd moved in with him a few months previously, but that might be a temporary situation, and in any case, none of Jolidon's business. 'For a while,' she answered. 'I haven't made any firm plans yet; it depends on what I decide to do next.'

He nodded, '*Bien sûr*. What made you think of

contacting me after all these years? There must have been a specific reason?'

'No. Only that I read somewhere that the company was dying. After I looked at the website, I figured there might be some value to extract from the corpse before the burial.'

He didn't believe her; with Esther Bonnard there was always another reason. He let it pass, *I'll find out sooner or later*.

TWO

Rolle, Suisse Romande, Switzerland
November, 2018

The vessel was still stationary and a voice intervened. *'Excusez-moi, Monsieur, Madame.* Are you getting off in Rolle? We're only here for a couple of minutes.' The deck officer pointed at the clock.

'Non, merci. We're staying on for the trip back to Lausanne.'

'Très bien, bon voyage.' He walked away, blowing his whistle to signal to the crewman to untie the mooring rope. A number of passengers had come aboard, all standing on the deck, enjoying the view as the ferry boat pulled slowly away, the sound of its massive horn echoing across the water.

The woman was quiet for a few minutes, and he lit a cigarette, brown and strong smelling. She grimaced and he held the cigarette away from her. *'Merci.* You'll have to get workmen in to drill the safes and take out the boxes, it'll take quite a while.'

'I figure it would take a month, more or less, depending how many there are left.'

'But they wouldn't know anything about the contents?'

'No, they'd just drill and extract the closed boxes, that's all. But there's another problem.' She waited expectantly, while he took a long drag, blowing the smoke away on the breeze. 'There's a young guy, Gilles Simenon, still working with me. He was head of the security box department, knows a lot of the clients, so I kept him on until we clear everything out, if we ever do. He spends all his time trying to find owners to get their property back to them.'

'Just the two of you?'

'There's a girl as well, but she just runs errands, she's no problem.'

'And Simenon, is he smart, I mean nosey, checking everything?'

'He's diligent, totally honest, not much imagination, very cautious and careful. He'll want to be involved in doing the inventories. It would be difficult to work around him without his catching on.'

'So he'd know what was in the boxes. Anyone else?'

'No more employees, but the owners have told me to hire a *huissier judiciaire*. You know, a kind of Swiss notary, to certify the inventories. It's to prevent fraud and for insurance purposes. They're very concerned about any potential liability.'

'Do they appoint him, or can you suggest someone?'

'I'm pretty sure they'd agree to whatever I propose if they think I'm going to take this headache away just like that.' He took another drag on his cheroot. 'Why? Do you know someone?'

'I can find a friendly candidate, no problem. This man Gilles Simenon is more difficult, I'll need to give it some thought, but I can usually find solutions, if the reward is sufficient, and in this case I think it will be.'

Jolidon was still unconvinced. 'So how exactly do we take advantage of the situation. You'll still have hundreds, maybe thousands of clients who will be looking to get their valuables back. It will take years and there might be nothing left.'

'Wait, one last question; how many of those owners filed a deposit statement or provided an insurance policy describing what's in their box?'

'I'd have to check, but it wouldn't be many, hardly any of them ever did. I'd say we had no proof of the contents for more than ninety per cent of the boxes.'

'And even for the few that you have, it's not really proof, is it? Think about it Claude, why do people hide money or valuables in safety deposit boxes in Geneva?'

'Because they're not insured?'

'And that means?'

He nodded his head, 'They're not declared to the tax authorities?'

'*Exactement!* You can be sure the majority of the contents are undeclared or illegally earned and the owners would have problems if they were discovered. Normally, they'd just come and open their box, take what they wanted and no one would know what it was. But if they had to go through a complicated procedure with you to prove ownership to recuperate something that was on your official inventory, signed by a *huissier*, it would be a real risk to them.'

'You mean, someone might report them to the tax people, and they could face charges?' He smiled, 'That's quite a threat.'

'The more difficult we make it for them, the more worried they'd become. And if they have no proof of their claim, what can they do? Most of them would give up and there'd be a lot of valuables left without an owner. That's without all those boxes out of contract where the owners may never turn up.'

He took a last deep drag and threw the butt over the side into the bluey-green water. 'You've thought this through very well, and you're right, there must be a lot of value there and it's a shame to let it go to waste. But there's another problem you haven't talked about. How do we get rid of the contents and get paid? Assuming I've understood your plan correctly, of course.'

'You'd be surprised, Claude. That's the easiest part and that's why you need me to make this work. I reckon we've got two or three years to make a fortune from this situation.'

She hesitated, knowing how corrupt the man was, but that she couldn't make it work without him. 'What do you say to a partnership?' She offered her hand.

'I'm willing to give it a try.' His hand was warm and sweaty, but she hid her distaste, there was a lot at stake.

'By the way,' she asked, as casually as possible, 'do you remember if Jenny Bishop has claimed whatever was in her box, no. 72?'

I knew it! She knows what's in that box. 'As a matter of fact, I know she hasn't, I would have remembered. I had a problem with her, a long time ago, a very complicated woman. Why do you ask?'

Esther tried to hide her emotions, but he noticed a tremble in her voice, 'That's a coincidence, I've had problems with her as well. She's not just complicated, she's dishonest. There's something in that box that belongs to me, just sentimental value, you understand, but it'll be a small victory if I can recover it.'

Once again, he didn't believe her. *It has to be something valuable. I knew it when Mrs Bishop first came with her friends all those years ago.* 'I'll be sure to take good care of it if this plan works.'

'Thanks, Claude.' Esther tried to calm herself down, her thoughts still racing. 'Is Zurich the only company still alive?'

'Yes. All the other subsidiaries were sold over the last few years. There were a lot of franchises as well, but I think they've all been taken over. I can check on it, but I'm pretty sure there's just Geneva and Zurich. They were the first and they're the last.'

'Pity, maybe you can check on it later. Now, we need to work out the details before we get back to Lausanne.'

Geneva Airport, Switzerland

Esther was waiting at the boarding gate for her BA flight to Heathrow when her mobile rang. Jolidon's name came up and she found a quiet space away from the crowd.

'What is it, Claude?'

'I've checked things out and I have some news for you.'

'Is it good or bad?'

'Could be good. I was wrong about the franchises. They've all been sold except for one. It was under contract, but it fell through and it's still for sale.'

'Where is it?'

'Santa Monica, Los Angeles. It's a small operation, less than 500 customers. It's still under the franchise name, *RH Security International.*'

'Right. Can you get me the details, the owners, price, selling agent and anything else you can find out?'

'I know the price. They were asking $200,000, but after the deal falling through, they won't get it. It's too small, a mom and pop type operation, no money to be made.'

'OK, send me the details by email, Claude. *Merci*, I'll keep you posted.'

Despite her usual nervousness, she had no problems at immigration control, her French passport in her maiden name of Esther Bonnard had been renewed a couple of years before and was still valid. Sipping a glass of champagne on the flight, she reflected on her current situation. Harry Fern-Chapman was a decent guy, successful, extremely good looking and not bad in bed, but Esther had been too spoiled by her Angolan lover, Raymundo d'Almeida, to settle for second best. Since his death at the hands of Jenny Bishop in 2008, she'd kept her sights set high. Although she knew she looked younger, she was now approaching 40 years of age, it might be the last throw of the dice for her. She wanted more, a whole lot more. And still burning inside her, as it had been every day for the last 10 years, was a desperate desire for revenge over Jenny Bishop.

Her brain whirling, she calculated, *I've still got $50,000 in Guadeloupe and $200k in my Almeida Enterprises account in Bahrain. If I can get that Santa Monica company for maybe $100K, it's worth the risk. There must be a lot more value than that in 500 boxes. With that money I can set up the structure I'll need to execute the Ramseyer, Haldeman project. Then the sky's the limit.*

As Jolidon had suspected, her real motive in contacting him was safety deposit box no. 72, inherited by Jenny Bishop from her father-in-law, Charlie Bishop. Ray d'Almeida had told her in 2008 that the diamonds in that box were worth at least $12 million. *It must be nearer $20 million today. And those diamonds are still there, I'm certain of it.* Esther had discreetly followed Jenny Bishop's fortunes over the last several years and she knew of the success of Bishop Private Equity, her investment business. *I know she had both the keys in 2010 but she didn't take anything out of the box. There'd be no reason for her to take them since then, she's already got more money than she deserves.*

Esther took her decision, knowing a $100K gamble could change her life once again, this time, definitely for the better.

She had only a travel bag with her and Harry was waiting at the Terminal 5 arrivals gate when she walked through. He was carrying a bunch of flowers and a bottle of champagne.

'I've missed you,' she whispered, as she wrapped him in a passionate embrace, earning disapproving stares from several female passengers and many more envious glances from the men.

'And I've missed you just as much.' He ignored the looks, basking in the feel of her body against his. *Just jealousy*, he said to himself smugly, she was the most beautiful partner he'd ever had, and he'd had many.

'Here let me take that.' He took the case and pulled it behind him as they walked to the car park elevators. 'How was your trip, successful?'

'I think so,' she answered, cautiously, 'time will tell.'

THREE

Marbella, Spain
April, 2019

'*Salud* and congratulations, Laura and Javier, and welcome to little Pedro. Even better looking than his grandfather.' Jenny Bishop leaned over the carrycot and kissed the damp forehead of the tiny, two month-old baby boy.

Laura Palomares laughed, '*Gracias*, Jenny, and thank you and Leticia for this lovely party.' Everyone raised their glasses and toasted her baby son, named after ex-Chief Inspector Pedro Espinoza.

'Not only better looking, but clearly a lot smarter, since his timing means we can save money by sharing our birthday celebrations.' The child had been born on February 5th, Espinoza's 65th birthday, and he was delighted by the coincidence. He raised his glass again, 'To my first grandson, Pedro Javier Palomares, a long, happy and successful life.'

There were over fifty guests, plus children, in the garden of York House, the Marbella property Jenny and her Angolan friend Leticia de Moncrieff had inherited from Jenny's father-in-law, Charlie Bishop. It was three in the afternoon, pleasantly warm, and most of the adults were sheltering in the cooler air of the huge marquee. The tent was lined with tables piled high with a selection of drinks, snacks and mouth-watering tapas, courtesy of

Encarni, Leticia's mother, who worked as their Spanish housekeeper and Lily Whittaker, the English housekeeper-nanny who'd been with Jenny since her daughter Ellen was born the previous year.

Outside, settees, chairs and loungers surrounded the pool, where the children were either splashing in the lukewarm water or playing a boisterous game of football on the lawn, under the supervision of Emilio, Leticia and Charlie's teenage son. Chester, Jenny's two-year old Westie, was running amok, chasing after the ball and adding to the general chaos. Balloons and streamers festooned the trees and bushes and there were enough sunshades and umbrellas, Jenny hoped, to protect everyone from succumbing to sunstroke.

'Look, Ellen, this is Pedro, a lovely new friend for you to play with soon.' Lily lifted up Jenny's twelve-month old daughter to show her the baby, and Ellen put her arms out to hold him.

'You'll have to wait a little, Ellen, he's sleeping now. Come with me, there are lots of friends you can play with.' Lily carried her outside to watch the activity.

Jenny looked gratefully after her, once again thanking her lucky stars at the choice she'd made almost two years previously. After recovering from her shock and delight at the miraculous news that she was expecting a daughter, she had quickly come to three important conclusions. Firstly, because of her work and life-style, she needed someone to help her at home and when travelling, and secondly, her semi-detached villa in Ipswich was much too small for three. The second problem was resolved when she found a large detached villa near the river, in a quiet area with a park in front, and less than a mile from her previous home. In a moment of pure nostalgia, she decided to name the villa, 'Durham House', a sister to York House.

Her next decision was fulfilled at the Ipswich RSPCA, where she found Chester, a six-month-old West Highland Terrier, who had been handed in as a tiny, homeless puppy, lovingly looked after by the staff until Jenny walked in. Cooper, her previous Westie, and the last link with her deceased husband, Ron, had passed away two years before, at the respectable age of 15 and she had been travelling too much to consider adopting another animal. Now, she would be staying in Ipswich much more and a friendly animal at home would be good for both her daughter and herself.

The third solution came in the form of Lily Whittaker, a no-nonsense Geordie who loved children and dogs, from Whitburn, just 5km from Sunderland, Jenny's original hometown. As well as caring for Ellen as if she was her own child, if there was anything Lily couldn't fix, make or organise, it was yet to be found. She now had a room in the houses in Ipswich and Marbella and Jenny didn't know how she'd managed to survive without her help. More importantly, Lily and Encarni got on like a house on fire, despite communicating mostly by using hand signals.

By three-thirty, everyone had filed in for lunch and the marquee resembled a restaurant, full of hungry, thirsty guests, chattering away noisily in several languages. Lily took her tired daughter off for her afternoon nap and Jenny found herself with time to eat something herself. She took a plate of tapas and a glass of rosé over to where Pedro Espinoza was sitting with his family and José, Leticia's

Angolan father. They were all still fussing over the baby and Espinoza turned to greet her, pulling a chair up a little away from the others. 'Jenny, come and sit here, close by me, otherwise I won't be able to hear a word you say.'

'Thanks, Pedro, I haven't seen you for ages, not since Laura's wedding. That's shameful, we have to get together more often.'

'If you would stop flying around the world buying up businesses everywhere, it would make it easier,' he chided her. 'I don't know why you don't buy your own private jet, it would be simpler and cheaper.'

Jenny laughed, but she knew this was true. Bishop Private Equity, the investment company she'd set up five years previously, was now more than just a hobby, it had prospered and grown into a diversified financial business, giving employment to a dozen employees and providing her with an interesting and fulfilling occupation as well as a regular uptick in her financial security.

'I've been thinking about that and you're right, Pedro, but for a different reason. From now on, I have to spend as much time as I can with Ellen. She's about to become a grown-up little girl and I want to enjoy every moment of it with her. Lily's marvellous, like an adoptive mother, but I can't keep leaving my daughter with her for the rest of her life. So, now, whenever I travel, Ellen will come with me, which means I'll have to cut down my travelling a lot.'

The Westie found her and poked his nose onto her lap and she stroked him. 'It will also be good for Chester, I know they both miss me when I'm away.'

'You have the luxury of choosing, unlike many people, and I think that's the best possible choice.' He raised his glass, 'Here's to staying at home. Although, as a matter of fact, this month it's my turn to go travelling, a very special journey.'

She looked expectantly at him and he went on, 'You remember I have a cousin, Ricardo, in Los Angeles?'

'I remember that you had hardly ever met him until a few years ago, is he well? Are you going over to see him?'

'Even better. We're going to walk the *Camino de Santiago*, together, the pilgrimage from St. Jean Pied de Port in France to Santiago de Compostela in Spain. Do you know anything about it?'

'I've heard of it, I know it's a spiritual pilgrimage, but I've no idea what's involved?'

'It's long, over 750km, and we have to cross the Pyrenees, so I think we can do it in about a month, if the weather's good and neither of us has a heart attack. And we want to do it in a simple way, no luxury hotels or fancy restaurants, just hostels and cafés.'

'It sounds really special, and you'll have plenty of time to get to know each other, very cathartic after all those years living in different countries.'

'I suspect Ricardo's thinking about retiring over here, that's why he wants us to spend this time together. I hope we get on well, it would be good for both of us.'

'When are you leaving?'

'I'm flying to Biarritz next week and Ricardo's coming there from LA.'

'I hope you have a memorable time; try to send me a postcard from somewhere on the way. Meanwhile, I'm going to invite Soledad and the family over for lunch or dinner while you're away. Little Pedro and Ellen have got to get to know each other. You have a wonderful grandson and I have a beautiful daughter. Maybe we should be planning their wedding already?'

Espinoza laughed and embraced her. 'You're right, we should start planning, that's just the project I need when I return.' He looked at his watch, 'Time to get back to the others and make the most of this lovely party.'

FOUR

Santa Monica, USA

May, 2019

It was 11am when Pedro Espinoza's taxi pulled up in front of the First Los Angeles Trust Bank building. His Iberia flight had arrived at 4pm the previous afternoon and he'd gone straight to his hotel to recuperate, ready for what he expected would be a difficult meeting. Espinoza was neither young nor wealthy and the thirteen-hour flight in economy, via Madrid, had totally exhausted him, adding to the strain inflicted by the dreadful news he'd received the previous week. Now after a good night's sleep, a shower and breakfast of croissants and coffee, he was feeling a lot better, ready to investigate what had happened to his cousin Ricardo. He couldn't turn back the clock to change what had occurred, but he could at least try to find out the cause and maybe do something about it.

He was taken up to the 22nd floor by a security guard with a gun in his belt, reminding him of his many years in the Spanish police force. *Strange*, he said to himself, *in 30 years of service, the first time I fired my gun was to shoot the lock off the pantry door in Jenny Bishop's house in Marbella and the second and last time was to kill that Angolan psychopath, d'Almeida.*

A balding man in a creased cotton jacket was waiting at the lift. 'Good morning Mr Espinoza, I'm Dustin

Greenwood, Head of National Customer Services. My office is just along here.'

As they walked along the corridor Greenwood made small talk, asking him about his flight and hotel accommodation then ushered him into a spacious, well-furnished office, with enormous picture windows running along the wall behind his desk. Espinoza accepted the offer of a coffee and went to look at the view. '*Maravilloso*,' he said, admiring the San Gabriel Mountains in the distance, ranged behind the spread of the city, still with a light dusting of snow.

'Pretty, eh? But you've got some beautiful scenery over there in Spain. You're from Malaga, right?'

He thanked the banker for the coffee and sat in the armchair across the wide, expanse of desk from him. It was bare except for a slim plastic folder with a few papers inside. 'Have you been to my city?'

'Not to Malaga, but quite a few years ago, when my kids were young, we took them on a tour of Europe. Spain was definitely our favourite, but we didn't see much of it, not enough time. I'd like to visit again, maybe after my retirement.'

He drank a sip of his coffee. 'Thanks for coming to see me, Mr Espinoza, your name was given in Mr Menendez's file as his nearest relative. I wanted to meet you personally, try to work out what happened here. How were you and he related?'

'He was my cousin, from my mother's side. Her sister married a Venezuelan-American and came to live here many years ago. Ricardo was born here, but he's been to Spain a few times in recent years. I didn't see enough of him, he was a nice man, quiet but good company.'

'He wasn't married, I understand.'

'He told me he never had time for it, building up his business, but I think he was a little afraid of women.'

'When did you see him last?'

'Just two weeks ago, in Spain. We were together for a month, walking the *Camino de Santiago*. It was a perfect experience. Do you know of it?'

'I've heard about it, friends of mine did the trek last year; sorry, pilgrimage I should say. It must be very special. Was your cousin in good spirits?'

'He was a very happy man. He'd just arranged to sell his business and was going to come back to live in Spain. I was looking forward to it also, I don't have many close relatives left.'

'So, there was no sign of depression or anxiety which might explain what happened?'

Espinoza was quiet for a moment. 'Mr Greenwood, before my retirement, I was a Chief Inspector in the Spanish police force, head of the Homicide Division in Andalusia. I'm now officially a private consultant, or detective if you like, although I'm not constantly occupied. I observe from what you've said that you don't know the background to Ricardo's actions. What exactly do you know?'

The banker looked slightly uncomfortable, sitting further back in his chair. He cleared his throat, 'I'm aware that his account was targeted by fraudsters while he was away and approximately a quarter million dollars was siphoned off. However, we had already agreed to reimburse the full amount this month.' He indicated the file on his desk, 'I suppose there had been some knock-on effects, but they could have easily been sorted out. We're the biggest bank in LA and we carry a lot of weight. We would have gone out of our way to help and I'm sure Joe Cunningham explained this to Mr Menendez, so I'm trying to understand why he would take such extreme action, murdering two people, when his financial situation would have been fully restored within a few days. It can only have been some kind of temporary insanity, there was absolutely no reason for this dreadful event. I've told the police department exactly the same thing and they saw no reason to disagree.'

Espinoza took an envelope from his jacket pocket. 'That's what I thought. I'm extremely sad and sorry for what happened to your colleagues, but the full story Ricky told Mr Cunningham before the incident is obviously not known by anyone else in the bank. I received this a few days ago, it was sent by my cousin on the morning of the tragedy. I'm afraid he had already decided what he was going to do if the bank wouldn't compensate him properly.'

'I don't understand. I just explained that he would be fully compensated, how could he not accept that?'

'Please read this letter, Mr Greenwood. It explains everything and you will understand why, in the space of two weeks, my cousin went from being a happy, contented man, to becoming a savage killer. It does not condone his actions, but it explains them.'

'My God! What an awful series of mishaps.' After reading and rereading the letter, the banker placed it next to the file on his immaculate desk. 'I just wish I'd been consulted. Like I said, I'm sure there was something we could have done. Poor Joe, a secondary victim of those frauds. And Ricardo, when that sale fell through and then losing his last insurance money, he must have been suicidal; in fact he obviously was.' He shook his head, 'As you say, it doesn't excuse the murders, but it helps to explain his state of mind. Have you shown this to the police?'

'Not yet. I have an appointment later today to tell them what I know and make arrangements for Ricardo's burial.'

'May I make a copy for our files, in case something comes up that might be relevant?'

There was a long moment of silence while he passed the three sheets through the photocopier, then, 'Is there anything at all we can do to help while you're here?'

Espinoza took out the pad with his scribbled notes. 'I suppose you'll still be reimbursing the funds to Ricky's company?'

'Of course, there are debts to be paid and we need to ensure the company is wound up in good order.'

'Do you have people who can organise that?'

'It's not part of our normal procedure, but I can arrange for an administrator, make sure that everything is closed off as it should be. Anything else we can do?'

Espinoza, hesitated, then asked quietly, 'The families of the two victims, Joe Cunningham and the other man. I suppose they will be properly compensated?'

'Absolutely. The bank will make sure they are adequately provided for, don't worry about that. You have enough on your plate without taking responsibility for your cousin's actions.'

'Do you think I should contact them to express my regret and condolences?'

Greenwood hesitated for a moment then shook his head. 'It's a kind gesture, but I don't think it would help and it might just stir up ill-feeling when they're starting to cope with what happened. I wouldn't advise it.'

'I understand, thank you, but if you ever get the chance, please let them know that I feel truly sorry for their loss.'

He nodded. 'Is there anything else I can help you with?'

'I don't know what else there might be, but can I contact you if anything comes up while I'm here in the US?'

Greenwood took out a card and scribbled on it. 'That's my mobile number, call me anytime, Mr Espinoza. If there's anything further I can do, I'll be happy to help.'

The Spaniard got up from his chair, looked at his notepad again. 'Oh, there may be one more thing you could tell me. What do you know about the company Mr Cunningham recommended, *RH Security International*?'

'I've never heard of them, but I can ask some questions. Ricky's letter says the business was sold and moved to San Diego.' They walked to the door and shook hands. 'I'll find out what I can and get back to you as soon as I know anything.'

Espinoza handed in his security pass and walked out into the bright Californian sunshine. It was now noon and his appointment with the Los Angeles Police Department was at 3pm. He strolled around for a while until he found '*Pepe's in LA*', a Spanish Bodega, US style. It was a warm, sultry day and he sat at a pavement table and ordered some tapas and a glass of Californian Pinot Grigio.

He took out his mobile. *Nine hours ahead in Malaga, just after 9pm, a good time to call Soledad.* He Facetimed her number.

'Papa? *Estás* in Los Angeles, you're in Los Angeles?'

'Laura, I didn't know you were with Mama?'

'Javier's in Madrid at a conference, so I came over with Pedro to keep her company, you know how she misses you when you're travelling.'

'How are you? How is Pedro, and Javier? Is everything going well?' Laura's husband, Javier Palomares, was a Detective Sergeant with the Malaga Homicide Squad of the Policía Nacional, and Espinoza was certain he would end up in the same job as he had occupied for eight years. He liked Javier and they got on well together, swapping stories about crime in Andalucía on their frequent visits from their home in Benalmadena, a few kilometres along the coast from Malaga.

'I'm fine and so is everybody else, especially Pedro,' his daughter was saying. 'How are things over there? I hope it's not too depressing. Poor Uncle Ricky, do they know why it happened?'

'Not yet, I'm just trying to understand what went on.' Espinoza hadn't divulged the contents of his cousin's letter to his family, not until he was certain of what had occurred and why. There were too many unknown factors and he needed time to work diligently through whatever he could uncover, if there was anything to be uncovered.

The waiter brought his first plate of tapas, *Calamares a la Romana,* hot and crispy looking. 'I'll have to ring off now. Tell Mama I'll call back in the morning. Enjoy your time together and a big kiss for Pedro.'

'We'll enjoy it. We're going shopping. *Adiós*, Papa.'

FIVE

San Diego, USA
May, 2019

Pedro Espinoza went to the door of the SouthPark Lodge at 10am the following morning and tested the temperature. It was already a pleasant 20°C and he put on his sunglasses and swung his light jacket over his shoulder before stepping out onto the busy pavement. The hotel was situated on 24th Street, between Broadway and the Martin Luther King Freeway and cost less than 100 dollars per night, including breakfast, which had been surprisingly good. After his interview with Sergeant Al Froberger at the LA Police Department, he had decided it would be cheaper and quicker to rent a small car than to use taxis and flights. It was a good decision, the 120 mile drive took less than 3 hours and there were several small hotels in the vicinity of his destination.

The meeting with Froberger had been short and totally unproductive. He had expected some kind of sympathetic reaction after sharing Rick's letter with the sergeant, but he was mistaken. The department had obviously already closed the dossier and classified the affair as murder and suicide by a bank customer with a disturbed mind and they were not interested in reopening the case. He assumed they had many open cases that might produce results, but this one definitely couldn't.

Even his questions about the security company were stone walled. 'Not in our jurisdiction and I don't see how it's relevant. Your cousin lost a lot of money and went berserk, killing two innocent people, even though he was going to be reimbursed. We don't have time to look into unproven accusations of fraud in San Diego made by a homicidal maniac.'

When the Spaniard tried to argue the case, Froberger had responded, 'You think there's something in it, go down there and find something. If you do, we might take a look, but right now, you're wasting your time.'

Que Dios tenga piedad de su alma, May God have mercy on his soul. Espinoza crossed himself again, turned away from the pale, white corpse of his cousin and walked to the door of the morgue. He felt quite sick, remembering the quiet, contented man who'd been his constant companion for more than a month in Spain, just a few weeks ago. A man he hadn't really got to know until those many days together, trudging along the well-travelled holy route and camping out in all kinds of basic accommodation each night. Unlike himself, Ricky was solemn, reflective, composed, risk-averse, but shared a great sense of humour. *I'll miss seeing him, even if it was only every few years*, he realised.

In the police administration office, he'd spent another hour confirming the arrangements for Ricky's funeral. Due to 'ongoing procedural matters', it would be at least two weeks before he could be laid to rest. Espinoza couldn't afford to come back to the US and he knew Ricky had very few friends. *Besides, who would want to attend the last rites of a crazed killer*, he reflected sadly. It was going to be a very quiet affair, in death as in life. He'd walked out of the precinct station, determined to find out what had really happened between LA and San Diego; where Ricky's $145,000 had gone, the straw that broke the camel's back.

Now, Espinoza checked the address he'd received from Dustin Greenwood, the only helpful gesture he'd received since arriving in the US. *West Coast Security Central* was, or had been, on Beech Street, about 2km away from the hotel. He managed to find a parking spot nearby and walked along until he found the premises, a double storefront with frosted windows and a painted sign with the name, and a logo of a large padlock on a chain over the words:

KEEP YOUR VALUABLES SECURE FOR YOU AND YOUR LOVED ONES.

Inside, there was no one at the untidy counter, nor in the office behind. He tapped on the only other door, at the side of the room. It was made of solid wood, with a steel frame across and around it and several complicated looking locks.

'Coming right now,' a voice shouted, and a few moments later a large, beefy woman in a floral print shirt and jeans came through the door, pulling it shut and locking it behind her. 'Howdy. Sorry about that, I'm Shirley, how can I help you?'

Although Espinoza's command of English was excellent, he adopted a very strong Spanish accent, 'Good morning, I was told you have a very good security service.'

'What kind of service are you looking for?'

'I need a safety box, to store valuables.'

The woman smiled dismissively. 'I guess you must have misunderstood, we don't provide security boxes. We gave that up last year. It's only business services now, no retail customers. Sorry if you came for nothing.' She turned, as if to show him out.

Espinoza said, 'That's strange. It was only a few weeks ago that my friend told me about your service.'

She looked impatient. 'Like I told you, we don't do that. Your friend must have mistaken us for another firm. Maybe it was San Diego Security Services, they're downtown, on Market Street. Look. I'm kinda' busy, so if you don't mind...'

He went to the door, 'Thank you for your help.'

Espinoza waited a few moments after the door closed behind him, then pushed it open and went in again. The wooden door was ajar and the woman was just going through it. In the corridor behind her, he could see a pile of security boxes stacked up, they looked as if they were open and empty. A burly fellow in tee shirt and shorts was taking a couple of them from the pile.

The woman turned and slammed the door shut again. 'What is it now?'

'Sorry, can you tell me where is Market Street? I've never been here before.'

Ex-Chief Inspector Pedro Espinoza sat in his rental car, noting, in his usual methodical manner, everything he'd just witnessed.

Shirley, if that was really her name, said they don't provide retail services, but their window logo says 'Keep your valuables secure for you and your loved ones'.

She said they gave that up last year, but Ricky was here

just a few weeks ago and opened his security box to find there was $145,000 missing. He couldn't prove it, because it wasn't declared, so he lost it.

There were several security boxes in the corridor, looking like they'd been emptied. They're getting rid of the evidence.

That's what happened to Ricky's box. It was brought down from LA, then plundered, then thrown away, just like his life.

All those other boxes were robbed in the same way and now they're getting rid of them.

Next, I suppose they'll close down the whole business and there'll be no evidence left of what happened. They've got away with murder, but I can't prove it.

He put away his notebook, inwardly seething with rage at his impotence, certain that Ricky's life had been destroyed by these people, just for money, a paltry $145k. In his career, Espinoza had witnessed many vile crimes committed for that same motive, but this time it was his own family and he felt a desire for revenge that he'd never experienced before.

He drove along the street to pass in front of the office. A notice was now stuck to the door, *Closed for Lunch*. He looked at his mobile, it was just coming up to 11am. *An early eater*, he mused. On a hunch, he drove around the corner and found a back alley which seemed to run behind the building. A grey Chevrolet truck with an open back was parked half-way down the alley. A man in shorts and tee shirt was pulling a tarpaulin sheet over the contents and he could see piled-up security boxes glinting in the bright sunlight. It was the man he'd seen behind the wooden door.

Over New Mexico, en route for Malaga, via Madrid
'Will you be having some dinner, sir?'

'No thanks, I'm going to try to sleep. Do you have another blanket, please?' Pedro Espinoza thanked his lucky stars; he'd saved almost $1,000 on a last-minute booking to Malaga, via Madrid, and had been allocated a window seat with no one else in the row. 'I'll have breakfast in the morning.' He smiled at the cabin attendant and spread himself out, enjoying the extra space. The hum of the engines calmed him and he started to feel drowsy, trying to leave behind the stressful events of the day that still filled his mind.

After exiting the alley behind the West Coast Security Central office, he'd gone back to his hotel room to think things through. He hadn't expected his cousin's story to be confirmed so quickly, nor that he would be so powerless to prove it.

I suppose they don't know about what happened with Ricky in Los Angeles; that might have put the wind up them. But after he came down here, found only $5,000 and walked away because he had no proof, it was just business as usual. They've finished emptying the boxes and got rid of them. The valuables will already have been taken away, so there's no way to prove anything except that they've closed down their security box business, just like she told me.

Moving the office and the boxes from LA was clever, he acknowledged grudgingly. When they close the San Diego business down there'll be nothing to show there was ever a criminal act. Clients will come down from LA and find an empty shop and no sign of their valuables. And I can't prove a thing; between the two jurisdictions it would be impossible to verify what really happened. The police here would be just like in LA, they won't be interested in my story because I've got nothing to show them. I'm just a tourist from Spain with a crazy conspiracy theory and they have more interesting things to do. Time to go home, he decided, disconsolately.

He'd called Soledad to tell her he'd made no progress and was coming straight back home. He thought she sounded a little disappointed, maybe enjoying her shopping with Laura too much. Espinoza hadn't told her the full story about Ricky's death and the murders, he'd have to find the right moment when he got home, it was much too dreadful to talk about on the telephone. He made himself as comfortable as possible, lying across the three seats, eventually drifting off to sleep, furious that he couldn't avenge his cousin's death and the destruction of his reputation.

London, England

Esther's mobile pinged at 6am. Harry was snoring and she crept quietly out of bed and went into the kitchen. It was a short message: *Premises empty. All goods delivered to buyer. Funds in your bank account. Boxes disposed of. Here are details for transfer. Shirley.* It was followed by details of a bank account in Puerto Rica. It would cost her another $50,000 but it had been a good investment. The cash was already sitting in her account in Guadeloupe. It could only get better.

She went back to bed and woke Harry up. She was feeling really good.

SIX

Zurich, Switzerland

May, 2019

'The US job produced just over $1 million net. There weren't many unclaimed boxes and not much value in them, but it was an excellent test run. That was good information, well done.'

The Frenchman took a drag on his noxious cigarette, carefully blowing the smoke away from her. 'Thanks. What's my cut?'

Esther and Jolidon were drinking a coffee in the Ramseyer, Haldeman offices in Stockerstrasse, Zurich. She'd come up by train from Geneva that morning. The premises reflected the past glory of the company, a well-appointed office on the 3rd floor of a prestigious building in the highly sought-after business centre of the city.

'$150,000; 15%,' she replied, 'as we agreed. Plus the fifty thousand for your work on the Geneva project. Then you'll have 25% going forward. Unless you're getting greedy already?'

He knew she was stealing from him, but there'd be chances for him to do the same, so he didn't mind. *Honesty amongst thieves*, he told himself. 'Ça va, ça va. If Geneva pays off like I think it will, 15% suits me fine.'

'Good, that's settled.' *And $1.1 million suits me just fine.*

The $125,000 she'd gambled on acquiring the Los Angeles RH business had produced almost $900,000 in cash. She'd collected this herself from the boxes, in San Diego in May, then $500k from the sale of the valuables, which Shirley had deposited in her Guadeloupe bank account and most of which was now in her account with the First Credit Bank of Bahrain. The goods had been worth more, but she'd decided to take a job lot price of a half a million, rather than risk trying to sell them on the open market. She supposed Shirley had taken a slice off the top, besides her $50k fee, but it was only to be expected and she wasn't unhappy with the deal; over $1million was not to be sneezed at.

Esther had made sure there were no risks attached after closing the San Diego office. She'd acquired the LA business through *Almeida Enterprises*, her Cayman Island company, via a Delaware corporation, owned in Curaçao by a UK company with a Panama lawyer as director and a registered office in a grocery shop in Manchester. The premises in San Diego had been rented for 3 months by a fictional tenant and there was no paper trail to follow. After learning the hard way from her losses in previous ventures, this time she'd taken the first $1.15 million, leaving enough for expenses and to be shared with the other 'partners'. Her bank balances were climbing nicely, she was becoming what she'd always wanted to be, a wealthy woman. The suite she'd booked in the hotel in Geneva cost a small fortune, proof of her new status.

'Where do you want the transfer, Claude? I can introduce you to a good bank, French speaking, no questions asked, no transparency.'

'Sounds perfect. Where is it?'

'Guadeloupe, the Credit Bank. I'll get the forms sent to you and make the transfer when it's set up.' She didn't mention that the managing director, an unhappily married sex addict, was most indiscreet after a bottle of champagne and a session of her personal attention. That was why she'd transferred most of her funds to the Bahraini bank, another lesson learned. Nevertheless, she could easily find out if Jolidon banked any funds she didn't know about.

He nodded and she went on, 'I haven't seen you for almost two months, going back and forth from London to LA was a real hassle, but worth it. It seems you've got the Geneva project under control, thanks, I'm impressed. Why don't you bring me up to date on the latest situation?'

'Sure. Everything's going like clockwork, no complications. Soon, Simenon will no longer be a concern. The inquest is scheduled to start in Geneva next Wednesday, they brought it forward because of the pending authorisation of the construction project, but I don't expect any problems. The reports from the engineers and the forensic experts are all conclusive. Definitely a tragic accident, most unfortunate. For Gilles, that is, not us.'

'That's true. But you got everything tied up before that?'

'Of course. Like I told you, everything was done according to the book. All the contents were inventoried by Simenon and certified by that *Huissier Judiciaire* you found, Maître René Christen.'

'What's he like, did I make a good choice?'

'Seems like a decent guy, bright enough not to ask too many questions and needs the money.'

'That's what I thought, good. Then?'

'I sent him here so he could certify there's no more

valuables in Zurich and that's when the accident happened.' He took a drag on his cheroot. 'We'd just finished emptying the boxes and inventorying the contents in Geneva.'

'How many boxes were there in the end?'

'Over 800 altogether, 400 out of contract and about the same number prepaid and unclaimed. Anyway, while he was away in Zurich, I went through all the items, identified the most valuable pieces and prepared the replacement list, with both signatures on it.' He laughed, 'I've learned a new trade, become quite a proficient forger.'

'Good, so as we agreed, you filed the less valuable one with *Edificio* and you've got the full one. Do you have my copies?'

He handed her an envelope and she pushed it into her bag. 'How many items on our inventory?'

'About 3,000, it's a complete list of everything the boxes contained. The one I gave to *Edificio* contains about half, the less valuable stuff. Our list includes the 1,500 best pieces. There's a lot of good merchandise there, a lot of value.'

At the sound of, '1,500 best pieces', a delicious shiver ran up her spine. 'Christen doesn't know about the Edificio list?'

'Of course not, he doesn't talk to them, I'm in charge of the business.'

'Where are the goods now?'

'In a warehouse on the other side of town, all with their box numbers attached. We were lucky, once the boxes were all emptied and I signed the contract with *Edificio*, no one was interested in them anymore. After the accident, they were only concerned with getting the permits through, they forgot all about the security boxes. I got everything shipped up quietly, no problems.'

'Good work, Claude, you've handled things really well. Does Christen know where the goods are?'

'I've never told him, but he'd be pretty stupid if he didn't have some idea.'

'You're not worried about that?'

'Like I said, he doesn't ask, and I don't tell him.'

'OK, I hope you're right.' She moved on to a less agreeable subject, 'What about the office move?' She loved the feeling of importance the smart environment of the Ramseyer, Haldeman premises gave her, but it was expensive and too high-profile, their new business wouldn't withstand the visibility.

'The owners accepted our notice for the end of the month. They've obviously got another prospect and our rent is quite low for this area. I'm sure they'll be happy to get rid of us. I've already rented a cheap apartment, further out of town. Here's the address.' He handed her a card with the name, '*RH Security Services*', and an address in *Badenerstrasse*.

'Where is it?'

'About 6 km from the centre, not far from the warehouse; a really tatty neighbourhood, hard to find, anonymous, no name on the door. Top floor on its own; five rooms, access to the roof and fire escape. There's enough space for a large office and living accommodation for me. The big advantage is that there's an intercom in the entrance lobby, or you need a key to get inside to the stairs or the elevator. I'll put a fake name on the mailbox, put some blinds on the front windows, install a CCTV camera outside the apartment door and I won't answer the intercom unless I'm expecting a visitor. I've bought a big, old-fashioned strongbox for the office, the saleable valuables can be kept in it, they're mostly small items of high value.'

She shuddered at the mental image, remembering too many places of that description, and worse, that she'd had to hide in over the years. 'What's your timeframe?'

'I'm moving in there this weekend and I'll sort through all the merchandise in the warehouse again and move the valuable items to the strongbox, like I said, about 1,500.'

'And you'll keep some warehouse space to store the stuff we're not interested in, with their box numbers? Not just the rubbish, but pieces that can be traced, like paintings or engraved items. You might need to return something if clients do manage to find you. It would be good for your reputation.'

Jolidon laughed then nodded his agreement and she asked, 'RH Security Services, that's not the same company?'

He shrugged cynically, 'No, it's just a name. I liquidated the old company after I bought it from Edificio 2000, as we agreed. It's in case they check on me, it looks the same but there's no company behind it and I don't expect to be giving the cards out to anyone else. I put the *Badenerstrasse* street address on the website for the same reason, but no apartment number, so it's virtually anonymous.'

'Sounds like you've thought of everything, well done. Now, what about the cash? How much was there?'

'I thought you'd ask that. Quite a lot, but maybe less than you might expect, seems people have less reason to hide cash in Switzerland than in other countries.'

'I assume it's not on the inventory?'

'All of it? You must be joking! You think I'm going to put all that cash on an inventory that's going to the *Edificio* bosses? it wouldn't be there for very long. They're Italian property developers, most corrupt business there is.' He laughed, 'Apart from ours.'

'So where is it?'

'In my apartment, with a separate list signed by Simenon and Maître René Christen.' He handed her three photocopied pages. 'Here. One million nine hundred and seventy thousand dollars in twelve currencies and notes of different denominations.'

SEVEN

Zurich, Switzerland

May, 2019

Two million dollars! That's about one and a half for me and the rest will pay off everyone else. Esther studied the list for a long moment, forcing herself to remain calm, considering potential issues. 'What did you put on the *Edificio* inventory?'

'A couple of hundred thousand, I had to put something.' He saw her worried glance. 'It's OK, they won't query it, I told them that most of the clients who had declared cash on their deposit statements had come to retrieve it and that's what was left unclaimed.'

'And they didn't try to grab it?'

'Not worth their risk. For two million they'd have manufactured an argument to keep the cash. *'For safekeeping, in an escrow account'*, something like that, but not for just two hundred grand.'

'Clever thinking. Did you actually check to see how many customers had declared they'd put cash in their boxes?'

'Of course. I looked through the original deposit statements for every remaining box. There's less than 100 clients who stated on their forms, 'Currency Notes'.'

'That's still a lot of cash, people are going to come looking for it, they won't just suddenly forget they put

$100k in a deposit box a few years ago. That's a real risk.'

He wagged his finger. 'Some of them are out of contract and none of them stated the amount of the cash.'

'You're sure?'

'Not a single one. They could have left $100K or $5k, or nothing; they have no proof, believe me.'

'You mean like the guy in LA; that's what happened to him.'

'Right. He had no proof that he'd left any cash at all, it must have been untaxed earnings, 'black money'. Like I told Shirley, he was lucky we gave him $5k to keep him quiet, but we know better now. No proof means no cash. Agreed?'

'Agreed. And the same goes for any valuables without a deposit statement.' Esther's pulse was racing. *Jolidon's smart, he's been in the business a long time and he knows I was right, why most clients won't dare to make a fuss, for fear of reprisals.* 'But there's still a problem. We can't launder that much cash; it would take too long. We need someone to handle it.'

Jolidon said, 'I know the right people. It'll cost fifteen per cent.' He held his breath, watching for her reaction.

'Fifteen? I thought ten was the going rate.' *Merde! I've just lost $300k, and he'll make a commission of at least $50k on the transaction*, she figured.

'The money's in thousands of notes and a dozen different currencies, it's not a straightforward bulk transaction. Can you do better?' he bluffed.

Esther looked at the listings again, she knew she couldn't. 'I assume that includes your 'handling fee'? I mean, you just get your 25%? That'll be about $400k, right?'

He shrugged, 'That's it, but I think we should give

Christen 5%, he helped to count it and we need to keep him close, so we can hardly leave him out.'

'Has he said anything about the accident?'

'I've never discussed it with him, and he's never brought it up. He'll have his suspicions, but I told you, he wasn't in Geneva at the time. He was here in Zurich.'

'How will you explain the funds?'

'I'll tell him it's an advance on his commissions from the sales we're organising. He knows where the cash came from and he won't believe me. It's just a game, but it'll give him deniability, that's all he wants.'

'Alright, I agree, it'll buy more loyalty.' *That's $1.2 million net for me. I don't have to pay fees to anyone else.* 'It's guaranteed safe, no comebacks, transferred to Guadeloupe?' She could move it to Bahrain later, no reason to trust him with those details.

'I can guarantee it, I've worked with these people before.'

She folded the photocopies and put them in her bag. 'OK, go ahead. Keep your cut and pay Christen then send the balance to my Guadeloupe account. And try to get the rate down to 12.5%, it's a shitload of money.' She knew he wouldn't try to improve the rate, it would cost him too much, but she had to show who was the boss. *And $1.2 million is a good day's pay.*

Jolidon relaxed. *She's not as sharp as she thinks, she should have asked for the original signed listings.* 'I'll get onto it today. Give me the account number.'

She consulted her phone and scribbled down a number for him. 'That's the IBAN, you don't need the beneficiary's name. Get rid of it after the transaction and don't mention my name, or we'll definitely fall out.

'Now, I've decided on the venue in Geneva for the first sale in September; a big one, Binghams, high profile, top prices if we're lucky. Switzerland's perfect for anonymous sales and that's where René comes in, he'll certify for them. We'll sell a batch of about 100 items of various values as a test run. Once we get going, we can ramp up the volumes, increase the number of outlets and sales. I figure we can run it safely for a couple of years, so you should calculate accordingly. OK with you?'

'Whatever you say. So far it's working fine and I'm not going to try to fix it.'

'I'm still worried about Christen. Are you sure he's dependable? He's the key man in this whole Swiss sales process.'

'Look, Esther. Christen is a decent guy whose life got screwed. He's become one of those people who don't want to know what's going on. If they don't see, or ask, then they don't know, so they're not responsible. He's bust, he needs cash and he can smell it's on the way. When he starts making some real money, he'll be fine. So stop worrying about him and get the programme organised, that's what we all want, sales and profit.'

'I'll take your word for it, but keep a close eye on him, he's important and potentially dangerous. You've got a lot to do, moving and equipping the new office and your apartment. Sorting the merchandise out with the valuable items moved to the strongbox and the rest of the stuff organised in the warehouse. Then it'll be time to get ready for the September sale. I'll come back when you're on top of things, and you can give me the final inventory and we'll agree on the sale items. I'll bring the details of the seller, the bank accounts and anything else Christen needs to prepare the documentation and enter the merchandise in the sale. He should be used to the process, so you need to learn everything he knows, just in case, OK?'

'Understood, he's an easy-going guy, I'll keep him out of the way until I've sorted everything out and I'm ready to prepare for the sale.'

Her brain was working through the new situation. *I'm going to have to set up a more complicated structure for the sales and funds, there's much more than I expected, it's too risky to work only with Guadeloupe. I've got no choice with Jolidon and Christen, but I'll have to watch them like a hawk and make it impossible for them to screw me.* Her work would be cut out to get everything ready for September, but she knew the right people in the right places to help.

Then, casually, she added, 'What about box 72, did you do what I asked?'

'It was unclaimed as I told you and I instructed Simenon to put it aside, unopened.'

'Wasn't he suspicious about that?'

'I told him I'd managed to contact Ms Bishop and she would be coming to open it herself. He wasn't very happy about it, but there was nothing he could do, I was still his boss.' He laughed, 'Anyway, it's not important now.'

'Right, of course. When was the last time she checked the box?'

'It was when she came to pay another five years' fees, in 2015. I didn't see her, Simenon took her down to the vault and he told me she'd taken nothing from it. Just opened it, looked at the contents then closed it and paid the fees until 2020.'

I knew it, the diamonds are still there. She clasped her

hands together to prevent them from trembling. 'Where is the box now?'

'I opened it afterwards and there were some old accounting books and a briefcase in it, locked. I threw the books away, they had no value, but the case is here in the safe, still locked. It's not on either of the inventories.'

Esther looked closely into his eyes, deciding if he was telling her the truth. 'And you've heard nothing from the Bishop woman since then? It's been over two years since you sent the letter, right?'

'Two and a half, January 2017, and I've heard nothing at all from her.' He shrugged, 'She may not have received the letter. I believe there was some confusion about her address.'

She relaxed and laughed, 'I see, you mean it was misdirected?'

He kept a straight face. 'It's possible, I told you before, there were quite a few addresses that may have been wrong, I just don't know.'

'What happens if she comes to check?'

'First, she has to find us, which won't be easy, since I won't be receiving visitors. And second, she has no proof whatsoever of what's in that case. It's bound to be some undeclared valuables and she can't afford to make a fuss, she's a respectable business-woman now, can't risk any scandal.'

He's right, she must never have declared those diamonds, along with Ray's murder it would have been a front-page press item.

He gave her a smug look and lit up another cheroot, keeping the smoke away from her. 'What is in it, by the way?'

'I'm not sure, Claude. I have an idea, but I'm not going to share it with you. I'm sure you have many secrets in your life that you wouldn't like to share; the same goes for me. This is one of my secrets and I don't want to talk about it again. OK?'

He spread his hands in agreement and she said, 'Can you fetch the briefcase for me, please?'

Esther took it from him, trying to supress her excitement as she held it in her trembling hands. It was a battered old leather briefcase, like a lawyer's document case; quite light, with two buckled straps and locks on the front. The clasps of the locks wouldn't open and there were no marks on them to show they'd been forced. She breathed a sigh of relief, it seemed he wasn't lying. *So, this is Charlie Bishop's briefcase and, God willing, what's left of his diamonds.* She knew that Jolidon had been aware since 2010 that the contents of box 72 were valuable. *But he doesn't know it contains a fortune of diamonds, millions and millions worth. Or he'd probably try to get rid of me or strike a better deal,* she reasoned.

'I'll keep this, Claude. It has some sentimental value for me,' she murmured, remembering again d'Almeida, the Angolan genius, her first and only real love, who had taught her everything she needed to know to succeed this time around. He had given his life trying to recover these diamonds, the fortune that had been stolen from his father by Charlie Bishop and his Angolan Clan. She cursed their names. Ten years after his death, she still missed him more than she could admit. She had named her Cayman Islands company, *Almeida Enterprises*, after him, hoping it would bring her luck and fortune. *And now,* she told herself, *my luck is turning and so will my fortune. I'll get revenge for him, and Jenny Bishop will pay for her father-in-law's deceit. The diamonds will be where Ray wanted, with me.*

'Just forget about it, Claude,' she said. 'It's probably nothing worthwhile.'

Jolidon hid a cynical smile; he didn't believe a word of it, but it wasn't the time to argue. *Be patient*, he told himself. '*Très bien.* When you come back, we'll look at all the valuables, have a glass of champagne.'

'Thanks, Claude. I'll call you on WhatsApp next week. Be careful.'

He admired her voluptuous figure as she walked to the door with the briefcase. *I wonder who or what's behind this? She's not working alone, she never does. What's in that case that got her so excited? Let's see what happens, maybe I could get lucky.*

Jolidon had been without a partner for quite a while and had been immediately attracted to the notary, René Christen, who had obviously been through a rough time and was showing it. He was even-tempered, a less complicated person than Esther, but Jolidon knew it would present too many hierarchal difficulties. *Anyway*, he thought, *it's good to work with a couple of intelligent people again after that brain-dead experience at RH. A breath of fresh air and maybe a fortune in the making. No need to push against an open door.*

EIGHT

Geneva, Switzerland

May, 2019

After leaving Jolidon, Esther took the train to Geneva and searched online for a locksmith. She found one near Cornavin station and arrived there at 4pm, with the briefcase, explaining that she'd left her keys in Zurich. It took only a couple of minutes and thirty francs for the assistant to unlock the clasps and hand it back to her, still unopened. By 4:30pm she was checking in at the Hotel Richemond, close to the lake and near the banks on the other side of the bridge. She had wanted to stay at the Hotel Mercury, where she and Ray d'Almeida had last made love, just two days before he'd been murdered, but it no longer existed, and she had to admit the Richemond was in a different class. Going up in the elevator with the smartly uniformed concierge, she thought of all the dreadful places she'd been forced to stay in over the last couple of years. Although she still had a great affection for *The Liffy Landing*, her bolt-hole pub in Dublin, where she had recuperated from many disasters, it reminded her too much of the bad times. *No more cheap accommodation for me*, she told herself. *Thanks to Jenny Bishop, now it's nothing but the best.*

The suite on the fifth floor had vistas across *Lac Léman* and the *Pont du Mont Blanc* to the old part of Geneva, but

Esther wasn't yet in the mood to look at pretty scenery. She sat at a coffee table by the window and with trembling fingers, undid the straps of the old briefcase and pressed the clasps open. The case was light because it was almost empty, and she took out the few contents and placed them on the table. There were ten chamois leather pouches, each tied with a string like an old-fashioned lady's purse. The only other item was a soft felt bag and she opened that first. It contained two picture frames, one made of silver and the other of wood.

Inside the silver frame was a one thousand dollar note with a picture of a moustached man from the forties, wearing a wing collar. *Why would anyone keep that?* she wondered, putting it impatiently aside. In the wooden frame was an old article cut from a newspaper, with a faded photograph. The date was written in the corner of the paper, '27th May, 1975'. *The year after the Portuguese Revolution of the Carnations,* she realised. The photograph was of a man in a business suit shaking hands with an army officer wearing rows of medals across his chest. Another civilian, Hispanic-looking, stood on one side with a broad smile on his face. Three more army officers stood on the other, with smug expressions on their faces. The caption underneath the photo read:

Primeiro-Ministro Gonçalves visita APA. Outra história de sucesso de Governo.

'Prime Minister Goncalves visits APA. Another Government success story,' she translated in her mind. *This must be Charlie Bishop and one of his henchmen in Lisbon, before they stole the diamonds from Ray's father and fled the country.*

Esther put the two frames back in the bag, then,

nervously holding her breath and praying silently, she unfastened the first pouch and emptied it onto the table. Her eyes opened wide and a sense of calm and serenity seemed to slowly envelope her as, one after the other, she opened the pouches and spilled out their contents. When the last was emptied, she sat back in her chair, gazing at the ten piles of cut diamonds that covered the table, sparkling in the sunlight, the brilliant-cut facets showing the reflection of every available ray of light. One pile was comprised of stones of about two carats, the other piles were of smaller stones, with a few of a half carat, but just as radiant. It was as if a bright fire had suddenly been lit on the table. Her breath was taken away by the lustrous brilliance before her and she suddenly began to sob, remembering the dramatic, deadly history of this fortune.

Tears flooded from her eyes as, after all this time, she finally looked at what Ray had searched for all his life. This was the fortune that had been stolen away from his parents and that he had been killed for, trying to recoup it from the Bishop family. She struggled to overcome her emotions, trying to come to terms with his obsessive search for justice, his tragic death, and the strange, fortuitous sequence of events that had brought the gems into her possession.

Esther took some of the diamonds and poured them from hand to hand, unknowingly just as Laurent had done, four decades before and Jenny Bishop had done, a few years ago. The stones flooded with light, like a stream of brilliantly lit clear water trickling through her hands. *They must be worth twenty million dollars. Ray's family could have lived a life of luxury and still left him a fabulous inheritance. Too late*, she said to herself, *too late*

*for Ray's family and too late for him. But not too late for
me to make amends. And I intend to do just that.*

She replaced the stones into their pouches, locked them
in the briefcase and went down to the front desk. 'Can you
lock this away for me until tomorrow morning?' she asked
the head receptionist and watched him place the case in a
large safe in the back office. *'Merci,'* she said and went to
get something to eat. And a glass of champagne.

The next morning, Esther went to the *Banque d'Epargne
Vaudoise* in the Rue Verdaine, where she'd had an account
in her maiden name since 2006, before her disastrous
marriage to Gaston Rousseau. It took only fifteen minutes
to rent a safety deposit box and place the briefcase in it.
Ironic, she thought, as she left the building, *from one box
to another. I hope this one's safer than the last.*

Divonne, French-Swiss Border

'You crossed the border.' The female voice from the
radio told Claude Jolidon what he already knew, he had
just driven across the border from Chavannes, in Vaud,
Switzerland, to Divonne, in the French Department of Ain.
Since the Swiss now adhered to the *Schengen Agreement,*
there was no border check; there were still customs posts
on each side of the frontier, but they were unmanned, and
the traffic flowed without stopping. He drove on for a few
minutes and turned into the car park of the Grand Hotel,
home of one of France's most successful casinos.

The man who was waiting for him near the rear entrance
was over two metres tall, with the shoulders of a rugby
prop forward; Rudi, one of the casino's two bouncers.
Jolidon had seen him throw unhappy customers bodily

out of the door and down the stairs. Rudi was Bulgarian and spoke very limited French; in his job he didn't need a larger vocabulary.

Jolidon opened the boot, to reveal two postal sacks tied with cord, bulky and heavy, and a smaller canvas bag, zipped up. 'Hi, Rudi, help me with these,' he said, in English, and went to pick one of the sacks up. The giant Bulgarian pushed him aside and hoisted them both onto his shoulders. Jolidon locked the car with the other bag in the boot and followed him into the building and along the corridor to an office labelled, *Pietro Minchella, General Manager*. Rudi dumped the sacks on the floor of the office without a word and went out, closing the door behind him.

'Ciao, Claude.' The casino boss was small and chubby with a goatee beard. Wearing a red shirt and suede boots, he looked more like a Santa Claus than a fully paid up member of the Italian family who ran twenty casinos throughout Europe.

'*Buona serata, Pietro.*' Jolidon shook his hand, then took a pocketknife and cut through the cord on the sacks. 'Just under two million, like I told you. It's all in packets of the same currencies, 12 altogether, easy to check.' He pulled out a couple of packets to show the Italian.

'*Bene, grazie,* Claude. It'll be counted and processed by the weekend. Give me the account details, I'll have the transfer routed through Hong Kong. *Bene?*'

'*Parfait.* Any chance of getting the rate down a little?'

'You're already making 2.5% from me, if you have a better deal somewhere else, take it. Cash is very difficult these days, if it wasn't for our long friendship, I swear I wouldn't touch it, the risk is too high.'

Jolidon looked disappointed. 'OK,' the Italian said and opened the desk drawer. 'Here's twenty grand of chips, you might have a lucky night. *Va bene?*'

The following morning, Jolidon took the canvas bag into the Geneva branch of the Swiss Bank of Oman, where he deposited CHF250,000 in banknotes into an account in the name of *Paris-Muscat Trading SA*. He had lunch at the Café St Pierre, with the bank manager, whom he'd known for many years, then drove on the motorway back to Zurich. It was a bright, clear day and he looked across at the Alps on the other side of the lake, thinking of how he'd handled the transaction. He was confident that Esther would forget about the photocopied list and that Christen would be more than happy with $100k, 5% commission on the net total of the original listings.

Jolidon was certainly happy with his reward. It was a long time since he'd made $900k in a day.

NINE

Pedro Espinoza reread the letter from the Los Angeles Police Department for a third time.

'What is it, *querido*,' asked Soledad, hearing his sigh.

He put it aside, deciding it was finally time to tell his wife the whole story about his cousin's death. 'It's the confirmation from the American police that Ricky's funeral finally took place. He was cremated in Los Angeles last week.'

'I'm sorry, Pedro, that's awful news to receive, but at least it's the end of a sad story. Whatever it was that caused him to commit suicide, you can put it all behind you now and remember him as he was before it happened.'

'Maybe not. It's a lot more complicated than you know, it's time I told you everything that happened over there. Just a second.'

He went to his study and retrieved Ricky's last letter. 'Here, read this, then I'll tell you the whole story.'

She read Ricky's handwritten account of his last few days, starting out with his feelings of peace, tranquillity and happiness after returning from his pilgrimage with her husband. As she read on, she could feel the change in his emotional state, the anger and despair building up in his mind, until the final paragraphs, which brought tears to her eyes.

Ricky had written: *Please pardon me, my dear cousin, for what I may have to do. I'm at the end of my tether, I can't see any future for me unless the bank compensates me for my losses in full, so that I can get my life back and come to spend my retirement near you and your family, my family. I desperately hope that they will show compassion and do the honourable thing to set things to rights.*

But if they cannot, or will not, I see no point in continuing. If I've lost everything and I'm looking forward to a life of poverty and loneliness, I think I may decide to end it all and get it over with. If that happens, there may be casualties, because I'm not sure how I will act until that moment occurs. But whatever comes to pass, Pedro, please forgive me and remember that I love you, Soledad and Laura and her family and I don't want to cause you pain. You are all that's left of my family and if I can't be with you, able to enjoy the rest of our lives together, then I don't want to face the alternative.

Dios los bendiga a todos, God bless you all.

Your loving cousin, Ricardo

'So, what actually happened in Los Angeles, Pedro?'

In an unemotional voice, Espinoza described to her the result of his investigations in the US, finishing with his visit to the shady security business in San Diego.

'*Dios Mio*, my God. How terribly sad.' She wiped her eyes. 'Everything just went wrong, one thing then the next until he must have thought there was some kind of a vendetta against him. To kill innocent people, then himself, he must have simply lost his mind. Poor Ricardo, he was the most peace-loving man you could find; he didn't deserve to become a murderer. It's just too awful to think about.'

They sat in silence for a moment then she asked, 'What did you mean, "maybe you can't put it behind you"?'

'If I could find out who was behind the purchase of *RH Security International* in LA, I might find a trail back to the people who stole Ricky's insurance money, the $150,000 that he kept for just such an emergency. That was what finally drove him to the limit, they are the people who were really responsible for those deaths.'

'Pedro, you're a 65 year old, semi-retired private detective in Malaga. How do you think you're ever going to find that out? Poor Ricky is gone, *Dios lo tenga en su Gloria,* God rest his soul, and the rest is all water under the bridge, let's leave well alone and get on with enjoying our humdrum, boring lives.'

'You're right, as usual, my dear. I'll pour you a glass of *Verdejo* before lunch.' He went to the wine fridge, *Stranger things have happened*, he said to himself, crossing his fingers.

Chelsea, London, England

'It's the most beautiful watch I've ever seen. Come here and give me a kiss.' Harry Fern-Chapman fastened the clasp of the gold Rolex on his wrist and pulled Esther into his arms, kissing her deeply and stroking her backside, thrusting against her. 'Thank you darling, it's really fabulous, the best gift I've ever received. You've been away for a lifetime, what were you doing, robbing a bank?'

Esther almost said, *No, but it seems like it*. That week she'd received confirmation from Guadeloupe that her account had been credited with $1.2 million from the cash in the Ramseyer, Haldeman boxes. She'd immediately transferred the total amount to Bahrain, where she now had almost $2.5 million. The explosion in her wealth was making her feel giddy. Calming herself, she answered carefully, 'My business is a bit complicated, it needs time to get results, but I had a very successful trip.'

'Do you want to tell me about it? It sounds interesting.'

'Not now, but I might, after you thank me properly. I've missed you.' She led him to the bedroom, 'Time to make up for it.'

An hour later, after the best sex she'd had in a long time, she went to the kitchen and poured two glasses of champagne. 'Cheers, darling,' she kissed him again. 'Let's go somewhere special for dinner. I feel like celebrating.'

'I'll book at the new Ivy café in Marylebone, I've heard it's really good.' He made the reservation then put aside the phone and sipped his champagne. 'You said you'd tell me about your business and I'm very intrigued. What exactly do you do?'

She thought for a moment, *I'd better nip this in the bud right away.* 'Harry, you've put me in a difficult situation. I'd love to tell you about it, but I'm in a business that requires strict confidentiality. The rewards are high, as you've seen, but I can never talk about what I do, or it could compromise my position and the wellbeing of my team.'

'Wow! You're some kind of spy, I knew it.'

'No comment, Harry. So, can we agree not to talk about it now, or ever in the future?'

'Sorry, just joking. I promise never to raise the subject again. OK?'

'Then I'll get us a couple more glasses and we can drink to that.'

She brought the drinks over and he said, 'I've got some rather good news to celebrate as well.'

Esther put down her glass and looked expectantly at him. 'OK, you've got my attention. What is it?'

He thumbed through a copy of the *Financial Times* to find an article. 'Here, read this. I think you'll be impressed.'

She raised her eyebrows at the headline to the quarter page item; '*Fern-Chapman's Olympic Funds Group hits £2 Billion*'. 'Congratulations Harry, that's amazing. Well done.' She scanned the article, 'It says you've averaged 12.5% return on your five funds for two years running. Is that right?'

'Since I set up on my own, that's right. I came out third in the UK fund management performance charts, so I'm pretty pleased. That's why we've attracted so much new money, almost £1 billion already this year. We're being recommended by all the UK investment managers and online platforms.'

'How do you make those returns? I thought the UK annual market performance was less than 10%, that's a huge difference.'

Fern-Chapman shrugged his shoulders, smiling with false modesty. 'That's what I've always done. When I was with Selchurch Peak, I was their star performer, with almost £10 billion under management. My reputation speaks for itself; I haven't lost the knack and the investment industry knows that.'

Esther's keen brain was calculating. *12.5% of $2.5 million is over $300,000 per year. My money's earning nothing in Bahrain. In fact, it's costing me fees and* *transaction charges every month. Maybe something to think about. Not yet, but maybe soon.*

Harry was saying, 'I can show you the details of our five funds if you like, what I look for and how I invest. It might be of interest to you, if you've got any spare money lying around.'

'Not now, Harry, maybe some other day. We've got time for something better before dinner.' She kissed him passionately again and pushed him back onto the couch.

TEN

Zurich, Switzerland

July, 2018

The meter showed ninety-five francs and Esther Bonnard climbed out of the taxi and gave the driver a CHF100-note. 'Keep the change,' she said in German, comparing the exorbitant price with a London cab, which would have been half the price for the same twenty-minute journey. *Never mind, I can afford it,* she comforted herself. She waited until he drove off, looking across at the cheap six-storey building with shops and a garage on the ground floor.

She hadn't been to the 'office' before and immediately took a dislike to it; the seedy building and surroundings reminded her of bad times in her life. But she was impressed by the anonymity achieved by Jolidon. It was several kilometres out of town, basically a tenement building inhabited by immigrants and with nothing to indicate there was any kind of commercial activity there, let alone the successor to Ramseyer, Haldeman & Company. *No wonder he said clients wouldn't be able to find him, he was right.*

Crossing the street carefully and holding tight to her handbag, she entered the hallway of no. 819. The name on the mailbox for flat 601 was Kruger and she pressed the intercom button. A voice answered, '*Qui-est-ce?* Who is it?'

'*Moi,*' she replied, and the door to the elevator unlocked. 'They're absolutely fabulous. Purest stones I've ever seen.' Claude Jolidon examined the larger of the diamonds through his loupe. 'Where did you find them?' Now, he was sure he knew the answer to the question, *the briefcase from Jenny Bishop's box no. 72, I should have kept it and done a runner.* But he knew he'd never have been able to get away with it, she'd have pursued him to the death. Besides, he didn't have the contacts to sell them.

Better the bird in the hand, he told himself, and when Esther replied sharply, 'I told you, some things I prefer to keep to myself,' he just nodded. 'Ok, I've got it. How much are they worth?'

'100 stones, worth between $1,500 and $2,000 per carat. I estimate the average size just over one carat, but Bingham's gemologist will give the exact weight. They should fetch close to $2 million. And there are more where they came from. Happy with that?' She saw his eyes light up, mentally calculating his share of the proceeds.

Esther had been busy the previous afternoon, in Geneva. First, she'd met René Christen, the *huissier*, at the *Luanda Banco de Credito, (Suisse) SA*, a branch of the Angolan financial institution. They introduced themselves to her contact, M. Alberto Cortola, who ushered them into a meeting room and produced a file of documents to open a multi-currency account. The only stipulation was that the balance would never be inferior to $100,000. The title of the account was *The African Benevolent Trust Fiduciary Account* and it could be operated only with the joint signatures of Mlle Esther Bonnard and Mâitre René Christen.

They showed their personal identity documents and gave

the address of Christen's studio apartment in Carouge, a suburb of Geneva. Esther handed over a file containing copies of the Trust's corporate documents, together with a cashier's cheque for $100,000 to fund the account. The banker examined the documents, then seeming satisfied, he looked the cheque over carefully. It was drawn on The Credit Bank of Guadeloupe and Esther had a moment of nervousness, but he didn't seem at all interested. It wasn't unusual for a customer to open an account with a deposit of $100,000.

The whole procedure took less than an hour and, relieved that the banker had asked no difficult questions, they walked out of the bank into the warm afternoon sunshine. She said to the notary, 'Claude doesn't know about this account and I don't want him to. The seller is an Angolan Trust, so it's normal that the fiduciary account is with an Angolan bank.' He nodded his understanding and she went on, 'Nobody can operate it alone, so the sales proceeds will be totally safe until we transfer them to the Trust's main account in Panama. Jolidon doesn't need to know the details, so let's keep them just between us.'

'Thanks for your confidence, Esther, that's fine with me. I'm used to fiduciary accounts, I won't be the one to abuse the situation, you can count on me.'

'I'll give him a copy of the Trust documents, so he knows who the seller is. He'll pass them on to you, so don't be surprised. *Merci et au revoir,* René, I'll see you after the sale, good luck and let's make a fortune together.'

Christen went off to catch his tram to Carouge and Esther walked across the bridge to the old town. *We'll see if he can keep his mouth shut. Claude can't keep a secret, so I'll soon know if he's let anything slip that he shouldn't.*

Esther never trusted anyone one hundred per cent, she'd encountered a lot of double dealing and deceit in her life. She'd also practised it extensively herself.

Ten minutes later she entered the *Banque d'Epargne Vaudoise*, where she retrieved Charlie Bishop's briefcase and returned to the Richemond in a taxi. Emptying the pouches onto the dressing table, she once again marvelled at the ten beautiful piles of diamonds, glistening in the sunlight from the window. She selected ten stones from each pile to make ten smaller parcels, wrapping the stones she'd chosen in tissue paper, in a padded envelope, sealed and sellotaped around, which she placed in the safe in her room, then replaced the pouches in the case.

The case was now safely back in the bank vault and she'd travelled by train to Zurich that morning with the envelope held tightly in her handbag. She'd enjoyed the journey through the Swiss countryside, thinking of how much her bank account would soon be boosted by the contents.

Jolidon reluctantly poured the stones back into the envelope. 'Well, wherever you got them, congratulations. Like you said, this will be a hell of a good sale. I'll show you the items I've chosen, see if you're happy with them.'

A massive steel strongbox stood behind him against the wall and he opened its three locks with separate keys, entered a code on the keypad and pulled the heavy door open. He took out a carton, laying the contents on his desk. There were about 100 items, ranging from diamond and sapphire necklaces, emerald bracelets and rings, to Cartier and Patek-Phillipe men's and women's watches. Each item was labelled with the number of the security box it came from. A dazzling display of beautifully crafted wearable ornaments lay before her, but all Esther saw was a large pile of Swiss Francs.

'What's your estimate?'

He showed her the list. 'We're hoping for a million and a half.'

'So, we could make over $3 million?'

'Something like that.'

She felt a quiver of anticipation. 'OK, here's the paperwork on the seller.' She handed him a folder containing various corporate documents. The name on the folder was *The African Benevolent Trust*. 'The trustee's name is Benjamin Appletree, that's his signature there. You can sign for him, just scrawl it as best you can, it's not important.'

Jolidon looked quickly through the Deed of Trust. 'Registered in Angola, very appropriate for selling those diamonds.'

'It's irrelevant, Luanda just happens to be a safe place for paperwork, not for anything else though.'

He raised his eyebrows but knew better than to ask questions. 'Right, I'll confirm everything to Christen and he'll get the paperwork done with Binghams.'

'What will you tell him about the valuables?'

'Nothing, and he won't ask.' He laughed, 'He's got a really bad problem if he doesn't remember seeing them before, when he signed the inventories.'

'You're absolutely sure he'll be OK? This is a big sale, we can't afford it to go wrong.'

'All the more reason he'll be fine. He's still broke, can't wait for his commission from the first proceeds. And don't forget, after this sale, he's in deep; he can't afford to cause any problems, so don't worry about him.'

She was confident he hadn't heard anything about the fiduciary account from the *huissier*. 'OK, if you say so. Binghams will want the valuables submitted by next week, to do the photographs and get the catalogue out in good time.'

'No problem, he knows his stuff. We'll make it, stop worrying.'

Jolidon put the carton of jewellery and Esther's package back into the strongbox and turned the three keys, which he placed in a smaller safe by his desk. 'Anything else?'

'Yes. I've been thinking again about the timeframe.'

'I'm listening.'

'Has there been anyone around, any visitors, enquiries, letters from clients looking for their property?'

'Well, you saw the name on the box downstairs is Kruger, but there's nobody in the building of that name. I never come in with any of the residents and I use the stairs, so I doubt anyone's even seen me around. The intercom's rung maybe a half-dozen times, so there's been a few people here, but I think they were just trying all the flats, to see what response they got. Maybe they were looking for RH, but I don't know and I don't care. When nobody answers, they give up and go away. There hasn't been a soul up to this floor since I came here a month ago.

'So far as mail goes, obviously none comes here. I opened a *Case Postale* at the local Post Office in my own name, with an address at my tobacconists' shop in Alstetten, a kilometre along the road. A few letters have been forwarded to me from the Ramseyer, Haldeman *Case Postale* in Geneva, that's all. I kept that one open with my name and this address so the Edificio 2000 people would see I was being diligent, but I don't think they pay any attention. They've got their hands full trying to get the final building permit. That's it.'

'What did you do with the letters?'

He opened the drawer of his desk and placed four unopened envelopes, addressed to Ramseyer, Haldeman, in front of her. 'You want to read them?'

She grimaced, '*Non, merci*. They might make us feel guilty, and we wouldn't want that, would we?' She tore them up and threw the pieces in the waste basket. '*Voilà*, filed away.'

'You said something about the timeframe?'

'Yes. I think it's too long. We can't afford to go slowly; we have to speed things up.'

'Why? Has something happened?'

'No, nothing at all, not yet. But those callers and letters could be a sign of problems to come. We've got 1,000 items to sell, and we can't do that safely with a couple of sales a year. It'll take 5 years, and in a five-year period, something will definitely go wrong, I can guarantee it. Someone will come along with a claim we can't fulfil, and we won't be able to stall them forever without it going legal.'

'What do you suggest?'

'There are three big auction houses holding sales in Geneva; McCallums in June, Binghams in September and Drewberrys in November. Then all of them have a sale in February. That's 7 major sales from now till the end of next year. If the Binghams' sale in September goes well, we should prepare to sell goods in all of them. We place 100 items of the best merchandise in all 7 sales and that's 70% sold. Christen's already talked to some local auction houses in Berne, Zurich and Basel, they'll get rid of the less expensive stuff. If we follow this plan, we can be out of this business by the end of next year with a fortune, no more risk, *merci et adieu.*'

'What about the diamonds, how many do you have left?'

She dodged the question, 'Enough for this programme.' *Plus another 300 for me to keep for my old age*, she told herself.

'You don't think it'll look suspicious, the diamonds? All those catalogues coming out with photos of virtually the same stones?'

'When they're being sold by an African Trust? This is Geneva, Claude. It's chickenfeed compared to the dodgy deals that get done every day. I should know, don't forget I worked with a Swiss bank, you can't imagine what goes on. And between you and me, we couldn't do it in London or New York, it's not so easy and I don't have the contacts in place. That's why Christen's so important, though I'd never tell him that. He's a Swiss notary, fully accredited, no one's going to question his signature. As long as he stays loyal and doesn't get too greedy, we've got the official stamp of approval.'

'So, after September we get ready for Drewberrys in November? Then you want to do three sales in February?'

'Can you be ready for them?'

'If we decide now, no problem. I'll get started on the November merchandise right away and I'll need the next batch of diamonds no later than September. Then we've got plenty of time until February.'

'OK, it's agreed, depending on the Binghams' results.'

In the train back to Geneva, Esther felt drowsy. The planning and preparation of the project had been exciting, but exhausting, though she was certain the September sale would exceed their expectations. She closed her eyes, *This time I've got everything right. No one's going to stop me taking back the fortune that was stolen from Ray's father. No one even knows what's happened to those diamonds. And if they ever find out, It'll be too late. I'll be rich and long gone.* She fell into a deep sleep as the train rushed through the darkening afternoon, taking her to her suite at the Hotel Richemond. Tomorrow morning she'd be back in Chelsea with Harry, they'd been invited to a party on Saturday by one of his rich clients to celebrate Boris Johnson's appointment as Prime Minister. She didn't care one way or another, but Harry was happy about it. Everything in Esther's life was good. For now.

Claude Jolidon was looking out of the window of the scruffy apartment, a lighted cheroot in his mouth. He was thinking about what Esther had said, *'we can be out of this business by the end of next year with a fortune, no more risk, merci et adieu.'*

We haven't even had our first big sale yet, and so far, I've made almost \$1 million from her idea. He decided it was time to start making future plans.

ELEVEN

'Very nice to meet you at last, Esther. Harry's been talking you up for a long time. I must say, he wasn't exaggerating at all, he's a lucky man. Cheers.' Sir Reginald Scarbrough clinked his champagne glass against hers.

'*Santé* and thank you for inviting me, Sir Reginald.'

He squeezed her hand. 'Reggie, my dear. That's what my friends call me and now I hope we're friends.'

'Very well, Reggie.' She pronounced it with a French accent, and he laughed, swigging back his drink and glancing again at her bosom. 'You have a beautiful home,' she went on, 'quite exquisite décor and furnishings.'

'I can take no credit for it. Like my title, I inherited the house from my late father and my wife had it redecorated a few years ago. Ah, here comes Nicola now, you can compliment her yourself.'

Esther turned and watched the woman walk across the enormous reception room towards them, greeting other guests on the way. She was about the same age as him, late forties, big-boned and ample, wearing a blue and gold silk designer outfit that must have cost the earth. The woman took her hands in hers, a condescending smile on her face. 'Such a delight to meet you, Esther. Harry has been hiding you for far too long, he's going to get a telling off from me.'

'I'll leave you to work out a suitable punishment.' Scarbrough kissed his wife's cheek and moved over to a nearby group of three couples. Esther thought she recognised one of the women from a popular television series. *Not as slim as she looks on TV*, she noticed with some pleasure, *rather chubby in fact*.

Standing near her and next to Nicola Scarbrough, Esther felt like a wood nymph, knowing how the understated pants suit showed off her slim, voluptuous figure, the low-cut blouse revealing just enough of her magnificent breasts to catch the attention, not just of Reggie, but of every man in the room. She felt totally comfortable in the midst of this crowd of elite, wealthy Londoners; she had a pile of money in the bank, a $20 million fortune of diamonds in a security vault and the best-looking man in the room was her partner, Harry Fern-Chapman. Esther had always had sexual allure, but she'd never had money. Now she had both and she loved the feeling. She hadn't felt so much at ease since her time as Elodie Delacroix, in Dubai, before the catastrophic ending when she'd had to flee back to Dublin like a criminal.

She pushed the thought from her mind and focussed on Lady Scarbrough, who was still burbling on about Harry. 'He's becoming quite a celebrity since he started out on his own. Clever move, using his reputation to steal some large clients and build a business quickly from nothing. Reggie and several of our friends are investing with him now, he seems to be getting a lot of attention. Look, that's Simon Mitchel, the TV actor, with his wife. He's making a lot of money now, I believe Harry and he have become good friends.'

Esther felt a pang of jealousy. *I thought he was managing funds for thousands of anonymous investors. He didn't tell me he had friends in such exalted circles. Why not, I wonder?* She said vaguely, 'I'm happy to hear he's doing so well, he never tells me much about his business.'

'Oh, my dear, I find it's best to stay out of these things. If the men want to throw their money around to impress their neighbours, let them do it. I actually find it all very tasteless. all this noise about stock markets, bonds, takeovers and exchange rates; just paper fortunes. One day they're making millions, the next they're preaching poverty. It has nothing to do with real wealth: land, property, family trust funds, that kind of old-fashioned wealth.'

She leaned closer to Esther, 'It's like this Brexit business, everyone rushing back and forwards to Brussels, making speeches and voting in the House of Commons and absolutely nothing changes. It's no surprise to me that Theresa May finally gave up, she never believed in leaving the EU in the first place. But Boris Johnson hasn't much chance of doing better with virtually no majority and so many cynical, treacherous MPs who refuse to do the people's bidding. I'm afraid it will die a death of attrition in the end, it's a great shame.'

'You're in favour of Brexit, then?'

'Of course, my dear. I know you're French and perhaps don't agree, but we've never been comfortable in the EU and you've never really welcomed us, only our financial contribution, and it's time we regained our sovereignty. I'm sure there were many ignorant, misguided people who voted to follow Farage and Johnson, but the same is true of any election or referendum and in the end, it's only the result that counts. When we finally had a chance to close our borders to all these foreigners who want to suck our social services and the NHS dry, we should have snatched it.'

Oblivious to Esther's shocked expression, she continued her rant. 'The most likely outcome after all this fuss and noise is that there'll be a general election and things could get even worse. If that pair of communist failures, Corbyn and McDonald, manage to grab power, then we really will have to worry about our fortunes. Sadly, I realise that my voice counts for nothing. We women still don't have much to say about things and the men can't agree on anything except disagreeing. But I suppose as long as it keeps them happy and doesn't affect our way of life or our fortunes, we should just ignore it, let them play their silly games and hope that common sense will finally prevail. Although I'm not very hopeful of that.'

Esther was speechless, trying to decide whether Lady Scarbrough was an empty-headed snob, a racist, or an astute thinker with her own opinions. She wasn't used to hearing English people speak so radically, complaining about immigration to a foreigner, and effectively rubbishing everything that was going on around them in the UK, including Harry's business career.

Remembering the Scarbroughs were amongst Harry's biggest investors, she decided the safest option was to change the subject, 'Reggie told me that you supervised the redecoration of the house. Would you like to show me around? It looks really beautiful.'

Esther spent the next couple of hours meeting a lot of people she didn't know and wouldn't remember, including billionaires, high flying businessmen, politicians and members of the House of Lords, and the usual collection of actors and personalities who were there to pose for photographs. She refused every offer; Esther couldn't afford to be recognised by one of the many people, official and unofficial, who were looking for her in several countries. She also refused to be drawn into a discussion on politics or Brexit, which seemed to be uppermost in everyone's mind, not just Nicola Scarbrough's. She had her own views on the matters, as a strong, independent woman with experience of living in many different countries, but she didn't believe in sharing such thoughts with strangers, whatever their title might be. She also heard a lot of comments confirming Harry's success in the investment world and decided to find out more from him when they were together in Chelsea.

It was 10pm and she was searching through the crowd for him to take her home when an attractive woman she didn't recognise came up to her and took her hand. 'Hello, please excuse me, but I'm sure I know you, and I'm racking my brain to think how. Haven't we met somewhere?'

Esther stiffened imperceptibly, faking a smile as she quickly studied the woman. *Handsome, not beautiful, strong features, accent may be Eastern European, about 40 years of age, fair hair tied back with a blue ribbon, good figure, sensible blue dress and silk wrap around her shoulders. Obviously not one of the high-flying celebrity guests.* She knew immediately they'd never met. *Who is she, how does she know me?*

'I'm sorry, but I think you've mistaken me for someone else. There's so many people here, it's easily done.' She looked across the crowd of heads surrounding them, 'I see my partner is searching for me, I'd better get over to him before he thinks I've left with some handsome millionaire. Nice to meet you, goodbye.' She strode off quickly into the adjoining reception room.

Esther racked her brain trying to identify the mysterious

guest but couldn't find her face in her memory. She considered discreetly asking Reggie Scarbrough about the unknown woman but decided it might cause more trouble than it was worth. *Just a mistaken identity*, she reasoned; at least she hoped so. A few minutes later, she managed to find Harry, lecturing about his investment policies to a group of expensively dressed middle-aged men. *More millionaire Olympic Funds Group candidates*, she supposed, as she dragged him away. He was quite drunk and she tried to talk him into leaving.

'Not yet, darling,' he slurred. 'The finale is yet to come.' He pointed to a butler, who was placing a silver salver on a sideboard. 'Come and try it, best in town.'

There was a general movement of guests towards the salver, many of them taking something from it. Realising what was going on, she pulled Harry back. 'You don't need to take that stuff. Come home with me now and I'll give you a much better time than that ever will.'

'What's wrong with both?' he laughed and reached for one of the twists of cocaine in the bowl.

Esther didn't want to risk staying any longer, the meeting with the unknown woman had unnerved her. 'I'll show you what's wrong.' She left him and went to find Sir Reginald, thanking him and explaining that she had a migraine and had to get home. It was cool outside, and she pulled her coat around her, walking briskly until she found a cruising taxi. Sitting back in the warmth of the cab, she went back over the events of the reception; *Who was that woman? Did she really know me, or did she just want someone to talk to? I'd remember if I'd met her before and I know I haven't.*

She tried to put the incident out of her mind and thought

about the end of the party. *So that's how the high and mighty spend their evenings.* She had heard about the increase in drug use by the middle and upper classes in England but had no idea how blatant and acceptable it had become.

Cocaine, probably exported from South America by a murderous cartel, smuggled into the UK by a dangerous criminal gang, distributed by dealers, often with police connivance. Probably delivered by some smart looking courier and then served by a Lord of the Realm on a silver platter worth more than most people's annual earnings. Things have changed in this country, and not for the better.

These people don't know how lucky they are. They've never had to suffer hardship, poverty, fear, cruelty, probably not even disappointment. Money solves everything, even I know that.

Esther never felt sorry for herself, but nor did she ever forget how hard life had been to her. She put her head back and closed her eyes. Memories floated across her tired mind, from her childhood in Toulouse: the beatings and abuse inflicted on her by her father, after her mother, his second wife, had died in mysterious circumstances. Her arranged marriage with his nephew, Gaston Rousseau, a homosexual sadist, who took her away from her few friends and installed her in Geneva. A cruel, cold, friendless marriage that she somehow managed to escape from, thanks to Ray d'Almeida. Now, the world was her oyster and after all she'd been through, she knew she deserved it.

Her reverie was interrupted by the taxi driver's voice. 'Here we are, missus. That's exactly twelve quid, please.'

Esther gave him fifteen, she was feeling generous.

TWELVE

Esther had drunk very little at last night's reception and had spurned the cocaine; she was easily addicted and wanted to avoid the temptation. Champagne was one thing, but drugs were another. But she hadn't slept well, her mind wrestling with the incident of the unknown woman who seemed to recognise her. She was absolutely certain they had never met before. *So, either she was mistaken, and she's seen someone very similar to me, or, she's seen a photograph of me, and that would be a very dangerous thing.* Her married name and photograph had been circulated by Interpol since 2008, but by using her maiden name and other pseudonyms, avoiding ever flying from a French airport and crossing borders selectively, thanks to the Schengen zone, she had managed to avoid being identified. *Perhaps until now*, she thought worriedly.

Nicola Scarbrough seems to be an opinionated, calculating, racist snob, but I need an excuse to speak to her to find out who the woman is, what she does, how she could possibly know me. Meanwhile, I have to sort out Harry's head. He's no good to me drunk or drugged.

She'd finished her coffee and croissant by the time Harry emerged from the bedroom, looking bleary-eyed and hungover. She let him make himself a double espresso, then sat at the kitchen table with him, ready for a row.

Before she could speak, he leaned across and took her hand, 'Sorry, Esther, I'm very sorry. I promise it won't happen again. I got a bit carried away, all those snobs sucking up to me. I'm still not used to it, it's quite an experience and it went to my head. I'll be more careful in future. Please forgive me.'

Esther was immediately suspicious. Harry seldom apologised for anything; she was the one who had to apologise after their occasional rows. *Why is he grovelling? What's going on in that head of his?* She got up and put her arms around him, kissed his cheek, *'Très bien.* I forgive you this time, but don't let there be a next time. Understood?'

She went to make two more coffees and took them into the living room. 'Come in here and take this with your coffee.' She gave him a paracetamol. 'You'll be fine in a half hour.'

Later, they were sitting chatting about the night before, when she said, 'Nicola Scarbrough was telling me how well Olympic Funds Group is doing; like the newspaper article said, growing very fast. She said Reggie and some of his friends are investing in the funds. I'm delighted for you.'

'Thanks, I can still hardly believe it, it's been a tough transition. You have no idea how difficult it is to get a good reputation in fund management. And it's even harder to keep it when you leave the umbrella of a big outfit. It's great that such a lot of experienced, skilful investors and fund managers have stayed with me since I started *Olympic*. Becoming a top manager with Selchurch

Peak was the right launching pad, I owe them a lot.'

She laughed, remembering what Lady Scarbrough had said. 'That didn't stop you from stealing as many of their clients as you could, did it?'

'That's not fair, Esther. I was with them for 10 years, from leaving university, and it was a great job and a fabulous experience. I learned a lot and made a pile of money with Selchurch but they made a lot more out of me. Then I risked my own savings to set up *Olympic* and some large clients came with me because they were happy with my management, so I'm not going to send them away. Then there's a lot of retail brokers who like my style and bring groups of small investors through their investment portfolio platforms.

'Anyway, there's more new money out there than you can possibly imagine, enough for all of us, and I'm attracting a decent slice of it. My specialist areas are popular and more importantly you've seen how good my results are, well above industry average.'

Esther knew more about banking and investing than she could disclose. 'You said you'd explain to me your funds and investment technique. What kind of opportunities do you look for?'

'The same markets I developed with *Selchurch*, I have five funds in basically five areas. Property and income trusts, well-backed hi-tech start-ups, oil and minerals mining, exploration and extraction, and smaller companies with niche market positions. I get quick capital returns or strong regular interest and dividend income from special situations that I spot. You have to dig really deep to separate the gold from the dross, but there are some valuable nuggets to be found.'

'Sounds like a fairly high-risk profile. You'll need better than average returns to justify that level of risk.'

He looked at her in surprise. 'You're absolutely right, and I do, average 12.5%, confirmed by the FT. You saw it, one of the best performances around.'

She wanted to say, *Mine is a lot better*, but just kissed him and said, 'That's great, Harry. I hope you keep it up and make a lot of money from it.'

'I didn't know you had such a good knowledge of the investment management industry,' he said thoughtfully. 'Have you been involved in banking?'

She backed off quickly. 'Not really. I worked in a bank many years ago, but I wasn't a banker or an investment advisor, just a secretary.' Esther had a fleeting image of Eric Schneider, the nose-blowing, sexually frustrated client manager at Klein Fellay in Geneva, where she'd worked in 2008. That was the first attempt to steal Jenny Bishop's fortune, ending in Ray d'Almeida's murder. Suddenly, for the first time since his death, she realised that she no longer felt sadness or remorse. *There's 20 million reasons in a bank vault in Geneva for me to be happy,* she thought, then switched her attention back to Harry.

He was saying, 'I don't believe you've ever been just a secretary, you're way too smart for that. I'm quite sure you're a very informed lady. I promised not to ask you again, but I know your trips to Geneva and elsewhere aren't just sight-seeing holidays. Most people don't come back from vacation with a solid gold Rolex for their boyfriend.' He grabbed her by the shoulders, staring into her eyes. 'I'm onto you, Esther Bonnard. What's your guilty secret? Share it with me.'

She froze for a moment, sure he'd seen through her disguise, somehow found out the truth about her past. Then he laughed and kissed her passionately. 'I don't care who or what you are. You're a mystery woman but you're my mystery woman and that's good enough for me.' He led her to the bedroom. 'Let me apologise properly for last night.'

'I've got some more good news for you.'

It was five in the afternoon. Esther looked up from the text she was reading on her mobile phone. 'I'm all ears.'

'Just look around this flat.'

She looked around at the mess they'd created in the room. It was a good-sized apartment, with a kitchen, two bedrooms, office and a living-dining room, where every chair and table seemed to be covered in papers and documents. *And it's always like this*, she thought. 'Sorry, I'll tidy up, but you have to pick up your own stuff, I don't know where it belongs.'

'I will, but that's not what I meant. The problem is, this flat's too small, it's always in a mess. We need more space, we both need a proper office, you need a dressing room of your own and we need proper reception rooms where we can entertain people, the kind of people who can help me expand *Olympic* even more.'

Before she could answer, he went on, 'Besides, Chelsea's no longer the top address it used to be. I think we deserve something grander, more in line with my reputation and the money I'm making now. And you deserve it too.'

'But I like Chelsea, it's just like a great big village and we've got everything we need here, shops, restaurants, parks. It's a great place to live.'

'How well do you know London, Esther?'

'Quite well, I suppose, but you know it better than I do. Where is it better than Chelsea?'

'Belgravia, that's the place to be.'

'So what do you have in mind?'

'Look at this.' He turned his laptop around so she could see the screen. 'This is our new home, I hope you like it.'

She looked at the majestic white stone façade of the Georgian house on the screen. *'Mon Dieu, c'est magnifique.'*

'It's on Eaton Square, with a terrace facing south-west across the gardens, so you get the evening sun. And it's just a few minutes' walk from Knightsbridge and Sloane Square. A perfect spot.' He scrolled through the photos of the beautiful penthouse apartment, room by room, each larger than the previous and all of them seemingly larger than their flat. 'What do you think?'

'It's amazing, but it must cost a fortune.'

'It belongs to Dr Horst Altwech, a German guy I know through the business. He's off on a two-to-three-year sabbatical in the US and wants someone trustworthy to look after it while he's away. He's more interested in security and careful treatment than a massive rent.'

'So he's making you a good offer?'

He named an amount that almost took her breath away. 'That's just what I said, a fortune.'

'Esther, it would cost more than twice that on the open market. Besides, I'm making a lot of money, I can afford to spend some on us, we deserve it.'

She looked at the photos again. 'It's full of beautiful furnishings. Is he leaving all those lovely things?'

'No, he's putting most of his stuff in storage, that's

where you come in. I want you to furnish it for us, you've got terrific taste and I know you'll do a marvellous job. What do you say?'

'When does he want us to take it?'

'He's been moving his stuff out for three months already and it will be empty by next month. That's another reason for offering it to me, I told him we can get out of our lease here with three months' notice. We can start furnishing it almost immediately.'

'And you've already decided?'

He put his arms around her and squeezed her to him. 'Not quite, I've got the rental agreement here, but that's where I'd like to live with you, if you'll agree.'

'Then I can't refuse. We'll open a bottle of Laurent Perrier to celebrate.'

THIRTEEN

Mayfair, London, England
July, 2019

'What a nice thought, inviting me for lunch. I love this place, Reggie and I have been regulars ever since we met, over 20 years ago.'

Esther was well aware of this, since the MD had come to the phone to take her reservation call personally when he heard whom she was lunching with. She and Harry had been to Scott's fish restaurant several times, but his name didn't have the pulling power of Sir Reginald Scarbrough or her Ladyship.

They ordered two glasses of Sancerre Sauvignon and after a few minutes of casual chit chat, she said, 'I wanted to apologise for leaving early the other night, Lady Scarbrough, I wasn't feeling at all well. Migraines, they really knock you out.'

'Please call me Nicola, it's much easier for both of us; and there's no need at all to apologise, my dear. I don't suffer myself, but I understand they're deadly. I hope you enjoyed the evening in spite of that, it was such a pleasure to meet you. I think we can be very good friends, here's to many pleasant lunches together.'

Esther forced a smile and sipped her wine. 'There's another reason I wanted to see you, Nicola, I have some news for you, something very special. Harry and I are moving from Chelsea in September. We're coming closer to your home; just across the park, Belgravia, Eaton Square.'

'Why, that's wonderful news, then we'll definitely become good friends. It's a lovely area, congratulations and here's to a trouble-free move.' She clinked their glasses.

'Thanks, I hope so.' Esther tried to look sheepish. 'But I want to ask a favour of you. I hope you won't mind.'

'Whatever it is, I'm sure I'll be delighted to oblige.'

Esther explained Harry's arrangement with Dr Altwech. 'So we have to furnish the apartment rather quickly, almost from scratch and I really don't know where to start, I'm virtually a stranger to London and I've never attempted such a job. Your home is so beautifully decorated and furnished, I was hoping you might help me to achieve the right result, tasteful but comfortable. Could you do that?'

'How flattering, of course I'll help, and,' she paused dramatically, 'I can introduce you to the perfect person to execute the work, Leonardo, my Italian Interior decorator. He's amazing, your worries are over. Just let me know when you want to meet him and I know he'll drop everything to fly to your assistance.'

Esther managed to get through lunch, which she insisted on paying for. Then, as they were about to get up from the table, she said, 'I almost forgot. There was someone I knew at your reception and we talked for a while, a wonderful person I used to know years ago, but for the life of me, I just can't remember her name and I was too embarrassed to ask.'

After some descriptions and memory searching, Lady Scarbrough snapped her fingers. 'Of course, it was Hugh

Middleton's partner. Reggie's on a committee with him, something to do with Internet or cyber security, he runs an institute of some kind, I believe. He couldn't come and she turned up in his place.' She pulled a face, 'A nice enough person, I think she's Latvian, or something like that.'

Esther had heard enough, 'Of course, now I remember, thanks so much. Now, about my meeting with Leonardo.' They walked out of the restaurant, Esther sure that Lady Scarbrough had already forgotten about the mysterious woman, just as she wished she could forget about Nicola.

After waving her off in a taxi, she hailed the next one to come along, 'Drive over to Brompton Road', she told the driver, 'I'm looking for a telecoms shop somewhere along there.'

A half-hour later, Esther was strolling the fifteen-minute walk to her apartment. It was cloudy with a cool breeze and she pulled her coat around her, holding tight onto the plastic bag with the cheap mobile phone and prepaid SIM she'd purchased at the Fony store. In the flat, it took her just a few minutes to find the *Institute for Global Internet Security, Directors: Dr Hugh Middleton & Ilona Tymoshenko*. There were photographs of the two principals and she recognised the woman who'd spoken to her the previous night.

She recognised the man also, hardly believing her eyes. Dr Hugh Middleton was none other than Lord Arthur Dudley, her old mentor and partner in the abduction of Leo Stewart, in 2010. *What a small world*, she said to herself. *Seems he's gone straight after his time inside. I wonder if he's still in love with me? This could be a blessing in disguise. But I'd better step carefully.*

She copied a couple of numbers from her mobile onto

the prepaid device and made several calls. It took a while, but she finally found the right answer.

City of London, England
'I assume that everything has proceeded like a well-oiled locomotive, Ilona?'

'The dossier went off just before 3pm, Hugh. Exactly as promised, the last day of the month. We've managed another miracle.'

'I expected no less, my dear. Well done and you may now advise your colleagues they are to relax for the rest of the week with my personal benediction.' Dr Hugh Middleton waved his hand extravagantly and went back into his office, closing the door behind him.

Ilona Tymoshenko sat back in her chair and poured herself a cup of hibiscus herbal tea from the porcelain teapot she kept in her office. She'd just made it for herself, the first time she'd had a moment's quiet all day. It was 15:30 and the report commissioned by the government of New Zealand, Innovations in Cybercrime in Banking, had been sent off, one hour before the 31st July deadline, in an encrypted file, which she hoped would stay encrypted. She had no more deadlines that week and was looking forward to catching up on less stressful tasks. But first, a cup of Ukrainian tea was called for. Imminent deadlines were a common occurrence at the Institute for Global Internet Security, and thanks to her impressive management skills and fanatical attention to detail, they came and went without too many catastrophes.

The business had outgrown their previous premises in Marylebone, and the 100 or so employees were now housed on 3 floors in a more efficient, but much less charming tower office block in Bishopsgate, in the City business area. Prior to setting up the Institute with Dr Hugh Middleton in 2012, Ilona had been a disillusioned information security official with the Ukraine Security Service. Now, after her successful application for UK citizenship in 2018, she considered herself to be British in every sense of the word, including being a Brexit supporter.

She sipped her tea and let her mind drift away from today's stressful deadline, finding herself reflecting on the lavish reception she'd attended the previous Saturday at Sir Reginald Scarbrough's home in Mayfair. In fact, she hadn't been invited, but owing to Dr Middleton's aversion to social events, she'd put on her best outfit and taken up his invitation. It had been quite an eye-opener for many reasons. She wasn't used to rubbing shoulders with the high and mighty of London society and found most of the people she'd chatted with to be entitled, shallow, self-obsessed and uninteresting. The cocaine had also been a shock, she'd never tried drugs and had no idea how prevalent the habit had become. It was no longer a dark and dirty street corner industry, but a social phenomenon which was destroying lives and relationships on a massive scale.

Then there was the woman in the pants suit whom she'd recognised. Ilona was a 'super-recogniser', a talent she'd acquired through her Ukrainian training; she never forgot a face, although she sometimes had difficulty placing it. This was one of those occasions and it was infuriating her, had been since the party. She hadn't asked the Scarbroughs about her when she'd said goodnight, worrying it might cause a problem with Dr Middleton's relationship, so she had to rely on her recuperative skills. Once again, she went through her routine of trying to place the woman's face in time, surroundings, circumstances, mannerisms. When none of these 'memory joggers' worked, she suddenly realised that she'd never actually seen her in real life, just a photograph. *Now I'm getting somewhere.*

Her mind went back over the events of the last few, tumultuous years, trying to fit the face into a situation she recognised. It was not until she explored her memory of the almost cataclysmic attempted Russian cyber-attack in 2016, involving Leo Stewart and General William Chillicott, that she had a flash of clarity. *That's her, the Belgian connection, Esther something or other, alias Tsunami. That's definitely her!* Ilona brought out her personal tablet and found the file she'd received almost three years ago from Chief Inspector Lucas Meyer, of the Belgian security service.

The photograph of the Scarbrough's mysterious guest jumped out at her; a French woman called Esther Rousseau, on the run since 2008, when she'd been involved in a robbery with Raymundo d'Almeida, an Angolan psychopath who was killed in a shoot-out with the police in Marbella, Spain. Under the pseudonym of Tsunami, Rousseau had reappeared as a key figure in the attempted cyber attack and then subsequently vanished from sight again. Until now.

There was also a *Daily Telegraph* article from 2010, which she remembered well, concerning Lord Arthur Selwyn Savage Dudley who had been imprisoned for non-declaration of accounts with foreign banks and was involved somehow with Rousseau. Dudley was none other than her partner, Dr Hugh Middleton, who had undergone a change of character during his prison sojourn, subsequently enrolling himself on the side of crime prevention, rather than execution.

Ilona had decided to give Dudley/Middleton the benefit of the doubt and keep his identity and history to herself. Besides which, one never knew when the knowledge she had obtained might become useful and valuable. Now, she had information which might be even more valuable. She closed the tablet and replaced it in the bottom drawer of her desk, locked it and put the key back in the filing cabinet where she kept it.

What price knowledge? A career criminal, guest at a reception of an English knight. And it seems that only I know who she really is. She slowly sipped the herbal tea from her home country. *I need to think about this for a while, mustn't do anything which could harm Hugh. No one knows except me, I've got time.*

Chelsea, London, England

Harry Fern-Chapman poked his head into the spare bedroom which Esther used as an office. 'You've been on that phone ever since I came through the door, I didn't come home early to watch you texting and calling all afternoon. Leave your multimillion-dollar deals for a moment and come and tell me what you've been doing.'

Esther put the mobile quickly into her pocket before he could notice it was a new one. 'Sorry, darling,' I had to execute something before five o'clock.' *I almost said, someone!* she realised. 'I'm finished now.'

'Time to switch your brain off and tell me about your morning. Did you find us an interior decorator?'

They sat on the settee, 'You won't believe what I've arranged.'

City of London, England

Ilona Tymoshenko was walking to Liverpool Street station to take the Metropolitan line tube to the Carluccio's café beside her flat near Regent's Park. She had stayed late to prepare the final account for the New Zealand Home Office contract, then to check the progress reports of their next big assignment, for the Malaysian Central Bank. Before she knew it, it was 10pm and she hadn't eaten since breakfast, she was starving. It was a cloudy, breezy evening and she was wearing her red parka and a warm woollen hat. Checking in both directions, she crossed Old Broad Street near the HSBC. The motorcycle had no lights on and she heard the roar of its exhaust too late to turn back. Ilona was thrown into the air and crashed down in the road, landing on her head and shoulders and leaving her with multiple fractures and wounds, unconscious and bleeding. The bike sped away into the night.

Thanks to passers-by who saw the incident and immediately called 999, an ambulance was there within seven minutes and transported Ilona to the Emergency Department of the Royal London Hospital on Whitechapel Road, just a couple of miles away. Immediate and professional treatment by capable paramedics in the ambulance and the A&E staff at the hospital kept her alive, but she was still unconscious and in a critical condition; it was touch and go.

Two police cars had arrived at the scene of the accident and the several witnesses who had gathered around Ilona's body to try to help, were questioned, but none of them could provide any further information. There was no CCTV at that juncture of Old Broad Street and they could identify neither the rider, the number plate, or even the colour of the bike, in the cloudy evening light. There are an estimated 150,000 motor bikes in London. The police enquiry began with no apparent starting point.

Chelsea, London, England

At 8:30pm Esther's phone pinged. It was a two-word text from the last man she'd spoken to that afternoon, *Job done*. The 'accident' had cost Esther £25k, but she knew it was money well spent. And that the woman had been a partner of her old admirer, Lord Arthur Dudley, was a bonus she hadn't expected. *He still owes me*, she thought, *but I'm getting it back*. Even without the effects of the champagne, she was in a very good mood.

'Everything OK?' called Harry.

She went across and kissed him. 'Everything's just fine. And I have news for you. For finding that beautiful apartment, I've decided to put $1 million into Olympic Funds Group, as a first step. Tell me which funds I should choose and what special discount you can take off for me.'

'Darling, for you, I'll take everything off.'

FOURTEEN

August, 2019

City of London, England

Lord Arthur Selwyn Savage Dudley, aka Dr Hugh Middleton, arrived at St Bartholomew's at 9am on Thursday morning, within an hour of receiving the call from the City of London Police station in Wood Street, a few minutes' walk from the hospital. Ilona had no family in the UK and lived alone, the only points of reference were her passport and the business cards in her handbag. It had taken them until then to track down his home address and telephone number. Sergeant Kevin Thompson was waiting at the entrance and showed him his ID and Middleton gave him his visiting card. The policeman walked him to the reception desk, where he provided as much information as he could to complete Ilona's dossier.

An astonishingly young-looking doctor then arrived, accompanied by a nurse, and introduced himself; in his anxiety, Middleton remembered Linda, the nurse's name, but immediately forgot his. They followed the pair to the intensive care unit, where they navigated through a series of curtained-off areas, all apparently occupied, until they reached Ilona's. Middleton took a deep breath and visibly paled when they went through the curtain. He sat by the side of the bed, 'Oh, my dear Ilona. What in heaven's name has happened to you?'

The policeman was observing him, looking for any unnatural or faked reaction, but he too was shocked by her appearance. Ilona looked as if she'd been involved in a savage battle. Her body was bandaged from the head to the waist and what little could be seen of her face was bruised and bloody. Her right arm was plastered and raised in a splint attached to a pulley suspended above the bed. Multiple tubes, attached to a bank of flashing, beeping dispensers, fed liquids into an IV on her left wrist and a mask over her nose and mouth was delivering air into her lungs, keeping her alive until her body recovered enough to function without assistance, if it ever could.

He read the doctor's name from his badge, 'Doctor Gaudille, how bad is the internal damage?'

'Her thigh, shoulder, arm and several ribs are broken, but they can all be fixed. The right lung was pierced by a rib and so was the spleen, but again, that's not our greatest worry. In addition, her skull was fractured and it's causing pressure to build up on the brain. Taken individually, none of these conditions is necessarily life-threatening, it's the combination of them all which worries me. It's a huge amount of trauma for the body to cope with and we must be careful not to attempt everything at the same time. It will take time and patience to sort things out one by one, or we'll diminish her ability to recuperate.'

They talked for a few minutes more, then Dr Gaudille excused himself, it certainly looked as if he had enough to keep him busy. Middleton and Sergeant Thompson sat for a while in silence, he with his eyes closed, silently reciting a prayer, the policeman respecting his anguished state. He opened his eyes, 'Can you describe to me what happened?

No one has yet provided any explanation, simply that Mme Tymoshenko had been involved in an accident. But what form of accident could conceivably cause so much damage and trauma? Please tell me what happened.'

Linda, the nurse, re-entered the room at that moment, motioning that she needed to check on Ilona. Sgt Thompson said, 'Let's step outside and we can talk without disturbing them.' They found two chairs in a quiet corner of the corridor and he took out his notebook. He examined Middleton's visiting card, noting the numerous letters after his name, some of which were genuine, and made a couple of notes. He explained what they knew, or at least had surmised from the witness statements, which was very little. 'It seems that the bike was accelerating at the moment of the crash, instead of braking, as you'd expect,' he finished. 'That's why I wanted to speak to you.'

'What?' Middleton shook his head vehemently. 'You suspect that this was a deliberate attack on Ilona? An attempt on her life? Nonsense! That's quite preposterous, she was the most wonderfully appreciated woman you could hope to encounter. We've worked together for over seven years, since she arrived in England. I can assure you that she was universally loved by every person who enjoyed the good fortune to be exposed to her charming personality and formidable intelligence. It's quite impossible that she was the target of such a grotesquely barbaric form of attack.'

Trying to take notes, Thompson realised that he might soon need a dictionary or a thesaurus, he had never been faced with such a loquacious character. He wrote down, *A Popular Person at Work*, then hopeful that he wouldn't sound too ignorant, he asked, 'What exactly do you do at the er...,' he read from Middleton's card, *The Institute for Global Internet Security*?'

'Is that relevant? In any event, it's not a secret. An oversimplified description of our activities is that we provide research and advice to large governmental organisations and NGOs on the causes and consequences of Internet fraud, cyber-warfare and their potential risks. We make recommendations for security practices, defence tactics and overall Internet management controls and no one ever takes any noticeable action to prevent or diminish the problems.'

Thompson wrote down, *Internet Fraud*. 'So, you work for the government?'

'We work for governments and government agencies all over the world; currently twenty-four, if memory serves.'

He wrote down, *Government Advisers*. 'Can you think of anything Ms Tymoshenko was working on that could have put her life in danger?'

'Ahah, now I understand your preoccupation with our professional activities, but I'm afraid that my response is still negative. The Institute remains anonymous and impartial in respect of our clients' activities; our only bias is in favour of increased control and security in the matter of Internet usage and commercial development. However, as I previously indicated, unfortunately to no avail at the present time.'

He wrote down, *No Business Threats*. 'And you know of nothing in her private life that could explain an attack of this kind?'

'Indeed not. Ilona's family is in the Ukraine, a very happy and peaceful family, I understand, with whom she is in constant communication. She lives alone in a charming flat near Regent's Park and has very few, but friendly and educated social relationships.'

Sgt Thompson wrote down, *No Known Enemies*, closed his notebook and stood up. 'Thank you, Dr Middleton, I assume I can contact you at either the Institute or at your home, if necessary?'

'I have no intention of departing from these shores, if that's what you infer. I shall remain at your disposal and sincerely hope to hear positive news from you in due course.' In fact, Middleton never left London, he suffered from hodophobia, an irrational fear of travelling, which explained his participation in international events only by video-conferencing technology.

He bade the officer goodbye and went back to Ilona's bedside. Linda had disappeared again and he sat alongside her, gazing at her bruised, damaged face. He put his fingers gently over her left hand, the only part of her body which seemed to be unhurt. 'Dearest Ilona,' he whispered, 'please get better quickly and return to the Institute. I'm afraid that I can't possibly manage without you, the business is destined to fail if we cannot depend on your brilliant stewardship, and you wouldn't want that to occur. So, you must summon up all of your legendary resources of energy and recuperate as quickly as humanly possible.'

As he looked at her damaged, broken face, still lovely to him, her immobile body, her breathing so light it was not even noticeable, Dr Hugh Middleton felt a feeling he'd experienced only once before. It was love, not like the jealous, passionate yearning he'd felt for Esther Rousseau ten years before, but a deep, almost paternal affection for Ilona that transcended their close working relationship. Tears fell from his eyes as he realised how much he loved and depended on her. He was sixty-nine years of age and he didn't know how he could face the future without Ilona Tymoshenko.

Chelsea, London, England

Esther bought the *Daily Telegraph* and the *Mail* the next day and the next, scouring them for news of the accident. Both Friday editions had a tiny report about Ilona Tymoshenko, a highly respected cyber-crime expert from the Ukraine who was in a critical condition in hospital after a motorcycle accident in Old Broad Street. The details of the accident were unclear, and the police were requesting anyone with any information concerning the matter to contact City of London Police Station. The name of the hospital was not given, but Esther liked the words, '*critical condition*'. She put the matter out of her mind and concentrated on her preparations for the upcoming September sale.

FIFTEEN

'This is Leonardo, my interior designer. I know you'll get on fabulously well together and he'll make a wonderful job of the apartment.'

Esther shook hands with the small, delicate-looking man in jeans and linen shirt introduced by Lady Nicola Scarbrough. *This is going to be expensive*, she thought, looking at the diamond in the ring on his middle finger. *Better make the right impression from the start, 'Piacere di conoscerti, Leonardo.'*

'You speak my language, that's wonderful. A pleasure to meet you too, Esther, may I call you that?'

They walked around the apartment, listening to the Italian's comments, suggestions and admiring the quick sketches he produced to illustrate his ideas. 'He's very good,' Esther said, 'I really appreciate your help, Nicola, I wouldn't have known where to start finding someone in London, but thanks to you, I don't have to try.'

'You speak a lot of languages, Esther, that's a wonderful gift. I'm totally non-lingual but Reggie can manage a few phrases in French, which is handy when we're down on the Riviera on the yacht. We'd be there now, if they weren't having such a dreadful heatwave in St Tropez.'

She ignored the not so subtle boast and immediately

regretted her clumsy showing off in Italian. 'It sounds better than it is, I speak just enough of a few languages to seem fluent, then I get into trouble when they start chatting away and I have to apologise and revert to French or English.'

They followed Leonardo around for a while longer and Nicola said, 'How is Harry, we haven't seen him since the party last month.'

'He's fine, on a business trip at the moment, then he's got his month-end reports to worry about. Have you known him for long?'

'Several years, since he was with Selchurch Peak. Also, he's a member of the Conservative Party, like us. Reggie's not very political, but I believe they are very alike in their thinking.'

'In what way?'

'We're very conservative in our family, Esther, and we have long memories. Great Britain used to be a world leader in so many areas, but since the last war we've seen it become diminished more and more. We were supposed to have been the victors in 1945, but it didn't seem like it, rationing and poverty for years afterwards, while Germany received all the money they needed to rebuild. Then, just as we were pulling things together, that treacherous PM, John Major, had a hat trick of failures; he brought down Maggie Thatcher, he negotiated us into the EU at Maastricht and he brought even more humiliation to us on Black Wednesday, in 1992, when sterling went down the toilet.'

Lady Scarbrough was in full flow. 'Do you remember what I said to you when we first met? I'm very sorry to have been correct. We're supposed to leave the EU on October

31st, come what may.' She laughed, humourlessly. 'That's the final date of the third extension, by the way. But it won't happen, Brexit will certainly be stalled again. Boris Johnson doesn't have the support to carry it through.'

'I heard today that he's talking about suspending Parliament until October, so that they won't have time to prevent it?'

'It won't work. They'll find all kinds of legal reasons why he can't do that and compel him to ask for yet another humiliating extension, the fourth. Then his only option will be to try to force a general election. God knows what will happen if he does, he doesn't even have a majority now, so we could be facing the economic destruction of the country under the Marxists.'

Esther was rapidly revising her opinion of Sir Reggie's wife. *She's no empty-headed socialite. Despite the dramatics, she's a knowledgeable lady with very decided opinions and the confidence to present them.* She thought about her investment in the Olympic funds, either Brexit or a Labour government would probably cause a market crash. 'Are you convinced that Brexit won't happen?'

Lady Scarbrough suddenly looked around, as if she had lost her bearings. 'That's Leonardo calling from upstairs. We'd better get up there before he decides everything without you.'

She had heard no call, but went up the staircase with her, wondering why she had suddenly changed the subject. *One moment she's rubbishing everything, the next she's afraid to say what she thinks. Why are the British such complicated people?* she wondered.

Chelsea, London, England

Esther got back to the flat three hours later, after approving a preliminary budget of £100,000 for some redecoration, some basic items of furniture plus Leonardo's fee of £25k. She estimated the final cost would be closer to a quarter of a million and she'd have to massage the numbers to avoid Harry having a heart attack, but she knew he could easily afford it. She'd break the news to him over a glass of champagne when he returned from Glasgow, where he'd been giving a presentation to investment brokers.

Ever wary of being identified, Esther had persuaded him to sign the lease on the apartment alone. 'I'll pay half the rent, but I can't be party to the contract,' she told him. 'I'm not resident in England, I don't even have a bank account here. I've got no credit rating; that's why I invested through my company, *Almeida Enterprises*.'

Harry was happy with her explanation, he loved the flat and trusted her absolutely; after all, the previous month she'd invested a million dollars with Olympic Funds Group. She was even more pleased with the arrangement, if anything went wrong, he would be left with a lease costing £40k per month and she would have invested some of her 'auction money' making a decent return. In her eyes, it was a fair deal.

City of London, England

Dr Hugh Middleton jumped up from Ilona Tymoshenko's bedside, stepped outside the private ward which she now occupied and called for the nurse. He had visited his partner each morning and evening since the accident more than three weeks ago, and there had been no apparent change in her condition. She had lain immobile, still bandaged almost everywhere but her face, where the bruises had gradually receded, leaving her looking almost as well and lovely as before, apart from the tube in her mouth sending nourishment into her body.

That was until a few seconds ago, when her eyes had flickered and a semi-smile seemed to flit across her lips. His heart leaped and he rushed outside to share the news with Veena, the duty nurse that morning. 'It seems Ilona may be recovering consciousness. I observed some movement in her eyes and mouth.'

They went back into the room and Veena checked the various monitors around the bed, then took her pulse manually. 'You're right,' she said happily, 'there's some signs of activity, that's wonderful. I'll fetch Dr Gaudille, he's just along the corridor.'

Middleton sat down at Ilona's side again, holding her uninjured hand, gazing at her face. Suddenly, she opened her eyes and saw him. Her eyes brightened and the tiny smile came to her lips again, it looked as if she was about to speak. He leaned closer, his ear to her mouth, hoping to hear her voice once more. All he heard was a soft exhale of breath and her eyes closed, the smile gone from her lips. Immediately, a bell on one of the monitors started to ring.

Dr Gaudille rushed into the room, looked at Ilona and quickly checked her pulse. He put his stethoscope on the side of her throat, moving it around to try to find a vital sign. 'Please wait outside, Dr Middleton,' he said and Veena escorted him into the corridor. Another doctor and nurse rushed into the room and the door closed behind them.

He sat alone in the corridor for he didn't know how long, his head in his hands, praying silently. Finally, the door opened, and the other doctor and nurses filed out without a word. Last came Dr Gaudille, who sat beside him. He shook his head, 'I'm sorry, Dr Middleton, it was too much to hope for, the damage was more than she could cope with. I'm afraid we've lost her. I'm terribly sorry.'

For once, Hugh Middleton was at a loss for words. He went into the room and saw Ilona lying peacefully, as if asleep. The feeding tube had been removed from her mouth and her face was almost unmarked, lovelier than he had ever seen her. He sat beside the bed and took her hand in his again, squeezing it as if to try to bring life back into her body. Tears ran down his face as he pressed the hand to his lips.

It was 8:25am on the morning of August 25th, 2019, when Ilona Tymoshenko passed away. She was 42 years old.

SIXTEEN

Geneva, Switzerland
September, 2019

'Three million, six hundred and fifteen thousand Swiss Francs, net.' Maître René Christen, the Swiss notary, handed Esther the statement of sale of the items he'd authenticated and entered into the Binghams auction on behalf of *The African Benevolent Trust*. He'd checked and signed the listing in their office at the hotel saleroom, then affixed his official stamp, his pulse racing as he calculated his 10% commission. *CHF350,000, free of tax, in my Luxembourg account. I can clear up some problems and even keep a little of it for myself.*

Officially, Christen didn't know who was behind the trust, because he'd never asked. Deniability was everything and he could show the submission documents, signed with an illegible scrawl, to demonstrate his good faith. All he knew about Esther Bonnard was that she was clever, unscrupulous and could make him debt-free and that was all he wanted to know. Now he was in her suite at the Richemond, where she'd taken up residence for a week while the sales were held. Esther was determined to enjoy her new-found wealth while she could, it hadn't come easily.

I've made two and a quarter million, she calculated, trying to keep her hand steady as she looked carefully over the statement, comparing it to the list she'd received from Jolidon the previous week. 'I see there were only five unsold lots,' she observed, mainly to show him she was paying close attention to their business.

He leaned closer to see the items she'd noticed, and she smelled alcohol on his breath. It was 10:30am. Moving away, she said, 'Can we get anything for them?'

'Old, unfashionable brooches or bracelets, I might be able to find a private buyer. The stones aren't bad, they can be used in more commercial pieces. But we sold 96 out of 101 lots, a great result.'

'Claude's advice was good. Keep the reserves low and move the merchandise. No point in having unsold valuables sitting around when it could be cash, even if it's not top price.'

'We discussed that together,' Christen said quickly. 'I was in favour of modest reserves, for just the reason you say. And it's proved an extremely successful strategy.'

She supressed a smile at his claim to fame. 'When will you receive payment?'

'I'll lodge this statement with the auction house tomorrow. They usually collect from the buyers within ten days, and pay a few days later, so it should be in the fiduciary account at the Luanda Credit Bank by the end of the month.'

'*Très bien*. I want the whole amount transferred to the Trust's account in Panama the day after we receive the funds.' She handed him a typewritten transfer request, signed by her and awaiting his co-signature. 'Just fill in the exact amount of the transfer. It's a Swiss Franc account in the name of *The African Benevolent Trust*; all the payments will be made from that account, so that our paperwork can't be faulted.' *And it will be almost impossible to follow the trail*, she hoped.

'Right, I'll complete it and take it into the bank myself as soon as the payment arrives.'

'Excellent. I suppose you want your commission sent to your Luxembourg bank in Swiss Francs?'

'*Oui, merci*.' He nodded his appreciation.

'You earned it.' *And I've earned my share of $2.25 million and I can keep my promise to Harry*. It looked as if Brexit wasn't going to happen and she'd told him she was considering investing another $1 million with him; now she could easily afford it. *I'm worth over $4 million. Nearly time to start looking at yachts.*

'As soon as I get confirmation of the transfer, all the fees and commissions will be paid immediately, there'll be no delays.'

He took her hand and shook it warmly, 'May I say congratulations on a fabulous sales result. A very impressive start to our relationship.'

She was surprised at the compliment. 'Thanks, René, it will be the first of many. I want you and Claude to get ready for the Drewberrys sale in November and the following three in February. We're going to repeat this result, or do better, every time. We've worked hard to get everything in place, now we're going to make the most of it.'

She thought of the number of 'assistants' she'd had to find and trust, or bribe, since the successful US test-run. After Maître René Christen, she'd found the others she needed; lawyers, accountants and bankers who avoided asking difficult questions, assisting her with offshore banking, corporate shopfronts, legal and financial arrangements and much more besides. The Panama account in the name of *The African Benevolent Trust*, incorporated in Luanda, Angola (*a very appropriate starting point*, she agreed with Jolidon) was just the second stop on the money trail. By the time it arrived at her Guadeloupe bank, then onto Bahrain, it would transit through companies and banks in several countries.

Esther had used the expertise she'd acquired in Swiss banking and then as a 'fixer' for a number of crooked and subversive projects at a very high level, including the Russian government, all of which had unfortunately ended in disaster. She had learned hard lessons from those experiences and was determined that this time it would be different. The competent and accommodating experts she'd hired were all kept carefully separate from each other and only partially informed. Apart from Christen and Jolidon, Esther was the only common point of contact. They were her key lieutenants, irreplaceable and the most at risk of discovery; that was why they were paid so well. Neither she nor Jolidon had attended the sale, only Christen was present. No one in the saleroom could be aware of any connection between them, it might lead to questions.

But the key component that guaranteed the success of the venture was the briefcase with Charlie Bishop's Angolan diamonds. In her mind, Esther was Ray d'Almeida's rightful heir; she had found the case and didn't intend to lose it again. The diamonds were her insurance that her partners would stay 'honest' because they were the cornerstone of the sales proceeds. The first batch of 100 stones had made over $1.75 million, 50% of the total proceeds. Jolidon and Christen had no idea where they were kept, and they would never know. As long as she protected her secret, they depended on her for their future fortunes.

Jenny Bishop won the first few rounds of our battle, she reflected, *but I've won the last and most important round, and that's how it's going to stay. I've got enough valuables to run this for a year or so and make a fortune into the bargain. Ray would be proud of me for finally turning the tables on the Bishop woman.*

Showing the notary to the door, she said, 'Well done, René. I'll leave you and Claude to get on with the local sales and prepare for Drewberrys in November. See you in Geneva next month.' He shook her hand and she again noticed the smell of alcohol as he walked out past her.

Esther went across to the desk and looked again at the list. *I'll have to watch that man. Drinking at ten in the morning. I wonder what else he does that I should worry about?*

London, England

'*Bonjour*, Claude. *Tout va bien*? Is everything OK?' Esther was strolling through Harrods in Knightsbridge, looking at designer outfits, when she received the WhatsApp call. She was immediately on her guard, he never called her unless it was something important, and that usually meant some kind of problem.

'*Oui, oui*. Everything's fine. Guadelope just confirmed the transfer, thanks, that was a great result. But that's not why I called. I just heard they've closed the inquest. The developers have got the final permits and they've started the demolition.'

'Really? That's fabulous news. So, that means no

possibility of more investigations?'

'Right. I only just learned about it yesterday. The verdict was an accident, so the permits came through immediately and they started the demolition a week ago. I went to take a look this morning and it's huge, the whole block is completely closed off. An off-limits building site full of wrecking machines, nobody allowed onto the premises.'

'*Merci*, Claude, well done, that's the last obstacle gone. Now we can get on with making a fortune. After the two small sales, next big event, Drewberrys, in November.' She decided to say nothing about Christen's drinking, Jolidon's mood was too good to spoil.

'Right, Esther. Nothing's going to stop us now. *Au revoir*.'

She collected several items and called over an assistant to help her try them on. *A good time to spend some money, make myself look good for Harry.*

On an impulse, she called him at his office. 'Hello, darling, I'm missing you, I hope you won't be late home? Good, I want to talk to you about that second investment with *Olympic*. I'm enjoying having my money working for me.'

SEVENTEEN

Dr Hugh Middleton was feeling tired and melancholy. The last six weeks had been the most emotionally draining in his life. For him, Ilona's death was not just a personal drama but a professional nightmare. Their business success was built on his ability to sell ice cream to Eskimos and obtain lucrative contracts from clients whose ability to pay was irrefutable; whilst her forte was to deliver the product on time and exceed all expectations, thus ensuring further mandates from the same customers in the future. The fact that the Institute's reports probably ended up unread, gathering dust in the archives of government departments, was disappointing and disheartening, but they had always hoped that someone, somewhere, would one day take their recommendations seriously and act accordingly. Now, compared to the tragedy of her death, it was almost irrelevant.

Events seemed to have passed him by without his active involvement, starting with the funeral, organised by Joan Philips, the office manager. It had all seemed like a bad dream, welcoming and saying goodbye to people he didn't know and would never see again. Ilona's family was represented by Mykyta, one of her brothers, her mother being too poorly to travel and the family unable to afford more than one fare. The only moment of reality came when Mykyta took him to one side to tell him how much the death would affect the family fortunes in the Ukraine. Apparently, Ilona had sent half of her salary every month to help them out and now he didn't know how they would manage.

When he discovered she had died intestate, Middleton had appointed a solicitor to look after the probate process, which would take some time and, he suspected, produce very little. Virtually his partner in the firm, Ilona was quite well paid and he remembered being surprised that she didn't own her flat, which he saw, on the couple of occasions he'd been allowed to visit, was sparsely and inexpensively furnished. *No wonder*, he realised, *if she was living on only 50% of her salary*. He generously calculated that she would be due 6 month's wages if she had been obliged to leave for any other reason and he offered it to the family. Mykyta told him they would be taxed if they cashed a cheque in Ukraine, and he arranged for the cash in $US, the brother's currency of choice. He left the UK with the banknotes in his backpack and Middleton never heard from the family again. He hoped the money had arrived safely.

Back at the Institute, he forced himself to think about continuity; Ilona was irreplaceable, but she had to be replaced. He chose Peter Findlay, a quiet, studious Scotsman, who had worked closely with her; he knew that would have been her choice. Findlay succeeded in meeting their deadlines, though Middleton was certain his reports would never be as absorbing and informative as hers had always been. There had been few occasions when a dossier was completed without a long and often argumentative exchange of ideas between them, resulting in brilliant exposures of the dangers surrounding cyber communications, and clear and present proposals to mitigate them. Now, those arguments no longer took place and he knew their recommendations were the worse for that.

There was no news from the police, apart from a message of condolence from Sergeant Kevin Thompson, who sent a wreath with a thoughtful message to the funeral. This didn't surprise Middleton; with Ilona's death, the pressure was off, and they had a million other priorities to attend to. Crime in London was rife and resources were limited. There was no point in hoping for a miraculous disclosure, Ilona's death was now just a statistic, a forgotten event in a file that would probably never again see the light of day.

Somehow life went on, and he began to face the mornings with less dread and without expecting to see Ilona each time he walked into the building. He knew he had to get a grip on his new situation. He believed he still had an important function to fulfil and for her sake and he continued to hope that one day, the *Institute for Global Internet Security* would somehow make a difference for the better, however small. He owed her that much.

Until now, he'd avoided the problem of Ilona's office. It remained untouched and he hadn't asked for it to be emptied. He steeled himself, unlocked the door and went inside; it still smelled faintly of her perfume. There were one or two personal items lying around, very few and nothing of importance; she had always carefully separated her professional and private life. *Although*, he thought sadly, *I don't think she had very much of a personal life.* Ilona kept a large business diary, which was still lying in her in-basket. He picked it up and opened it where the page-marker ribbon showed. The pages covered four days, 28 – 31 July 2019. On the 31st she'd noted, *New Zealand – 4pm*, the day of the accident. He remembered the usual last-minute rush, as well as the effusive reception the dossier had generated. On the facing page, 28th, was written, *Sir Reginald Scarbrough, 8pm.* He searched his memory, *Of course, one of those celebrity-ridden evening parties I detest. She kindly stepped in to save my face and represent the firm. Poor thing, I never asked her about it, I hope it wasn't too boring.*

He looked through her desk drawers, finding nothing but business papers and supplies. The bottom one was locked, but he found the key in the filing cabinet where she kept it. The drawer contained some personal papers and letters, and her tablet. He switched it on, but the screen remained dark; the battery was flat. Middleton found the cable, plugged it into the wall socket and after a moment, it lit up. He knew the password, she'd shared it with him in case of an emergency; *Ukraine*11*, the year she'd arrived in the UK. Ilona had switched it off without closing the programme and on the screen appeared the last item she'd looked at. Dr Hugh Middleton was looking at a newspaper article, with a photograph of himself, named as Lord Arthur Selwyn Savage Dudley.

Geneva, Switzerland

Esther Bonnard walked across the Pont du Mont-Blanc in the crisp autumn sunshine to the left bank, where she had tea in *Walther*, an old-fashioned chocolate shop. At the *Banque d'Epargne Vaudoise*, she retrieved the briefcase then took a taxi back to the Richemond.

As she'd done in July, Esther prepared an envelope with 100 diamonds of differing sizes and stored it in the hotel safe. After returning the briefcase to the bank vault, she came back to the hotel for a glass of champagne, then an early supper in *Le Jardin*, the hotel's restaurant on the park.

The next morning, she caught the 09:42 train from Cornavin station to Zurich, the envelope safely in her handbag, locked with the clasp. Claude Jolidon was waiting for her when she arrived at Zurich Oerliken exactly 3 hours later. They took a taxi to 819 *Badenerstrasse* and went up to the sixth floor of the building, into the apartment with no name plate. She hid her dislike of the 'office', Jolidon had to spend every day there and didn't complain, so she held her tongue.

'The stuff for the next two small sales is already with Christen, it's worth about 750k,' he said, 'but I'll show you what we've chosen for Drewberrys, see if you agree.'

'I'm not going to second guess you, Claude, we're partners. If you and René are happy with it, that's fine with me. What's your estimate?'

'Between 2 and 2.5 million. The total reserve is CHF2 million, so I think we'll exceed it again.'

She took out the sealed envelope from her handbag. 'There's another 100 stones here, exactly like the last ones, so we could break through the 4 million barrier.'

'*Fantastique*, I'm pretty sure we will. René told me the jeweller who bought the first batch has been hassling him about getting some more, so we should see some competitive bidding. I'll make the same reserve, one point-five. OK with you?'

She nodded and he put the envelope in the strongbox

and locked it. 'Anything special to report? Any problems?'

'Not a thing. It's like being a hermit here, I never see anyone. I'm glad you accelerated the sales programme, another two years in this apartment, I'd be going gaga.'

She grabbed the opportunity. 'I know what you mean, I'd hate to be stuck here, it gives me the creeps. After the February sales, why don't we look for a better place? It'll be more than 3 years since you wrote to the clients about closing down. I doubt there'll be much risk by that time.'

On the train back to Geneva, Esther thought of what she'd accomplished already that year. She'd increased her fortune by over $4 million, with another 6 major sales still to come, as well as the smaller auctions. *What am I going to do with all that money?* She pinched herself, *No, it's not a dream, I've really done it.* She dozed off, dreaming of making love to Ray d'Almeida on a Caribbean beach.

EIGHTEEN

Belgravia, London, England
September, 2019

Esther was thinking about the $2 million she'd invested into Olympic Funds. The share prices had continued to rise and she wished she'd taken a bigger gamble. She took her mobile to check her Bahrain account, when it rang in her hand. René Christen's name appeared and she stepped out onto the balcony. It was a cold, rainy day, but the magnificent centennial trees and shrubs in the square were still showing their colours, hundreds of subtle shades of greens and browns. *Summer's almost over*, she thought, *what a hurried year it's been.*

'*Bonjour, René*, how are you?'

'Fine, Esther, thanks. The proceeds from the two small sales in Berne and Zurich have arrived in the fiduciary account. What are your instructions?'

Esther listened carefully to his voice, wondering if he'd been drinking, it was impossible to tell. She knew that regular drinkers found ways of hiding their addiction, carefully managing their movement and speech whatever their condition. He was probably no exception and so far, there had been no ill-effects. *He's producing good results from these sales and that's all that matters.* She had already been informed of the sales results, a total of CHF980,000 after commissions. *That's $600,000 for* *me, rien d'extraordinaire, nothing special*, had been her reaction, then she remembered how grateful she'd been, just a few years ago, to steal a paltry $25,000 to add to her pitifully small life savings in Guadeloupe. Now those savings amounted to almost $5 million. *I'm getting spoiled,* she realised, *$600k is more than most people make in a lifetime.*

Esther had no qualms about the source of her earnings; she had suffered for years at the hands of the Bishop family, losing her lover and several potential fortunes. Now it was payback time and if a few wealthy, careless people got caught in the crossfire, too bad.

'Esther?' Christen was waiting.

'*Pardon, René.* I'll send you a signed instruction for the fiduciary account by registered, express mail today. Just countersign it and take it into the bank please.'

'*D'accord.* I'll go to the *Banco de Credito* ....'

'Quiet! No details on the telephone, it's the fiduciary account, no need to spell it out. And your account's the same, right?'

'Same as usual.' He didn't make the mistake again.

'Is everything on target for Drewberrys in November?'

'I've just received the proof for the catalogue. Everything's in there, 110 items, it's going to be a great sale. I'll courier you a copy as soon as it's printed.'

'*Parfait, René*, see you soon.'

She switched her mobile off. *Imbécile! Giving bank details over the phone, it's just inviting trouble, who knows who's listening these days? I wonder if it's the effect of the drink?* Esther knew she was becoming paranoid, but she had never had so much to protect.

'Everything OK?' Harry had come out onto the balcony

and put his arm around her.

'No problems, just a business call, everything's fine.'

'I suppose *Almeida Enterprises* just closed another big deal?' He was careful to avoid questions about her business.

'Let's say, I might be getting a bit too cash-heavy again. How are we doing?'

'Wait till you see my Q3 report, you won't be disappointed.'

She kissed him on the cheek. *If my Olympic funds are up by 5%, it seems crazy to leave all that money earning nothing in Bahrain. Maybe it's time to take another plunge?*

'I was thinking,' he said. 'This apartment's looking really fabulous, you've done a great job. Just a few odds and ends to finish off and we'll be settled for the next two or three years.'

Amazing what almost half a million pounds can achieve, she said to herself. Aloud, she said, 'Thanks, darling, but if it hadn't been for Nicola Scarbrough and her Italian genius, Leonardo, I would never even have known where to start. I don't deserve the praise.'

'That's what I had in mind. Why don't we invite the Scarbroughs over one evening, show them how the place looks and have a quiet dinner?' Before she could protest, he added, 'We can get it catered, you don't have to do a thing.'

Carouge, Geneva, Switzerland

'Bitch!' René Christen slammed his mobile down on the table in his rented studio in Carouge.

He poured himself a generous glass of wine and sat in

the kitchen, ignoring the news programme on the TV, thinking about his conversation with Esther, reflecting on his involvement with her and Claude Jolidon. After his acrimonious divorce two years previously, when his ex-wife had extracted every last penny from him (on pain of divulging his nocturnal activities in Geneva's old town), Christen had been forced to sell the villa in Fribourg he'd inherited on his father's death. Louisa had taken everything, leaving him with only their debts; the final ignominy being when he was declared bankrupt. But despite the financial sacrifice, word somehow got around Fribourg and within a year, he had lost most of his clients and all his staff. His professional reputation in the canton was in tatters. What was worse, under Swiss law, he was still liable for his debts, even after the bankruptcy. He was ruined, both professionally and financially.

He didn't miss his family life; he'd been married for 12 seemingly interminable years to a vain, aspiring, disappointed woman and they'd had no children. Nor did he miss her cabal of pseudo-intellectual, posturing friends, always competing with him, and succeeding better than he. But he desperately missed the family villa, the memories of a happier life as an only child, then a student, coming home from school and college to a loving family home and proud parents. It had broken his heart when they were taken from him a few years before, killed by a drunken driver in Neuchatel. Most of all, he missed the professional status he'd achieved as a *huissier;* almost, but not quite, a notary. Still, a worthy profession that had helped him gravitate to a social circle that had welcomed, then destroyed him.

Moving to Geneva had been a relief, an escape from the

shame and embarrassment of encountering past friends and acquaintances in the street; Fribourg is a very small city, smaller than most towns. But Christen was still faced with a mountain to climb; at forty years of age, it seemed his life had fallen apart. He had debts to reimburse and was devoid of any real professional activity, managing to find work as a menial clerk-accountant in a legal office. He began to drown his problems in drink, if he could afford it after the monthly debt instalments. Soon, there was less and less money for the instalments and he struggled to cope in his new job. His meeting with Esther Bonnard had been a Godsend, offering him a chance to recover his life and his fortune.

She had done her homework well, knew every detail of his fall from grace, but avoided speaking specifically about his situation, merely dangling the carrot of substantial rewards for doing what he'd been trained for and loved, acting as a *huissier*. He made a point of never asking searching questions, it was better to remain ignorant, a childish method of avoiding responsibility. But he knew that she and Claude Jolidon, whom he liked, but couldn't quite figure, were planning a major heist, when he was appointed by Edificio 2000 to certify the inventory of the valuables from hundreds of security boxes at Ramseyer, Haldeman. And he wasn't very surprised when Simenon disappeared in the 'accident' while he was in Zurich on Jolidon's instructions. He didn't officially know who was behind *The African Benevolent Trust*, though he could easily guess that it had nothing to do with Africa. And his opinion of Esther Bonnard hadn't changed, he knew she was a cunning, callous villain, but he needed her ability to make money.

The price of lending his name and professional credentials to their plan was to pretend that he didn't know what was behind it, that he turned a blind eye to them stealing and selling the unclaimed contents of the boxes. And he knew, or suspected something else, something of great value. After their meeting in Geneva to open the fiduciary account with the Luanda bank, he had followed Esther to the *Banque d'Epargne Vaudoise*, waiting across the street until she came out and took a taxi from the nearby rank. She was carrying a briefcase, the same old-fashioned leather briefcase he had seen Jolidon take from security box no. 72 after the fire. He was sure he knew what was inside that case – a huge treasure of Angolan diamonds.

So far, Christen had made over half a million Swiss Francs from the arrangement. He was gradually clearing his debts, but it would take a lot more than that to clear his conscience.

He poured himself another glass of wine and opened the *Tribune de Genève*, turning to the male escort pages.

City of London, England

Dr Hugh Middleton was putting two and two together and he didn't like the sum total. He knew it wasn't a coincidence that Ilona had been knocked down by a speeding motorcycle on the same day she'd been looking at photographs of himself and Esther Rousseau. Sergeant Thompson had been right; Ilona had been cruelly murdered, and he'd lost a wonderful person he cared about and the finest business partner anyone could ever hope for. He was angry, but he was also scared, knowing he might be next on Esther's list. She had a lot to hide and if she thought she'd been found out, was prepared to stop at nothing. He was sure that included murdering a clever, innocent woman, to keep her past and her real identity hidden from scrutiny.

Somewhere, Ilona must have seen Esther Rousseau and recognised her from the Tsunami photograph. In addition to his formidable intellect, Middleton was a highly intuitive individual and he knew it was too much of a coincidence to be otherwise. For three years, his partner had kept his true identity and criminal background to herself. She couldn't have shared it with anyone else, or he would have already been confronted. Then, for some reason, she'd suddenly dug the file out again. Why? The most likely explanation was the item in her diary, the reception at the Scarbrough's place just two days before the attack. *She must have recognised someone and that someone was Esther.*

Somehow the French woman had found this out, tracked her down and arranged for her murder. *If I'm right*, he forced himself to accept, *she must also know who and where I am. But she can't know I've worked out that she's the murderer. If she suspects that, it's strange she's taken no action, maybe worried that she'd show her hand and be caught out. Or she might be biding her time, waiting for a propitious moment to strike and clear away any remaining links to her past.*

Ilona was gone, murdered, and he needed to know more, but how? An idea came to him. He checked his diary; the *Home Affairs Committee on Cyber-Crime and Internet Security* was meeting on the afternoon of October 21st in Whitehall. Both he and Scarbrough were on that committee and they usually enjoyed a glass of wine together afterwards. He had the Tsunami photograph, he just needed to think up a plausible reason for asking about

Esther. He was confident he could manage to invent one over the next few weeks.

Belgravia, London, England

'What a superb dinner, it was really delicious.' Lady Scarbrough put down her napkin and took a sip of the dessert wine. 'Well done, Esther.'

Before Sir Reginald could add his compliments, Esther said, 'I'd love to take the praise, but Harry knows the truth. *Table d'Hôte Catering*, on Ebury Street, near the station. He found them and now it's going to cost him a fortune, because I'm never going to cook again.'

Harry smiled to himself, the evening had been a great success, Esther was a natural hostess and had made the Scarbroughs relax from the moment they'd walked through the door. That was important to him, especially with a client who'd invested £10 million into Olympic Funds and was encouraging many of his wealthy friends to do the same. Though his investing record was good, Harry wasn't the only game in town and socialising with the right people was a necessary evil. But with Reggie and Nicola it wasn't hard work, he liked them, and the two men had similar views on many things.

Esther served coffee in the drawing room and inevitably, the talk turned to Brexit, Lady Scarbrough once again being outspoken. 'I simply can't believe that the Supreme Court would side with that dreadful woman, Gina Miller. It's a public humiliation, I'm quite embarrassed to be British, and a woman, for that matter.'

'I haven't been following events, has anything actually happened, or is it still just a never-ending political drama serial?'

'The short version, Esther, is that Boris Johnson did manage to close down Parliament until October and the High Court decided that it was a political decision which didn't concern them. But it has now been overturned by the Supreme Court after the interventions of treacherous politicians and businesspeople with money. So there'll be more arguments in the Commons and we'll never reach an agreement on us leaving. The next deadline is October 31st and I'm sure that nothing will happen by then. Boris Johnson says he won't request another extension, but he's going to be forced to. So, to quote your excellent English phrase, it's still a never-ending political drama serial.'

As the others continued to discuss the stalemate, Esther's calculating mind wandered elsewhere. *It sounds like Brexit is never going to happen. That means the markets and sterling will strengthen. I'll be making at least another $2 million in this month's sales. Good timing.*

The Scarbrough's car took them off into the cold, rainy night and Harry pulled Esther close to him. 'Well done, darling, you've made us friends for life, and I've got one very happy important investor.'

'Not just one. I've decided *Almeida Enterprises* will take another *tranche* of a million.'

NINETEEN

'Just a little further along this street and Mammy will show you the prettiest, sparkliest thing you've ever seen.' Jenny Bishop puckered her lips and blew a kiss to the little blonde girl in the pushchair. It was late morning, a warm, sunny autumn day in Geneva, a perfect moment to take her daughter, Ellen, for a stroll along the lakeside.

She clapped her hands and shouted, 'Mama', reaching out to her. Jenny lifted her from the buggy and they walked slowly along, hand in hand into the Pâquis area, a cosmopolitan mix of cafés and bars, sprinkled with more dubious establishments, many featuring groups of scantily clad women in their doorways. Jenny hadn't been here for almost five years and was surprised at the increase in the numbers of working women and shifty-looking men since her last visit.

From the sublime to the ridiculous, she thought, holding tightly to her daughter's hand, comparing the pristine lawns and pathways she'd just left with the grubby streets and buildings now surrounding her. *And the UN and other NGO headquarters are just five minutes away*, she remembered, wondering how such a rapid change could occur in an elegant, international and apparently well-controlled Swiss city. A police car went slowly by, helping to alleviate the sudden apprehension she'd felt for herself and her daughter.

She walked around the corner to her destination, 'Here we are, it's ....'

Jenny stood stock still, turning her head this way and that, looking along the street and back again, a blank expression on her face, thinking she'd taken a wrong turn but knowing she hadn't. She was definitely in the Rue de Mauvergny, but no. 475 was no longer a solid six story edifice faced in white stone with a brass plate at the entrance announcing, *Ramseyer, Haldemann & Company. Sécurité Privée et Commerciale.* In fact, when she got her bearings, she realised the building was no longer there; in its place was a vast, tent-like canvas structure. A giant yellow crane towered over the tent, a massive black bucket dangling from the jib, as it swung away to dump its load in a lorry parked alongside.

Finding a spot from where she could see inside the canvas, she saw it surrounded the remains of the demolished building above the ground and an enormous excavation, dozens of metres long and wide, filled with the remains of massive concrete pillars and walls, iron rods poking out from the shattered masonry below the surface. Amongst the piles of debris, workmen in hard hats and hi-vis jackets were demolishing the reinforced concrete with a huge machine on tracks and a dozen pneumatic hammer drills. A wrecking ball on a chain swung into the walls, gradually weakening them until they could be brought down by the other machinery; the noise was deafening. The sight suddenly reminded her of the words of Gilles Simenon, the young manager, who had informed her in 2008 that the walls were 'constructed from triple layers of reinforced concrete'. She knew there were at least two floors underground and it seemed they were now destroying them with a great amount of effort and noise.

Her heart in her mouth, Jenny looked in disbelief at the sight before her, racking her brains to try to work out what on earth was going on. Why would they take such trouble to knock down such a beautiful building that was virtually indestructible? What's happened to Ramseyer, Haldeman? What's happened to the security boxes?

A billboard in front of the site advertised *Centre Mauvergny*, a mixed-use development of apartments, retail space and offices, due for delivery in 2022. But there was no mention of the security company whose safety deposit vault had guarded Charlie Bishop's briefcase, and the Angolan diamonds it held for more than forty years.

Ellen was becoming distressed by the deafening racket and Jenny lifted her back into the pushchair and walked to the end of the street, hoping to see a sign directing her to the new address, but there was nothing. It was as if the company had never existed. Trying to supress the feeling of panic that swept over her, she went back to the demolition site, where she found someone who looked like the foreman, asking him, in her rusty school French, *'Où est Ramseyer, Haldeman, securité?'*

She repeated the question in various formats as he shrugged and shook his head, finally pointing to the bottom corner of the sign, where a dark blue logo, in the form of a swooping eagle was featured above the words, *Agence Suisse, Aigle Immobilier SARL*. She noted down the address and telephone number then thanked the man and manoeuvred the pushchair quickly away from the chaos, frantically wondering what she could do next.

Going towards the Rue du Mont Blanc, an idea came to her and after a brisk fifteen-minute walk, she arrived at the main branch of the *Banque de Commerce de Genève*, where she had maintained her Swiss accounts since her battle with Klein, Fellay in 2010.

The manager, Valérie Aeschiman, came out to reception, a warm smile on her face. 'Jenny, what a nice surprise, and little Ellen is with you, my how she's grown, she's beautiful.'

'Bonjour, ma jolie, viens avec moi.' She picked the child up and led the way to her office, chattering away in her lilting French accent about her daughter, Camille, who was now in senior school. 'I wasn't expecting you until the end of the year to review your investments.' She sat Ellen on her knee. 'What can I do for you today?'

'I see that Ramseyer, Haldeman, the security company, has moved from Rue de Mauvergny. Do you know where their new offices are?'

'That's the building that burned down earlier this year. I don't know where they've moved to. They started demolishing it a few months ago, not before time, it was awful, like a big toothless monster.'

Jenny's heart jumped into her mouth. 'The building burned down? That's impossible, it was a massive place, with a solid stone façade. How could it burn down?'

'I don't know. There was an investigation at the time, but I don't think it was ever discovered exactly what happened. There was a rumour that it was, you know,' she put her finger to her lips, 'an insurance fraud, but nothing was ever proved. Something to do with the electricity system, I think they said.'

'But the underground vaults with the security boxes,

they couldn't have burned. There were several floors of them, built in reinforced concrete. I've just seen them demolishing the walls and it's an enormous job.'

'You've been down in their vaults? Did you have business there?'

Jenny swallowed, saying as little as possible, 'Leticia and I had a safety deposit box there. I need to know where their new offices are.'

'I'm sorry, Jenny, all I know is there's a new development starting as soon as the demolition is over. It will help to upgrade the area, it's looking awfully seedy these days.'

'When did the fire happen? Do you know the date?'

Mme Aeschiman shook her head. 'I don't remember exactly. Let me check, we've got an assistant manager who used to work there. Just a second.'

Ellen was becoming restless, picking up and putting down everything she could grab from Valérie's desk. Jenny took her back on her knee while she looked up the diary on her mobile. The bank manager was speaking on the phone in French. '*Le cinq avril? T'es sûr? Ah oui, je me rappel.*' She turned back to Jenny, 'It was in early April.'

'That's more than six months ago!' She found the date she was looking for. 'I was last there in March 2015, to pay the fees up to the end of this year. That's why I came today, to pay for the next five years.' She shook her head. 'I've never heard anything from them since then. Nothing about the fire or their new address or what's happened to the security boxes.

'I knew the manager of the safekeeping department quite well, Gilles Simenon, a very efficient young man,. He'd have made sure I was advised of the fire and whatever new arrangements they were making.' She saw the banker's expression. 'What is it?'

'Gilles Simenon, that's the name Richard just mentioned. I'm sorry, Jenny, he told me he was killed in the fire. They were very good friends apparently.'

'What?' Jenny suddenly felt sick and tears welled up in her eyes. 'Gilles was killed in the fire?' she blurted out. 'It's not possible, how could that happen?' She took out a tissue and wiped her eyes, thinking of the quiet, handsome Swiss man she'd known distantly for ten years, always friendly and polite when she'd called at the offices. Hugging her daughter to her, she asked, 'Did he have a family?'

'I don't know, Jenny, but I'll call Richard in and you can ask him yourself.'

TWENTY

Richard Claireaux was a tall, bearded man in his mid-thirties, who stood to attention as he addressed her in perfect English, just as Simenon had done, Jenny remembered.

'I wasn't with RH when the fire occurred, hadn't been for years,' he explained. Most of the personnel were paid off in 2016, after the company went bankrupt and the building was repossessed by the bank, that's when I left.'

'The company went bankrupt in 2016? And then the building burned down this year? My God, I don't believe it!' She held tightly on to Ellen, as if to protect her from the revelations of the last few minutes.

'I'm sorry, Mme Bishop, I thought you knew about it. They'd been struggling since 2012, closing offices and firing people in the companies around Europe. Then in 2015 when they were finally facing bankruptcy, they closed down the other Swiss companies, until there was only Zurich and Geneva left, but everything went bust the following year. The Geneva building was sold to a development company, and a few people were kept on, to clean up the ongoing business. Gilles stayed because of the problem of the security boxes.

'About the fire, I heard the story from one of the

security guards who was there, it was a dreadful accident. It occurred at night and there were just Gilles and two guards in the building. The others escaped, because they were in the office area, but Gilles was down in the second-floor vault chamber.'

The second floor vault, Jenny remembered, *that's where Charlie's box was; no. 72, a quarter size door on the bottom row. Why did Gilles have to die there?* she asked herself, unreasonably. 'Why was he in the vault at night? That can't have been normal.'

'I wondered the same thing. The last time I saw him he told me they'd taken out all the boxes and were going to send the contents to the Zurich office. He'd been asked to stay on to try to find the owners to return their possessions, but he wasn't keen to move to Zurich.'

'But if they'd already removed them, why would he be in the vault, especially at night?'

'The report from the inquest said he was checking that all the rented boxes had been safely removed, so they could close the building down. Maybe he didn't have time during the day, I have no idea.' His voice cracked as he went on, 'They found that the fire knocked out the electronic door systems and he was trapped there, couldn't get out.'

She shivered and held her daughter tightly, dreadful memories flooding back into her mind. *I've always known those diamonds were cursed, so many deaths; Charlie and his partners, Adam and my husband Ron, probably more, all because of Ray d'Almeida's pathological obsession with the Angolan diamonds. And it means the contents must still be somewhere, maybe in Zurich, waiting to be claimed.* Jenny felt more apprehension than relief at the thought.

'Did they find out how the fire started?'

'The security guards said they heard an explosion in the machine room, then the electricity system went berserk and fires started to appear everywhere. It was an old construction, full of previous-generation technical and automated equipment, so when it went wrong it affected everything, throughout the building.'

'Is the inquest over?'

'It was closed last month.'

'What was the coroner's verdict?'

'An accident caused by an unknown technical defect in the electric circuitry. Gilles's death was caused by the smoke circulating through the air conditioning system.'

Jenny's mind was suddenly filled with an image of Gilles Simenon, surrounded by a cloud of poisonous smoke, struggling to open the steel doors which guarded the enormous, circular room with hundreds of safety deposit boxes around the walls.

Ellen squealed and she realised she was squeezing her too tightly in her anxiety. She calmed her and asked, 'Was Gilles married, did he have a family?'

'He'd been married a few months before, to Marie Costoni, an Italian girl. She stayed a few months in their flat in Meyrin, but then went back to her family in Turin.'

'Do you have her number? I'd like to call, just to say how sorry I am.'

He found the number on his mobile and Jenny jotted it down. 'Do you know what's become of Ramseyer, Haldeman since the fire?'

'I don't know if there's anybody still working there, except maybe the man who was in charge of Geneva and Zurich when I left.'

'Do you remember his name?'

'Claude Jolidon, a Frenchman, but I don't know if he's still there.'

She noticed his grimace, remembering the man Adam had described as a 'Shifty-looking bloke with bad breath'. 'Monsieur Jolidon; I met him about ten years ago. I didn't like him either.' She thought about him for a moment. 'Did he order Gilles to work at night?'

He shrugged. 'I've no idea but if the company's still in existence, you might be able to find him and ask him yourself.'

She shook her head, 'I can't believe they went bankrupt. Gilles told me they had offices all over Switzerland and Europe, he said it was a huge business.'

'It was, but after the founder, Dr Haldeman, died in 2000, his son, Patrick, went into all kinds of crazy deals where he lost a fortune. He was a technical graduate, not a businessman and I heard he was defrauded out of his own fortune, through his naivety. Then he mortgaged the company buildings to try to recoup his losses, but the 2008 crash wiped him out. The banks foreclosed on him and everything was closed or sold off until there was only Geneva and Zurich remaining. After the fire, I doubt if there's anything left.'

'And the other partner, Ramseyer. Couldn't he prevent Patrick mortgaging everything?'

'There wasn't another partner. Dr Haldeman's mother's name was Ramseyer and he added it to make the firm sound more substantial. He built the business up single-handed.'

'And then Patrick brought it down single-handed; with the help of the bankers, of course.' With the exception of

Valérie Aeschiman, Jenny's experience of Swiss bankers was not a happy one. 'I suppose everything must have gone downhill very quickly?'

Richard gave a cynical smile, 'It's fairly logical. If you're in the security business, the last thing you want is to have problems with the banks to ruin your reputation.'

He went to the door, 'I'm sorry to bring you such bad news, Mme Bishop, I wish you and your daughter a safe trip back to the UK.'

TWENTY-ONE

Richard left Mme Aeschiman's office, Jenny still trying to cope with his revelations.

'What an awful story, Dr Haldeman must be turning in his grave.' She shook her head, 'It seems that Patrick Haldeman destroyed the business his father had spent his whole life building.'

'No doubt at all. I don't know any details because we never had any dealings with the firm, but between you and me,' Valérie leaned across the desk and whispered, 'he had a terrible reputation, Patrick. I don't think it was just the crash, he was a crazy spender.'

'What do you mean, crazy?'

She looked around the empty room then went on, 'I heard he would rent a private jet, to take him to the South of France, or Italy or England, to play golf. The pilot would wait for him to play, have drinks and dinner or whatever, all night,' she raised her eyebrows, 'then he'd fly him back the next morning. Do you know how much that costs?' She shook her head and sat back in her chair.

'I see what you mean. What happened to him, do you know?'

She shrugged her shoulders, 'No idea.'

'So we still come back to the same problem. How can I

get in touch with whoever is running the business now?'

'Isn't there a notice or a sign at the site with their new address?'

Jenny described what she'd found at the building site. 'Could you call this Aigle Agency and ask what's going on? My French isn't up to it.'

By now, it was almost time for Ellen's lunch and she was becoming restive. Jenny took a banana from her bag and gave it to her daughter, who messily pushed the soft fruit into her mouth. Mme Aeschiman dialled the number and put the speaker on, Jenny trying to follow what was said. She gave up listening after what seemed like hours as the call was transferred several times, Valérie finally speaking in Swiss German to Herr Widmer, the company's General Manager in Lucerne, the guttural dialect grating on her ears.

At last she put the phone down and consulted her copious notes. 'Let's see if I can get this right. The building was bought from the bank in 2016 by Edificio 2000, a Swiss property company, subject to getting approval for a new development. The fire occurred in April and they started demolishing the building after the result of the inquest, when the council rushed the permit through. Three years is not a long time to get a building permit in Geneva. There's a shortage of accommodation in the area, so they probably got priority by building a lot of apartments.'

'And Ramseyer, Haldeman, the security boxes?'

'He said the unclaimed boxes were removed and he thinks the contents were sent to their Zurich office.'

'So there must be a process for clients like me to claim their property. It's sure to be on their website.'

'I'll look it up, just a minute.'

Ellen was yawning and rubbing her eyes and Jenny cradled her in her arms, stroking her face as she fell into a doze. She looked up as Mme Aeschiman found the page.

'Yes, here it is. Hmm, not a lot to it, it looks like a temporary site'. She scrolled down through the articles. 'No, wait, there's a notice here addressed to former clients with safety deposit boxes, I'll print it out, it's easier.'

The printer hummed and she handed Jenny a single sheet of paper:

RAMSEYER, HALDEMAN & COMPANY SA
IMPORTANT NOTICE TO CLIENTS OF OUR
SAFETY DEPOSIT SERVICE

Dear Clients, as you have already been informed by our registered mail of January 15th, sent to your address of record, we are withdrawing our safety deposit box service, effective immediately. You are kindly requested to remove all your possessions from your box(es) before December 31st 2018 and to make alternative arrangements to deposit them. If you have paid your safekeeping fees in advance for a period after this date, please contact the accounting department at our Zurich office, details below, to obtain a refund of any amounts due. All boxes will be opened by June 30th 2019 and any unclaimed contents will be kept by us in safekeeping until December 31st 2019. We will advise you subsequently if the contents are moved to another safe depository. Any such contents can be claimed by contacting our Zurich office and providing identification and proof of ownership.

Ramseyer, Haldeman & Company thanks you for the trust and confidence you have placed in us over the years and we sincerely apologise for any inconvenience caused

by our decision.
   Case Postale 1201 Genève: Stockerstrasse, 71, Zurich
   March 31st 2017

'I don't believe it!' Jenny was becoming more and more worried and exasperated. 'I never received that registered letter from them in January 2017, and nothing at all since then. So they're keeping any unclaimed contents until December but what happens after that? There must have been a lot of possessions left in those boxes, I can't be the only one. Maybe there's some kind of time limit, like a Statute of Limitations for claims. But they can't dispose of clients' property if it wasn't claimed because we weren't informed.'

She read out the address given on the bottom of the notice, 'Stockerstrasse, 71. Is that the current address of their Zurich office?'

Valérie checked it with the website, 'No. It seems they've moved offices to Badenerstrasse 819.' She frowned. 'But that seems strange.'

'Why?'

'The Stockerstrasse address is near the centre, where the banks and insurance companies are, that's where you'd expect it to be. But this new address is a long way from the business district, five or six kilometres I'd say, and not in a very good area. I'll look it up.'

A moment later, she turned her laptop toward Jenny. The building shown on the screen was a 6-story red and white concrete apartment block next to a couple of shops and a car showroom, a dozen second-hand cars on display outside. There was no sign of an office in the name of Ramseyer, Haldeman.

Jenny stared disbelievingly at the screen. 'The company seems to have disappeared completely. Can you look at the Stockerstrasse address?'

Valérie looked it up, then shook her head. 'It's the Swiss office of *Christenhelm*, a Scandinavian hotel company, nothing to do with security.'

'But if they're still in business, they must have a proper office somewhere.'

'I'll call them. Perhaps they've moved again or something like that.' The phone rang out a dozen times, then the call failed without any message. 'It's almost midday, maybe they've closed for lunch,' she said hopefully.

This must be one of my nightmares. It can't really be happening, Jenny sat silently, looking blankly at the phone.

'Wait, we've got one last option.' Valérie looked up another number. 'I'll try the developers, Edificio 2000. I see they're in Locarno, in the Tessin.' This time there was a reply and she launched into an explanation of Jenny's plight, then was transferred to Carlo Favrini, Customer Services Manager.

When Mme Aeschiman finally ran out of breath, he quickly interjected, in heavily accented French, 'I'm sorry, but what was left of the Ramseyer, Haldeman business was sold almost a year ago, before I started working here, so I don't have any information. Give me your client's details and I'll have an email sent right away,' he paused, and she heard the rustle of paper, 'to M Jolidon, that's who's listed as Director. I'm sure he can sort it out for you. That's all I can do.'

Jenny grimaced as she heard the name over the speaker. *So it's Claude Jolidon who's behind all this. I knew he was a crook, the first time I saw him.*

Mme Aeschiman gave him Jenny's details and rang off. 'I hope there's nothing of great value in that box? I don't mean to be inquisitive, but you seem very upset about it.'

Only fifteen or twenty million dollars' worth of Angolan diamonds. And they weren't declared or insured. No one knows they were there except Leticia and me. Her mouth was dry as she answered, 'Mainly sentimental value, Valérie, but still very precious to me.'

Jenny saw her glance at her watch and pulled herself together, gently waking her daughter. 'I'm sorry, it's time for your lunchbreak. I'll be off now and think about what to do next.' Mme Aeschiman gave Ellen a last hug and Jenny placed her in her pushchair and went to the door. 'Thank you, Valérie, you've been very helpful, as always. I may come to see you again soon, depending on what I find out.'

TWENTY-TWO

Esther Bonnard was staying in the Hotel Richemond again. She'd taken a great liking to the place, especially suite no. 520 on the 5th floor, and was becoming known by the staff, which helped to ensure even better service than their usual level of excellence. Harry was on a two-day investor seminar in Manchester and she'd decided to slip quickly over to Switzerland to keep tabs on Claude Jolidon. So far, he seemed to have been fairly honest in their dealings, but she'd been let down so often in her life, she was suspicious of everyone. Besides, he had about $10 million of her valuables in his strong box, more than enough temptation for the most honest of crooks. She took the Zurich train then a taxi to Badenerstrasse 819 and followed a resident into the hallway. Esther walked up the stairs to avoid the smell in the lift, it reminded her too much of the times she'd had to hide out in places like that.

'Hi Claude, it's Esther,' she called speaking up to the CCTV camera.

A moment later the two Yale locks snapped back, and he peered round the door. 'What are you doing here, something wrong?' He looked around the landing and ushered her into the apartment.

'You told me you were fed up being alone here, so I thought I'd pay a visit.' She saw his wary look. 'Just to cheer you up, that's all.'

'Thanks, that was thoughtful.' Jolidon pulled up a hardbacked chair by his desk for her. 'I'll make a couple of coffees.' He went into the kitchen and Esther looked around the office, regretting that she'd come all this way to visit him. She didn't like this place. It was sparsely furnished; a cheap wooden desk with a lamp on it, a table and a couple of chairs. A laptop was on the desk, the screen dark. Metal filing cabinets stood around the walls with a big old-fashioned steel strongbox and the table was littered with piles of files and papers placed between them. The only item of decoration was a poster of the 2018 French World Cup football team with Hugo Loris holding the cup aloft. The closed blinds on the only window made it dark and dismal and she felt nervous and uncomfortable. She decided to persuade him to move as soon as possible.

Jolidon was asking himself why she'd travelled all the way from London to Zurich to cheer him up. *She's just keeping me honest, surprise visit, hoping to catch me with my hand in the till. She'll have to do better than that.*

He thought of the two dozen high-priced items he'd removed from the strongbox and was selling, a few at a time, through his casino friend and fence, Pietro Minchella, in Divonne. The $100k net he'd received so far had gone into his account with the Swiss Bank of Oman, in Geneva, so her friend in Guadeloupe wouldn't see it. The items were not on the final inventory he'd given to Esther before the sales and René Christen would never remember if they'd been sold or not, he was a nice guy, but half-cut a lot of the time. Even if René did spot a discrepancy, he could say the client had come with proof of ownership and he'd handed the valuables over.

'Thanks, Claude,' she said as he put the coffees on the desk. 'So, how's everything going? You said you're bored, so I assume there've been no problems.'

'Not problems, lucky breaks, actually. A couple of clients have managed to find their way here, I'm not sure how, actually knocked on the door and I saw them on the CCTV.' Seeing her worried look, he went on, 'It's OK, I recognised them each time, nobody special. Their items were in the warehouse with the box numbers, so I returned them and they were happy to get everything back.' He laughed. 'It impressed the clients and made us look like a serious company.'

He sipped his coffee. 'The only other visitor is some guy who's been a couple of times. He came upstairs and knocked and rang the bell, but I just ignored it and he went away.'

'You didn't recognise him?'

'I couldn't see who it was on the CCTV, he was wearing a cap and scarf and didn't look up. I don't know why he's come twice, just ringing and knocking and then pissing off. Apart from that, we got a few more letters that I threw away and a few buzzes on the intercom. A couple of phone calls, but I ignore them if I don't recognise the number.'

'I told you. They must be a bunch of crooks, most of these clients, hiding their spoils in boxes in Geneva. We're doing them a favour, making sure they don't get investigated. And that's all there's been in, what is it, 4 months?'

'That's all. Until this morning.'

'What happened this morning?'

'I got this email from *Edificio*.' He handed her a printout from his laptop.

Geneva, Switzerland

Jenny Bishop pushed her daughter's buggy down the Rue du Mont Blanc towards the Hotel Richemond, thinking of what she'd told the bank manager, *'Mainly sentimental value'. The last part of Charlie's legacy, 1,000 diamonds that Adam hadn't managed to sell. They'd been in that anonymous box since Charlie and Nick rented it in 1976 to start the Angolan Clan business. I left them there in 2008, because I didn't know what to do about them. Leticia's probably forgotten all about the box; she doesn't know I have both keys. And now they're worth more than fifteen million dollars. After what we already received from Charlie's other legacies, it's too much, far too much and neither Leticia nor I need it, thank the Lord.*

Jenny had always had misgivings about receiving money without earning it, she knew it often brought more problems than it solved, and she had seen the consequences at first hand. Besides which, with the help of Patrice, Leticia's banker husband, their successful investments meant they would never be short of money. And *Bishop Private Equity*, the investment company she'd set up five years previously, was now more than just a hobby, it had prospered and grown into a diversified financial business, giving work to a dozen employees and providing her with an interesting and fulfilling occupation as well as a regular uptick in her financial security.

She was now just across the park from the Richemond and took out her mobile. 'Hello Lily, we're just arriving at the hotel, can you come down and give me a hand?'

Putting away her phone, her mind returned to the problem of Ramseyer, Haldeman and box no. 72. *It seems ridiculous, she thought to herself, but the truth is, I'm glad those diamonds have disappeared. I never wanted to have anything to do with them, they brought such pain, death and misery. Good riddance to them, I'm pleased they're gone. The best thing to do is forget all about them as if they never existed. Leticia's never going to ask about them, so let's let sleeping dogs lie and they'll never be mentioned again.*

Ellen was wide awake again and Jenny walked with her through the park to the hotel with a new spring in her step, a sense of relief flooding through her mind, feeling as if a huge burden had been removed from her shoulders. Lily saw them from the hotel entrance and strode towards them, wearing her usual friendly expression. Ellen saw her approaching and waved her arms happily, chattering away. Looking at her daughter's laughing face, Jenny suddenly thought of Emilio, the son born to Leticia and Charlie, who was now thirteen years old, a clever, lovable boy with his whole life ahead of him. She remembered the moment in 2008, when José Luis, Charlie's lawyer, had revealed Emilio's birthright to her and Leticia.

According to Charlie's will, he becomes co-owner of the diamonds on his twenty-first birthday. I'm being thoughtless and selfish. Whatever I or Leticia think, we can't just write off his inheritance without his knowledge or consent.

As she slowly reconciled herself to this fact, Jenny's steely determination kicked in and her mind settled, the decision becoming clear to her. *I have to find out what happened and what's going on at Badenerstrasse 819, if there really is an office there. And if Claude Jolidon is involved in some kind of conspiracy, I'll have to deal with him and recover those diamonds if I can, it's my duty to Charlie and to Emilio. If I succeed, after that it's not up to me what happens to them.*

Lily took the pushchair from her. 'How was your morning? You look very pensive, is everything OK?'

'I'm not sure,' Jenny replied. 'Time will tell.' She cleared the thoughts from her mind. 'Let's have a snack in the park, then Ellen can have her nap and I'll do some work. If it's still warm and sunny, we can go out later for a walk and an early supper in the old town.'

TWENTY-THREE

Zurich, Switzerland
October, 2019

Esther Bonnard's heart started pounding as she read the email from Edificio 2000. She tried to sound nonchalant. 'So, Jenny Bishop has found us, I'm not really surprised. It was bound to happen sometime, she's a smart lady.'

'You're right, but she's only got as far as Geneva, Zurich's another thing altogether. But what's more important is proof, or rather, lack of it. She can say what she likes, but she has nothing to prove what was in that box.'

'You don't seem at all worried.'

'I'm not. We've got all the cards. She's got nothing to show, just a receipt for the fees from 2015. Some clients paid the fees even when the boxes were empty, keeping them for their kids or whatever, or taking stuff out and then replacing it later. There's absolutely nothing to prove there was anything in that box.'

'What about *Edificio*, won't they be suspicious, or worried?'

'Same thing applies. It's not their problem. I'm the guy who bought the company so they could get on with their construction without worrying about the RH legacy. And, don't forget, there's nothing on their inventory about box 72 or Charlie Bishop's briefcase - even less, what was in it.'

He gave her a quizzical look, but she ignored it.

'What will you tell them?'

'It's already sorted.' He handed her the printout of his reply. *'Thanks for your message re Ms Bishop and I have checked the relevant documentation. As you'll see from the certified inventory, box no. 72 doesn't appear at all and there is no record of anything in Ms Bishop's name. Our files show her last visit was in 2015 and if there was anything in the box, I imagine she removed it at that time. If she contacts us, I will try to assist her as best I can. Thanks again for your diligence. CJ'*

'What if she finds her way here? She must know you're here, the *Edificio* people would tell her.'

'So what? If that happens, I'll handle it. Believe me, Esther, Jenny Bishop is not going to mess up our business, take my word for it and forget all about her. Now, is there anything else we need to discuss?'

Esther was impressed. She'd always assumed Jolidon was a softy, a pushover, but she was revising her opinion. *That's what a few millions of dollars can do to someone,* she reflected. Aloud she said, 'OK, Claude, I'll leave Jenny Bishop to you, thanks.' She cleared her mind. 'There's another thing you should know about. It's Christen, I'm pretty sure he's an alcoholic.' She told him of the incident at the Hotel Richemond at 10:30 in the morning.

'I know. I've noticed it several times, maybe not an alcoholic but definitely a regular drinker. But if that's how he manages to perform, and he's actually doing a great job, that's all we want. We can't live his life for him, he's been through a really shitty time, and more importantly, he knows this is probably his last chance to get back on his feet and he can't afford to screw it up.'

'You don't think we should worry?'

'You can worry all you like, but it won't make any difference. Look at the facts, Esther, we can't afford to change. Where are we going to find another Christen? We've got a sale coming in a few weeks' time and he's the official representative of the seller. You knew he wasn't perfect when you hired him, that's why he took the job. And drinking's not the worst problem he could have, believe me, I know a lot worse.'

Esther bit her lip, irritated by the implied criticism. She thought of the fiduciary account at the *Luanda Banco de Credito* in Geneva, Christen was joint signatory on the account. She couldn't afford to take any risks with him, but she knew Jolidon was right. '*Très bien*, it's too late to do anything, but keep him on a short lead, let him know you're looking over his shoulder.'

'I'll watch him like a hawk and if I see the slightest threat to our business, I'll sort it, right away. Alright?'

'I suppose so, but don't let me down, there's too much at stake, for both of us.'

'Esther, when you're playing for stakes as big as these, there's bound to be some problems on the way, but we're both smart enough to resolve them. Is there anything else you wanted to talk about?'

She decided to wait for a better opportunity to talk to him again about moving office. 'No, that's it. We're through here, I think, Claude. I'm glad I decided to come over, you're doing a great job, well done, and keep it up. I'll get on my way.'

'What time's your train back? I'll take you down to the station, the public transport around here's not suitable for a lady.'

In his car, she checked her watch. She could make the 2:10pm train back, there was always plenty of room in first class. That meant she'd be back to the hotel at about 5:30, comfortably in time to get to Cointrin Airport for the 7:55pm Heathrow flight with BA. With the one-hour time difference, she'd be in London at 8:30pm. Esther called the airline and changed her return flight then rang the hotel to advise them she was checking out.

Jolidon pulled up in front of the station and she climbed out. 'Thanks, Claude, I promise to come more often to break the monotony.' They shook hands and she watched him drive away, Esther didn't invite any familiarity from him. On the train, she settled back in her first-class seat and fell into a doze, thinking through the day's events. A couple of unexpected problems had arisen - Christen's drinking and Jenny Bishop's appearance - but she knew Claude was right, they were smart enough to sort them out. With 20 or 30 million dollars on the line, solutions could always be found.

TWENTY-FOUR

Geneva, Switzerland

October, 2019

Esther Bonnard packed the remaining items in her carry-on bag and took a last look around suite 520, nothing forgotten. It was coming up to 6:00pm, *Perfect timing, pay the bill and grab a taxi for the airport.* She wheeled the bag out of the room and called the elevator to take her down to reception.

A moment later, Jenny Bishop and her family came into the hotel, returning from their walk and Ellen's early supper. Lily left the buggy with the hall porter and they walked across the hall to the twin elevators.

Both lifts were in use and several other guests arrived with their bags. The elevator on the right arrived and they entered with some of the others. As they turned around inside, a woman in a smart suede coat emerged from the other elevator and pushed her wheelie bag between the waiting guests across to the reception desk. Jenny was immediately drawn to her; the woman's face was hidden from her, but somehow, her figure, posture and walk rang a bell in her mind. She tried to place the recollection but before she could react, the doors closed, taking them to the 5th floor.

Who was that? I'm sure I know her. She racked her memory but couldn't make the connection.

She was still puzzling when Lily put the key in the door of their suite, no. 521. *Probably just a coincidence, it can't be that important.* But Jenny didn't believe in coincidences; she knew she'd met the woman somewhere. *But where?*

'Time to play Ellen's bedtime game,' she said to Lily. Her daughter understood and clapped her hands. 'Bedtime game,' she repeated.

London, England

Harry was waiting at the platform in Paddington when Esther arrived, delighted to have her back so soon. She liked Harry, he reminded her of Clo-Clo, a cocker spaniel her family had in happier times when she was a child in Toulouse, faithful, loving and a complete softy. Besides, she now had $3 million invested with his firm and he was making a lot of money for her.

'Let's get a takeaway on the way back.' She squeezed his backside. 'We'll have champagne and a Chinese supper then make love all night.'

Geneva, Switzerland

'Yes, this is Marie. Who's calling?'

At 8:30 that evening, when Ellen was fast asleep in her cot and Lily was engrossed with social media on her mobile, Jenny had called the number in Italy given to her by Richard.

She quickly explained who she was, 'I just wanted to say how sad I was to hear about the accident, Gilles was a fine young man. I hope you're settled back in Turin and getting over your loss.'

There was a long pause, then, 'I'm sorry, but I don't understand who you are. How well did you know Gilles?'

'Only as a client of Ramseyer, Haldeman. I met him just a few times over the last 10 years, but he was polite and helpful and I appreciated it. I just wanted you to know that.'

'How did you hear about it after all this time? The company's been closed for months now, since the fire.'

'Richard Claireaux told me about it today, at the *Banque de Commerce*. I know how difficult it is to cope with such dreadful events, I'm sorry if I've upset you.'

'No, I'm alright, thank you, it's been a difficult time, but I'm with my family now and feeling much better. Thank you for calling, it was very thoughtful.'

Before she could ring off, Jenny asked, 'Marie, do you know why Gilles was in the vaults that night?'

Another pause. 'I don't really know. He told me he'd been ordered to make a control, to be sure that all the unclaimed boxes had been removed, so they could close the building down before the demolition. They had to certify to the planning department that the building was completely empty.'

'That's what Richard told me, but I don't understand why he was doing it at night?'

'I'm not sure, he didn't tell me why he was working that night, but I think he was just too busy during the day.'

'Why was that?'

'He was doing the inventory of the contents with a notary, it was a long job, hundreds of boxes to go through. Then the notary had to leave for a couple of days, so he was on his own and he didn't have time during the day. I guess it was just bad luck, no one's fault.'

'I see; yes, it was very bad luck. Do you know who instructed him to make the control?'

'It was his boss, M. Jolidon. He told me the day before the accident.' Jenny heard a sob in her voice, 'I have to go now. Thanks again for your kind wishes.'

Jenny switched off her mobile and sat thinking about the day's events and this latest information. *Claude Jolidon ordered Gilles to carry out a control, knowing he wouldn't have time to make it during the day and he's now in charge of the business after Edificio sold it. Too much of a coincidence, there's definitely something crooked going on. What else do I know?* She snapped her fingers in irritation, *I forgot to ask Marie for the name of the notary. He might have seen or heard something that might help.*

She picked up her mobile again, then put it away. *I can't call her back, she was too distressed and it's not her problem, it's mine. I'll have to find out some other way*

Jenny opened up the browser on her laptop, typing in, *Ramseyer, Haldeman.*

TWENTY-FIVE

Zurich, Switzerland
October, 2019

At eight the next morning, Jenny gave Ellen a long hug and many kisses, then leaving her in Lily's safe care, she went down to the car waiting at the entrance for her. '*Bonjour,* Rachid, this is where we're going.' She handed the chauffeur a note with the Zurich address. It was a bright, sunny day and the drive through the autumn colours of the Swiss countryside was spectacular. Three hours later they arrived in the Swiss-German city and found their way to Badenerstrasse.

She had spent a couple of hours the previous evening searching for information about Ramseyer, Haldeman. There were many newspaper reports concerning Dr Deitrich Haldeman, covering the years of hard work and dedication that led to the creation of his company, a global success story, and his humanitarian activities in later life. After the death of his beloved wife, Velma, he had channelled his still formidable energy into working with charitable causes, championing liberty and opportunity, and opposing discrimination, oppression and corruption. He had left an enviable legacy, both in commercial and humanitarian terms.

The articles about his only son and heir, Patrick, were less flattering. Married several times and living the life of an international playboy, he was everything that his father opposed. He had been a brilliant student at the *EPFL*, the Swiss Federal Institute of Technology, in Lausanne, graduating with honours in Electrical and Mechanical Engineering. But after his father's death, he reinvented himself as a deal-maker, with catastrophic results. There were many items from 2009 to 2012, detailing his fall from grace, until it was announced in 2015 that he had been declared bankrupt and had left Switzerland. After that, it seemed the press had lost interest in him and she found no more mention of him. There were some photographs of him in 2015, a tall, fair-haired man, in his forties, good-looking, but already showing the effects of a life of drinking and partying.

The last items were mainly newspaper reports of the fire and the death of the young Swiss man, Gilles Simenon, but her French wasn't good enough to glean much from them. There were a number of articles concerning the inquest and a Maître René Christen, *Huissier Judiciaire,* was mentioned, whom she guessed was the notary who'd been working with Gilles, but she couldn't be sure. She looked up his name but found only a one-page entry dated 2016, giving an address and telephone number in Fribourg. On the off chance, she called the number and listened to a message in French and German, which she couldn't understand. She noted the details to follow up the next day.

Finally, she scrolled through the current Ramseyer, Haldeman website and any previous versions she could find, all of which were out of date or provided nothing more than the one fact she already knew - the address of the Zurich office.

After taking her decision that afternoon, Jenny had booked a chauffeur to drive her there the next morning. She didn't know what she'd find, but she was determined to do everything she could to recover Emilio's inheritance. *Perhaps it's all a mistake and Jolidon's got the clients' possessions stored in a warehouse somewhere and I can retrieve Charlie's briefcase and the whole matter will be settled.*

But she didn't believe it would be that simple, the whole story of the fire and removal of the valuables to Zurich was too clouded in mystery. And Jolidon was not a man who inspired confidence. She knew she had to be prepared for complications and maybe to fight a battle. This didn't worry her; she'd done it before, several times, and emerged successful.

No. 819 Badenerstrasse was a twenty-minute drive from the centre of town, and they finally pulled up in front of the apartment block she'd seen on Mme Aeschiman's computer screen. Jenny put on her sunglasses and climbed out to stretch her legs, looking around at the second-hand cars, the doorway with no. 819 on it and five floors of dirty concrete above, searching for any sign that Ramseyer, Haldeman might be housed there. There was nothing to be seen except for a couple of shoppers, emerging from the grocery store next to the car showroom. *Probably Eastern European immigrants*, she decided. She knew from her business studies that over a quarter of Switzerland's 8.5 million population were of foreign extraction and since the country had become part of the Schengen zone, there had been an influx of immigrants from Eastern Europe.

Jenny pushed open the door, finding herself in a small, scruffy lobby, with post boxes and intercom buttons on the wall. She looked at the post boxes; they all had family names, mostly Eastern European, with a couple of Spanish or Portuguese. A dirty, cracked glass door led to another lobby, but it was locked. Through it she could see three apartment doors, a metal door, marked **TREPPE**, and an elevator. She turned the handle and pushed the door several times, but it was firmly locked. Stepping back to go outside, she managed to avoid a man coming into the building. He was carrying a briefcase and seemed to be in a hurry.

'*Pardon, Monsieur*,' she said and stepped aside, looking in her handbag, as if she'd forgotten something. He nodded brusquely, put a key in the lock of the glass door and went through to the elevator. '*Merci*,' Jenny stepped in behind him. '*Quel étage, Madame?*' he asked, and she searched her schoolgirl French vocabulary, '*Premier, s'il vous plaît.*' He pressed the button for the first floor then the sixth.

Cautiously looking him over behind her sunglasses, she saw he was smartly dressed, polished shoes and a well-fitting suit. *Quite out of place for this part of town*, she thought, as the door slid to and they ascended. It was not yet midday and she was surprised to notice a definite smell of alcohol in the air. The man seemed nervous, checking his briefcase lock and looking at his watch. He nodded to her again as she got out and walked across the landing, taking off the sunglasses as the door closed again behind her.

Like the ground floor, there were four doors, three bore family names and the third, marked *Treppe*, was unlocked and opened onto a staircase. She climbed the stairs and checked each floor; they were all the same, three doors with family names plus the staircase door.

On the sixth floor, a short corridor led from the stairs to another door which opened onto a fire escape at the back of the building. There was an access hatch in the ceiling above her head, but there was no staircase going up. After looking around to make sure of her bearings, Jenny went quietly through the door to the landing and found a light switch. Here, there were only two doors, one of which had the word '*Hauswirtschaftsraum*' and a lightning bolt painted on it. She assumed it was a utilities room. *That means there's only one large apartment up here*, she realised. The other door had the number 601 on a small plaque by the bell push, but no nameplate. There were two Yale locks on the door and a CCTV camera was fastened to the ceiling above.

This has to be it, there's no other door without a nameplate and it's obviously one large flat. And the camera clinches it, why would a private individual or family need such security in an apartment building like this. This is where that man with the briefcase was coming, so there must be someone in there. Stooping down, she put her ear to the door and could hear the muffled sound of voices but couldn't make out the language. *Yes, I've found them.* She hesitated for a few moments, her finger over the bell push, wondering if this was a wise move, then she pressed the button.

TWENTY-SIX

'You're certain you weren't followed?' The frenchman in the skin-tight jeans asked. He went to the window, peered through the blinds and surveyed the scene outside.

'*Biensûr*. Of course,' the visitor replied. 'There was a woman waiting for the elevator when I arrived, but she got out on the first floor.'

'Is that your car outside? The black Mercedes?'

'A Mercedes? You're joking. You know I always come by train then take the bus here. With my Travel Card it's cheaper than driving, and more relaxing. What's got into you today, Claude? You're as nervous as a kitten.'

Jolidon said nothing about the email from *Edificio 2000*, nor his discussion with Esther. 'I've been checking the website. There were a lot of visits yesterday and that's unusual. We haven't had one for weeks and now we get a half dozen. And there was a phone call in the afternoon, a Geneva number. Someone is trying to get hold of us and I'm wondering why.'

'Well, I'm afraid I can't help you there. Is the package ready? They're expecting it today. I've already delivered the rest of the lots.'

'It's here.' Opening the strongbox, he took out Esther's padded A4 envelope and placed it on the table. René

Christen picked it up, weighing it in his hands.

'These things weigh nothing. How many are there?'

'The same, one hundred stones, about 100 carats. They're just as good, wait until you see them.' He relocked the strongbox and put the keys in the safe under his desk.

'Are there many more where these came from?' he asked innocently, thinking about the old leather briefcase.

'I don't know and if I did I wouldn't tell you. Esther gave them to me yesterday and I didn't ask her where they came from or how many more she has and if you'll take my advice, you shouldn't ask her either. Let's not rock the boat. OK, René?'

'I didn't mean anything by it, just wondering, that's all. It's not every day you find a source of fabulous Angolan diamonds, so there has to be an interesting story behind it.' When Jolidon didn't answer, he went on, 'I've arranged to have their gemologist look at them tomorrow, but it's a formality. What do you think they'll fetch?'

'Same as last time, they're worth up to two million, but the one point five reserve is to be sure they sell. Happy with that?'

'No harm done. If they're as good the others, there'll be buyers at the right price. I told you, I've had a lot of interest since the last sale.' He was quiet for a moment, counting. 'We could hit four or five million on this sale if it goes well. My ten per cent commission is looking better all the time. Well done, Claude.'

As he reached out to shake hands, the laptop screen lit up and showed a hallway and a woman's head and shoulders from above. A moment later, the doorbell rang.

'*Merde!* Who the fuck's that? I knew something was going on,' the Frenchman whispered. He gave Christen a suspicious look and put his finger to his lips, went to the screen on the desk, manipulating the CCTV camera in the ceiling above Jenny's head. She heard the slight movement and looked up.

'I know there's someone in there. Is that you, Monsieur Jolidon?' she said to the camera. 'Please open the door.'

'*Putain*. I don't fucking believe it!' The Frenchman stared at the screen in amazement. He hadn't seen the woman for ten years, but he was never likely to forget her. It was Madame Jenny Bishop, the owner of box no. 72 at Ramseyer, Haldeman in Geneva. 'Don't say a word, just wait until she goes away,' he whispered. Christen nodded his head and both men sat absolutely still and silent, listening to the noise outside.

Jenny knocked on the door and rang the bell for a minute or two, finally shouting at the top of her voice, **'WHOEVER'S IN THERE, OPEN THE DOOR OR I'LL CALL THE POLICE.'**

There was no sound from the apartment, then a door opened on the floor below and she heard a woman's voice echoing up the stairwell, *'PARE COM ESSE BARULHO OU EU VOU LIGAR PARA A POLÍCIA'*.

Jenny knew the language was Portuguese, but the only word she recognised was *policia*. She forced herself to be calm and assess her situation realistically; she was in a locked, private residential building where she didn't belong and if she continued to make a commotion the police would come, not to help her, but probably to arrest her for trespassing. She knew there were at least two people in that apartment, they could see her, via the CCTV camera above her head, although she'd avoided looking up at it again after her initial reaction.

Even if she could get them to open the door, she couldn't prove this was the Ramseyer, Haldeman office, or that there were valuable items in her security box which she wanted to claim, or even that she was a client. She cursed herself silently for being so careless, leaving an undeclared fortune in diamonds in an uninsured security box, but it didn't help her present predicament. *I have no idea who's in that apartment. It might be just some worried citizens with extra security. A lot of people have CCTV cameras these days, mostly innocent people.*

However, Jenny didn't believe it for a moment, this was the address on the website, and it was the only apartment which fitted the bill. *Besides,* she reflected, *if they're innocent people, why would they not open the door when they see a harmless woman knocking?*

'I'LL BE BACK, WITH THE POLICE,' she shouted at the door. *Fairly feeble threat,* she told herself and reluctantly walked back down the staircase, checking the name plates again at each door, but finding nothing more than she'd already seen; apartment 601 was listed as Kruger, but she knew that wasn't the name of the inhabitant.

Her driver was waiting in the car and opened the door for her. 'Are we going back now, Mme Bishop?'

She checked the time, it was almost midday. 'Wait, Rachid. Let me think for a moment.'

Jenny looked up at the shuttered sixth-floor windows. There was an opening in the blind and something moved across, but she couldn't make out who or what it was.

They saw me on the CCTV feed but didn't open the door. I'm sure it's Jolidon and that man I met, and now they know I'm on their trail. I wonder? She said to the driver, 'Go down to the next corner, then come back and park on the other side of the road, try to keep out of sight.'

TWENTY-SEVEN

The men in the window watched through the blinds as the Mercedes drove away. 'How do you know that woman? Who is she?' The *huissier* looked shaken by the intrusion.

The Frenchman lit a cheroot, inhaling deeply. 'Don't worry, just someone I met years ago. An English woman, used to do business with us in Geneva, I don't know what she was doing here. Was that who was in the elevator with you?'

Christen said, 'I didn't get a proper look on the screen, but I don't think so, it was a younger woman, wearing sunglasses, French-speaking.'

'Good, so she's seen neither of us, doesn't know who's here.'

'But she called you by name. Why would she think you were here?'

'Because she knows that I used to be the Swiss manager, there's nothing strange about that. Forget her, she's harmless. See how she pissed off when we didn't answer, she won't be back. Just concentrate on the sale, we need it to go well.' He opened the door and checked the empty landing, '*See you soon, René.* Travel safely and send me a copy of the valuations when you can.'

Jolidon closed the door and turned both Yale locks,

went to sit at the desk, conflicting thoughts crossing his mind. He called a UK number 'That Bishop woman was here. Yes, here at the office but she doesn't know if there was anyone here.'

He listened for a moment, '*Non*, she didn't see me or René. We saw her on the CCTV, and she left when no one answered.' He listened again. 'Of course. I'll keep my eyes peeled, but I don't think it's worth worrying about. She's got nothing to show the police, they'll just laugh at her. And even if she comes back with a sledgehammer and breaks the door down, she's got no proof of anything. I've told you a dozen times, I've got no idea what was in that briefcase, the contents of the box were never declared, there's nothing on the inventory and no way she can prove otherwise.'

He lit up another cheroot. 'Forget her and look forward to the next sale. René's on his way to Geneva with the package. I'll see you next month. *Salut*.'

Jolidon took a deep drag of his cigarette, remembering his previous skirmishes with Jenny Bishop. He went back over the Ramseyer, Haldeman plan in his mind from start to finish, worrying that they'd made a mistake somewhere. *How much does she know, apart from me being here? Edificio mentioned my name and she's found me; but that's all. She's concerned only about the contents of the briefcase from box 72, and there's nothing she can do about it because it doesn't officially exist.* Edificio had already shown they weren't at all interested in Ramseyer, Haldeman and even less with a claim for something that didn't appear on the inventory.

He was now certain that the diamonds produced for the first two sales had come from the briefcase in Jenny

Bishop's box, but he wasn't going to upset Esther by talking about it again. As far as the fire and Simenon's death were concerned, the questions had all been asked and answered at the inquest. The building was off-limits and being demolished, so there was nothing to be found there. He knew the Bishop woman was a force to be reckoned with, but this time he was certain she was on the losing side. At least, he hoped she was.

Belgravia, London, UK

Esther put her mobile down. *So, Jenny Bishop has managed to find the office. Well done her!! A day earlier and she might have bumped into me, my luck has definitely turned for the better. She's been looking for the diamonds, but she doesn't know where they are and she's got no proof that they ever existed and neither has Jolidon. This time I'm in the driving seat and it's her turn to worry about losing her fortune.*

She went into the living room, where Harry was watching the news. He turned to her, laughing uproariously. 'You know that Boris was supposed to ask the EU for another extension after October 31st?'

'Didn't he say he'd rather die in a ditch before he'd do it?'

'You're right, he did, but the Remainers have tied him up in knots, so he's had to write the letter.'

'Well, I'm surprised you think it's so funny, you're a staunch Brexit supporter, aren't you?'

'That's not the funny part. He didn't even sign the letter, and he wrote another to tell them he didn't think it was the right thing to do. So he didn't exactly die in the ditch as much as crawl out with his head held high.'

'So what?' She answered, thinking back to the conversations they'd had with Lord and Lady Scarbrough. 'It won't change anything. The Remainers will still find a way to stop him getting Brexit done.'

Esther saw him start to formulate an argument and put her hand across his lips. 'Can we please forget politics for a while? I need champagne and sex. Which shall we start with?'

Zurich, Switzerland

Jenny sat back in her seat as she watched the smartly dressed man walk into the *Hauptbahnhof*, the central train station. Her short wait opposite no. 819 had been worthwhile. A few minutes after their return, he had come out, this time carrying his briefcase closely under his arm. He walked to a nearby bus stop and climbed on to the waiting bus, and they followed it slowly towards the city centre. She tried several times to get a photo with her mobile but there was too much traffic and she couldn't get a clear image from the inside of the car. At the station, they watched from nearby as he left the bus and walked quickly inside, giving her no opportunity to get a shot.

'OK, Rachid,' Jenny said, annoyed that she hadn't as much as a decent picture of the man to show from her day's excursion. 'Let's get back to the hotel. We'll be just in time for me to have tea with my daughter.'

The driver said nothing. He was trying to work out who Jenny Bishop was and why she was following a man in Zurich.

TWENTY-EIGHT

'Good health, Hugh, and thanks for the impressive presentation, an excellent afternoon's work. If that doesn't put some fire up their arses, nothing will.' Sir Reginald Scarbrough took a swallow of the Château Latour Pauillac. 'Hmm, delicious, one of my favourite Bordeaux.'

'And to you, Reggie. Unfortunately, after many years of presenting similarly realistic disaster scenarios, my expectations of action of any kind are depressingly low. Meanwhile, the incidence of damage caused both privately and on national and international levels continues to escalate.'

Middleton bided his time, until Scarbrough had consumed most of the £120 bottle and was more loquacious. 'That reminds me', he said, 'I believe we have a friend in common.'

'I'm sure we have many, Hugh, which one are you referring to?'

'It's a little embarrassing, a younger woman I used to know quite well, if you take my meaning.'

'Well I never!' He raised his eyebrows and slapped his hand on the table. 'You old dog, I was somehow under the impression that you weren't keen on the ladies. No offence meant, of course.'

Middleton's past history didn't permit him to take offence, especially when it was so close to the truth. He attempted to give a sly smile. 'None taken, but I came by your house the evening you threw that bash a couple of months ago. I was on my way to a prior engagement and I dropped my partner, Ilona, off on the way. You'll remember she attended in my stead?' He was certain that Reggie was unaware of her death.

Scarbrough pondered a moment, 'Of course, I remember her, pleasant enough young woman, from Bulgaria or somewhere over there?' He took a sip of his wine.

Hiding his distaste at Sir Reginald's unspoken prejudice, he answered, 'Ukraine, actually, very clever lady. Sadly, she was killed in a traffic accident a few months ago, a tragic loss.'

Scarbrough said only, 'Sorry to hear that, must have caused you some problems at the Institute.'

Middleton nodded his thanks. 'In any event, as I was leaving your house, I'm certain I noticed the young woman in question walking into the property and I thought it might be amusing to get in touch again. You never know, she might have fond memories of me.'

He fished in his pocket and pulled out a small photo he'd produced from the Tsunami image. 'That's the woman I mean, although the photo was taken a few years ago. Do you remember her?' He put his trembling hands together on the table, dreading Scarbrough's reaction.

Sir Reginald put on his spectacles and scrutinised the poor-quality print. 'I don't believe it! That's Esther, Esther Bonnard, Harry Fern-Chapman's partner. We were just round there the other evening, lovely apartment they have on Eaton Square, costs a fortune. What a coincidence, it's a small world, isn't it?'

Middleton supressed his reaction to the news. *I've found her, though she's changed her name.* He tried to sound disappointed, 'That's her, that's Esther, but sadly, it seems that my attentions wouldn't be reciprocated, a great shame. Who is this Fern-Chapman? I don't believe I know him.'

'He's an investment fund manager, cut his teeth at Selchurch Peak, then set up on his own a couple of years ago, as Olympic Funds Group. He's doing very well, you might want to take a modest punt, many of my friends have.'

'I'll certainly look at the opportunity, though my resources may be inadequate for such a high-level relationship. What is the name of the organisation?'

Scarbrough finished off the Pauillac and they walked to the door. 'I sincerely hope, Reggie, that this story will remain between us. I have no wish to blight Esther's relationship with Mr Fern-Chapman, it sounds as if she has found a fine partner in her life and I wish her the very best of luck and happiness.'

'My lips are sealed, Hugh. I'm just sorry that I couldn't give you better news. She's a very attractive woman, you must be quite disappointed. Still, you have the memories, eh? I'm rather jealous, actually.'

Back at his flat Middleton took out the note he'd made, *Partner of Harry Fern-Chapman, Olympic Funds Group. And she's now calling herself Esther Bonnard, I wonder where that came from?* He had known her only as Esther Rousseau, in London, or Elodie Delacroix/Tsunami, in Dubai, and had never heard her maiden name, but it was the same Esther who'd been involved in the Leo Stewart kidnapping fiasco in 2010, ending up with his imprisonment and her disappearance. *She's fallen on her feet yet again.* He marvelled at her resilience, recovering from one misfortune after another.

He looked up Fern-Chapman's profile, following the story of his successful career at Selchurch Peak, then the two years of rapid growth of his independent fund business. *Impressive returns,* he said to himself. *Reggie was right, I could do with that kind of performance for my pension pot.* But he knew that was a bad idea for two reasons; the modest amount of his savings would be of no interest to a manager like Fern-Chapman, and secondly, it was too close to home. If Esther somehow found him via Olympic Funds, he wouldn't live long enough to spend whatever profit he could achieve.

Middleton reflected on the situation. He had no proof that she had been involved in Ilona's accident, and it would be impossible to find a hit and run murderer after all this time. Despite being convinced that she had arranged it, he knew there was nothing he could do. As far as their past records were concerned, it was checkmate. She knew who and where he was, and in his elevated position as adviser to governments, he couldn't afford the scandal of disclosure. He now had the same information about her, and she probably didn't know that. If she did, she'd have already gone after him and he wouldn't be sitting here worrying about it.

On the other hand, he tried to reassure himself, *killing someone who is forewarned isn't all that easy and she has a lot to lose, living with a millionaire investment banker.*

In one of his previous lives, Middleton, then Lord Arthur Dudley, had been a high-flying, wealthy man, until his ingenious, but highly corrupt methods of amassing wealth brought him crashing back down to earth, in the form of his term in Ford Open Prison in West Sussex. He was still fascinated by all kinds of money-making schemes and out of interest, he searched for the descriptions and subscription documents for Olympic Funds. He studied all five of them, then sat back in shock, astonished at the composition of the portfolios of investments.

Without exception, they included an abnormally high percentage of unquoted and Over-the-Counter, OTC, traded shares in hi-tech start-up and small or medium sized 'special opportunity' businesses. *There is no liquidity there at all,* he reflected. *If there's a scare in the markets and clients want to recover their investments, however modest, those shares will have to be sold at whatever price can be achieved. Fern-Chapman will be at the mercy of the traders, they'll drive the price down and the funds will suffer massive losses and so will his clients. That man is playing a dangerous game.*

Intrigued, he looked up Selchurch Peak, and found many of the same investments in their funds; high-risk illiquid shareholdings, which no doubt dated from before he left the company, two years ago. *It's not quite as bad as Olympic, but a high risk of problems if the markets take a shock.*

Middleton now had information about Esther and her high-risk investor boyfriend. He remembered what Ilona had always said to him, 'Information is power, guard it well'. He didn't know what he could do with the knowledge he'd obtained, but he somehow felt better prepared for whatever might happen.

Belgravia, London, England

'Bonjour, René, how are things in Geneva?' It was a rainy Monday morning and Esther was alone in the apartment. She listened carefully, trying to detect if he'd been drinking, but his voice sounded clear and confident. At his news, her mood immediately brightened. 'CHF820,000, that's not bad for two small sales. I'll sign a transfer instruction and send it to you by registered, express post like before, you'll get it in two days. You can countersign it and take it to the Geneva bank.'

Esther switched off from listening to his usual self-serving explanations of how cleverly he'd calculated the reserves and helped to push the prices up with a fake telephone bidder. She was busy calculating her new net worth. *That brings my Bahrain account back up to $2.5 million. Plus $3 million with Harry; over $5 million.* She gave herself a mental high-five. *Not bad, after starting with $250k just a year ago.*

Noticing the *huissier* had stopped talking, she said, '*Oui, oui*, René, that's great. I'm a bit busy right now, I'll send you the transfer request this morning and I look forward to seeing you next month. *Au revoir.*'

Christen's phone went dead, her condescending response resonating in his mind. He took a swig from the glass of white wine on the table. *Arrogant bitch, I'm making her a fortune and she doesn't have the courtesy to say, 'well done' or 'thanks'.*

He knew from Jolidon's bragging that he received 25%; his own share was only 10%, which left 65% for Esther and her 'expenses'.

There are virtually no expenses on these local auctions; that means over 500k for her, 200k for Claude and only

82k for me and I organised them both single-handed. He looked again at the summary he'd made of the sales proceeds and disbursements. She had made almost $5 million, Jolidon, $2 million, and he had received about $620k. *I'm in the limelight, managing the sales, signing on the fiduciary account, taking all the risks and what do I get? Chickenfeed.*

He poured himself another glass of wine, it was helping him to clearly see the injustice of it all. *Why did I agree to a paltry 10% commission? I was stupid, or desperate, or maybe both. If I'd known what was involved, the risks I'd have to take, I'd never have agreed to it.* The catalogue for the November sale at Drewberrys was on the table, and he flicked through the pages. *I know where every one of those items came from, they're all on Gilles Simenon's inventory and I've got a copy of it. The briefcase isn't on there, but I know where she keeps it and what's inside it. As for Simenon's 'accident', one word from me and the enquiry into the fire would be reopened like a shot. Things have to change if they want to continue with these sales; without me they'd be locked away in prison with no business at all.*

After just 6 months, René Christen, bankrupt Swiss *Huissier Judiciaire*, became aware of his importance to Esther Bonnard and the damage he could do to her organisation. He finished the last of the wine. *Patience, René, it's not worth starting a fight this time over only 800k. I'll wait for the big sale, next month. Then, with 4 million at stake and needing my signature to release the money, we'll see who's calling the shots.*

TWENTY-NINE

Marbella, Spain
November, 2019

'Listen to this, Jenny, what does it remind you of?' Leticia read out, '*One hundred rare, unmounted Angolan diamonds, totalling 105 carats. These magnificent stones of between .05 and 2 carats are graded: purity finest white, clarity VVS1 or VVS2 with a round brilliant cut. The privately-owned stones have never previously been offered for sale and are from the pre-independence period; known provenance, guaranteed not blood diamonds.*

'They're just like the stones we saw in Charlie's security box in Geneva. Look, lot number 900, don't they look the same to you?' She handed her the glossy catalogue. 'Although that's impossible, because they're locked away and we don't know who's got the other key. That's a shame, just look at the reserve price, one and a half million Swiss Francs. The whole batch in the box must be worth at least fifteen million.'

Jenny turned away from her laptop and took the book, trying to hide her shock at this sudden interruption. It was the catalogue for the Drewberrys November auction sale of jewellery in Geneva. A half-page photograph showed the beautiful gems, spilled out on a blue velvet cloth, artfully lit with soft lighting reflecting from the multiple facets of the brilliant cut stones. She gasped, sure these were Charlie's Angolan diamonds, remembering what they had looked like in the Ramseyer, Haldeman vault all those years ago, realising her vague suspicions were probably true. The fire had been an act of arson and the contents of box 72 had become anonymous lot 900 in an auction sale, probably stolen by Claude Jolidon and the man she'd seen going up to the apartment in Zurich.

That's what was going on, she realised, *the man with the briefcase was bringing or collecting some of the diamonds for the auction. Clever, they're selling them in batches, to escape too much attention and avoid driving the price down.* She wondered for a moment if the man might have been Patrick Haldeman, the son of the founder, but quickly put the thought aside, he didn't resemble the photographs she'd seen online and hadn't looked like a playboy, more like a lawyer or banker.

Maybe it was the notary, René Christen? He seems to have disappeared along with Ramseyer, Haldeman.

The day after her trip to Zurich, Jenny had called Christen's Fribourg number again and listened to the same message. She played it to the concierge, who told her that the office was closed until further notice; no further information was given, nor could she find any trace of the *huissier* in the online phonebooks. *Another dead-end*, she thought despondently.

She spoke to Valérie Aeschiman, hoping she'd heard something further from *Edificio 2000*, but she hadn't. In a last attempt, she called the company in Locarno and asked for M. Favrini, who, thankfully, spoke excellent English.

'What can I do for you, Madame Bishop? he asked in a formal tone.

'I'd like to know if you've sent an email to M. Jolidon and if anything has transpired.'

'I'm afraid I can't tell you that; in fact, I can't tell you anything. I've examined the matter with our inhouse lawyer, and we find that you are not eligible for repatriation of any property from Ramseyer, Haldeman. Neither your name nor the security box number you quoted appears on the certified inventory we received from them. There is no record of any possessions relating to you at all.'

Jenny couldn't believe her ears. 'But, box no. 72 has been rented by me for over 10 years and it was there with my property in it at the time of the fire.'

'Madame Bishop, I went to the trouble of searching for the inventory in our files and checking it with our lawyer. I repeat, that box is not on the list and there is no property on it in your name. Frankly, I don't understand why you're making these claims to *Edificio 2000*, instead of to RH Security Services in Zurich. Perhaps it's for financial reasons? However, the position of my company is that we have nothing further to do with these matters and we accept no liability of any kind; if you think you have a claim for property, you must address yourself to our successors in Zurich.'

'I've tried that,' she managed to interject. 'I went to their office yesterday and no one answered. I'm sure the office was occupied, but they ignored me, and I was obliged to leave empty-handed. That's why I'm calling you.'

'I've already explained to you that there is no legal basis for you to question my company about this and we cannot accept any responsibility for your claims, especially since they are not borne out by the certified inventory. Now, I'm extremely busy with a CHF300 million property development and I have no more time to waste on this matter. Goodbye, Madame Bishop.' The line went dead.

Jenny sat for a long while, the conversation reverberating in her mind. *I'm completely stuck*, she realised. *Jolidon must have removed my box from Gilles' inventory and he's selling Charlie's diamonds from that locked apartment in Zurich. Edificio's lawyer is obviously worried about any potential liability, and I can't prove a thing.*

After despondently trying the HR Zurich number several times again, with no success, Jenny knew there was nothing further she could achieve by staying in Switzerland. Her London business required her presence and Ellen needed to get back to her home surroundings. In addition, Jenny needed time to think about the implications of what she'd discovered, somehow try to formulate a plan to recover the diamonds, and she couldn't do that in a Geneva hotel. *I've no choice but to go home.*

They flew to the UK the following day and spent a couple of weeks at her home in Ipswich, Jenny commuting to London to catch up on progress in *Bishop Private Equity*. Her firm now comprised 25 holdings in private companies in almost every area of activity, all trying to plan for what might happen if and when the country left the EU; with or without an agreement. Brexit seemed to be the only subject of discussion in the UK, though no one seemed to know what they were talking about, and she was happy to leave again with Ellen for Marbella.

Leticia's husband, Patrice, was now General Manager of the Spanish arm of *BIP, Banque Internationale de Paris*. Since he had refused to leave Marbella when he was promoted, he was on one of his regular trips to Madrid and she had come over to York House with Sebastien, her youngest son, to spend a few nights. Her mother, Encarni, was in the kitchen with Lily, preparing dinner, the children already fast asleep in bed and Chester lying on the floor across her feet. He was happy to be home after two weeks in the kennels and was determined to stay close to his mistress.

Jenny flicked through the catalogue. Pages and pages of beautiful gems; diamonds, sapphires, emeralds, rubies, opals, unmounted or mounted in fabulous gold and platinum pieces of jewellery; in rings, necklaces, brooches, watches and every type of wearable ornament. Many of the items bore captions like, '*Property of a Lady*', or '*From the estate of a Titled Family*'. The caption to lot no. 900 read only, '*Private Investment Trust*'.

How can they control where all this jewellery comes from? she asked herself. *It's not possible. There's so much of it and it's worth millions and millions. I wonder how much of it is like Charlie's diamonds? There must have been a lot of other unclaimed valuables stolen, just like his. 'Hundreds of boxes,' Marie told me. And most of it was probably not declared or insured, so even if it was subsequently discovered, it's impossible to prove ownership. But the cleverest part is that no one knows or cares where the proceeds go, Drewberrys get paid for the items, take their commission and transfer the funds wherever they're told. The simplest form of money laundering there could be.*

She looked through the pages again, finding and counting dozens of items with the same caption, '*Private Investment Trust*', convinced they were like the Angolan stones, stolen from the Ramseyer, Haldeman coffers.

Leticia's question broke her reverie. 'Don't you think they look the same?'

Her thoughts returned to the present predicament. *I have to tell Leticia the truth. I left them in the briefcase in that box for all these years and didn't tell her about the keys, and now I'm sure they've been stolen, and Emilio's legacy may be lost forever. It can't be avoided any longer.*

She handed the catalogue back. 'Where did you get this? I didn't know you followed the Geneva auctions.'

'Patrice gave it to me. I'm probably not supposed to tell you, but he works with all the big auction houses, helping them when they come to Marbella to find clients. They have valuation days to encourage people to sell their valuables at their sales. There's a lot of residents here with jewellery to sell, mostly older people, and just as many younger ones with new money, jet set types, looking for expensive bling to show off to their friends. He calls it the ultimate recycling business; the jewellery gets bought and sold time after time and usually the price keeps going up. Diamonds especially, Patrice told me they've been one of the best investments over the last twenty years.'

'And even better is that no one knows where the valuables come from, nor where the proceeds go. Recycling and laundering, like a Chinese laundry.'

'Sorry, Jenny, I'm not following you. What are you talking about?'

'Just a minute, I need to look something up.' She went online, looking for catalogues of recent auctions. There were none, but she found items showing selected high achieving lots from the previous auctions that year. In the report of Binghams' September auction of over 200 million Swiss Francs, she scrolled through the photographs of magnificent jewellery until she came to lot no. 687. Jenny caught her breath as she looked at virtually the same photograph, the diamonds spilling onto a lavender velvet cloth, with the captions, *'One hundred rare, unmounted Angolan diamonds, totalling 101 carats.'* *'Private Investment Trust'*. The sales price achieved was CHF1.75 million.

The screen became dim as tears came to her eyes. Now she knew for certain that Gilles Simenon's death was not an accident. *He was deliberately sent on duty by Claude Jolidon to be murdered in the blaze because he knew the owners of the boxes and what was in them. Hundreds of boxes. He would have made sure they were contacted and could collect their valuables. Who knows how many of the goods in these sales are from Ramseyer, Haldeman? Stolen goods worth countless millions. And what about Christen, the huissier, is he part of the conspiracy?*

Her thoughts turned to Marie Simenon, Gilles' widow, still grieving over his death. For her sake, Jenny wanted to prove that her husband hadn't died in a tragic, pointless accident, but the fire had been an act of arson; by criminals, for profit. She had to somehow try to bring the culprits to justice so Marie could find some sort of closure. *Murdered, just for money, it's always about money. After being hidden away for more than 10 years, those diamonds are still causing murder and mayhem.*

'What's wrong. Why are you so upset?' Leticia put her arm around her as she saw the tears. 'Are you thinking about Ron and Charlie? It was such a long time ago, I never thought. I'm sorry if it brought back bad memories.'

Jenny wiped her eyes. 'It's not your fault, I'm alright now. Hang on, I want to check one more thing.' She found the results of the top selling items in McCallums' sales in June, but there were no batches of loose diamonds. *The fire was in April, too late to prepare for the June auctions. So, they sold 100 stones in September and there's another 100 coming up this month. That's twenty per cent of Charlie's diamonds. 800 still left, somewhere, probably in that apartment in Zurich. Almost a quarter of Emilio's inheritance gone and it's my fault.* Her mood began to change from sadness to anger. *It's time to put a stop to it,* she told herself. *I must do something to save the remaining diamonds, and find the murderers of Gilles Simenon, but how, what can I possibly do?*

She put aside the laptop, wondering how to break this terrible news to her friend. *It's not the right time to tell her,* she reasoned, *I need to find out more about what's going on and try to prevent it.* One more thought came to her. 'Do you think you might still have the catalogue at home for the last Bingham's sale, it was in September?'

'I'm sure I have it, you know me, I never throw anything away. Why do you want it?'

'Oh, nothing special, just something I want to check on.' Then, on an impulse, she asked, 'Why don't we take a trip to Geneva? We haven't been there together since 2008. We could go to the auction if you like, it's in a couple of weeks. I'm sure it's fascinating, watching people bidding millions for this beautiful jewellery. We might even find something we can afford. And we can go back to the *Park des Eaux-Vives* for dinner. What do you say, a weekend in Geneva, like old times, just the two of us?'

Leticia's eyes lit up. 'What a great idea. I'd love to come and I'm sure Pascal won't mind. I'll ask him when he gets back on Saturday. But what about the children? I don't think we can take three youngsters with us. We won't be able to go out on the town with the kids in tow. On second thoughts, I'm not sure if Patrice would trust me going to Geneva with you. After our adventure there the last time and what happened with Leo in Dubai, he thinks you're a dangerous influence on me.' She pulled a face and winked, reminding Jenny of the innocent young woman she had first met in Marbella in 2008.

'Don't be silly, that's all in the distant past. Thanks to him, you're now a mother of two and I'm just a boring middle-aged private equity investor, so he can't complain if we go off for a girl's weekend to recharge our batteries. Lily will look after the children and Chester as well; they can all stay in the house with her and your mother can spoil them rotten. They'll have a great time, and so will we. What do you say?'

Leticia laughed out loud, 'Sold to the lady in the blue dress. See, I'm practising already. If it will cheer you up, then of course we'll go. Get the calendar up on your screen and we'll work out the dates. It'll be wonderful, like you said, just like old times.'

A feeling of foreboding suddenly came over Jenny as she turned to her laptop. 'It'll be even better, I'm sure,' she said.

THIRTY

Marbella, Spain
November, 2019

Jenny was sweating and filthy, her hands and bare feet raw and scratched from the gravel path and the rough, rock face of the tunnel walls. The roof above her was so low, she had to stoop or crawl to move forward and her back was aching. The metal box she was carrying seemed to weigh a ton and she had to stop and lay it down time and again. She could see a faint light in the distance, *the mouth of the tunnel*, she realised, it seemed miles away. Behind her, she could feel the heat of the flames, hear the sound of multiple explosions, like percussion drums, beating out a dreadful, constant rhythm of death. The air was unbearably hot, smoke and dust swirling around her until she could hardly breathe. She already had a handkerchief tied over her nose and mouth and now she closed her eyes to shut out the flashes and the dust whirling around her, stumbling forward like a blind woman, the box seeming to become heavier and heavier with every step.

'Ouch!' Her head bumped into something hard, she pushed forward with the box and was rewarded by the sound of a metallic barrier clashing against it. Opening her eyes, she saw from the reflection of the flames behind her, a heavy metal gate which barred her way. Jenny put the box down and reaching forward, she grasped the bars, trying to pull or push the gate open, in vain. Desperately, she examined it, tears running from her eyes as she squinted through the smoky haze in the gloomy half-light. It was fastened with a large iron padlock attached to an iron frame set into the tunnel wall. She looked around the narrow, low passageway; there was no way out, unless she returned towards the fire. She heaved at the bars of the gate, rattling it madly, willing it to open, but it remained immovable.

Jenny sat down on the security box, holding back her tears of frustration, desperately trying to think of a way to escape from this nightmare. She pulled the handkerchief closer over her nose, breathing through her mouth to keep out the smoke. But she could feel it was beginning to affect her. Her mind started to wander, remembering previous occasions when she or her family had faced grave danger. She leaned back against the rock wall of the tunnel, a kaleidoscope of thoughts rushing through her mind; *April 2008, when she'd learned of the death of her husband, Ron, then her father-in-law, Charlie; the night of Adam Peterson's death in Marbella in the fatal gunfight between d'Almeida and Pedro Espinoza; the abduction in South Africa of her nephew Leo in 2010; Leo's imprisonment in Dubai and the foiled Russian cyber-attack in 2017.*

I've had my share of adventures and survival, she thought. *Everything comes to an end. This time it's different, there's no one here I can fight, or convince, or outwit, it's just me and the fire.* She had a vision of Ellen, tucked up in her bed in York House, under the watchful eye of Lily Whitaker. *Thank God she's safe and well and surrounded by good people who love her.*

Now the smoke was increasing, and Jenny found herself

falling asleep. She stood up, holding the handkerchief over her face, fighting to keep her eyes open, willing herself to stay awake as long as she possibly could. The noise of the explosions had died away, and it was quiet, though she could see the flames still approaching behind her. Somewhere, in the far reaches of her consciousness, she thought she heard a new sound; it was a woman's voice, calling. A faint light was flashing in the mid-distance.

She cried out, 'I'm here, please help me!' The flashing light came nearer, and a voice she knew called, 'Hang on, Jenny, we're almost there.'

A moment later, two figures emerged from the gloom, shining a flashlight onto her. 'Thank God we got here in time.' The torch turned around and she saw Leticia and her husband, Patrice. 'Stand back,' he told her, as he attacked the frame of the gate with a crowbar.

A few minutes later, as her friends helped her towards the entrance, Patrice carrying the security box, Jenny looked back into the tunnel. In the glow from the fire she saw the figure of a woman, standing by the broken gate, watching them escape. The woman turned and walked slowly away, disappearing into the gloom. There was something about her walk that Jenny recognised, a distant memory that she couldn't quite bring to mind, but she knew it wasn't a pleasant memory.

Jenny woke in a sweat, she hadn't had a nightmare like this since 2017, when Leo had been imprisoned in Dubai. She was still trembling from the fear she'd experienced, the vision clear in her mind, the delusion of escaping from the fire in the vault at Ramseyer, Haldeman, with Charlie's security box. From all her previous experiences, she knew the nightmare was telling her something and she thought she might know what. She went to shower and have breakfast with Leticia and the children, trying to show a brave face, despite her misgivings.

THIRTY-ONE

Belgravia, London, England
November 2019

Esther took a tray with two coffees into Harry's office. She had a copy of the *Financial Times* with her. 'What happened to Olympic Funds this week?' He'd been away for a few days and she'd been buying it to check on the performance of her investments. She wasn't happy with what she'd read; after the many previous disappointments in her life, Esther was terrified of losing her newly acquired wealth.

He looked up from his laptop. 'What are they saying?'

She opened up an article on the UK markets. 'It says here that there've been a number of large withdrawals that have driven the fund prices down and the November results will be poor.'

'A temporary blip, darling, nothing to worry about.' He sipped his coffee. 'A couple of investors reacting to the General Election announcement. The government is in such a crap state of weakness that everyone with money is terrified that Labour could manage to get in, then we really would see a massive fall in the markets. Maybe even a wealth tax as well, so there's a lot of nervousness around, people moving their money to offshore tax havens, that kind of panic activity.'

'But look at this, I checked the share prices and two of

my funds actually fell in value, by a couple of per cent. How did that happen?'

He turned from his computer. 'We had to liquidate a few holdings to meet the withdrawals. It's normal procedure, Esther, we don't hold too much cash, it's not worth it, cash earns nothing these days.' Seeing she was unconvinced, he went on, 'I told you when you came on board, the three funds you're in are the most profitable of the group, but they're also extremely safe. You know I wouldn't expose you to any unnecessary risk, trust me. And despite that little slowdown, you're still ahead Esther, still showing a profit. I promise when the election's over, the markets will turn around and you'll see our strategy will bring you terrific rewards. You can't be an emotional investor, reacting every time some minor event causes a panic attack, you have to be patient and go with the flow for a little while.'

Esther remembered her conversations with Nicola Scarbrough about the threat of a Labour government. 'But if Boris Johnson loses, you think the markets will be in trouble?'

'There's absolutely no chance of that. I'm sure that Corbyn and McDonald will put the frighteners on everyone, and Boris will find a way to get a working majority, so please stop worrying.'

Esther was still worried. 'You're absolutely sure my investments are safe?'

'I wouldn't say it if it wasn't true.' He was becoming irritated. 'Look at my investment history and think about the huge number of investors who've made a fortune with me over the long term. I can't offer you a better guarantee than that. Right now, it's a very nervous time for everyone but when the election's out of the way, you'll see what I'm capable of. Now I need to get this finished, so please forget about an insignificant blip in the markets and think about the future opportunity.'

I suppose he's right, she told herself, *I'm being paranoid. And I should make about $2 million from next month's sales, so better not lose any sleep if it's just a market fluctuation.* 'Promise me I'll be the first to know if there's a problem?'

He had turned back to his screen, 'Of course, Esther, I told you. Just leave it to me and you won't be disappointed.'

She immediately started worrying about the Geneva sale and went into the kitchen to ring Jolidon. He was surprised, she seldom called him. 'What's up?'

'Just checking. Is everything in good shape for Drewberrys? It's in two weeks' time.'

She heard him take a drag on his cheroot. 'Of course, everything's fine. I promised you I'd do nothing all day but make sure that Christen's doing his job, and he is. You've seen the catalogue and everything's in there, it looks great.'

'OK, I just thought a last-minute check wouldn't hurt.'

'You seem very nervous, what's the problem?'

Realising she'd sounded weak, she said, 'There's no problem. I'm just making sure nothing goes wrong because of René's drinking.'

'*Bien*, I'll go through everything with him one last time, but don't call me again, now you're making me nervous.'

Geneva, Switzerland

René Christen was in Drewberrys' Geneva office, having an argument with Bernard Villeneuve, their Swiss lawyer, when his mobile rang. He saw Jolidon's name and moved away from Villeneuve. 'Claude?'

'How's everything going?'

'Who wants to know?'

'The boss just asked me to check everything's OK for the sale.'

'The boss? So now, she calls herself 'The Boss', does she? Who the fuck does she think she is?'

Jolidon was shocked, he'd never known Christen lose his temper before. 'Calm down, René, she doesn't call herself that, I was having a joke.'

'Well, you can tell her I'm at Drewberrys right now, have been all morning, arguing about the authenticity papers for our merchandise, so I'm not in the mood for jokes. Their lawyer has been checking the catalogue descriptions and he's not 100% happy with our documentation.'

'What's the problem?'

'You should know what the problem is, this bloody *African Benevolent Trust*. It's got them nervous, there's been so many scandals in the Swiss banks lately, they're scared shitless about money laundering. Especially when it's to do with Africa. And you'll have to get me a certification signed by that trustee, Benjamin Appletree, confirming that they're not conflict diamonds. These people are a damn sight more professional than Binghams; this lawyer's putting my balls through the wringer, so I've got my work cut out. If I don't do this right, we'll have nothing in the sale. Then the 'boss' wouldn't be very happy, would she? I mean if she didn't get her 60% of the sales proceeds, right?'

Jolidon said, 'OK, I can get the certification today. Appletree's in Angola. He knows they're pre-revolution stones. Send me the text they want and I'll get it signed and scanned and to you this afternoon. I'm sorry you're getting beat up over there, but I know you can sort it out, hopefully without too much trouble.'

'Thanks, but I'm also still up to my neck in the laundering paperwork and there's nothing you can do to help with that. Now you better leave me to do what I'm best at, making you guys very rich.' He put the phone away and went back to his argument with Villeneuve.

Jolidon put his mobile on the table and walked to the window, lit up another cheroot and looked down at the busy street below, '*Merde*.' He remembered what Esther had said to him on one of her infrequent visits to Zurich, '*As long as he stays loyal and doesn't get too greedy, we've got the official stamp of approval.*'

What happens when he gets too greedy, he asked himself?

Marbella, Spain

'I brought you that catalogue you asked me for. I've never looked at, so keep it for me, please. I've got quite a collection of them now.' Leticia handed Jenny the Bingham's auction catalogue from the September sale in Geneva.

'Thanks, I'll look at it later. We've got to get to the market before it gets too crowded.' She called Ellen and Chester and they went out to the car to drive to La Cala Saturday market, a highlight of the weekend.

After supper that evening, Jenny leafed through the catalogue and found what she was looking for. Like the Drewberrys November catalogue, there were at least 100 items with the caption, *Private Investment Trust. More stolen goods*, she knew. *They're selling off all the valuables they've stolen from the security boxes, one sale after the other.* She felt a huge wave of anger sweep over her. *How can such a massive fraud be committed and be seen by no one but me? It's grotesque: murder, arson and robbery, with millions of dollars of reward to the perpetrators. It has to be exposed and the culprits punished, but I can't even prove that Charlie's box was in the vault when it was emptied.*

I have to share the whole story with someone, she decided. *And it can't be Leticia, not yet, not until I've worked out what we can do, if anything, otherwise it will only frighten her. I need a reasoned, independent opinion from a reliable and trustworthy person. Then maybe I can decide if going to Geneva is the right thing, or not.*

She picked up her phone and called Pedro Espinoza.

Westminster, London, England

Hugh Middleton opened up the FT financial markets quotes and scanned down to Olympic Funds Group. He was in the Tube on his way to a meeting at the Ministry of Defence. The Permanent Secretary had called him, ostensibly to ask about possible whistle-blower hacking in one of their dozens of departments. Middleton wasn't fooled, he was usually called in to glean free information from him about what other nations were doing about Internet security and why. He had bought a copy of the newspaper, to read on the train and check on Fern-Chapman's performance, as he had done a couple of times each week. So far, he'd been disappointed at their steady performance, but since the General Election date had been announced, he wondered if there had been any negative reaction.

He felt a sense of *schadenfreude*, guilty satisfaction, when he saw there had been a drop of between 2% and 3% across all five funds. There was also a report of substantial withdrawals, causing the sale of a number of illiquid shares at a loss. *Exactly what I expected, it had to occur, and it will happen again. If the election goes badly, or we get some other kind of bad news, it will get much, much worse.*

Middleton was leafing through the other pages when an article about Fern-Chapman's previous employer caught his attention. Entitled '*Flitter bankruptcy costs Selchurch Peak £1 billion*', the piece concerned the bankruptcy of Flitter, a start-up, hi-tech online real-estate management business into which the fund manager had invested substantial amounts in shareholdings, high-interest corporate 'junk' bonds and syndicated loans. After five years of R&D work and over £1 billion of losses, the company had failed to develop the technical platform they had promised. Finally, interest charges, overhead and rental commitments had drained their cash until they were forced into liquidation the previous month. It was expected that shareholders and unsecured creditors would receive nothing from the liquidation proceeds. The share price of several of Selchurch Peak's funds had fallen by up to 2% as a result of the losses.

He gave a grunt of satisfaction when he read that Flitter had been selected by Selchurch Peak's previous top investment manager, Harry-Fern-Chapman. He didn't remember Flitter being listed on any of the investments of the Olympic Funds he'd looked at, but his prognosis was being proved faster than he had imagined.

How can I take advantage of this situation? A germ of

an idea came to mind. *Maybe. Not yet, but maybe soon,* he told himself. He folded up the newspaper and placed it into his computer bag. *Time to start keeping a file on these people,* he told himself.

THIRTY-TWO

Mijas, Spain
November, 2019

'It's been months since I've seen you and I want to hear all about your family, especially little Pedro.' Jenny needed to share her suspicions with someone unemotional, shrewd and intuitive and ex-Chief Inspector Pedro Espinoza fitted the bill perfectly. She'd invited him for lunch to *Da Bruno*, an Italian restaurant in Mijas, midway between their homes, an easy drive for both of them. Ellen was in Leticia's care at her apartment in Puente Romano; she was unaware of her worries, one of which was to explain what had happened in Geneva when she'd lost confidence in Adam Peterson and taken the second key from his jacket. She'd been wrong not to tell her friend sooner, and Jenny hated being wrong.

She sipped her glass of *Muga* rosé and listened to Espinoza describing the delight he and Soledad felt in finally having a grandchild. He spoke in fluent, but pleasantly accented English, a very calming and thoughtful presence in her worried state. He talked a lot about his son-in-law, Javier, obviously proud that the young man was following his own career path in the Malaga Police Force.

The waiter brought their first course and Jenny said, 'I almost forgot. The last time you came to Marbella, you were about to go on your pilgrimage with Ricardo, the *Camino de Santiago*. It must have been a wonderful experience. I want to hear all about it.'

Espinoza's heart sank. He'd been dreading this moment since she'd called him. No one outside of his family knew what had happened in Los Angeles, neither he nor Soledad had spoken about it to anyone. Even Laura and Javier knew only that Ricardo had committed suicide, but not about the other killings. Nobody else in Spain knew Ricardo and he hadn't wanted to besmirch his name with the dreadful story. *Let sleeping dogs lie*, he'd decided, but now he had to face one of the few people he couldn't lie to, someone who knew him too well.

Jenny saw the change in his expression. 'What's wrong, Pedro? Didn't it go as you hoped? If you don't want to tell me, I understand, it's fine.'

He took his decision, he'd been bottling the dreadful events up inside himself for too long, he needed to tell the story and Jenny was the right person to tell. She had had her share of problems, but she'd always faced up to and overcome them, sometimes with his help. In many ways, he knew she was stronger than he. It would help to talk to her, it might bring him some kind of closure.

'It's not a happy story,' he began. 'I've told no one else and I must ask you to do the same.' She said nothing, just sat listening in silence, her meal forgotten as, in a quiet, unemotional voice, Espinoza recounted to her the fatal sequence of events which had caused his cousin to commit murder and suicide six months ago. He missed out nothing, the investment scams and the knock-on consequences which destroyed his business, the safety deposit companies in LA and San Diego, and the disappearance of Ricardo's last financial lifeline. Then, holding his emotions at bay, he told her of the meeting with Joe Cunningham and its deadly results. Finally, he described his futile trip to the US and his suspicions of the closure of the LA and San Diego companies.

She almost interrupted when she heard this, but kept silent, *Ricardo's tragedy couldn't have had anything to do with Ramseyer, Haldeman*, she told herself, *that would be too much of a coincidence.* Jenny didn't believe in coincidences.

Espinoza stopped speaking, silent for a long moment, looking vacantly across the room, then he said, 'Our walk to Santiago de Compostela was wonderful. Ricardo was relaxed, content and happy, he was selling his business, which he'd never really liked, for a very good price and he was planning to retire here in Malaga, to be close to us, his only remaining family. His life was full to the brim with wonderful plans.' He took a deep breath. 'Then, everything was lost, and so was he.'

Jenny waited until he had recovered his composure, distressed by the dreadful events, but touched that he had confided in her. There were questions burning on her tongue, remembering only too well her own experiences of the terrible consequences that money, or the desire for it, could provoke.

Espinoza finally looked at her and she took his hand. 'Thank you for sharing that with me, Pedro, it must have been more difficult than I can imagine. It's a dreadfully sad story, but I hope it helped you a little to share it with me. Poor Ricardo, it was as if his life had suddenly been wiped out and it was too much for him to cope with, easier to just give up. Until we're faced with such dire threats, we never know what we're capable of. We both understand how it feels.'

He nodded, knowing she was thinking back to the dramatic scenes in York House in 2008, when she had tried her very best to kill Ray d'Almeida, who finally died from a bullet from Espinoza's gun. 'The difference,' he sighed, 'is that two innocent people were killed, for no justification. As a policeman, it's hard for me to reconcile myself with murder, especially by my own cousin.'

He picked up his glass of rosé. 'Salud. I'm relieved to have told you, Jenny. I feel better and I am never going to mention it again, to anyone. *Gracias, querida*, you are a good friend.'

Jenny changed the subject to safer, family matters until they had their coffees, then she asked, 'Do you remember the name of the security companies in Los Angeles and San Diego?'

He frowned, 'The second one was called *West Coast Security Central*, I remember it because I got the name from Dustin Greenwood at the bank and I went down there and saw the empty boxes. But the office in LA was already closed and I didn't go there. It was six months ago and I'm afraid I can't bring the name to mind. It began with two initials, I remember. Something like *RL Security* or similar, why do you ask?'

'Could it have been *RH Security*?'

'I'm not sure. Is it important?'

'It could be very important and perhaps connected with a problem I have at the moment, the reason I wanted to talk with you.'

'I'll check as soon as I get home, it's in Ricardo's letter.'

'Thanks, Pedro. I might be wrong about this, but it's too important to ignore.'

'Do you want to tell me what it's all about?'

She called the waiter over. 'Let's get two more coffees. This will take some time.'

Marbella, Spain

Chester came bounding over to Jenny as she came through the front door at York House and she was tousling his head, when her mobile rang.

Espinoza said, 'You were right, Jenny, it was *RH Security International.*'

She caught her breath, a sick feeling in her stomach. '*RH Security International,*' she repeated. 'Ramseyer, Haldeman by another name'.

Leticia came from the living room to greet her and she said, 'Thanks Pedro, I'll call you tomorrow morning and we can talk about it.'

She put the mobile away and her friend asked, 'Did I hear you say, Ramseyer, Haldeman? What was that about?'

'Oh, nothing special, Pedro mentioned a security company and it just made me think of them.'

'Oh, I see. It's a long time since I've heard you say that name. I suppose Charlie's diamonds are still sitting in the security box. I wonder whatever happened to that second key, but I suppose we'll never find out. That reminds me, have you booked the flights for our Geneva trip?'

She ignored the first remark, it wasn't the moment to tell Leticia the truth, it might never be. 'We'll plan our schedule tomorrow, make sure Patrice agrees with everything when he gets back. Right, I got some giant prawns for supper. I suppose Ellen's having her afternoon nap, so you can help me to shell them. Come along, Chester, time for supper.'

THIRTY-THREE

Marbella, Spain
Saturday, November 23, 2019

Jenny hardly slept that night, her head full of questions that she couldn't answer. She was bathing Ellen at 8am when Espinoza called back. Lily took over and she went to her bedroom to talk to him.

He wasted no time. 'We have to tell Leticia and Patrice the whole story and we have to find who's behind this conspiracy. That man, Jolidon, can't be working alone. It's a well-organised fraud that's been carried out in at least two countries, there must be several perpetrators. If we can find whoever caused Ricardo to do what he did and who was responsible for the Geneva fire, it might just be possible to bring these murderers to justice and recover your diamonds.'

'Do you really think we can do anything? I've been to their Zurich hiding-hole and got nowhere. If it's such a well-organised group, they must have a lot of resources, what chance do we have of stopping them?'

'One thing at a time, Jenny. The first thing to do is, talk to your friends, explain to them what happened in 2008 and why. Then we can start working out our next moves. It's been 12 years, my dear, you need to get it off your chest.'

She made her decision. 'Right. There's no time like the

present. It's Saturday, Patrice is getting back from Dubai today and he's coming here to pick up Leticia and the children at around 4pm. Will you come over and help me out? He knows nothing at all about the diamonds or Ramseyer, Haldeman and I really don't feel up to being cross-examined alone.'

'Of course, don't worry, I'll be happy to come.' A pause. 'Do you mind if I ask Javier to come with me? He's very smart and he's also authorised to carry a gun.' She heard him laugh quietly. 'And Jenny, can we please not speak about the murders in LA? I don't think it will help us to share that with anyone, it might complicate our task and it would destroy our memories of a fine man.'

Belgravia, London, England

'Fern-Chapman's Olympic Funds Group sheds £200 Million amid severe market correction.'

The quarter page article was on page 5 of the Saturday *Financial Times*. Harry was in Edinburgh for the day and Esther had finished her shopping and was having a sandwich in a coffee bar in Kensington. She read carefully through the item, her heart in her mouth, seeing there had been more substantial withdrawals from some of his funds and they'd been forced to sell holdings again, driving down the share valuations. There was a reference to *Neil Woodford*, another investment manager, whose name was unknown to her, referring to the suspension of funds under his management the previous June. She checked the funds she'd invested in, *Olympic Equity Income, Triple Lock and Special Opportunities*. All three had fallen by between 3% and 5% since the last time she'd looked. The other two Olympic funds were down even more.

Esther looked up Neil Woodford online and found dozens of articles about him and his investment group. His story was similar to Harry's, a successful manager with a well-known management company who'd set up his own organisation, amassing £15 billion of punters' money in a number of funds. After a few years of underperformance, his £4 billion flagship Equity Income Fund had been suspended the previous June, following massive withdrawals. Woodford was fired as investment manager in October and the fund was handed over to new managers for liquidation. The investment portfolio included a high percentage of unquoted and secondary market shareholdings and it was expected that the remaining investors would make further substantial losses.

That's exactly the kind of investments Harry was boasting about. Comparing the story with Olympic's recent history, Esther felt suddenly sick. *I'm losing money now, even after the gains in the third quarter. If this continues like it did for Woodford, I could lose millions. That's not what I signed up for. I have to talk to Harry about selling, before it gets worse.* Fern-Chapman's mobile didn't answer and she walked back to the apartment in Eaton Square, worrying about her money.

City of London, England

Dr Hugh Middleton was reading the same article Esther had seen. He was in his office at the Institute, catching up on their too busy schedule. Since Ilona's death, he missed not only her physical presence with him every day, but also her super-efficient management, which meant he never had to check anything. Now, he seemed to spend every weekend reading the weekly progress reports and worrying that they'd meet their deadlines.

He'd paused for a while to make himself a coffee and read his favourite newspaper, the Olympic item immediately catching his attention. He smiled when he saw the comparison with Neil Woodford then, turning to the market pages, he checked each of the Olympic funds, once again feeling guiltily satisfied. *That's a fall of almost 10% in the last two weeks. If the election looks like going badly, we could be facing a collapse of confidence.* He thought again of the vague idea he'd had two weeks before and decided it was time to put some meat on its bones.

Middleton was a very organised man, he took out the dossier containing the several articles he'd cut from the newspaper over the last few weeks and re-read them, writing his notes by hand. If anything went wrong, it was easier to destroy sheets of paper than to worry about his laptop being interrogated. Then he started jotting down various ideas, considering the potential effects and risks. *This has to be very well thought out, I can't afford to be seen to be behind it.*

Edinburgh, Scotland

Harry Fern-Chapman saw his mobile light up with Esther's name, but he couldn't take the call, he was locked in a discussion with Alex Cameron, the CEO of Cameron Overview. Authorised by the UK Financial Conduct Authority, Cameron's company was effectively the Managing Director of the Olympic Funds Group. Fern-Chapman was the originator and Investment Manager of the group, a very highly paid position, but with no direct responsibility for the well-being of the funds he advised.

He apologised and put the phone away and Cameron

continued reading the extract from the prospectus for *Olympic Equity Income.* 'If fund assets are depleted by unusually large liquidations or the share price falls by 10% or more in any month, we must consider suspension of share trading to protect investors from panic selling. The clause applies to all five funds.'

'You can't seriously be considering suspending those funds based on a couple of week's poor performance?' Fern-Chapman banged on the table. 'I'm not responsible for Boris Johnson calling an election, or Brexit still being in limbo, or the Labour Party promising a Marxist paradise with a magic money forest. This will cause panic selling, not prevent it. It will destroy the whole group.'

'Harry, I don't disagree with your political argument, but that's not the reason for what's happening. We both know what the real problem is and it's very simple; it's all the bets you've taken on untested, start-up companies that are still making losses. We've had a few years of bull markets and a few high-flying tech start-ups, like Uber and Lyft, going berserk. Obviously, when the markets are strong and bullish, everything's fine and dandy and your picks follow the trend, but when there's worry and uncertainty, as there is at the moment, with an election coming up, it becomes a really big problem.'

Before Fern-Chapman could respond, he went on, 'And the publicity around Selchurch Peak's losses from the Flitter bankruptcy last month didn't help. Word's been going around that you picked that company as a potential 'Unicorn' while you were there. It's absorbed a billion of punters' money and now it's bust. That hasn't helped to maintain confidence in your stock-picking expertise.'

'I resent that implication. Flitter was a guaranteed

multi-billion-dollar company when I picked it and it was steaming ahead while I was with Selchurch. But since I left, I've never put a penny of Olympic money into it, because once I was out of the picture, there was no one to help them make it happen. I took a good decision. My policy is, don't invest into businesses that you can't influence. What happened afterwards had nothing to do with me and it has nothing to do with Olympic.'

'I'm not going to argue with you, Harry. The fact is, almost all your funds, especially Equity Income and Special Situation, are full of unquoted and Over-the-Counter illiquid shares in small companies like Flitter, which are hard to sell without causing a fall in value. The large amounts of withdrawals over the last few weeks have drained us of cash and we've had to sell shitloads of those unquoted shares to avoid a default. It's a double whammy. First of all, we have to find a buyer for shares that can't be sold on the market, and that's not easy at the moment. Then when the traders see us selling, they immediately mark down the prices and we end up making a loss, driving the price further down into the bargain. That causes other investors to sell their shares and so it goes on. It's a self-fulfilling spiral and we can't let it continue without taking action to mitigate investors' losses. At the moment, we're down 8% on the month with substantial depletion, you can't argue with those facts.'

'So you want to suspend the funds, just like that? Without giving me a chance to sort things out?'

'My duty is to take action by the end of the month in which losses of 10% occur. After the Woodford scandal, I'm not going to risk being accused of any delay, or of trading investors' money away. But I won't do anything until we see what the total fall is at the end of this month, that gives you a week to see what miracles you can perform. Then I'll take my decision. That's the best I can do.'

Marbella, Spain
'My God! That's the most incredible story I've ever heard. How come you've never told me before?' Patrice Moncrieff looked from Jenny to his wife.

Jenny held up her hand, 'Wait, Patrice. There's another thing that not even Leticia knows about. I have a confession to make, something else happened that weekend that I've never told her.' The two women had managed to relate the story of Charlie Bishop's Angolan Clan over the course of the last hour, repeating, interrupting and correcting each other, finally finishing with the death of Ray d'Almeida, the disappearance of Esther Rousseau and the missing key to box 72.

'What have you never told me, Jenny?' In the heat of the moment, Leticia's usually perfect English deserted her.

Jenny opened her purse and took out the two keys to Charlie's security box, each with an elastic band through the hole, one yellow and the other green. She placed them on the table. 'That's what I never told you.'

Leticia stared in amazement at the keys. 'You have both keys? I gave you the green one, but Adam lost the yellow one. Where did it come from? How did you get it? I don't understand.'

'I took it from his pocket, the coat that was in his bathroom in the hotel, you remember? I took it and kept it, because I didn't trust him. And afterwards, when we found the contract in Charlie's laptop, I saw I was right. The price for the remaining diamonds was $12 million, not $10 million. He was trying to steal $2 million from us, because we didn't know the real value of the stones.'

'Of course I remember, but I didn't know about the key. All these years and you never told me you had them both; I can't believe it.' She looked suspiciously at her, her voice rising in anger. 'What's happened to the diamonds, are they still in the security box? Is that where the diamonds in the auction came from?'

'Don't be silly, Leticia, you just told us that Jenny saved your life, and Emilio's as well. Do you honestly think she's going to steal whatever's in that box? I think you should apologise.'

'It's OK, Patrice, she's right, she has good reason to be upset. I should have told you years ago, Leticia, but I didn't because you were worried about the risk to you and Emilio. You gave me your key to keep and you didn't want to hear anything more about it. So I've kept the two keys with me all these years and I just left the diamonds in their box. They were to be part of Emilio's inheritance when he's twenty-one, that's what Charlie wanted. It never seemed to be the right moment to tell you, and I suppose I just kept putting it off. But now,' she looked anxiously at Espinoza for help, 'something's happened and we have to talk about it.'

'Leticia, Patrice, what Jenny has told you is exactly correct, and she's done nothing wrong.' The ex-Chief Inspector took up the story. 'I know this because, strangely, more than 10 years since our paths crossed for the first time, there has now been a second occasion. Let me tell you about my cousin, Ricardo.'

THIRTY-FOUR

'We believe the security box scam at RH Security Services in Los Angeles and the fire at Ramseyer, Haldeman were organised by the same people. It's too much of a coincidence to be otherwise.' Espinoza summed up their lengthy explanations in his usual objective manner.

Leticia reached out and took Espinoza's hand. 'I'm so sorry, Pedro. It was awful what happened to your cousin. And for you, to have to go over there for such a dreadful reason. I'm sure you're right, these people caused Ricardo to kill himself, just as if they took a gun and shot him themselves. And now whoever they are, they've burned down that beautiful Ramseyer, Haldeman building, killed Gilles Simenon and stolen all the valuables, along with Charlie's diamonds. They've already caused so much pain and death, and now they'll turn up again in the Drewberrys sale next week. After all these years, I can't believe it's still going on, murder and robbery, just for a case of diamonds from my country.'

She went to Jenny and put her arms around her. 'I said a very stupid thing to you, I'm sorry. I had such a shock when I saw those keys. Like a bad dream coming back to haunt me. I hate thinking about what happened, and you've kept it away from me all these years. Thanks for that, and for telling me everything, it was a very brave thing to do. I don't blame you for leaving the diamonds in the security box. It should have been the safest place for them.'

'But it wasn't.' Javier spoke for the first time. 'The fact is there's some kind of murderous gang out there who caused the deaths of Uncle Ricky and Gilles and now they're cashing in millions of dollars of your inheritance. That's arson, murder and grand larceny. What are we going to do about it? That's why we're here, to work out a plan of action.'

Belgravia, London, England

'I've decided to take a week off. I'm going 'stir crazy' being in this crappy apartment for the last six months and there's nothing I can do here while the sales are on. René's on top of that, so I'm redundant. You OK with that?'

Esther heard Jolidon light up a cheroot and take a deep drag. 'You deserve it. Where are you going?'

'The weather's beautiful in the *Tessin* and I need some sunshine, so I've booked at the Tivoli in Lugano. You might not believe it, but I actually like walking by the lake, very peaceful and invigorating.'

She laughed. 'I'm jealous already, it's pouring here and the forecast for Geneva is freezing cold and damp.'

'When are you going?' Jolidon asked. 'I suppose you're staying at the Richemond, as usual?'

'Yes, I should get there about midday on Tuesday.' She double checked her flight confirmation. 'The sales run from Friday to Sunday. I won't be going there, of course, but I'll go to the viewing, just for the experience. And at least I'll be able to see Christen from time to time, keep him on the straight and narrow.'

'Well, there's nothing more I can do, but if you need to talk to me, call my mobile.'

Her antennae immediately went up. 'Is there something I might want to talk to you about?'

'Nothing special, but René's been a bit difficult this last couple of weeks.'

'You mean the business with the lawyers at Drewberrys?'

'He handled that well, he's doing a great job, but he seems to be in a touchy mood, I think he's feeling neglected. It would be a good idea to maybe invite him for lunch or dinner while you're there. Show him your appreciation, you know?'

'I'll do what I can. And Claude, just a thought. You don't think there's any chance of Jenny Bishop coming back to the office while you're away?'

'I don't see why she would, but it's irrelevant. She ran away with her tail between her legs because she knows she can't prove a thing. Even if she does, I'll see her on the CCTV feed, probably crying into her milk.'

'We should think about moving offices again. Not right away, you're too busy, but it would help to confuse her and anyone else who might be looking for RH.' Esther didn't emphasise her dislike of the Zurich apartment, hoping Jolidon might agree to a change.

'Not a bad idea, mix things up again. I'll think about it when I get my head above water. I've got the February sales to prepare for, that's top priority, but I promise to look at it asap.'

'Right, understood. I have to go, Claude, I'll call you from Geneva.' Esther had just seen the taxi pull up outside the apartment building. She'd been looking out the window since Harry had called from City Airport, wondering how best to address her worries about Olympic. Any potential problems with Christen and that bitch Jenny Bishop could wait. *One thing at a time.*

She poured two glasses of champagne and went to open the door. 'Welcome home, darling. I hope you had a good day in Scotland.' She hung up his raincoat and they went into the sitting room. 'Cheers. How's everything?'

'Cheers,' he clinked her glass. 'Everything's fine, just a bit tiring, up there this morning and down this afternoon. But no problems, everything's going well.' He sounded tired and worried and didn't look her in the eyes.

'That's good,' she said, not believing it. 'So, the FT today got it wrong today?'

'You saw that disgusting article? It's complete rubbish. There were a few more withdrawals and we fell by a few points, but it's nothing like as bad as they're saying.'

'Why would they write something that's not true?'

'Did you see the name of their correspondent, the journalist who wrote it?' She shook her head. 'Terry Owen's his name. He used to work for me at Selchurch Peak. A useless git; didn't understand basic market psychology or value investing. He wanted to join me at Olympic Group and I told him to fuck off. Selchurch fired him after I left, and he couldn't find another job in the industry. He calls himself an independent financial analyst now and he hates my guts. He'll do anything he can to bring me down, but he's pissing in the wind.'

He took a gulp of his champagne. 'What's happened is a purely temporary setback, a combination of political weakness and general apprehension. Investors are over-sensitive to even small events, so they're terrified by an election, but in the end it's value and performance that count. I've told you not to worry, Esther, I've handled bigger problems than this before and I'll do the same again, you'll see.'

She had never seen him so agitated, using language she'd never heard him use. 'Who's this Neil Woodford they mention in the article? They say his funds were similar to yours and they were suspended.'

'More bullshit. There's no similarity at all. I've personally handpicked all the companies in my portfolios and there's not one of them I'd willingly sell. They've all got fabulous prospects and once this election's over and we get a Conservative government, you'll see how quickly the share prices will bounce back.'

Esther couldn't help being impressed by Harry's infectious positivity and determination. She wavered, 'You don't think the fall will continue, it's not permanent?'

'Definitely not. It's nothing that can't be fixed within the month.'

'How do you intend to do that?'

'I've already started, that's why I was in Scotland on a Saturday. My whole team is working on it right now, right through the weekend, and we've got a lot of positive actions we can take. These things happen, Esther, market confidence is fickle, but if there's no underlying asset value problem then it will quickly turn around. You're off to Geneva on Tuesday for a few days, right?' She nodded. 'I promise you, by the time you get back, I'll be turning the situation around.'

She asked him one last time. 'Harry, if you think I should liquidate my holdings now, even at a loss, you should tell me. I won't complain, but I need to know the truth.'

'I never advise liquidating when share prices fall. On the contrary, that's the time to invest, not that I'm asking you to, it's up you to decide. But you should definitely wait until this volatility passes, then you can take your decision calmly and I'll do whatever you ask.'

She made her mind up. '*Bien*. We'll wait until I get back from Geneva. But if things haven't improved, I'll be selling, so be prepared.'

Harry Fern-Chapman nodded and took another swig of champagne. 'Whatever you say, darling, but I won't fail to perform.' He went into the bathroom to hide the emotion and worry written on his face. *How the hell am I going to sort this out? I could lose everything, Esther, my friends, my fortune, my reputation. Everything's on the line this time.* He splashed some water on his face and came out with a smile, 'Now, what are we doing about our Saturday night dinner?'

THIRTY-FIVE

Marbella, Spain
Saturday, November 23, 2019

'What did you see at the apartment in Zurich?' Javier was going through the notes he'd made that afternoon.

'Nothing at all. It's very well hidden away; an anonymous apartment in a rundown building, the whole of the sixth floor with a CCTV camera above the door. I saw the man who went up there, but I don't know him. Then I could hear voices inside, but not what language they were speaking, and I got no reply when I knocked and shouted.'

'Would you know that man again?'

'Yes. I saw him come out and followed him when he took the bus to the station, I didn't manage to get a photo, there were lorries and buses in the way, but I'd remember him. I think he'd been drinking, I smelt it in the lift when he asked me which floor I wanted.' Jenny explained that she suspected him to be René Christen, the *huissier*, notary, but she could find no trace of him online.

'I can get that checked out, maybe find a photograph somewhere so you can confirm it was him. What did he look like?'

Jenny searched her memory and gave him a vague description, which he scribbled down.

'What about this Frenchman, Jolidon? What do you know about him?'

'I haven't seen him since 2008, the first time we went to Ramseyer, Haldeman, but I'd know him anywhere. He's a creepy looking guy and I never trusted him. I'm certain he's involved, stealing the remaining valuables to sell at auction sales. It's a brilliant plan, selling untraceable goods for cash.'

'You think he was responsible for the explosion and fire?'

'It's more than likely; sending Gilles to do the audit knowing he didn't have time during the day.'

Patrice said, 'It was clever of him to convince Edificio 2000 to sell him the company and then take over the restitution of the unclaimed valuables. Maybe he's the mastermind behind the whole plot.'

'I can think of only one other person who could possibly profit from this plan.' Jenny gave them a shortened history of Patrick Haldeman, the founder's son, and his fall from grace.

'And you don't know what happened to him?'

'No, all I know is he was a playboy and a terrible businessman, and he brought his father's company to ruin.'

Javier shook his head, 'It doesn't sound like he'd be able to dream up a plan like this. I agree with Patrice, my bet is on Jolidon, he must be running things from Zurich.'

'Perhaps.' Jenny's dream, and her sixth sense, were telling her it wasn't so, but she said nothing more.

'Do you think he's that clever?' Leticia shook her head. 'I don't think so. He seemed like a small-time crook, trying to get duplicate keys to our box.'

'He tried to get duplicate keys?'

'I'm sure he knew there was something valuable in

there and he wanted us to leave the keys so he could have duplicates made. He said it was in case we lost one.'

Espinoza interjected, 'Don't forget, Leticia, most big-time crooks start out as small-time crooks.'

'What does he look like?' Javier asked, and both women dredged up their memories of the foppish man with long, greasy hair, wearing a too-tight suit, trying to look 10 years younger than his 40 years.

'Right, and he's about 50 now? What about the stolen goods? Do you think they're in that apartment?'

'It would make sense, with the CCTV and the anonymity of the place. The valuable items they've stolen won't take up much space, they'd probably fit into a large safe.'

'Maybe that's why the man you saw was visiting. To bring or take merchandise for the sales. Maybe he is the notary.'

'That's exactly what occurred to me.'

'You mean there might be valuables worth tens of millions of dollars sitting in that crappy apartment in Zurich? There's no chance of them ever letting anyone in.' Patrice grimaced, 'This is a very dangerous situation, if they've already committed murder to steal those goods, they won't hesitate to do it again.'

'First we have to see if Jolidon's in that apartment and there's only one way to find out. How easy would it be to survey the building, watch who comes and goes? If we got a photograph of one of these men coming out, we'd be halfway there.'

'I didn't get one, but it should be easy for a professional. There's a petrol station with a little café on the other side of the street. It's directly across from the building and you can see into the entrance.'

'I'll get onto that right away. What about these sales in Geneva, when are they?'

'There's only one auction house having sales, Drewberrys. The exhibition starts today at the Mandarin Oriental, and the auctions are next weekend over three days, Friday to Sunday.'

'How do we know when the diamonds are to be auctioned?'

'We don't know exactly, just which session they'll be sold at. There are over 1,000 items in next week's sales, starting with the least expensive objects, going up to the mega-millions. They're having morning, afternoon and evening sales, to get through all the lots. Look.' Leticia showed them the catalogue, opened at lot number 900.

'Wow! What fabulous stones, all the way from Angola, when it belonged to Portugal, before the 1974 revolution. Incredible! It says the seller is a 'Private Investment Trust'.' Patrice laughed, 'That can hide a multitude of sins.'

'Patrice, the point is these crooks have found the perfect way to sell their spoils. Auction sales are ideal for ....'

'Recycling and laundering, like a Chinese laundry,' Leticia finished for her. 'That's what you meant when you first looked at the catalogue.'

'I remember.' Jenny flicked through the catalogue, pointing out the many items with the caption, '*Private Investment Trust*'. 'There are over 100 lots and I'm sure they all come from the security boxes. Leticia found the September catalogue from Binghams and there were another 100 items. Charlie's diamonds sold for 1.75 million Swiss Francs, so the total value of those valuables must be several millions. All stolen goods, but how do we prove it?'

Patrice shook his head. 'I don't know the answer, Jenny, but it looks like you could be right.'

'Can't your people find out who's behind that trust?' Leticia asked him.

'I doubt it, we don't have that kind of expertise. We sometimes help to set them up, but it's almost impossible to go back through an existing structure if it's been well-organised. These people are obviously very professional. We don't know the name, where it's registered or by whom. It's sure to be an offshore tax haven, and it's probably hidden by fake companies all over the world. There's big money involved here, so they'd do their homework.' Patrice shrugged, not realising he'd perfectly described Esther Rousseau's structure.

Espinoza was speaking quietly in Spanish to Javier. He asked, 'Which sessions are they being sold in?'

'Here.' Leticia took a list from the catalogue, 'The smaller items are being sold between Friday and Saturday, and the diamonds are the last lot at the Saturday evening session. That's a week from today, the 16th.'

'Another question please, I've never been to one of these auctions. Can anyone attend?'

Patrice explained, 'During the exhibition anyone can visit to look at the valuables, but to be present at the auction and make bids, you need to be accredited.'

'Sorry, what does that mean?'

'If you're not already a client, you need confirmation of your financial status. In other words, that you have the capacity to bid and pay for what you purchase.' Patrice shrugged, 'It's all about money, not acquiring works of art.'

Espinoza thought for a moment, 'Presumably, your bank could provide that confirmation?'

'Of course, we do it all the time. Any bank can do it.'

Javier and Espinoza exchanged glances. 'Let's talk about that, we may have an idea.'

A half hour later, Jenny and Leticia were talking together when Espinoza came to say goodbye. 'You don't have to decide this evening,' he said. 'It's a big decision. Sleep on it and we can discuss it in the morning.'

'No need, Pedro. We've already agreed. It's all or nothing.'

Delmas, Mpumalanga, South Africa

It was 10pm on a warm, balmy evening, with a three-quarter moon in a clear, star-filled sky that extended forever. Marius Coetzee was walking his dogs across the fields that surrounded the farmhouse he shared with his wife, Karen, in Delmas, near Johannesburg. Since 2018, when their adoptive daughter, Abby, had been married and moved to London, there were just the two of them at home, and that suited him perfectly. He'd almost managed to forget the lost two-year period after Karen had walked out with Abby in 2008, when he'd poisoned himself on alcohol and tobacco; preferring to remember their reconciliation at the time of Leo Stewart's abduction in 2010. Somehow, he'd been able to save Leo and his own marriage, and he never stopped giving thanks for the miracle of finding his family again.

The greater miracle was, of course, surviving the gunshot wounds he'd suffered after the foiled abduction. It happened on a beautiful night like this, walking his dogs, thinking about Emma Stewart's book, *An Extravagant Death*, when he was ambushed by Zimbabwe hitmen, then shipped off to hospital for a month. Since then, he'd recovered, built a new cyber-security business, Abby and Leo had been married and he and Karen were happier than they'd ever been. Now he was enjoying his few minutes of solitude, walking with his hounds, still missing the cheroots he'd given up all those years ago.

Coetzee was whistling for the dogs to return to the farmhouse when his mobile rang. It showed a Spanish number and he answered, 'Jenny Bishop! Great to hear from you. How are you, how's everything in Marbella?'

'Sorry to disappoint you, Marius, but it's not Jenny calling.'

'I don't believe it, Pedro Espinoza? How the hell are you?' Then, his suspicious mind taking over, 'What's the problem? Is everybody OK?'

'Don't worry, everything's fine here in Spain and I hope it's the same with Karen and you.'

Coetzee laughed in disbelief. 'OK, Pedro, let's have it. Why are you calling me at ten o'clock on a Saturday night? What's the problem?'

'You're right, I confess. There are a couple of things I thought you could help me with. Do you have a few minutes to talk?'

THIRTY-SIX

Marbella, Spain

Sunday, November 24, 2019

'We've been married for 10 years and you've never breathed a word to me about the security box and the diamonds.' Patrice took his wife's hand. 'I wish you had, it might have helped, to share the secret, I mean.'

'It wasn't a secret; it was just something Jenny and I agreed never to talk about. She was right, I never wanted to hear about that key, or the diamonds, or the security box. I was frightened something like this would happen and now it has. That man, d'Almeida, was crazy. He killed Charlie and Ron and so many other good, innocent people, trying to steal the diamonds and I'm sure he would have killed us too. Even after he stole $12 million from us, he didn't want us alive, he was a madman.'

He put his arms around her, as she broke down in tears at the memory of the fatal night in Marbella. 'He shot Adam and he was trying to kill Emilio, it was horrible, he knew he would be caught and he just wanted to kill everyone he could. Finally, Pedro had to shoot him. I know he hated himself for that, but it was the only way.'

'But once you knew he'd been killed, why were you still so worried about keeping the key?'

'Because d'Almeida was dead, but his accomplice was still alive, Esther Rousseau, the woman who worked at

Klein, Fellay. She was a wicked person, as bad as him; I never told you much about it, but she was involved in Leo's kidnapping in South Africa, trying to get Jenny to pay a ransom. She disappeared, but I was terrified she would find us and come for the diamonds. That's what caused all those deaths, all those horrible memories; Charlie's diamonds. I had nightmares for months afterwards, I didn't want anything to do with them, we'd inherited enough money from him, we didn't need more. I was still frightened inside for a long time, until we were married, then it was better. Now, I'm scared that it might start all over again and somehow hurt us or our family. I didn't sleep again last night, worrying what might happen.'

He held her close, 'Shhh, it's OK now, Leticia, Esther Rousseau's in the distant past. Don't worry about Jolidon, or his cronies. We've got Pedro and Javier on our side, and I'll be with you all the time. I'm a banker, not a fighter, but I swear I won't let anything happen to you or the boys.'

'Wait, Patrice. You still don't know everything. It's like Jenny's story, there are many chapters, other things I haven't told you. I didn't want to complicate our lives more than they already were. But now it's time to tell you the whole story. It didn't end when d'Almeida died.'

He sat silently, wondering what else she'd held back from him during their almost 10 years of marriage.

'I told you about the night in Marbella when he stole that money from us by Internet. But what I didn't tell you,' she paused, fearful of his reaction, 'is that two years later, Jenny persuaded Klein, Fellay to reimburse us the full amount.'

'The bank accepted total responsibility for d'Almeida's Internet transfer?'

'Twelve million dollars, they reimbursed us. I don't know how she did it, but we got every penny back.'

He thought for a moment, then, 'You didn't have to tell me that, Leticia. It makes no difference to me, or to us. We don't need that money and I'd just as soon forget about it.'

'Patrice, we can't forget about it and it does make a difference, because of Emilio. It's the same as the diamonds, he inherits half of that money when he reaches twenty-one. Jenny placed it in an investment account with our joint signatures, and we've never touched any of it. Here, this is the last statement.'

He looked at the total on the document. 'My God, our son is wealthier than us! I was wrong, this does make a difference.' Patrice crossed his fingers, he knew where there were huge amounts of money involved, there was huge danger, especially for Leticia and Jenny.

Malaga, Spain

'Did you have a private investigator in Geneva for the Angolan Clan business?' Soledad and Laura were out enjoying the sunshine with the baby and their husbands were discussing the first steps in the plan they'd agreed with the others.

'No, it was a cop I knew at the time, Inspector Andreas Blaser, a very helpful guy, but I don't know if he's still on the force. He was around 50, so he might have retired. You're thinking about the surveillance of the office in Zurich?'

'Yes, I don't have any contacts in Switzerland and I don't think you want me to start an investigation here in Spain.'

'You mean because of Ricardo? You're right, no need to rake up family dirt in our own backyard. But I think we should stay away from the police altogether.'

'Any special reason?'

'We may have to operate outside the law in this business. Are you OK with that?'

'I'm fine with it. I don't see how we'll be breaking the law by trying to stop a gang of murderers and thieves.'

'Good, and you're right about the surveillance, we need a good private investigation firm in Switzerland.'

'It'll be expensive.'

'Jenny's ready to spend whatever's necessary to sort this out. She thinks it's her fault the diamonds have been taken. She's wrong, but we need an investigator, so let's hire one. Here, try this man, he's highly recommended.' He handed Javier a scanned business card.

'*Privatdetektei Huntzer AG*, Franz Stenmark, Senior Investigator'. He's in Zurich, perfect. How did you get his name?'

'I still have a few contacts here and there, you'd be surprised. Give Stenmark a call in the morning, tell him they were recommended by Marius Coetzee.'

'Who's he?'

'Coetzee's the nearest thing we've got to another armed officer, like you, but he's in Africa, Johannesburg. You might be lucky enough to meet him, depending on what happens.'

Marbella, Spain

'Are you sure you can take a few days off next week? I don't want to cause you problems at the bank.'

'Don't worry, Jenny, you're forgetting, I'm the boss now. I asked myself for a week's leave and I agreed. Besides, Drewberrys is a BIP customer and I've never been to any of their sales.' Patrice laughed, 'I could charge the trip on expenses as 'Client Relations Travel'.' His manner became more serious, 'Also, I've been thinking about the risks involved. I'm not a tough guy by any means, but I'd like to provide some moral support if I can.' He said nothing about Leticia's revelation. *The less said the better.*

'Thanks, Patrice, I appreciate it, but I don't foresee any problems, not at this stage. Maybe later, if we win this first round, but one step at a time.'

'I hope you're right, but I'm still coming. When do you want to go?'

'I'd like to visit the exhibition first, see if they really are Charlie's diamonds, though there's no doubt in my mind. If we go Wednesday, we can visit on Thursday, before the sales start, and check everything out.'

'Fine with me. I'll get my secretary to book the flights and find us hotel rooms.'

'No, Patrice, I'll do it. It's my fault we're in this mess and I want to get us out of it. That includes any costs we have to incur, they're for my account.'

He knew better than to argue when she spoke in her schoolteacher's voice. 'Whatever you say, Ms. Bishop. Who's coming?'

'Just as we agreed; you, me, Leticia and Pedro. Javier can't just take time off and leave Laura with the baby, so he can stay and coordinate with the detective agency they've found in Zurich.'

'They've found an agency? That was quick work.'

'Pedro called Marius Coetzee.'

'Coetzee? I see, so you do think there might be trouble, that was a smart move. And he knows an investigator in Zurich?'

'Marius knows everyone and everything, including how

to kill people with his bare hands. I hope we won't need him, but he's on standby if things get out of hand.'

Delmas, Mpumalanga, South Africa

'You won't believe who called me last night while I was out walking the dogs.'

Karen Coetzee looked up from her newspaper. 'I'm not even going to try to guess. Who was it?'

'Spoilsport.' He kissed her forehead. 'Pedro Espinoza, you remember, the Spanish detective who solved Leo's abduction mystery?'

'Oh dear!' She put the paper aside. 'So this must have to do with Jenny Bishop and that means there are problems around. What is it this time?'

'Nothing to worry about.' He recounted part of his conversation with Espinoza. 'All he wanted was an introduction to a good agency in Switzerland. It's nothing to do with us, no need to worry. I scanned him the card from Franz Stenmark, at *Huntzer*, the guy who helped us with that banking cyber-attack in Zurich.'

Karen was a clever, intuitive woman with a successful career in journalism, reporting on social and educational inequalities in South Africa, prior to her break-up with Marius, when she gave up full-time work to move to the Delmas farmhouse with Abby. 'I see,' she said thoughtfully, 'and what else did you talk about?'

'OK, sorry, mind-reader. It seems Jenny might be the victim of some kind of fraud. They're going to Geneva this week to check some things out and they'll let me know what happens.'

'You mean they'll call for help if they need it?'

'I suppose so, but that's what I do best, right?'

THIRTY-SEVEN

Malaga, Spain
Monday, November 25, 2019

Franz Stenmark spoke perfect English with a slight American accent, using a lot of trendy expressions, making Javier feel a little self-conscious at his own inability to pronounce some words with the right accent. He said, 'I hear you know Marius Coetzee, in Johannesburg?'

'My father-in law knows him from a few years ago, but I've never met him. Have you?'

'Sure, once, a couple months ago. That was enough.'

'You didn't like him?'

'On the contrary, I liked him a lot. I guess it's just that ... Well, to tell the truth, he made me feel really ineffective.'

Javier laughed, 'What did he do?'

'He doesn't need to do anything. He just looks at you and you know he's thinking like a week ahead of you, waiting for you to catch up, and he's already up for anything that might happen.'

'OK, I'm impressed, but there's nothing he can do for us in Johannesburg. We need an experienced man in Zurich right away, are you available?'

'What kind of job?'

'Surveillance and identification. It's a simple job, but there's a lot at stake.' He gave Stenmark an edited version of the history and the probable occupants of the sixth floor, omitting the suspected murder and the value of the lost diamonds.

'Just watch the building for a few days and photograph everyone who goes in and out? Hell, you don't need me for that, we've got junior people at half my rate. My hourly fee is ...' He gave an amount in Swiss Francs.

Javier's eyes watered when he mentally converted it to Euros, it was more than twice his salary rate. 'We want the best we can get. Coetzee says that's you, so if you're free, I'd like you to do it personally.'

'You're the boss. I'll take a quick look at my schedule. OK, if you really want me, I can delegate some other jobs and be free by tomorrow. Let's check out the actions you want me to take, so we don't have any misunderstandings. It's purely surveillance, right? Photos, descriptions, but no interaction with possible suspects?'

'That's it, but you can ring the bell occasionally, see if someone comes to the door.'

'Mistaken address, right, OK, I'll do that.'

London, England

'Reggie, great to hear from you, how are you and Nicola?' Harry Fern-Chapman was in his London office when his secretary, Mandy, passed the call through. He was immediately on his guard, and considered telling her he was too busy, but decided it would cause more harm than good. He took the call, worried that Lord Scarbrough had heard the stories that were beginning to circulate about him and Olympic Funds Group.

After the usual pleasantries, Scarbrough asked, 'How are things at Olympic? We just got back from a cruise in South America and I haven't had time to catch up, thought I'd get it straight from the horse's mouth, as it were.'

Fern-Chapman listened carefully but couldn't spot any signs of doubt in his voice. He decided to plant a few seeds himself, 'Apart from some temporary volatility, not much to say. The markets have been a bit jittery with the election looming, but I'm sure you know that. A few nervous sellers around, but Olympic's in good shape, terrific value, compared to a lot of our competitors. Last week, I met with the Cameron Overview people, our FCA Corporate MD you know, in Edinburgh. They're happy with everything, so that's good news.'

'That's on the up and up, is it Harry? You'd tell me if there was anything amiss, wouldn't you? I've brought a lot of business to Olympic, wouldn't like to lose face with my friends.'

'You know I'm always dead straight with you, Reggie, how could I be otherwise after everything you've done to help me? What made you think there might be something wrong?' He waited nervously, wondering what Scarbrough had heard. He knew by heart the number of investors introduced by him and the amounts involved, close to £100 million. Olympic couldn't survive withdrawals of that magnitude from one group of shareholders. It would sound the death knoll.

'Oh, nothing special. There was some talk on the ship about Selchurch Peak and the Flitter bankruptcy. That almost cost me a bit, but happily I got out of it when I started with you and Olympic, lucky escape. I was just worried in case we had any positions that might suffer.'

'Absolutely no exposure of any kind.' He repeated what he'd told Alex Cameron. 'Don't worry, I don't back start-ups where I can't influence their growth, it's a mug's game.'

They talked for a few more minutes and Lord Scarbrough said, 'We must get together again soon, at our place this time. I'll get Nicola to call Esther and arrange a convenient date.'

He rang off and sat silently looking at the email he'd found on his laptop that morning on his arrival in Mayfair.

It read, '*Watch out for Woodford, Part 2, from the man who brought Flitter to Selchurch Peak*'. The sender's address was ***enough@stopfraud.com***. Lying on his desk was Saturday's FT, open at the article by Terry Owen, which he'd read before making his call. Lord Reginald Scarbrough had made the same calculation as Fern-Chapman - he and his friends, on his recommendation, had invested a total of £100 million in Olympic Funds. The question was, what should he - or could he - do about it?

Malaga, Spain

'Javier confirmed the Zurich agent will start the surveillance tomorrow morning. He persuaded Franz Stenmark to take the job himself. He's their top man, very expensive, but you said you wanted the best.'

'Pedro, I got us into this mess, and I owe it to Leticia and Emilio to try to get us out of it. If that means spending some of my money, I'm happy to do so.'

'I understand, Jenny, I just hope it's worthwhile and we get something from it,' the ex-policeman replied. 'Unfortunately, in my experience, that's not always the case with surveillance, you need a lot of luck.'

'We'll give it a week and see what happens. That seems to be their office, so he should see someone going in or coming out. Now, good news, I managed to get the last four seats to Geneva with Swiss, on Wednesday at 2pm, so we should be at the Metropole by five.'

'Thank you, Jenny,' he said. 'It's many years since I was last in Geneva. Where exactly is the hotel?'

'It's on the other side of the lake, about a ten minute taxi-drive from the Mandarin Oriental. That should be a safe enough distance.'

'You mean in case someone recognises you?'

'Exactly. If the man I saw in Zurich is the notary, he'll probably be there and maybe Jolidon as well. I don't want to be spotted and ruin the whole plan.'

'Neither of them knows Patrice or me, so we can check things out first.'

She could tell from his voice that Pedro was looking forward to the trip, happy to become a detective again for a while. 'Just be careful. You're not as young as you were in 2008.'

'You don't have to remind me, Jenny, Soledad does it regularly. By the way, she sends her best regards and says I should look after you.'

'Does she know why we're going?'

'Not exactly, I just said you have to make a business trip to Geneva and you needed a bodyguard, so she agreed I could go.'

'Don't you ever worry that she's trying to get rid of you for your life insurance policy?'

Belgravia, London, England

Esther was in her nightdress. Her BA flight to Geneva was at ten o'clock the next morning and she'd set her mobile alarm for 6am, which gave her enough time for any last-minute packing before taking a taxi to Heathrow. She came into the living room, 'I'm going to get an early night, I'll sleep in the guest room and try not to wake you when I leave in the morning. Don't be too late.' She kissed him and went off to bed.

Harry Fern-Chapman poured himself a large whiskey with very little soda. He looked around at the beautiful furnishings in the apartment. *That was a quarter of a million well spent*, he told himself, *provided I manage to hang on to it*. The TV was on and he stretched out on the oversize settee to watch that night's election debate. As always, the primary subject was Brexit, and it was hard to see who was carrying the argument. After a half-hour, suddenly realising he was falling asleep and hardly registering anything they said, or didn't say, he flipped to Classic FM and sat looking out at the lights in Eaton Square.

Harry was worried, not about the investors in Olympic Funds, they'd taken a risk that might or might not pay off; it wasn't up to him, the markets would dictate. It was his personal financial and reputational situation that was worrying him, it wasn't looking good. The call from Reggie Scarbrough had shaken him; if he lost the confidence of him and his clique, it would be the death knoll of Olympic Group, his sole source of income and virtually his only asset. He couldn't permit it to go down, he'd be wiped out, not just his reputation, but the lifestyle he'd created after many years of hard work and clever, intuitive investment '*nous*'.

He had made a lot of money with Selchurch Peak and left with £10 million in the bank, a lot of which he'd invested in setting up Olympic. He'd made that money back in fees over the last couple of years, but in a desperate attempt to reduce the damage to the fund prices, he'd taken nothing recently, which meant he'd left more than $4 million on the table, a table that would collapse in an expensive heap if he couldn't find a way to convince Alex Cameron not to suspend trading next week. Afterwards, only a strong Conservative government would bring the markets back, but that didn't depend on him and it would be too late.

Harry had an encyclopaedic knowledge of 20th Century investment management companies. He made himself a coffee and went into his office, with the beginnings of an idea. For the next two hours, he searched online for several investment failures and successes, starting with a long-forgotten company called Investors Overseas Services, its founder, Bernie Cornfeld, and its 'saviour', Robert Vesco.

THIRTY-EIGHT

Tuesday, November 26, 2019
City of London, London, England

Dr Hugh Middleton finished his morning perusal of the **Financial Times,** feeling quite disappointed when he found no reports about Olympic Funds. He bought the paper every day now, hoping to see further news about Fern-Chapman's inevitable demise. He checked the fund prices, *Hmm, no real change. Well, must be patient, it's just a matter of time.*

Heathrow Airport, England
'I'm at the airport and the flight's on time. I'll call you later today from Geneva. Love you, take care.' Esther switched off her mobile and walked towards Gate 15, supressing the apprehension she always felt at immigration or police control points. She tried to always travel with only a carry-on bag, so she could check in online and avoid the double passport check at the baggage counter. This trip was one of the most important of her life, it could double her wealth in just a few days, she couldn't afford any problems. The automated procedures that most airports had installed were an advantage, no one looked very carefully at ID documents anymore and she walked down the alleyway to the plane, feeling like a million dollars.

Belgravia, London, England

It was just before 9am when Fern-Chapman called Mandy to tell her he was under the weather and wouldn't be coming in to work. He coughed a few times during the call and spoke with a raspy voice. 'Seems like I've caught something, I feel rotten. I'm going to see the quack this morning, I'll call you later if I can't come in. I don't want to infect everybody if I've got a bug.'

Harry's reading the night before had concretised in his mind a plan to save Olympic Fund Group. The first step was to accumulate $10 million in an anonymous place that couldn't be traced back to him. Opening up his laptop, he went online to double-check the account for Benelux Mineral Holdings SA, at the Luxembourg Fiduciary Deposit Bank. The balance was a little over $7.5 million, what was left of his Selchurch and Olympic fees, but his name appeared nowhere; BMH was a South African company with bearer shares, whose director and signatory was *Econovest Bruxelloise SA*, a Belgian entity whose sole shareholder was Andorra-Dubai Holdings Ltd, incorporated in Nassau, Bahamas. The sole director of *Econovest* was Guillaume Fric, a Luxembourg lawyer Fern-Chapman occasionally used for confidential, personal business. The trail ended there.

He went through his calculations for the purchase of shares in his target company, Atlantic Offshore Oil & Gas SA, a Luxemburg semi-privately held exploration company, still controlled by the founders, the Boillat family, who owned 75% of the total of 50 million shares. The other 12.5 million shares, 25% of the capital, were in theory, available on the Over-the-Counter Market, however all of the OTC shares were owned by Harry's three top Olympic funds. Olympic had paid $5 per share a year previously and had a right of first refusal on any further sales by the Boillat family. In reality, there was no market for Atlantic Offshore shares unless Olympic or the family sold; and none had changed hands since that transaction. Since there had been little news, either positive or negative, that wasn't surprising. At that share price, the company's market cap, the value of its total 50 million shares, was $250 million.

He searched his laptop for a contract he'd executed a couple of years previously and compared it with his notes for the proposal to Atlantic Offshore; it suited his purposes perfectly. He printed out the 12-page agreement and marked it up with a black felt pen; he preferred editing documents by hand. Then he pulled up the original contract on his screen again, made the changes and added the requisite signature names for BMH.

Next, Fern-Chapman composed a letter from Olympic Funds, renouncing their right to subscribe for 3 million shares of Atlantic Offshore Oil & Gas SA at a price per share of $10. He saved the contract and letter in his laptop and printed them both for the Atlantic Offshore file in his cabinet. Lastly, he prepared an email for Guillaume Fric and attached the contract to it.

It was now 11am and Harry prepared and signed a payment order for the Olympic Funds Group London general account at Lloyds, for $2.5 million, labelling it, '*H. Fern-Chapman, on account of unpaid Management Fees; January – September*'. The receiving account was at HSBC, in his own name. He emailed the order to his CFO, Tom Newman, asking him to call his mobile for confirmation. Tom called a few minutes later and he answered with the same raspy voice and cough. 'I just got back from the doctor's, seems I've picked up the flu, so I'll be staying home today. I feel like shit; can you tell Mandy not to bother me unless it's vital. I've got some personal things I can attend to while I'm stuck here, and I'll need those funds please, as soon as you can.' Newman was aware that the amount was just a part of Harry's outstanding fees, and despite his misgivings, he confirmed the payment would be made immediately.

Right, I've got the money I need. Harry breathed a sigh of relief and checked the time again, it was 11:30 pm. He called Guillaume Fric, his Luxembourg lawyer, on his mobile number. 'I want you to make an offer to the Boillat family on behalf of Benelux Mineral Holdings for 3 million shares of Atlantic Offshore at a strike price of $10 per share, that's $30 million. You have to do it today to close on Friday.'

After a moment's silence, the lawyer said, 'What about Olympic Group's right of first refusal?'

'You can tell them you've been assured that Olympic won't bid at that price. If they agree to the deal, Olympic will confirm in writing they won't exercise their right, nor prevent the sale.'

Fric sucked in his breath. 'You did the Olympic purchase at $5 just a year ago and now you're offering $10 through BMH? Fucking Hell, you're doubling the value of their company.'

'Exactly, except it's not me offering, I've got nothing to do with this transaction. Is that clear?' he replied.

'OK. What do you know?'

'What a lot of people would love to find out, so no comment. You're acquainted with Gérard Boillat, the head of the family, so you can call him personally.'

'I can do that. What about the contract?'

'It's ready, I'm sending it to you now. I want you to save it, print it out then wipe my email off your system. You'll act for BMH and when it's agreed, you'll sign for *Econovest Bruxelloise*, you're their sole director. I repeat, I'm not involved, nor is Olympic, understood?'

'Of course, I heard you, go ahead.'

He pressed *Send* and heard the *beep* as his email with the contract arrived on Fric's computer.

'OK, it's here, I'll save it with my own fingerprint, print it out and delete your entire message, OK?'

'I'm doing the same.' Fern-Chapman double-deleted the e-mail from his laptop.

'Does BMH have the cash?' the lawyer asked.

'Not exactly, there's a down payment of $10 million, then four six-monthly payments for the balance.'

'So it's a two-year deal?' The lawyer sounded sceptical.

'Don't worry, at that price he won't refuse the transaction.'

'If you say so. Where's the $10 million?'

'There's $7.5 million in the BMH Luxembourg account now. The remaining $2.5 million will be there tomorrow. When you execute the deal, just transfer the $10 million from BMH to your custodial account to pay Atlantic, so it can be seen to come from BMH, OK?'

'Understood. You want to do the trade direct, or through the OTC?'

'Ask him to make an option available on the OTC and BMH will buy the shares there.'

Fric knew there was a lot Fern-Chapman wasn't telling him, but he was careful not to ask the wrong questions.

'OK, Benelux Mineral Holdings wants an option for three million shares made available on the Over-the-Counter Market by Friday in accordance with your contract and we'll acquire them for $30 million. Right?'

'That's it. But listen Guillaume, one last time, it's a BMH deal, I'm not involved, and I don't want my name mentioned to Boillat or anyone. I'll call you tomorrow and we can go over any comments they might have. You can get it finalised and signed by Thursday and the OTC transaction can be executed on Friday. I'm relying on you.'

'If it's do-able, I'll get it done, you know me.'

'Thanks, Guillaume, I'll call you tomorrow.'

He rang off, the lawyer wondering what discovery could possibly double Atlantic Offshore's value overnight. He made a couple of calls to reschedule previous arrangements then he began calculating his fees and commission for the week's work. He was having lunch with Gérard Boillat at his club in a half hour, no need to call him, he'd be more receptive over a glass of port.

THIRTY-NINE

Tuesday, November 26, 2019
Geneva, Switzerland

Esther Bonnard swiped the entry card and pulled her bag into suite 520 at the Richemond. *It's just like coming home,* she thought to herself. On the side table was an ice bucket with a bottle of Laurent-Perrier chilling, fruit, flowers and a handwritten card from the Hotel Manager welcoming her back. She took off her coat, threw it on the bed and went to the window. It was a cold, clear afternoon and she could see the *Jet d'Eau*, the Geneva landmark fountain, rising one hundred and forty metres into the sky on the other side of the lake. To the right, standing above the old town, was the steeple of the St Pierre Cathedral; near the bank where Charlie Bishop's briefcase, still containing over $10 million of Angolan diamonds, was in safekeeping.

She had read the *Financial Times* on the flight. There were no articles about Olympic Funds and the share prices hadn't budged since the previous week. She felt a little less anxious, hoping Harry's strategy was working, or at least would be by the time she returned to London. A fight with him was the last thing she needed, apart from losing some of her money, it would probably mean losing him too. *Let's concentrate on the sale, that'll be at least $2 million more insurance in the bank. Time to worry about Harry* *and Olympic when I get back next week.*

She checked the time, it was almost 1pm. *Perfect time for an aperitif*, she decided. Her mobile rang as she was coaxing the cork from the bottle; she saw Christen's name and took the call.

'Have you arrived safely in Geneva, Esther?'

'I'm at the Richemond, just got in, the flight was a little late, but no problems. How's everything?'

'Everything is in good shape. I'm at the Mandarin Oriental, looking at the sales rooms. They're fabulous, the best I've ever seen. Are you coming to view?'

'I was planning on coming tomorrow morning, but I don't think we should be seen there together. What do you think?'

'I agree, we need to be careful. I don't have to be here in the morning, so come whenever you like. I would like to see you before the sale, when you have the time.'

She tried to interpret his mood, his voice sounded sharp, positive and relaxed, *no signs of any problems, or of drinking.* 'Of course, we should meet, but not here at the hotel. Why don't we have dinner tomorrow night? I'll have seen the sales display and we'll have time for a chat, talk about the next steps in our business.'

'Do you want me to reserve? I know a very good Italian restaurant in *Pâquis*, near your hotel, a quiet place where we won't be noticed. I'll text you the address and we can meet there at 7pm.'

Esther poured herself a glass of champagne, trying to work out what Christen wanted to talk about. *It has to be money*, she reasoned, *that's the only reason he's in this relationship. Maybe I bargained too hard with him. I can afford a reasonable bonus, that should keep him motivated and satisfied. We're in this business for just another year or so. How much can it cost me to keep him happy until then?*

Belgravia, London

Harry Fern-Chapman received a call from his contact at HSBC confirming his account had been credited with a transfer of $2.5 million, from Olympic Funds. He checked the time, it was 10:00 am in the Bahamas. 'I'm sending you an order right away to forward the funds to another account, OK? You can call me back to confirm the details.'

By the end of the afternoon, the funds had transited through an account at the Nassau Credit Trust Bank and finally arrived in the Benelux Mineral Holdings account in Luxembourg, via a last detour to Valletta, Malta. The lawyer now had access to the $10 million that Fern-Chapman was certain would seal the Atlantic Offshore deal. More importantly, it would be virtually impossible to trace him, or Olympic Group to the transaction.

Harry poured himself a beer, switched on Classic FM and sat in the living room, trying to calm his racing pulse. *If this works, it'll get Cameron off my back and fix everything until after the election, then nobody knows what will happen. If Labour gets in and the shit hits the fan, it won't be my fault. If it doesn't work ... I'm definitely fucked.*

Marbella, Spain

'I'll be back from Geneva on Sunday night, so you and Encarni have a few days to spoil Ellen and Sebastien rotten.' It was a warm, sunny afternoon in Marbella and

Jenny and Lily were watching the little girl throwing a ball for Chester near the large pond Charlie had built at the top of the garden.

'We're both much stricter than her doting mother, so it'll do her the world of good.'

Jenny laughed, 'You're right, but she's my daughter, so I'm excused.'

Lily was quiet for a moment, then she said, in her straightforward Geordie fashion, 'You seem to have been a bit preoccupied these last few weeks. I hope everything's alright. I mean with you and your business.'

She's got the wrong end of the stick, but it must be rather obvious something's wrong, Jenny realised. 'It's a bit of a complicated time, to be honest. You think the past is gone and done with, then once in a while you're suddenly reminded that it's still there, I suppose it will always be there.'

'Well, I don't imagine there's anything I can do, but you only have to ask.'

'Thanks, Lily. but I'll be in good company with Leticia, Patrice and Pedro, and things will get sorted, one way or another. What I really need you to do is look after my daughter while I'm away, as you always do. You'll have your hands full, with her, Chester and Leticia's boys, so don't worry about me, I'll be fine. I promise if I think you can help in any other way, I won't hesitate to ask you.'

Malaga, Spain
'Hello Franz, how was your first day on the job?'

'Is that a joke, or what? It was bloody freezing and unproductive. I'd forgotten how long and boring those surveillance days can be. Thank God it gets dark at 5pm, so I could go for a burger and an espresso. I'm in a café near the building now, nothing to report.'

'You didn't recognise anyone?'

'Nobody resembling the two descriptions you gave me. I checked all the names from the mailboxes, and everyone who came or went was a typical resident, mostly Spanish or Portuguese, a few Eastern Europeans. You can read it in their clothes and the way they behave and talk, definitely no smart businessman or sleazy-looking Frenchman. I would have made them right away.'

Javier wasn't surprised that the businessman hadn't shown. If he was the notary, as he suspected, he'd probably be in Geneva for the sales. Jolidon was a different story, he was unlikely to want to leave the valuables unattended, if that's where they were. 'Can you see into the apartment?' he asked.

'It's got blinds on the only front window and the others are small and in an alleyway, so I can't see inside.'

'Did you manage to get inside the building?

'You bet, I followed a Spanish couple in. Told them I was visiting the Kruger family on the sixth floor, but they didn't know anything about them. Said they'd never seen anyone coming or going to that floor.'

'What about the apartment itself?'

'Just like you described, CCTV camera and no nameplate on the door. I knocked and rang the bell couple of times but couldn't hear anything from inside, so I've got zilch to report there either.'

'The CCTV? You could be identified.'

He heard Stenmark laugh, 'Don't worry, I know how to get out of camera. I'm invisible around those things. They'll know someone was there, but not who. From what you told me they'll think it was a client looking for his valuables.'

'Right, well done, but nothing to get our teeth into.' Javier sighed. 'Thanks Franz, get yourself home and have a whiskey, that's all I can recommend. I hope you have more luck tomorrow and it sounds like you should wear warmer clothes.'

Geneva, Switzerland

'Just thought you'd like to know; I got a transmission of a visitor from the CCTV camera at the apartment a few hours ago. Nice to know it actually works.'

Esther caught her breath. 'Was it the guy you told me about, who's been before?'

'He didn't look up at the camera, but I don't think so. It must be absolutely freezing in Zurich, he was really well wrapped up. Probably just another client. If he's serious he'll come back when I'm there and I'll cope with it. Don't worry, just keeping you informed, that's all. How's everything in Geneva?'

'Christen told me the salerooms look fabulous. I'm going to visit tomorrow morning.'

'Be careful. It's not the time to be recognised.'

Marbella, Spain.

Jenny had the house to herself when Espinoza rang at eight that evening, Ellen was in bed and Lily was in her room chatting to her son in England on WhatsApp. She was watching TV, Chester draped across her lap, fast asleep.

'Franz Stenmark had nothing to report from Zurich,' he told her, repeating what Javier had reported.

'They're probably both in Geneva for the sales, assuming

I was right about Jolidon and the notary.'

'We should find out if you're right on Thursday, all being well. Did Patrice confirm he has everything he needs?'

'Everything's ready for our flight tomorrow. I'm looking forward to it. It's time we took the initiative in this business, time we took control.'

'One thing at a time. I'll see you at the airport check-in desk at 13:00. Meanwhile, be calm and sleep well. Goodnight, Jenny.'

FORTY

Esther waited until midday before going to the Mandarin Oriental, calculating there would be fewer visitors at lunchtime, reducing the chance of her being recognised. She was always on tenterhooks in Geneva, having lived there for six years, during and after her marriage to Gaston Rousseau; until her ignominious escape on a flight to Luton, where Ray d'Almeida had failed to arrive to take her to Panama, a trip she would never make. After almost 12 years, apart from the peculiar coincidence of meeting Ilona Tymoshenko at the Scarbroughs' party, she had never been seen or recognised, but since Interpol, the trans-European police agency, became interested in her, she never took it for granted. She didn't know if it was due to their incompetence, or her clever travel planning, but it didn't matter. It had worked until now, and she had to keep it up for another year or so, before she disappeared from Europe with the fortune she'd worked so hard to amass.

Her timing was good, the exhibition rooms were busy, but not crowded and she felt more at ease once she'd cast her eye around the magnificently converted ballroom and two adjacent rooms. The smartly dressed visitors were much too busy examining the vast array of beautiful jewellery, watches and gemstones to notice her. Small, discreet tables were available where dealers and expert gemologists could examine the valuables more closely and appraise them with their loupes. Esther knew from the catalogue the sales comprised almost 1,200 items, but she looked around in awe, dazzled by the huge quantity of valuables that filled the dozens of glass-topped cabinets lining the walls of the room.

She walked around in a reverie, looking at the greatest display of wealth she'd ever encountered. At Klein, Fellay, the Geneva investment bank where she'd worked, while Ray d'Almeida's accomplice, she'd become used to meeting prosperous clients and seeing statements of substantial fortunes, but this treasure trove was beyond her wildest dreams.

Drewberrys was the largest of the auction houses and Esther knew their previous sale, in February, had comprised less than 1,000 pieces, with a sales value of a quarter of a billion Swiss Francs. *This collection must be worth even more than that, she imagined. And I was worried that our paltry 4 million or so might be noticed. It's a drop in the ocean.* She relaxed, enjoying being surrounded by such riches, knowing that, like many owner-sellers, she was now a wealthy woman in her own right.

Touring the rooms, she looked out for the items being sold by the *African Benevolent Trust*. Jolidon had done his work well, it was an eclectic collection of very wearable jewellery, watches and ornamental items, she was confident they would reach the reasonable reserve prices he'd estimated. The jewel in the crown was lot no. 900, Charlie Bishop's Angolan diamonds, presented as they were in the catalogue, spilling onto a blue velvet cloth, the multiple facets reflecting the lights shining onto the glass case. She looked at them fondly, remembering the many hardships she'd had to withstand before they finally came into her possession.

Esther returned to the Richemond feeling happy and positive; the sight of 'her' objects amongst that immense treasure of valuables was just the tonic she needed. She went down for a light lunch in the *Jardin* restaurant and her thoughts turned to René Christen. She wondered what her dinner appointment with him would throw up, but was confident she could cope.

Belgravia, London, England

'How did it go?' Harry was at home speaking to Guillaume Fric on his mobile, he hadn't gone to the office in case he was overheard talking to the lawyer. He kept his voice steady, but he was holding his breath, dreading a negative answer.

'Boillat's hooked, I'm sure of it. Has to go through the contract and present the transaction to his Board, of course, but it's a formality.' Guillaume Fric's eyes were shining, he'd never made an easier €100,000 in his life. 'How come you were so sure he'd take the bait?'

Fern-Chapman breathed out with relief, 'Simple. First, he can't refuse that price, he'd be a laughing stock; and second; Brexit. It's a Luxembourg company and subject to EU regulations. Olympic's right of first refusal means we can obstruct any further share sales. They've never been comfortable with that restriction, but that was the price of the deal. If Brexit gets done, it will get even worse. The EU will never let a UK fund group exercise such a right on a Luxembourg company. The European court would go bananas and it would end up in litigation and he'd be stuck for years. This is the only opportunity he's got to get rid of some more shares before everything gets clogged up in the Brexit works. And at that price, he'd be crazy not to sell, even if he has to take the risk of two-year payment terms. He gets $10 million cash and he's got a precedent for challenging Olympic's refusal rights in the future, so he can dispose of more shares. Piece of cake.'

'That's smart thinking, but in that case, why did you price it so high?'

'I have my reasons; you'll find out in due course. Is he going through the contract?'

'He's looked at it and said he'd get his lawyers to go through it today and tomorrow. Complained about the overtime fees they'll charge him.' Fric laughed, 'I recognised that contract, I wrote the original for Olympic a couple of years ago. It's a good piece of work; you should take up the profession, I'm looking for a partner.'

Harry didn't comment on the compliment, he knew Fric's fees would also be exorbitant, but if it worked out as planned, he could afford them. 'OK, call me on this mobile when you've got any news,' he said. 'Don't forget, Friday's the deadline.'

Geneva, Switzerland

'*Soyez-les bienvenus à l'Hotel Métropole, Messieurs, Mesdames.*'

The liveried concierge opened the taxi door, helped Jenny and Leticia out, then went to supervise the bellboys carrying in their baggage.

'Portuguese,' Leticia whispered to Jenny as they walked up the staircase to the reception desk. 'Nothing's changed in 12 years.'

'Just like being back home in Angola, Leticia. You can drop your French for a while.'

'They're smart people, the Swiss,' she replied, 'Everyone knows the Portuguese are the best workers in the world, outside of their own country, that is.'

Jenny checked her watch. 'Almost six o'clock. Time to freshen up and have a drink before dinner. Let's meet in the bar at 7:30pm. We'll discuss tactics for tomorrow.'

'Whatever you say, Mme Bishop.' Patrice winked at Espinoza, 'Best know who's in charge,' he whispered.

'With Jenny, there's never any doubt,' answered the Spaniard.

Malaga, Spain

'Any better news today, Franz?' It was 7:15pm and Javier had been waiting anxiously for the call.

'You mean apart from the icy rain?'

Javier felt embarrassed, it was a beautifully warm day in Malaga. 'Oh, sorry, I didn't see the forecast, was it that bad?'

'No sweat, I'm getting used to it and I took your advice, two layers of clothing, I'm fine, and I've got some news.'

Javier's ears pricked up, 'You saw someone?'

'I did, but neither of the guys you're looking for. Definitely not a resident and not the kind of visitor I'd expect to see there, completely out of place. I'm guessing he wasn't going to see any of them.'

'Did you get a shot?'

'Some really crap ones, it was pissing down and I could hardly see across the road. I'm sending them to you now, hang on.'

A moment later, three photos arrived on his phone

Franz was right, the visibility must have been very bad. It was a tall, well-built man, probably around fifty, wearing a mackintosh and what looked like a golf cap, with a scarf around his face and carrying an umbrella. Javier couldn't make out his features, but he didn't match either of the descriptions Jenny and Leticia had given.

'I see what you mean, not what you'd expect. Did he go into the building?'

'Eventually. He walked up to the entrance and went into the lobby, but I guess he couldn't get inside, just hung around until he could follow someone in, it was the Spanish couple I met yesterday.'

'So he didn't have a key?'

'Definitely not, he was just waiting for someone to come in.'

'Did he know the couple?'

'Pretty sure he didn't. Never spoke to them, just walked inside after they opened the door.'

Javier asked, 'I don't suppose you followed him in?'

'Nope, I don't have instructions for that. Anyway, I didn't want to spook him and ruin the surveillance.'

The Spaniard cursed silently, he knew it wasn't in Stenmark's brief. 'OK, my mistake, sorry. How long was he in there?'

'Less than 5 minutes at most. Went in, came out and walked down the street to the bus stop.'

'So, he might have gone up to that apartment, couldn't get in and came straight back out. When was this?'

'Four o'clock this afternoon. I didn't follow him to the bus, but it was the city centre route, it goes to the main train station.'

'Did you go over to check on the apartment again?'

'Sure. I went a couple of times, followed residents who came in, I recognise them all now. Last time was at 6pm, 30 minutes ago. I went late to see if anyone had come in after dark and I'd missed them in this shitty weather, but there's still nobody on the sixth floor. There's been no one in that apartment for two days.'

'You're sure of that?'

'As sure as I can be without going inside. By the way, that stranger who went in is probably on the CCTV recording and they'll see it whenever they come back. That's good, they might think I'm the same guy out of camera when I go up to look around.'

'Right, either that or an unhappy client. Anything else?'

'A sauna? Hot bath?'

Geneva, Switzerland

Espinoza examined the photos he'd just received from Javier. 'He's dressed for the rain, and with that scarf you can't make out the features at all.'

'It's been pouring in Zurich, but it's neither of the two men we're looking for.'

'I'll show them to Jenny, but I'm sure you're right. I wonder who it was, whether he was going to the RH apartment?'

'Franz was sure he wasn't visiting any of the residents. If he was up there and couldn't get in, it probably confirms there's no one there.'

'Makes sense. He's convinced there's been nobody there for two days?'

'Certain. He's checked several times during the day and again this evening and the place is always empty.'

'So, it's likely they're both here in Geneva for the sales.

That could be just what we need.'

'Maybe we're wasting our time in Zurich.' Javier sounded disappointed. 'I'll call you again tomorrow evening if I get anything worthwhile from Franz.'

'Give my love to the family.'

'And you take care. If those people are in Geneva, things could become complicated.'

Lugano, Tessin, Switzerland

'It was the same guy I told you about, who's been a couple of times, but he was wearing a cap and a scarf again and I couldn't see his face. He knows the camera's there and didn't look up. He was only there a couple of minutes, knocked and rang a few times like before, then went away. My guess is he's a client looking for his valuables, but he's not making much progress.'

Esther relaxed. 'I suppose so. If he didn't cause a riot, it must have been some law-abiding citizen. That makes two of them, so it's not exactly a procession. That's good work, Claude, but I'll be glad when you get back to Zurich.'

Jolidon gave a grunt, 'I may never go back. Have you seen the weather there? It's like Siberia in the rain. I'm just fine here in the Tessin until the sales are over.'

FORTY-ONE

Chez Mario was just 10 minutes away from the hotel. It was a dry, but freezing cold evening and Esther walked briskly along, glad to enter the warm atmosphere of the restaurant. René Christen was already sitting at a corner table when she arrived, and he stood up and shook her hand.

He took her coat off and draped it over the spare chair. 'Would you like a glass of *Chasselas*? It's really excellent.' He was referring to the local white wine, grown in almost every village in Switzerland, under many different names. There was a half-empty carafe on the table and he poured her a healthy measure. 'Cheers and good health, Esther. It's nice to see you again.'

'*Santé*, René. That's delicious, thanks. How's everything? I went along to the exhibition this morning. Very impressive, and our valuables look great, very saleable. *Félicitations*, well done.'

'*Merci*, there were some problems with provenance, their lawyer didn't care for the *African Benevolent Trust*. A very suspicious man, worried about money laundering and conflict diamonds, those kind of things, but fortunately...' he took a swallow of wine, looked at her.

'You sorted it out and everything is in place for a very

successful sale. Another one. Claude and I are delighted with the way things are going, we'll all come out of this a lot better than we came in.' She waited for his response, eyeing him up. The *huissier* was just a few years older than her, a little overweight and starting to show the signs of over-drinking. But he was still a good-looking man and, she could imagine in another life he might have appealed to her, but now he was simply another problem to be dealt with.

'Yes,' he replied, pouring himself another glass. 'I sorted it out, like I've sorted out a lot of things since we started working together. I'm sure you've noticed?'

'We have no complaints, if that's what you mean. You're doing a good job and it's greatly appreciated.'

The waiter came to take their order and the *huissier* asked for another carafe of wine. Esther took the opportunity to change the subject. 'Where are you living now, I remember you told me you weren't happy with your apartment.'

'I'm still in the same place and still not happy with it.'

She realised she'd put her foot in it, given him the perfect opening. 'I'm sorry to hear that, is it difficult to find a good apartment in Geneva these days?'

'Not if you can afford it.' He laughed cynically and emptied his glass.

She knew where he was going with this and decided to get it over with. Dropping her voice, she asked, 'You've made a lot of money recently, have you managed to clear your debts?'

'Not even close. With the interest accumulating every month, it'll take me at least another two years, maybe three.'

'Even if we have six sales next year, as planned?'

'With 10% of the profits, I'll still be working for my creditors. I might be clear by the end of the following year, if I'm lucky.'

Esther knew he was lying to her. *He's probably spent half of his commissions on bars and boyfriends.* She hadn't told him that she intended to pull the plug at the end of next year and she knew Jolidon had said nothing. She was considering her response when the carafe of wine arrived. Christen poured himself another glass, '*Santé.*' He looked quizzically at her, waiting for a reaction.

'It sounds as if you're not happy with our arrangement.'

'Not particularly. If I'd known what was involved, I wouldn't have accepted your offer, that's for sure.'

She knew he'd been desperate to accept any offer that would pay him more than the pittance he'd been earning. 'But you've made about 600,000 Swiss Francs this year. With this sale, you'll be at almost a million. Not many people make that kind of money, even in Switzerland.'

He smiled, 'Not many people make over 6 million. Six times as much, with a fraction of the risk.'

'We're all running a great risk, René, that's why we're making a lot of money. And if you're complaining about me, don't forget who spotted the opportunity, who made the investment, brought the banks, the lawyers, put the whole structure together, and,' she dropped her voice to a whisper, 'who brought the main asset, the diamonds, to the table. Without them, this would be a nickel and dime operation, not a multi-million-dollar opportunity for everyone concerned.'

'That's my point, Esther, this is not a multi-million-dollar opportunity for everyone concerned. Just step back and look at our situations. You don't live in Switzerland and you're hiding behind some kind of complicated structure with an Angolan front which I'm sure is impenetrable, so you're virtually risk-free. I'm here in Geneva, signing my life away in full sight every time I enter a lot into a sale; so far, dozens of times. And I'm co-signatory to a dodgy account in a bank, also based in Angola, which I'm sure could get me put away for a very long time.'

He took another swig of wine. 'More importantly for both of us, unless I continue to take those risks, there will be no more sales and no more profits for anyone. So I don't think you can calculate the risk or the reward as six times more in your favour. Do you?'

'*Bon appétit, Monsieur, Dame.*' The waiter placed their meals on the table and filled up Christen's glass again. Esther had hardly touched her wine and the carafe was almost empty again. She was astonished at how much the notary could drink, but even more surprised that the wine appeared to make him become increasingly lucid and eloquent. *He's prepared his presentation very well, I underestimated him.*

'*Bon appetit,*' she said, 'it looks delicious. Thanks for the invitation.' They started eating the pasta dishes and she changed the subject, thinking of her conversation with Jolidon and the unknown visitor, but didn't mention the incident. 'How are you getting along with Claude? No problems there?'

'We get along fine, but I don't see him that much, except when I go Zurich to pick up the valuables. He's got a great job, getting paid a fortune for sitting in an office sorting out goods from the strongbox to sell. I wouldn't mind being in his place and making what he's making.' He reached for the wine carafe again.

He always finds a way to get back to the partnership shares. Two can play at that game, she decided, *time to take a risk and put some pressure on him.* Esther pushed her plate aside. 'I've suddenly lost my appetite, René, well done. I'll leave you here to finish your wine and hope you're in a better mood the next time we talk. It would be a good idea if you told me what you want, instead of what you don't want, so we can put this disagreement behind us. It would also be a good idea if you didn't drink yourself stupid when I'm trying to have a sensible conversation with you. Don't forget, you're not the only *huissier* in Switzerland and I have excellent contacts to find another if you don't want to continue. *Bonne nuit.*' She grabbed her coat and walked out without looking back.

The *huissier* watched in dismay as she stormed out. *Merde, I didn't expect that.* His pretence at bravado was suddenly replaced by the fear and uncertainty he'd suffered since his divorce. He took another gulp of wine, the only thing that was holding him together now. Christen couldn't afford to overplay his hand; he desperately needed a large amount of money very soon. That week he'd finally received something he'd been dreading since he'd been made bankrupt. Several years previously, he'd been appointed trustee for a substantial family fortune, settled by Raphaël Comina, an elderly friend and one-time business partner of his father. Despite the bankruptcy, because of their close relationship, and probably because it was too much trouble to change, Comina had continued to maintain him as trustee.

Inevitably, a couple of months ago, the old man had finally passed away and the Comina family and their lawyer were now trying to discover why an amount of a half a million Swiss Francs seemed to be missing from the trust funds. For the moment, they were giving him the benefit of the doubt, and he'd been asked to attend a meeting with them in Fribourg on Friday afternoon.

That meant he'd miss the first afternoon and evening of the sales; the *African Benevolent Trust* had 36 items in those sessions, with a total reserve of almost CHF700k. Depending on the outcome of the discussion, he didn't know if he'd be able to attend the Saturday sales either, when the rest of their valuables were being auctioned. If the discussion went badly, they might report it to the Cantonal Police and he could be arrested immediately. Between that and his other overdue debt repayments, he desperately needed a million francs very soon. Whatever happened, René Christen was between a rock and a hard place and he somehow had to convince Esther Bonnard that he deserved a very big bonus.

His hand shook as he took another swallow of wine, reflecting on his problem. *Neither Esther nor Jolidon will know if I'm at the auction. I don't have any official function, just observing for my client. I'll have to take the chance; the goods will sell whether I'm there or not and I've got to try to convince the Comina family not to take any action.* His thoughts shifted to the argument they'd just had. *She seemed really pissed off. On the other hand, it doesn't change anything, we've got a sale in progress and we'll soon have 4 million in the fiduciary account. She needs my signature to release that money, then I must be able to make enough to clear up this Fribourg business. We'll see who's calling the shots. Esther's bluffing*, he tried to convince himself, *she can't afford to make a change,*

*even if she could find another huissier to replace me. I
know too much. I'll get my money, enough to push back
the problem anyway.*

He drank the rest of the wine then called the waiter over
and asked for a cognac and the bill. He didn't go into the
old town that night, somehow he wasn't in the mood.

Geneva, Switzerland

Espinoza's mobile rang again while he and the others were
enjoying a drink in the bar of the Métropole. He didn't
recognise the number and walked out to the corridor to
take the call. 'Who's this, please?'

'Hi Pedro, it's Coetzee. How are things going?'

'Marius, great to hear from you. We just arrived in
Geneva, that's where we think the action will be. By the
way, we hired Franz Stenmark to monitor the apartment
in Zurich, he seems very professional, thanks for the
introduction.'

'I know, I hope you don't mind but I talked to him earlier
today, he told me there's nobody in that apartment.'

'That's what he thinks, but he can't be sure, obviously.
Why the interest?'

'I've been thinking about the situation and I've had a
few ideas. Want to hear them?'

'I'm always happy to listen to ideas, but I don't have
much time.'

'OK, put simply, the only way you'll ever get anything
out of that apartment is to bug it, both visual and audio.
If there's nobody in there at the moment, then now's the
perfect time.'

'We thought of that, but Stenmark can't do it, it's illegal
under Swiss law and he'd lose his license. Thanks, Marius,

it's a good idea but unfortunately impossible.'

'I agree. He can't do it, but someone else could, someone who doesn't have a licence to lose.'

'I wouldn't know how to find such a person. There's a CCTV camera outside, it requires a lot of expertise. If the occupants are here in Geneva for the sale, they'll probably be returning on Sunday. We don't have the time or the local knowledge to find a trustworthy person with those skills.'

'We both know someone who can do it with his eyes shut, well within the time frame.'

Espinoza's pulse quickened, 'Who are you talking about?'

'Me.'

'You mean you could fly up to Zurich in time to do the job?'

'I'm sitting on the plane now: it leaves in 20 minutes and I get in at 6am tomorrow. I figured you'd agree, so I didn't want to waste any time.'

Geneva, Switzerland

Esther lay awake for a long while, assessing the situation. The conversation with Christen had shaken her, he obviously wanted a lot more than she'd imagined. She had the same thought he'd had; *In a couple of weeks with 3 or 4 million Swiss Francs in the fiduciary account, he'll have the upper hand. I can't afford that. On the other hand, he obviously needs the money and he can't get it without my signature, so it's touché. We need each other so there's bound to be a solution that can satisfy us both.*

She finally fell asleep, dreaming, as she often did, that she was lying on a beach next to Ray d'Almeida. She slept like a baby.

FORTY-TWO

Thursday, November 28, 2019

Geneva, Switzerland

'**Coetzee called me from Zurich airport.** He got in late on account of the weather, there was a huge storm there last night. He was going over to meet Franz Stenmark at the RH apartment. Apparently, he's got his bag of tools with him, whatever that means. I don't think I want to know.'

'I wish I was up there with them, doing something useful. I'm getting frustrated sitting here in Malaga just making phone calls,' Javier said.

'I know what you mean, but remember, police work is 99% patience and 1% action, and we'll need you for that when we get back.' Espinoza checked the time, 'I've got to meet the others for breakfast now, then we're going to the sales viewing. I'll call you this evening to catch up.' He put his mobile away and went down to the dining room.

'Has he arrived?' Jenny hadn't been too surprised when she'd heard Coetzee's plan, she knew what he was capable of and how quickly he reacted. She had immediately suggested he should join them in Geneva.

Espinoza brought them up to date. 'If there's still nobody in that apartment, we should have both visual and audio observation when he gets here. I'm assuming he can install it that quickly?'

'If anyone can, it's Coetzee.' Patrice thought back

to their showdown with the Chinese cyber crooks in Shanghai, two years previously. 'He seems to be an expert at most things involving intervention.'

'OK, it's almost nine o'clock and we need to be at the exhibition when it opens at ten, so that Leticia and I can get to the bank before midday.' Jenny assumed her schoolteacher persona. 'Let's run through things once more, make sure we've got our act together. The sales start tomorrow, we've got to be well-rehearsed.'

Belgravia, London, England

'How are you this morning, darling? Missing me?' Harry Fern-Clapman was working at home when Esther called his mobile. He was staying away from the office until his BMH deal was done.

'All the better for hearing your voice. Of course I'm missing you. What's happening in Geneva, making a lot of money?'

'Not yet, but I'm hoping to. I saw from the news that the markets were quieter yesterday, you must be relieved.'

'Not really, quiet doesn't do it for me. I'm working on something that will make a lot of noise and turn our funds around just like I promised you.'

'Great, what is it?'

'No comment, you'll have to wait for the announcement like everyone else.'

'Well, I've got a busy day ahead, so I'll love you and leave you. Call me tonight if you have a moment.'

Geneva, Switzerland

'Good morning, René, how are you feeling?'

Esther heard the *huissier* coughing and clearing his

throat and after a moment, he answered, 'I'm fine, Esther, I hope you are too, looking forward to some very successful sales this week.'

'Good. Exactly what I wanted to talk about. Sorry for walking out of our dinner last night, but I was a bit tired after travelling and we didn't get off to the best start.'

He shook his head, trying to get over the hangover. 'Nothing to apologise for, maybe I overdid my request for a better deal; after all, it's well overdue.'

You didn't request anything; that's the problem, she thought. *Just bitched and moaned and got drunk*. Aloud, she said, 'No problem, René. I agree we need to revise our arrangement and I have a suggestion, *d'accord?*'

Christen's mind suddenly cleared. 'I'm listening,' he said cautiously.

'Why don't we wait to see what the sales produce this week and use that result to work out a new formula. I'm sure you agree that it's better to use real numbers rather than expectations.'

She could almost hear his mind cogitating over this unexpected proposal. *What might be in it for me? What are the risks? How might she try to screw me? There'll be maybe CHF 4 million of leverage in the fiduciary account. I only need a million and it needs my signature.*

Finally, he said, '*D'accord*, Esther. I think that's a very fair suggestion. Let's see the numbers and decide on a fair percentage.'

Esther was relieved. *That's won me a few days, and it should keep him happy during the sales.* She called room service and ordered breakfast, with a glass of champagne.

Zurich, Switzerland

'Nice to see you again, Franz. How've you been?' Coetzee greeted him in German as he stepped out of the taxi outside the petrol station in Badenerstrasse. He had only a travel bag with him.

'Fine until this week.' The agent shivered and coughed into his gloved hand. 'This job is going to kill me, I should have doubled my rate.'

'I see what you mean, it's quite a change from Joburg. At least it's stopped raining after last night's storm, it was pretty bad up there; I was wondering if we'd make it in.' He pulled his heavy army coat tighter around him against the cold wind. 'Let's get a coffee and have a chat while you warm up.'

They sat in the window of the café, where they could partially see the entrance to no. 819. The storm had blown away the clouds and rain; it was still freezing, but the visibility was good.

'Have you seen any visitors this morning?'

Stenmark shook his head. 'Only a couple of residents going to work or coming in with shopping. I haven't been over yet, but I'm sure the apartment is still empty.'

Coetzee opened his bag and took out a leather satchel. 'What kind of lock's on the door?'

'You mean the downstairs hall? It's a Yale, but it's easier and safer to wait for someone to come in or out. You don't want to get seen picking a lock at the entrance, the Swiss police don't care for that. I've never had to wait for more than 10 minutes or so, it's no big deal.'

'OK, I don't want to get you in trouble.' He checked the time, 'It's 9:30, we'll get another coffee and I'll wander across in a half-hour or so. There's bound to be people coming and going around ten o'clock.'

Zurich, Switzerland

'OK, I'm here. See you in 15 minutes,' Coetzee whispered. He was at the top of the staircase in the apartment building, where he could see the CCTV camera but was out of its range. He'd followed a young couple into the hallway and walked quietly up, his antennae registering every detail on the way.

'Be careful.' Stenmark ordered another coffee, glad to be out of the freezing cold. He pulled the South-African's bag closer, wondering what was in it.

Marius opened up his leather satchel, revealing an array of electronic instruments, several smartphones and a miniature screen and keyboard. At the security checkpoint in O.R. Tambo airport in Joburg, he'd shown his state-issued permit to the officer and, as usual, had been waved through without a search. He recognised the CCTV camera above the door; it was a popular commercial range using Cloud connectivity. It took him a couple of minutes to identify its signal on his diagnostic screen and he froze the screen and cut the sound detector, without switching it off. He then added the IP address of his screen to the camera menu, so that it transmitted simultaneously to him and the unknown occupants. He took three smartphones from the satchel and linked them also.

A moment later he'd opened the Yale locks on the door and was inside the apartment. There were five rooms; two bedrooms at the back, a living room and kitchen and a large office facing the street, with closed blinds on the windows. In the office, he installed a WiFi voice transmitter on the underside of the desktop, hidden with black tape and linked to the CCTV unit. Via the camera, he'd be able to see what the occupants could see on the landing and hear what was said both inside and outside.

There was a large, old-fashioned steel strongbox standing against the wall and he considered trying to open it. It was a three-key model with a keypad, and he knew it was impossible to do it in the time he had available. The same went for a smaller safe under the desk and a bank of filing cabinets with padlocks; mechanical locks had never been Coetzee's forté, Yale locks were easier. He took several photos of the room, checked that there was no sign of his entry, then went out and relocked the apartment door. Standing at the top of the stairs again, he unfroze the camera system and ensured that the picture was being received on his phone. It would register a pause of about 10 minutes, but the owner would see nothing untoward, since there had been no movement or sound recorded.

Coetzee walked down the stairs and across to the petrol station and joined Franz Stenmark for another coffee. 'Now you don't need to stand outside all the time if it's freezing or pissing down.' He handed the SwissGerman the smartphone and showed him how to locate the CCTV channel. 'It's an anonymous prepaid phone, untraceable. It's just a gift from a friend, so you've done nothing wrong. Keep it safe.'

Stenmark looked at the screen showing the empty corridor outside Jolidon's office. 'Is there any point in continuing with this outside surveillance?'

'Unfortunately, yes. We can't monitor comings and goings without someone watching the building. I'm going to Geneva this afternoon and I'll talk to Pedro Espinoza. Maybe we don't need such an expensive, high-powered guy kicking his heels here. I'll call you later and we'll sort it out. By the way, that room in front with the blinds is the office.' He described the layout of the apartment.

Coetzee checked the time, finished his coffee and shook hands with the agent. 'Thanks, Franz, it's been good to see you again, take care.'

He pulled the wheelie bag out of the café and crossed the road towards the bus stop, just in time for the next bus to the central station, where he would take the train to Geneva. There was one leaving at 13:00, so he had time for a meal.

Franz Stenmark watched the South-African get onto the bus. His feelings of inferiority hadn't been diminished by that morning's exhibition.

FORTY-THREE

Thursday, November 28, 2019
Geneva, Switzerland

It was just after 10am when Jenny and the others arrived at the Mandarin-Oriental and were shown into the sale rooms. Although they all carried a copy of the Drewberrys' catalogue and had leafed through it many times, nothing could have prepared them for the real thing, it was far beyond anything they'd anticipated. They walked slowly past the succession of cabinets, each laden with beautifully crafted precious stone and metals, the last containing impossibly large and seemingly priceless emeralds, diamonds, sapphires and rubies. Unlike Esther Bonnard, the previous day, they admired the beauty, not just the value of the 1,200 pieces. When they reached lot no. 900, Jenny gasped, and tears came to her eyes. She now knew for certain they were her father-in-law's diamonds from Angola.

Leticia took her hand. 'We were right, there's no doubt at all.'

Jenny nodded and wiped her eyes. 'Right, time to allocate lots,' she said, and they returned to the main room, comparing their catalogues with the physical valuables and making notes on the pages to confirm the reserve prices and the session when they would be sold. It took them an hour to identify all the items labelled, *Private Investment*

Trust; there were 110 of them, with reserves ranging from thousands of Swiss Francs to CHF1.5 million for the diamonds.

'That's everything, and they're all being sold on Friday and Saturday. That makes our job a bit easier,' Jenny announced and ushered them out of the sale rooms. As they walked down the corridor to the lobby, she suddenly stopped and turned to examine a painting on the wall. It was an old, hand-coloured engraving, a landscape, showing a view of the *Lac Léman* in 1867.

'That's pretty. I didn't know you were keen on old engravings.' Leticia stood beside her to admire the picture as two men, conversing in French, walked past them towards the exhibition rooms.

Jenny waited there until the men had disappeared into the ballroom, then took Leticia's hand and hurried to catch the others up. They walked away from the hotel and she said, 'That man in the dark suit was the fellow I saw in Zurich. We were right, he must be Christen, the *huissier*.'

'*Ojalá*, lucky break,' Espinoza exclaimed. He looked around, 'Wait in that café on the corner and we'll go back in to find him, so we'll know him in future.'

The women were enjoying cups of hot chocolate when they returned, Jenny sitting with her back to the window. 'I'm sure that was one of the conspirators, the notary. He must have been involved in the fire and Gilles' death. And he certified a fake inventory which doesn't contain Charlie's briefcase or the diamonds. He looks so ordinary, it's hard to imagine he's a murderer and a crook.' She shuddered at the mental image. 'I definitely can't appear at the sales, in case he sees me, but now you know what he looks like and you can keep your eye on him.'

Espinoza's mobile rang and he moved away from the table, speaking quietly for a minute or two. 'Coetzee will be at the Métropole at 5pm,' he announced as he sat down again.

'He's finished at the apartment?'

'I imagine so. You know Coetzee, he doesn't waste time on explanations. Anyway, he wanted to be sure you've booked him into the same hotel. Apparently, he needs some sleep, I can't for the life of me think why.'

'When you told me yesterday evening, I booked him in and got their last room. I think it must be the Royal Suite, it's costing a fortune.'

'And he'll probably sleep on the floor,' laughed Patrice.

'If he's given us eyes and ears into Jolidon's office, he can sleep on the roof if he likes.' Jenny became serious again, 'Now, Leticia and I are meeting Madame Aeschiman in a half-hour, so let's agree on the final list of lots and the total requirement.'

Geneva, Switzerland

'Thanks for receiving us on short notice, Valérie, I know how busy you are. This is my dear friend, Leticia da Costa Moncrief, Emilio's mother and my co-signatory on his trustee account.'

'*Enchantée*, Mme da Costa, it's a pleasure to finally meet you, after, what is it, nine years? Emilio must be almost 15 years old now.' Valérie Aeschiman shook her hand, marvelling at the woman's appearance. Leticia was now forty-three, but could have passed for thirty. Even after having two children she still retained the striking beauty she'd inherited from her Angolan parents.

'*De même, Mme Aeschiman*,' she now spoke four

languages fluently, after living in Spain with a French husband and English friends, plus her native Portuguese, which she would never lose.

'That's enough showing off, I'm not going to embarrass myself by attempting to speak in French.' Jenny sat at the desk and patted the other seat for her friend. 'Valérie, this has to do with the problem we talked about last month, Ramseyer, Haldeman. But first, I have to apologise, I wasn't totally honest with you. There were valuables in the security box and it belongs jointly to Leticia and I.'

'There's no need to apologise, Jenny, I suspected as much. You were so shocked and distressed I realised it must have been an important matter. If there's something I can do to help, I'm at your disposal, as always.'

'Thank you. We have a plan of action and it will require quite a large investment. We want to remain as anonymous as possible and we thought you could help us to do that. Let me explain what we have in mind.'

A half hour later, the two women walked back across the bridge to the Hôtel Métropole, Jenny clutching her handbag tightly. The envelope inside contained a letter of credit issued to '*Durham House Investments Ltd*' by the *Banque de Commerce de Genève*, in the amount of 5 million Swiss Francs.

Luxembourg, EU

'The lawyers have got a few picky points on the contract, got to justify their fees, but basically, we'll have a deal to sign tomorrow. Congratulations, Harry. I think you paid over the odds, but you have your reasons and it's not my business.'

'And the OTC registration?'

'They'll have it filed first thing Friday morning. BMH can execute its option as soon as it's registered. I'll need to send them the first refusal renunciation letter from Olympic, do you have it?'

'I've got it ready. I'll send it as soon as I ring off. Don't forget to erase the email after you've saved and printed it.'

'No problem, send it right away and I'll forward it from my own saved file.'

'Thanks and well done, Guillaume, you earned your fee, as usual.' Harry paused, 'One more thing.'

Fric said nothing, wondering what was coming next.

'There'll be a lot of noise around this, it'll be a big story. People will be asking the same question as you; What's happened to warrant a 100% increase in Atlantic Offshore's valuation? There must be no answers from BMH or anyone else, especially nothing about Olympic or me.'

'I told you, Harry, you're not involved. As a matter of fact, neither of us is involved. It would take a brigade of lawyers and tax agents to find who's behind BMH and they'd need a criminal subpoena. It's not in anybody's interests to help them. Don't worry, Mum's the word, I know how to play the game; you should know that by now.'

Fern-Chapman ended the call and found the letter of renunciation on his laptop. He changed the date, attached his electronic signature and forwarded the PDF to Fric, with a note; *Don't forget to delete.* Relieved and delighted at Fric's news, he poured himself a beer and called Esther, it was almost 1:00pm. She'd probably be having her pre-lunch cocktail of champagne and peach schnapps.

Geneva, Switzerland.

'Hello darling, how's everything going over there?'

'No problems, Harry. Apart from missing you, as usual. I saw it's raining in London, is it miserable?' Esther was in the bar at the Richemond, on her second cocktail, trying to fill in time during the sales days; she was desperate to attend, but knew it was the worst thing to do. She'd called Christen, who'd told her the morning viewing had been very busy, with a lot of interest in their lots. She was hoping it would materialise into good prices, so she could afford to be generous with him and get things back to normal.

Fern-Chapman said, 'Just a typical, rainy London work day. When are you getting back?'

'I'll be finished on Sunday, arriving in the evening at Terminal 5, I can't wait.'

'Email your flight details and I'll pick you up, the motorway will be quiet. I assume you're making piles of money.'

'It's looking promising. How about you?'

'Sorry, privileged insider information, I could be arrested if I divulge anything. You'll have to wait until next week to find out, but you won't be disappointed. Love you, see you at Heathrow on Sunday.'

Geneva, Switzerland

'How do you do, Monsieur Tournier? It's a pleasure to meet you,' Patrice said in French as he handed the Drewberrys Swiss MD a visiting card, showing his name as Financial Director of Durham House Investments Ltd.

'That's a very English name for a Bahamas company,' Tournier answered in perfect English.

He switched languages, 'You're quite right, the owner is English, but has businesses in several countries. You know how it is these days, everything's multi-national.'

After a few minutes of small talk, Tournier asked, 'So what can I do for you, M de Moncrieff?'

Patrice handed him the letter of credit. 'I wanted to establish our credentials for this week's sales. We intend to acquire quite a lot of items, and I hoped to arrange a reasonable buyer's premium.'

Tournier glanced at the document, seemingly unimpressed. 'Our standard fee up to that amount is 13.5%. As you know, we don't charge a seller's fee, so we have to cover our costs somehow.'

Patrice said nothing and after a moment, he added, 'I could exceptionally offer you 12.5%, but I'm unable to go lower. You won't find a better rate with any other house.'

'Then I appreciate the offer, let's agree on 12.5%.'

'Excellent. May I make a copy of this LOC for our files? It's normal practice when we provide accreditation to new clients.'

It took only a few minutes to complete the documentation and Tournier said, 'I hope you manage to acquire the items you've chosen. I look forward to seeing you at the sales. Thanks for deciding to become part of the Drewberrys family, I'm sure you won't regret it.'

'By the way,' said Patrice, 'we're interested in lot no. 900, the Angolan cut diamonds. I know that they're not subject to the 2000, Kimberley process, that only concerns rough diamonds, but I suppose you've satisfied yourself that they are not conflict diamonds?'

'Of course. We insisted on a certificate from the owners; I can't show it to you because I'm not allowed to reveal the sellers' name, but if you're fortunate enough to win them, you'll naturally receive the document.'

The two men shook hands and Patrice left him, happy that he'd fulfilled his mandate. *Durham House Investments Ltd* was now an accredited client of Drewberrys Auction House Ltd, subject to the terms and conditions of their live auction sales rule book. *Now it's game on; my kind of game*, he said to himself.

FORTY-FOUR

'How are they doing, Guillaume? Their lawyers seem to be making a mountain out of a molehill. This is the best deal they've been offered in the life of the company, why isn't it done?'

'Calm down, Harry. Best or not best deal, it's a $30 million transaction and they can't afford to fuck it up, especially with the Brexit complications. Your strategy was spot on, but it's not simple. You know that EU law never uses one word where ten will do, so just be patient, we'll be through this by this evening.' He paused, 'Hang on, they've just sent me a revised contract. I'll read it through and call you straight back.'

Harry waited impatiently for what seemed like an hour, praying nothing had gone wrong. Fric's name came up again. 'So?'

'Everything's agreed, they've made a couple of changes, but nothing of any importance, just to earn their fees. But there's one snag.'

'What is it?'

'They want an original signed letter from Olympic renouncing the right of first refusal.'

'But you gave them the one I sent you, no?'

'They've got that, but the lawyers are saying if Brexit goes ahead and there's ever a dispute over a future transaction, they want to be able to show an original document, not an electronic one. I hate to admit it, but they're right, that letter could have been faked.'

Fern-Chapman looked at the time, it was almost 5pm, he realised he'd started sweating. 'So what am supposed to do? We need this deal finished tomorrow morning; I can't get a courier service to guarantee to get it there in time.'

'You'll have to bring it yourself, Harry, it's the only solution.'

'Shit! Let me check the flights, I'll call you back.'

Fifteen minutes later, Fern-Chapman was booked on a Luxair flight, leaving Heathrow at 20:15, returning from Luxembourg with KLM at 13:00 on Friday. He quickly packed an overnight bag, checked that the letter was in the Atlantic Offshore file and threw his laptop and the file into the bag and ran downstairs for a taxi. Now, he was really sweating.

Geneva, Switzerland

'Cheers, Marius. It's wonderful to see you again, wonderful and totally unexpected. Thanks for coming, it means a lot to us.'

'My pleasure, Jenny. I wouldn't pass up a chance to see you and your friends again. And to sleep in the Royal Suite; even the bed is bigger than my farmhouse.' He raised his glass, 'I'm glad I could be useful at the same time.'

Strangely, Jenny had known Marius Coetzee since 2010, but had never met him or his wife Karen in person, until they came over to London for Leo and Abby's wedding in 2018. Unknowingly, she echoed Karen's thoughts, *It seems I only contact him when I'm in some kind of trouble.*

He gave her the second smartphone he'd programmed at the apartment and explained how it worked, showing her how to find the CCTV channel. 'That's all you see outside, just an empty corridor, unless someone comes to the door, but no one has, since I was there. Franz just called me, he's feeling fairly useless. I got a couple of photos of the inside, nothing special except that steel strongbox, must weigh a ton.'

The others passed the photos around. 'That's the key to this dreadful business, no doubt about it.' Espinoza shook his head, thinking of Ricardo and their time together on the *Camino de Santiago*.

Coetzee asked, 'What's this really about, am I allowed to know?'

'It all goes back to my father-in-law's death, in 2008,' Jenny said. 'The short version is, Charlie had placed valuables in a security box and they've been stolen.'

He didn't miss a beat, 'Right. And you think they're in that apartment in Zurich?'

'We're pretty sure of it, that strongbox seems to confirm it.'

'So why are you all in Geneva?'

'Because the thieves are selling them here at the auction sales.' She handed him the catalogue, showing the photograph of lot 900.

'Wow, fabulous stones!' He nodded his head, 'Clever buggers! That's hard to prove, unless Charlie left a receipt or some kind of document that shows they were in the box.' He looked around at their blank expressions. 'He didn't. OK, so what's the plan?'

'There's a lot more besides just the diamonds. We'll tell you over dinner.'

Delmas, Mpumalanga, South Africa

'My word, Marius, you don't often call me when you're travelling on business, what's wrong?'

'I'd like you to do something for me, Karen, and before you ask, yes, it's for Jenny, really.'

'I see. And does that involve flying to Geneva?'

'No way, I know you hate flying. You can do it at home and it's actually something you'll enjoy. Intellectually stimulating, better than watching over the security business.'

'Marius, stop selling! What's this about?'

She listened in silence as Coetzee repeated the stories he'd heard from Espinoza and Jenny that evening. 'My God, poor Jenny and Pedro. Those diamonds are cursed, they've brought nothing but bad luck.'

'Karen, this is not about the diamonds, it's about the crooks who are after them and probably have been since Charlie was killed. These people, whoever they are, are murderers and criminals and they've hurt our friends. We can help to stop them and maybe even catch them red-handed.' He explained the plan they'd discussed that evening. 'We're going to need an expert to back it up, I think you could be that expert.' He explained his idea to her. 'Will you do it?'

'How much time do I have to graduate?'

'Less than two weeks, but it's a piece of cake for you, you could learn Chinese in that time.'

'No need to butter me up, Marius. What about arguing the case, if necessary?'

'We can do it on a video link, no need to fly anywhere.'

Coetzee slept well in his enormous bed, happy that he

might help to resolve a few problems for his friends. Maybe it would also relieve Karen's boredom and thirst for knowledge for a while.

Zurich, Switzerland

'Another wasted day, no one and nothing in sight. It's already pitch-black outside and freezing, but at least it's stopped raining.' Franz Stenmark was making his daily report to Javier. 'I'm still wondering what's the use of me hanging around here when we can see everything that's happening - which is zilch - from the camera.'

'We're expecting someone to return to the apartment tomorrow or Sunday, so you've probably only got a couple more days. It's not worth changing now, we'll review things again on Sunday, OK? Just think of all that money you're making for sitting in a café.'

FORTY-FIVE

Friday, November 29, 2019

Luxembourg, EU

'**Are you happy with it?**' **Harry Fern-Chapman was reading through the contract a second time,** not having made a single change. He was in Guillaume Fric's office; it was 7:30am and the lawyer's staff wouldn't arrive for another hour. Fric had watched him quietly, until now, as the Englishman read the final page again.

'It's OK. Like you said, twice as long as necessary, but they haven't changed any material points.'

'So, we can go with it?'

'I've got a flight at 1pm, tell them we need it signed by 11am. I want to take it with me.' He took the printed letter of renunciation from his Atlantic Offshore file, signed it and handed it to Fric. 'I've signed in blue, to show it's original. Here you go, make a photocopy of it for me and don't tell them it almost caused me a heart attack.'

Aware of the potential consequences, the lawyer studied the letter carefully. 'This isn't correct,' he announced.

'What do you mean?' Fern-Chapman's heartbeat shot up.

'It's dated November 26th, that was Tuesday, the day you wrote it. It should be today, the 29th. That's when you're handing it to me.'

'Damn, of course, sorry, it's all this rushing about,

thanks, Guillaume. I'll link up to your printer and change it.' He pulled out his laptop. 'What's your WiFi password?' When he'd acquired the printer connection, he pulled up the PDF from its file. It still had his electronic signature attached and he removed it, modified the date, then printed it out. He replaced his signature and saved it again.

Fric checked the printed letter carefully, 'OK, you can sign this one.'

He scribbled his name. 'Can we please finally get this bloody deal done, Guillaume?'

'I'll email them now to set it up,' the lawyer said.

'Great, please bring the contract to my hotel as soon as you get it signed.'

Lugano, Tessin, Switzerland

'Don't you know I'm on holiday? It's not even 8am.'

'*Bonjour*, Claude. Sorry, but the sales start today, and I just thought you'd like to know how things are going here, and of course, with René Christen.'

'OK, what's happened? Anything I should worry about?'

'I don't think so. The exhibition looks great and the valuables you chose are perfect. We should hit our numbers, up around four million, for sure.'

'Thanks, and René?'

'That man drinks like a fish, I've never seen anything like it, but he seems to function just as well, it's incredible. He gave me a hard time; he's not happy and wants a much better deal.'

'What did you say?'

'I walked out to show him I wasn't impressed with his attitude, but I called him yesterday and we agreed to discuss it when we know this week's results.'

'So, he'll be OK during the sales?'

'Of course, it's in his interests to get the best possible result before we renegotiate his deal. That's why I'm calling.'

Jolidon didn't miss the implication. *So, she expects me to participate in his new deal. She can forget that. I like René and he deserves a lot better, but she's got the most to lose if he gets difficult and refuses to sign on the fiduciary account.* 'I don't want to get involved in any negotiations, it would just confuse things,' he said. 'And then we'd end up renegotiating both deals. I don't think you want to go there, do you?'

Merde, he's smart and he's right; one unhappy partner at a time is quite enough. 'Fair enough, I hired him and agreed his deal; I'll work it out with him. Don't worry, as soon as we see the sales results, I'll get it sorted. Enjoy Ticino, *Ciao.*'

Geneva, Switzerland

'This morning's just for watching and learning the ropes, there's nothing in this first session we want to buy, they're all low value items.' As the person most familiar with the auction process, Patrice was rehearsing his troops, prior to going to the Mandarin Oriental to attend the 10am sale. 'Stéphane Tournier's allocated two seats for us, the room's going to be very busy, so we'll take it in turns to occupy our places and rotate, and no one will stand out unduly. Watch the process, it's not complicated, but look for the serious buyers; they usually come in late in the bidding. It frightens the amateurs off, unless they've simply fallen in love with the item, then you just have to wait to see how far they'll go. The professionals have a firm limit and they don't get carried away. We'll do the same, come in late and scare the tourists off if we can.

'You should make a couple of early bids this morning, just to get the knack, but drop out before the end. We'll start buying at this afternoon's session from our list. All the items we want are up this afternoon, this evening and at the three sales tomorrow, then we've got nothing to do on Sunday. Remember, you represent Durham House Investments Ltd, and we're accredited buyers; the auctioneer knows we have a decent budget, so you have status. Anything else, Jenny?'

'Just to thank Marius for his idea of getting Karen involved, it could make all the difference to the outcome. Now, have fun everyone, sorry I can't come along.' She would dearly have liked to be part of the action, but knew it was too risky.

'Take a look at the Zurich CCTV image on the mobile. You might see something happen.'

'Not likely, Franz Stenmark is getting paid to watch that, I'm going early Christmas shopping, try to find some fun things for the children.'

Geneva, Switzerland

René Christen looked around the busy sale room with satisfaction. A few faces he recognised and even more he didn't. He was standing at the side of the room where he could see everyone and everything. The bidding for the cheaper valuables was going well, some goods selling well over their reserves. The *African Benevolent Trust* had 27 pieces in this first session, all estimated at under CHF15k; it wasn't a big deal but a very good test of buyers' interest.

As always, he was keeping a tally of the hammer prices; all of their lots had exceeded the reserve prices so far, a total of CHF160k, and he was jealously impressed by Claude Jolidon's ability to pick out highly saleable valuables from the steel strongbox in his office.

If it continues like this, we'll hit that 4 million Swiss Franc mark, he said to himself. *Then Esther will have to make me a really serious offer if she wants the proceeds to leave the fiduciary account. That means a million, anything less and we're all going down together.*

All 100 seats in the converted ballroom were occupied and there was a small crowd standing behind them; he knew that would increase over the weekend, the excitement of an auction was contagious, and a lot of the crowd were just there to watch. Simon Tomlin, the English auctioneer, was at a table on the platform at the head of the room, on one side of him was Daniel Altermatt, the Drewberrys notary who was the legal official at the sale, and on the other a young woman at a laptop. A large screen behind them showed photographs of the valuables, the results as the bidding progressed, then the final result, sold or unsold. So far, almost every lot had found a buyer at the reserve price or better. At the side of the room was a long counter, with a bank of telephones, only a few were in use at the moment, but Christen knew they'd all be busy on the high-value sales days with phone-in bidders. On the other side were two dozen agents on their mobiles or tablets, representing overseas buyers, in addition to the online customers, whose bids would be monitored by Altermatt.

Christen noticed a change in the allocated seating area, an attractive woman, who had made a few early bids, but dropped out quickly, was leaving seat no 47. The front section of 60 seats were assigned by Stéphane Tournier, the Drewberrys Swiss MD, *which means she must have passed the accreditation test. So, she's a high stakes bidder,* he told himself, *not interested in the cheap stuff.* He'd seen her talking to the man in the adjacent seat, no. 48, who was still sitting there. He was smartly dressed, wearing a suit and tie, *could be a banker*, Christen thought, but the man had also made a few desultory bids before dropping out quickly.

The woman's place was taken a moment later by a solid, tough-looking fellow with a tanned face and dark hair, cut short, military style. He spoke briefly to his neighbour then looked around the room and his eyes met the *huissier*'s. He nodded and smiled, but the smile didn't reach his eyes.

The beauty, the brains and the brawn. Maybe some kind of a syndicate, high-class criminals perhaps. That would be good news, they'll be keen to spend their funds; launder their spoils and help push up the prices. Crooks buying stolen goods with stolen money. What goes around comes around. Christen supressed a smile and made a mental note to check the accreditation list for seat numbers 47 and 48. He was sure they'd be spending money in the bigger-value sales, otherwise they wouldn't be there. The *huissier* had a good feeling about this auction and about the new deal he'd be able to negotiate with Esther Bonnard afterwards.

After the hammer came down again on the next lot, the could-be banker got up to vacate his chair. Christen noticed that he left his catalogue on the seat, and it was quickly picked up by the man who replaced him, an older, shorter chap, with receding red hair. *Definitely a syndicate,* he decided.

Espinoza looked through the catalogue, noting the prices marked by Patrice against the *Private Investment Trust* lots, all in excess of the reserves. *They're getting good prices*, he thought, *I hope our credit line is enough for the job.*

'You see the man in the dark suit standing at the back?' Espinoza whispered.

'Looking around at the bidders and making notes after each sale?'

He nodded, 'We think he's Christen, the notary.'

'That's the guy Jenny saw in Zurich?'

'It is, but we don't want to draw attention by asking anyone, it might alert them.'

'Right. But if it is him, we can't have him standing there right through the sales, it'll look suspicious, all of us only bidding for the trust merchandise.'

'Then we need to bid for other goods and drop out before it gets serious. That will look less suspicious. We'll tell the others to do that.'

'And maybe I'll have to sort something out, keep him away somehow.'

The Spaniard knew Coetzee had ways of doing things he wouldn't approve of, so he said nothing.

The morning session ended at 12:30, all of the *African Benevolent Trust* items being sold and fetching CHF410,000. *Almost 50k over the estimates*, Christen calculated, *un excellent début!* He left the hotel and took a bus to his apartment to pack a bag and get something to eat, with a couple of glasses of wine. Then, pulling his travel bag, he went for the tram to Cornavin station in time for the 2pm train to Fribourg. It would get him there at 15:33 precisely; his appointment was at four o'clock, for one of the most important meetings of his life. He was too preoccupied to spot the man who'd followed him from the Mandarin Oriental, waited outside his flat, photographed him and watched him climb onto the train.

Coetzee walked back to the hotel to make his switchover with one of the team. *Why is he on a train to Fribourg if he's busy selling millions of francs of valuables?*

Luxembourg Airport, EU

Harry Fern-Chapman placed the contract signed by Guillaume Fric, on behalf of Benelux Mineral Holdings, and Gérard Boillat, for Atlantic Offshore Oil & Gas Ltd in the file in his travel bag and shook the lawyer's hand. 'Thanks again, Guillaume, you've done a good job. Call me this evening after you exercise the OTC purchase and send your invoice to my private email address. It'll be paid immediately by BMH.'

In the cab to the airport, he called his secretary. 'Just thought you'd like to know I'm feeling a lot better. I'll check with the doc this afternoon and if nothing changes, I'll see you on Monday morning. Have a great weekend, Mandy.'

His KLM flight was on time and he would arrive in London, via Amsterdam, at 4.30pm. Esther was arriving on Sunday evening and he'd come back to Heathrow to pick her up. He'd have great news for her and she'd never know he'd been anywhere but Belgravia.

FORTY-SIX

Friday, November 29, 2019
Geneva, Switzerland

'Thank you, sir. Twenty-one thousand, I have twenty-one thousand francs, do I hear twenty-two? Anyone? Madame, do you want to follow?'

A woman in the second row shook her head, 'No? Very well, I'm selling at CHF21,000. The auctioneer banged his gavel, 'Once, twice, three times; for the last time, at CHF21,000, sold to the gentleman in row five.'

As the sale result appeared on the screen and was translated in French over the tannoy, Espinoza nodded and marked the price against the item in the catalogue, lot number 320, a ruby and diamond ring set in platinum. He'd had to bid 20% over the reserve to clinch the purchase, the sixth of the *Private Investment Trust* items, all of them so far in that Friday afternoon session. He took out his notepad and added it to the summary sheet he was keeping. The Spaniard liked writing things down, it helped him to think clearly and work out a plan of action. So far, he had spent CHF85,000 and Leticia, sitting next to him, had notched up CHF72,000.

Following his suggestion to Coetzee, they were also bidding for other items and pulling out when the battle between the serious buyers started. The Angolan woman glanced at his calculations and winked at him; she was thoroughly enjoying herself, buying lovely jewellery with no price limit, so far. Leticia da Costa had the feeling she was finally doing something useful, something to pay back the awful people who had murdered and terrorised her family and stolen her son's inheritance. She leaned closer to the ex-chief inspector, '*Parece que te estás divirtiendo.* Look's like you're having a good time.'

Espinoza put his hand over hers, 'It's the first time in my life I've had so much money to spend. I think it's going to my head, I'll leave you to buy the next items, while I recover my senses.' He looked around the saleroom again and saw that the notary, Christen, still wasn't present. *I only hope Coetzee didn't hurt him too badly*, he prayed.

The auctioneer announced, 'A magnificent pair of diamond earrings by Cartier, each half a carat, marquise cut, set in white gold. I'm starting at twenty-five thousand Francs. Do I hear twenty-seven?'

Espinoza was about to whisper, 'Off you go,' when Leticia waved her catalogue. 'Thirty thousand,' she called. He realised she wanted to cut the session as short as possible. He didn't disagree.

Geneva, Switzerland

'Thank you, ladies and gentlemen, that's the end of this afternoon's session, thank you for attending and participating in a very successful sale. I look forward to seeing you all again at 7pm this evening, meanwhile, I think you deserve a glass of champagne in the lobby bar, courtesy of Drewberrys.' Simon Tomlin, the auctioneer, packed up his papers and walked out of the saleroom, shaking hands with several participants as he passed.

Marius Coetzee and Patrice were now occupying seats

47 and 48; they stood up and stretched their bodies. 'Well done, Patrice, so far so good, you've set this up very well.' He looked at the summary sheet which he'd inherited from Pedro Espinoza. 'We got all fifteen lots from the Private Trust, total cost, CHF320,000. I'm glad it's not my money, I'd be having nightmares. On the other hand, I don't have that kind of money, so I guess it would never happen.'

They walked out to meet Espinoza and Leticia in the nearby café. Coetzee was still puzzling over the *huissier*. 'I wonder why Christen didn't come to the sale.'

'I thought you'd arranged that?' Patrice said, surprised.

'Who told you that?'

'Pedro, said something about an accident.'

'I don't believe it; he thinks I'm a killing machine. I've never laid a finger on him, but I'm surprised he's not here. I saw him go off on the train to Fribourg at two o'clock. With millions of francs at stake, if he is the notary, you'd think he'd be watching the shop.' Coetzee's suspicious mind was telling him something wasn't right, but he put it aside. 'Why don't you call Jenny, she'll be wondering how we're doing, tell her the good news, good guys plus fifteen, bad guys minus fifteen.'

Fribourg, Switzerland

René Christen had been acting his heart out for an hour, the tears came to his eyes as he explained what had gone wrong with his investment of the misplaced funds from the family trust. He confirmed that he'd placed the money with a reputable currency trader and showed a copy of an agreement between himself, on behalf of the Comina Family Trust, for five hundred thousand Swiss Francs to be managed by *Multi-Currencies Ltd*, a UK company, with an address in Brighton. The agreement was dated over three years previously, nine months before his bankruptcy.

'There's a guaranteed minimum return of 10% per year,' he told them, taking out copies of bank statements from his dossier. 'Look, you can see the dividend credited on the last day of each quarter.' He pointed out a regular credit entry of CHF12,500 since the date of the contract. 'The last payment was on September 30th; you've never missed a dividend.'

This much was true, he had personally sent the amount every quarter to avoid or at least delay any suspicions for as long as possible. 'The original contract is in Raphaël's files,' he added.

'We found it, René, and of course we believe you,' said, Nicole, the widow. 'It's just that Serge tried to contact that company to check on the contract, and he couldn't find them. There seems to be no such company in Brighton. That's why we called you, we're rather worried, it's a lot of money for the family and we need it, what with the inheritance taxes and all the costs we've had since Raphaël's passing.'

Christen's brain was working at high speed. 'Of course, now I understand, I should have told you; I apologise, but with my personal problems and being away from Fribourg, I completely forgot. When the Brexit threat became severe, they moved their offices to Brussels, because they have so much international business. I've got their number here in my dossier, I'll call them. He looked up a number and called from his mobile. 'There's no reply,' he said and pressed the speaker button so they could hear the phone ringing.

'No surprise there,' Serge said, 'it's after 5pm on a Friday. They'll be closed for the weekend. That means we can't sort this out before Monday. I'd better call our lawyer and tell him the situation, I promised to keep him up to date. He couldn't come today, but he said he'd be available in the morning, if we needed him.'

'How soon do you need the funds?' Christen asked, 'I can probably arrange to cut the contract short if it's urgent, I think it's a 30-day notice period.'

'Are you staying in Fribourg tonight? We could meet Hans tomorrow and agree on everything so you can arrange to terminate the contract.'

He's a smart man, the notary realised, *not as naïve as I thought, but this could work in my favour*. 'That's a good idea,' he answered. 'We can execute an instruction to terminate the agreement and I'll make the arrangements on Monday.'

René Christen walked away from the Cominas' house, thanking his lucky stars. At tomorrow morning's meeting he was sure he could win a month's reprieve then get back to Geneva in time for their big sale item, the Angolan diamonds, lot no. 900. He called a friend's number to arrange a free night's accommodation. He was making progress, but he wasn't out of the woods yet.

Belgravia, London, England

Harry was in a cab from Paddington when the lawyer called. 'BMH exercised the option this afternoon. Congratulations, they've acquired 3,000,000 shares of Atlantic Offshore Oil & Gas. I just hope you know what you're doing; $30 million is a bunch of money.'

He checked the time, 5pm; *perfect for this evening's market news*. 'Don't worry, Guillaume, you'll find out soon and you won't be disappointed.'

It had stopped raining in London and the city was quieter than usual. He sat back in the taxi seat, feeling better than he had for a long time. *This will change everything. Harry Fern-Chapman is not so easy to bring down.*

Geneva, Switzerland

'Altogether, in the two sessions, we bought 35 pieces out of a possible 36, for a total investment so far of CHF780,000.' Patrice handed Jenny Espinoza's summary sheet. 'Tonight, there was a very lovely and determined lady who wanted a pearl and diamond necklace at any price, so we finally let her have it. But overall, we calculate they've netted CHF440,000; and we're at almost twice that. If we can keep this up tomorrow, we'll be in a very strong position.'

They were sitting in the bar of the Métropole, with a glass of wine and snacks, it was 9:30pm and no one wanted supper at that hour.

'That's great, Patrice, well done all of you, but our line of credit is for five million. So tomorrow, I want you to buy every single lot, including Charlie's diamonds of course, no matter what the price. If we break the budget and anything goes wrong, I'll cover it. I hope that's clear.' Jenny looked around the table, challenging any unlikely objection to her instructions.

'Jenny's right.' It was Coetzee who spoke. 'We've got them by the ankle at the minute. Next is the balls and then the throat. Otherwise it's just another game of ladies' tennis.'

There was a moment's silence, then Patrice said, 'I'd better order a second bottle of Burgundy.'

Later, after calling to say goodnight to Karen, Marius Coetzee lay awake for a while, his mind churning. *Why wasn't the notary there? What was he doing on a train to Fribourg? It means something and I wish I knew what.*

Fribourg, Switzerland

'Esther, I hope it's not too late for you.'

'Hello, René, thanks for calling. It's never too late if it's good news.'

'It's not good, it's great. Everything sold! We're way over budget. CHF1.22 million against reserves of a million, right ahead of the game.'

She felt a thrill of excitement. 'That good, eh?'

'Better than good; great atmosphere, great punters and, more importantly, great prices. It was a fabulous day and tomorrow is going to be even better.'

'That was worth staying up late for, I hope you're right and we can hit that magic four million number, then we can sort out your concerns. Thanks again and *bonne nuit*, René.'

The notary switched off his mobile. Fortunately, it was not a video call, since the sight of the *huissier* in his underpants might have caused Esther some concern. He had looked up the auction results via his online access. As seller's representative, he could see real-time results of the sales, but no information about the buyers. It didn't matter to him who they were, as long as he could convince Esther he'd been at the sales. Seeing the hammer prices, he'd been even more excited than her and it sounded like she was ready to talk sensibly. His gamble was looking better every minute.

He opened the bottle of Chivas Regal he'd bought at

the supermarket and poured a couple of glasses, went into the living room where his friend was watching TV in the nude. '*Santé* Michel, it's great to be back in Fribourg,' he lied.

In Geneva, Esther called Claude Jolidon and relayed the good news. 'If it keeps up, I should be able to make René an offer he can't refuse, put these disagreements behind us and get on with making us all rich.'

Jolidon just grunted. He was busy calculating his 25% share.

FORTY-SEVEN

Saturday, November 30, 2019
Edinburgh, Scotland

'Good morning, Harry. That was a stroke of luck. Saved by the bell.'

'Sorry, Alex, a bit too early for me. What are you on about?'

Olympic Group's Corporate Managing Director laughed. 'Don't tell me you didn't know about the Atlantic Offshore transaction?'

'Atlantic? All I know is that I refused to pay an exorbitant price and agreed to renounce Olympic's right of first refusal. Why? Has something happened? I've been out of it with a bug for a couple of days.'

'You missed their big deal then. Yesterday, they sold 3 million shares at $10. Twice the price Olympic paid last year.'

'Shit! I thought they were trying it on when they asked me. Who paid that price?'

'Some private investment company out of Belgium, Benelux Mineral Holdings; never heard of them, have you?'

'Doesn't ring a bell. Atlantic didn't mention a name when they offered me the deal.'

'When was that?' Cameron asked.

'On Wednesday, when I was recovering from the flu, but I didn't take them seriously. That's why I agreed to drop our first refusal right.'

'I was wondering about that, what happened?'

'They told me they'd had an offer at \$10 and did I want to exercise our right. When I refused, they asked me to confirm it. So I emailed them a renunciation when I was up and about again.'

'But you don't know why BMH would bid that price?'

'Sounds like someone knows something. Maybe I should have a closer look.'

'You're still missing the point, Harry. Three of our funds hold twelve and a half million shares between them. Plus, the markets were still open when the news got around yesterday and there was some buying in. They've all gone up by over 4%, so you're finishing the month at less than 4% down instead of almost 10%. Year on year, you're actually in the black and I think Monday will continue the trend.'

'Shit! I must still be groggy, I wasn't thinking. That means there's no question of suspension of any of them; thank God for Benelux Holdings, whoever they are.'

'Right. We'll postpone next week's meeting and I hope you get more good news before the end of the year. Well done; that was a great pick and I'm really happy for you and for Olympic. Take care and have a great weekend.'

Harry put his mobile down, a tired smile on his face. *So far, so good. It looks like it might work, at least for the time being. Now, all we need is for Boris to pull it off and we should be out of the woods.* It had cost him all the money he had, but he would have lost everything anyway, if he hadn't taken the risk. *All in all, a good decision*, he thought, and went to fix himself a coffee.

Edinburgh, Scotland

Alex Cameron hung up then rang his assistant's mobile.

'Sorry to disturb your weekend, Moira. I want you to do an in-depth investigation into a Belgian company. You have a pen handy? It's called Benelux Mineral Holdings and I'd never heard of them until they just popped up on the last day of November to save Fern-Chapman's Olympic Group from suspension. It all seems a bit too convenient to me. Get onto it as soon as you can, please, see if there's more to it than meets the eye.'

South Kensington, London, England
'Atlantic Offshore Oil and Gas Share Value Doubles after OTC Transaction.'

Dr Hugh Middleton was reading the Weekend FT in the tube on his way to visit the Natural History Museum, when the article on page 13 caught his attention. Despite a predominantly negative point of view, honed by many unfortunate experiences in his earlier life, he envied success, and enjoyed reading about it. His attention was suddenly captured by the journalist's final paragraph: *'The main beneficiaries of this unexpectedly generous share transaction, apart from the founding Boillat family of Luxembourg, are Olympic Fund Group, the only other shareholders in Atlantic Offshore, holding 12.5 million shares in several of their funds. Olympic Fund share prices rose on average 4% after the announcement and subsequent buying in the European and US markets.'*

Well, well, well, Middleton said to himself. *This deserves some examination. What are the chances of a little-known company, a lot of whose untradeable shares are held by Fern-Chapman, receiving an offer of twice their market price just when Olympic Funds are in the doldrums?*

He knew the answer to his rhetorical question was, *slim*,

but how he might prove it was, for the moment, beyond him. He folded up the newspaper and got off the tube to stroll to the museum. His weekend treat.

Luxembourg, EU

Guillaume Fric couldn't refrain from laughing when he read the article. *I should have seen through that scam from the beginning. Well done, Harry.* Then, as lawyers always do, he considered his position. *It's a very dodgy deal; definitely 'Insider Trading' if it comes out.*

If it was exposed as a criminal act; was he vulnerable? He reviewed the facts; he'd received instructions from Andorra-Dubai Holdings Ltd, the Bahamas shareholder of BMH, to negotiate a share purchase. BMH had bought the shares with funds from its own bank account. Where the money came from was not his concern and in truth, he didn't know. Neither did he know who was the ultimate owner of BMH, since he had no visibility of the ownership of the Bahamas company.

He filed the article away in the BMH dossier and checked again that he'd double-deleted all of Fern-Chapman's email documents and deleted the calls on his mobile. Fric considered changing the phone, but it was far too complicated and he could do that if it became necessary. He went back to his statement of fees to BMH, increasing the total by 50%. *Harry can hardly complain*, he decided, *I've just helped him save his business.*

Geneva, Switzerland

'Why didn't you call to tell me?' Esther sounded upset.

'Sorry, darling, I couldn't tell you until it was finalised and I've been busy with phones and emails since then, I just forgot. Anyway, you know about it now and I hope you're happy.' Harry had decided to play a different role with Esther; he needed her to believe that he'd brokered a great deal, saved Olympic Funds and her investments into the bargain.

'Four per cent up, that means I'm making money again. Well done, Harry, I hope this is just the start of the improvement you've been promising.'

'Absolutely. There'll be more activity when the markets open on Monday, all positive. Then when Boris wins his mandate, you're going to see terrific returns. Maybe not as good as in Geneva, but a solid performance, just like I promised. How is everything there, by the way?'

'It's looking good. We should have a lot to celebrate when I get home. Things couldn't be better.'

Fern-Chapman put his mobile away, relieved that Esther's mind was back on track. As always, he wondered what she was doing in Geneva and how it was so profitable, but he knew better than to ask, it was obviously a touchy subject.

Geneva, Switzerland

'Mission accomplished, Oh Exalted and Worshipful Leader. She who must be obeyed.'

Jenny giggled, 'That's enough of that, Patrice. Just the results, please.'

He handed her the summary sheet, updated with that morning's sales results. 'We bought all 18 items, making a total of 52 lots for an investment of CHF1,300,000 to date.'

'There's some really beautiful pieces, Jenny. You'd love them.'

'You know I don't get the occasion to wear jewellery like that, Leticia, I'm not married to a high-flying banker. Anyway, that's great news, well done. Does that mean we've got them by, excuse me, the balls now, Marius?'

'We'll be there by this afternoon, then tonight we go for the throat; death by five million Swiss Francs, or is it ten? I'm losing count.'

'We've just got time for a sandwich and glass of wine, I booked a table for 12:30.'

They walked through to the café and she asked, 'Was it very busy? I'd love to have been there, must be a great atmosphere.'

'It was packed, I've never seen so many people trying to get rid of their money all at the same time.' Espinoza shook his head, 'It's like a bear pit, everyone waving their paddles or catalogues, shouting out bids. Especially Leticia,' he laughed.

'I know. I got a little carried away, Pedro, but I didn't miss a single item.'

'Actually, Jenny, you could have come, Christen wasn't there. I'm starting to wonder if the man we all saw really is the notary, or maybe we're on the wrong track. It can't be normal to miss auction sales where you're selling 4 or 5 million francs of stolen goods. It doesn't make any sense.'

At 2pm, Leticia and Coetzee were back in seats 47 and 48, Coetzee peering around the crowded room for the man they assumed was the notary.

'He's still not here,' he whispered to her. 'There must be someone else watching over the sales, but I can't see the wood for the trees in this crowd.' Coetzee didn't understand what was going on and when he couldn't understand something, he worried.

'Forget it for now and get your paddle ready,' she said. 'You're buying the first lot.'

Fribourg, Switzerland

'This should be sufficient.' Hans Unterhelm handed René Christen a two-page document.

The *huissier* checked the time. It was after 2pm. He'd have to get a move on to be back in Geneva for the evening auction session, featuring the Angolan diamonds. He put the document on the desk so the lawyer wouldn't notice his hand trembling and read it with mixed feelings of relief and apprehension. Either he could convince Esther to give him the money or he was down the toilet, but now he had a month to work it out.

'*Das ist perfekt, Hans, danke.*' He signed the paper with a flourish.

A half-hour later, after many apologies and a glass of schnapps, to compensate for his hurt feelings, Christen was in a taxi on his way to catch the 3:35pm train to Geneva. He'd make it to the Mandarin Oriental in plenty of time for the evening auction at 7pm. The train was almost empty and he accessed the auction website to check the morning's results. He felt a shiver of excitement; once again, every lot had sold at well over the reserve prices.

Esther's not going to be able to short-change me after these results, he told himself. He didn't feel like speaking to her and sent a text with the good news. *She might get the implicit message as well. All the better.*

Then Christen lay back in his seat and caught up on his sleep, it had been a tiring day, and night.

Geneva, Switzerland

Esther read the text as the *huissier* had intended. She knew he was still unhappy with her and would remain that way until she made a significant gesture. But if the sales results continued like this, it wouldn't cost her much, it would mostly be the cream off the top. And Harry's news was the icing on top of the cream, she was making money hand over fist now; things were going so well, nothing could stop her from achieving her dream, the dream that Ray d'Almeida had instilled in her; her rightful place amongst the world's wealthy.

She didn't call Claude Jolidon, she'd wait for the afternoon and evening results and bombard him with good sales results, *I'll be the queen bee, especially if the diamonds sell well.*

Geneva, Switzerland

'We've still only missed that one item, from yesterday. The tally is 68 out of a possible 69, for a total of CHF1,850,000, I think we've reached Marius's ball control point.' Patrice handed Jenny the updated summary. They were in the lounge at the Métropole, reporting on the afternoon sale, delighted that everything had gone according to plan.

'We're not having to bid so high, I noticed,' Espinoza said. 'I think the other serious buyers have seen that we really want the items we bid for and they're giving up more easily.'

'But we're still paying consistently higher than the reserves, so, whoever these *Private Trust* people are, their overall sales proceeds will be looking good to them. And, it's the Saturday evening sale next. It'll be even more packed, so I expect there'll be some silly bids.'

'Do you think anyone might be suspicious that we're only buying the *Private Trust* items?'

'I don't think so, the advantage is there are two auctioneers working alternately, so it's less obvious than one person seeing it at every session. It's Rupert Jennings, the senior guy, at tonight's session.'

'I don't think Drewberrys care,' said Coetzee. 'Every successful hammer price is another 12.5% in their pocket; they don't give a shit. And by the way, that guy wasn't there again; I'm still wondering who he is and if he's been replaced by someone I haven't spotted.' He shook his head in frustration.

'OK, let's work this out. We've spent about CHF1.75 million and there are 12 remaining lots plus the diamonds this evening with total reserves of about CHF2 million. Assuming a worst-case scenario, let's say 2.5 million, including the buyer's premium we should still be comfortably within our budget.'

Coetzee said, 'That's fine in theory, but if we don't get Charlie's diamonds, this whole plan has been for nothing. We have to buy them at any price.'

'Agreed, Marius, we've got to get them,' said Jenny.

'Right,' Patrice pulled his hand across his neck, 'throat time.'

At that moment, a loud ping sounded, and Coetzee and Jenny looked at their mobiles. 'It's the Zurich CCTV.' He simultaneously activated both connections and the others crowded around to see.

The camera in the Zurich building showed a man, wearing a cap and with a scarf around his face about to swing something at the lens. Then the screen went dark.

FORTY-EIGHT

Saturday, November 30, 2019
Zurich, Switzerland

'Did you see that?'

'I sure did, he's smashed the unit. Sorry, I was just about to leave, it's really dark here now. I went to the toilet and missed him going into the building, but I figure it's the same guy who came the other day.'

'Can you get over there and grab him?' Coetzee asked.

'You're forgetting, I don't have a mandate for that, but I'll try to get a shot. The audio is still working and it sounds like he's trying to get into the apartment,' Stenmark responded.

'He's hiding behind a scarf, get a clear picture if you can.'

'I'm going across right now to wait inside the lobby, I'll do my best.'

'Send it to Javier, OK? We've got to go into a meeting now.'

'OK, will do, have a good meeting.'

Lugano, Switzerland.

'Fuck, *merde, putain.*' Claude Jolidon looked at the blank screen on his mobile. His reaction had also been fast enough to catch the moment of the attack. *What the hell does that mean? It's the same guy who's been a few times. Who goes around smashing CCTV cameras?* He could hear noises over the audio feed; the man was trying to open the door. Then the sounds stopped and there was silence. Relieved, he checked the time; the evening sale, their last, would be starting in 30 minutes; the largest reserve values, plus the diamonds. Was there a connection?

He thought of calling Esther, she wouldn't have been alerted, but decided to wait until he knew more about what was going on. He hesitated, then pressed Christen's name on his mobile.

Carouge, Geneva, Switzerland

René Christen was on the tram, on his way to the Mandarin-Oriental for the evening sale. He'd taken a shower, changed his outfit, had a snack and celebrated with a half bottle of Chasselas to control his nerves. This was the most important sale he'd ever attended, it could make or break him, and now he was sure it would make him. He'd accessed the afternoon results online and seen that every item had sold well over the reserve prices, bringing the total to date to over CHF2 million. With the evening lots, plus the diamonds, it was certain they would break the four million barrier.

He'd sent a quick text to Esther, to show he was on top of things. This was just the argument he needed for his meeting with her. He was confident he could sell her his proposal, maybe do even better, so he'd have some spending money until the next sales in February.

He was thinking about his discussion with her when Jolidon's name came up on his phone. 'Claude, how's the Tessin? I hope it's warmer than Geneva.' His mood quickly changed as he listened in silence to the Frenchman. 'And you didn't recognise him?'

'He had a cap and a scarf around his face, and it was only a split second before the camera went dark. He didn't get into the apartment, but I was worried it might be to do with the sales. Is everything alright there, no trouble?'

'I'm standing outside the salesroom now,' Christen replied, 'it couldn't be better. You must have had the results from Esther until this morning? It continued this afternoon; it's been a terrific day; we're selling everything like ice cream on August 1st. We're at over CHF2 million now and we'll double it at tonight's session. I don't know what happened in Zurich, maybe a disgruntled client, looking for his valuables, but it's not going to change anything here. Don't worry, you're going to make a lot of money.'

'I didn't tell you, but the same guy's been a couple of times, just visiting. Now he comes back with a hammer. I suppose you could be right, just an unhappy client, but I'm thinking about moving office again. Esther and I were talking about it a while ago. I'd better call and tell her what happened.'

'Don't do that, Claude. Wait until we've got great results to announce and it will be just an insignificant event.'

Reluctantly, Jolidon agreed, Christen didn't want anything to upset Esther Bonnard's mood until he'd extracted his money, every penny of it.

Geneva, Switzerland

'We've got to get back to the sales. Franz will call Javier if he gets a photo or there's anything more to tell.' Coetzee and the others put on their coats.

'OK, I'll hold the fort here. Good luck, and remember, throat time.'

Jenny was in her suite when Javier called. 'Franz managed to get a shot, it's not great, the guy was running out the door. I'm sending it to you and Coetzee now.'

'How long had he been upstairs?'

'He waited in the lobby for him about ten minutes, not more.'

'And did he go up see what had happened at the apartment?'

'Yes, Marius was right, the guy tried to get in. Stenmark said someone tried to open the Yale locks. There was a broken piece of a plastic membership card on the floor, but the door was still locked.'

The photo arrived on Jenny's phone and she put on her glasses, squinting at the small picture. 'Hmm, he's still well disguised, but you can see his eyes this time.' She paused, wondering why he looked somehow familiar.

'Do you recognise him?'

'I don't know. There's something in the eyes that rings a bell, but I can't bring it to mind.'

'I hear the plan's working well, we're getting what we want.'

'That's right, it's a great plan, thanks to you and Pedro. But tonight is the clincher, we need the diamonds to make this work, so they've got to make sure nobody else gets them.'

He rang off and Jenny looked at the photo again. There was something she recognised, but she couldn't put her finger on it. She put it aside and made her regular evening call to Elsie, making sure all was well with Ellen, Chester and the other visitors at York House.

Delmas, Mpumalanga, South Africa

In the two days of researching online since Marius' call, Karen Coetzee had printed out enough articles from the Internet to form a substantial book. Her mind clear on how to present the idea, she called George van Wyk, the Features Editor at the *Johannesburg Sun*. After her acrimonious divorce from Marius in 2008, Karen had moved to the farmhouse in Delmas with Abby and given up her full-time career as an investigative journalist, finding a job at the local winery. The editor had begged her to accept a monthly assignment which she could manage from home; she was their star journalist and he didn't want to lose her. Karen jumped at the offer, she knew she'd go mad without intellectual stimulation. Besides, the pay from the *Sun* was more than she made from her job at the winery. The arrangement had been beneficial to both parties, Karen was still a widely read writer on many controversial subjects, with almost 200k followers on Twitter, Facebook and Instagram, and the *Sun* circulation and online reader numbers took a hike every time her articles appeared.

Van Wyk was now Editor in Chief and when Karen outlined her proposal, he was immediately hooked. They spent an hour discussing various approaches to the article. 'We'll have to run it by the lawyers,' he told her, 'but we'll be able to syndicate it all over the world, I love it.' Mentally thanking Marius for the opportunity, she experienced a feeling she didn't get very often these days, the feeling of making a difference. They agreed on a 10-day delivery for legal approval and publication in the Saturday edition in two weeks' time.

Karen took the dossier out onto the porch, sat down

in her most comfortable chair and started her in depth research into the subject matter.

Geneva, Switzerland

At 18:55, Marius Coetzee and Leticia de Moncrieff took their places in the fifth row, seats 47 and 48, for the sixth session of Drewberrys auction week. Pedro and Patrice were waiting for their changeover in the bar. As they sat down, Coetzee whispered, 'The notary's back, did you see him?'

She shook her head, 'Where?'

'Sitting by the telephones along on the left.'

She glanced over. 'Does that worry you?'

'It would have done if it wasn't the last sale. There's no chance he can screw things up now, even if he wonders why we're buying all his lots. I just wish I knew why he wasn't at the other sales. If he really is who we think he is.'

René Christen had managed to get there early, with time for another glass of wine in the bar, before taking his seat in the saleroom. *Beauty and the beast, still here*, he registered, *excellent*. He hadn't had time to check who they were, but their accreditation for the second day meant they had a lot of money to spend.

Rupert Jennings, the senior auctioneer, walked onto the podium; Daniel Altermatt, the *huissier* and the woman assistant were already at the table. 'Good evening, ladies and gentlemen, welcome to the Saturday evening session, the sixth in this week's Drewberrys auction sales. We have 100 beautiful items to present to you, so we'll waste no time. Please open your catalogues at lot no. 801. This magnificent Patek-Philippe 3940J gentleman's watch/chronometer is dated 1990 and is considered one of the greatest complicated automatic wristwatches of the twentieth century. It features a perpetual calendar function powered by a 22k microtor, indicators for the leap year, month, date, day, day/night, as well as moon-phase. It is accompanied by its original certificate and sales receipt in a Patek Philippe wallet. Who will start the bidding at CHF35,000?'

Once again, bidding was strong and the first five lots sold at good prices. The sixth, the first of the *Private Investment Trust* items was a diamond and emerald pendant. 'I love this piece,' Leticia whispered to Coetzee as her final bid was accepted.

'Shame you'll never get to wear it,' he answered, squeezing her hand.

In the first hour of the session, they bought all seven of the goods they wanted, leaving five more for Patrice and Espinoza to acquire, plus Charlie Bishop's diamonds. They'd tossed a coin to decide who would get to bid for the top prize; the losers were most disappointed.

At the changeover, Leticia called Jenny, who was waiting nervously in her room. 'So far, so good. We've got the first 7 items for just under CHF300k, so the others have got a good budget for the rest. By the way, that man you saw is back again, he was watching us every time we bought something, I think you were right that he's the notary.'

'I knew it. Good work, Leticia. And Javier sent me a photo of the person who broke the CCTV camera in Zurich, but I don't recognise him, maybe something in the back of my memory, but I can't think from where. Are you and Marius coming back to the hotel now?'

'Patrice thinks it will look more normal if we wait until the end, like members of a company or syndicate would do. We should be back by 9:30pm. We're going in to watch from the crowd. Anyway, Jenny, I want to be there when we buy our diamonds back.'

FORTY-NINE

Saturday, November 30, 2019

Geneva, Switzerland

René Christen was drunk and very nervous. He'd watched all 10 of his lots that evening go under the hammer to the group he'd labelled as 'the syndicate' and he was wondering why. He'd noticed that they had made offers on many other items, but always pulled out when the bidding got serious. On the *African Benevolent Trust* valuables, they had always won the final bid. So far that evening, they had bought everything with good premiums; he couldn't complain at that, but he had a nagging feeling that it wasn't a coincidence. After his near escape in Fribourg, then the incident in Zurich and several glasses of wine, he felt very anxious. He'd tried unsuccessfully to find out the names of the buyers of the 97 pieces sold in the previous five sales, when he was absent, but the information wasn't available.

At the moment, the older man was bidding for their last lot before the Angolan diamonds, a solitaire 2 carat diamond ring, and he seemed determined to get it at any cost. He finally bought it at 20% more than the reserve, looking delighted, and offering a high-five to his partner, the banker. Christen calculated that the diamonds would come up in 15 or 20 minutes. He left the saleroom and went into the auction office, where there was only a young woman working; everyone else either assisting at, or simply enjoying the bidding battles.

He pulled himself together, trying to sound like a notary. '*Bonsoir Madame*, I'm Maître Christen, the representative of *The African Benevolent Trust*, I'm sure you've seen my clients' name, we have over 100 items in the sales.'

'*Bonsoir, Maître*, I've certainly seen your client's name. What can I do for you?'

'I've been watching this session and I wondered who the bidders are in seats 47 and 48, I seem to know them from somewhere.'

She consulted her files. 'We're not supposed to divulge buyer information, but since you're a notary representing a substantial seller, I'll make an exception. It's a company called *Durham House Investments*.'

He scribbled the name down. 'Thank you. Have they bought many items before this session?'

'I'm afraid I can't give you that information, but they have been very active throughout the sales, that's all I can say.'

Christen checked the time, went into the bar for another glass of *Chasselas*, then came back to the crowd at the back of the packed saleroom. He pushed his way through nearer the front, from where he could see the two men were still sitting, watching the bidding for lot 894.

Patrice saw him from the corner of his eye. 'Make a few bids on the next lot, Pedro. That notary fellow has just come back in, try to fool him for a while.'

Espinoza was becoming quite an expert at measuring the intensity of the audience, he made four bids, then dropped out before the finale. 'I'm not sure this is the best tactic,' he whispered. 'Do we still have a good margin?'

Patrice checked his figures. 'We should be well under 5 million, including the premium. What do you have in mind?'

'There's a lovely pearl and diamond necklace coming up now, very traditional, much more Jenny's style, with a CHF25,000 reserve. Why don't we get it for her? She'll be delighted and we might fool the notary.'

'My turn,' said the banker. Waving his catalogue, he called out, 'Twenty-six thousand.'

Christen watched the hammer come down on Patrice's last bid of CHF32,000 for the necklace. *Maybe I was wrong about them*, he thought. *They just happen to like Claude's choice of jewellery.*

At 9:20pm, Rupert Jennings announced, 'Now we come to the highlight of this evening's sale, lot number 900. A collection of very rare Angolan, cut diamonds, certified by the owners to date from before the 1974 Portuguese Revolution, when the subsequent civil war in Angola caused the closure of the diamond mines. There are 100 diamonds in this collection, weight ranging from 0.5 of a carat to two carats, with a total of 105 carats. Our experts rate these exceptional stones as purity finest white, clarity VVS1 and VVS2, round brilliant cut, and without doubt of Angolan origin. I'm starting the bidding at CHF1.5 million, do I hear more?'

Espinoza and Patrice watched for a minute or two, the catalogues, paddles and hands going up until the bidding was at CHF1.8 million. There was a hum in the room, it was by far the highest bid so far in the sales, the audience was becoming involved, the atmosphere was electric

'Do I hear CHF1,850,000?' asked Jennings.

'Time to make a move,' said Espinoza, holding up his paddle.

The noise from the crowd increased until Jennings had to shout to be heard. 'Thank you, the gentleman in row 5. I have one million eight hundred and fifty thousand Swiss francs for these rare and exceptional diamonds from pre-independence Angola. Is there a higher bid out there?'

René Christen was still standing in the crowd at the back of the room. He had drunk almost a litre of white wine and his tiredness was catching up. He saw the under-bidder shake his head. It was the jeweller who had bought the previous lot of diamonds at the Binghams sale. I can push this price higher, he said to himself. *Guarantee that Esther will pay me what I need.*

Rupert Jennings announced, 'No more bids? Very well, ladies and gentlemen, I'm selling at CHF1,850,000. Once, twice....'

Christen pushed forward and waved a catalogue 'One million nine hundred thousand francs,' he called, then stepped back into the crowd.

After another rush of noise around the room, there was a sudden hush, everyone looking around the room for the new bidder. Rupert Jennings had seen only a catalogue being waved, he didn't know if it was a genuine bid from an accredited buyer or an enthusiastic bystander. He turned to ask Daniel Altermatt, the notary, if he could identify the bidder. There was a resounding silence, a silence that beckoned a response, all eyes now on the ex-policeman from Malaga, the under-bidder in the saleroom.

Patrice said nothing, just placed his hand on Pedro's sleeve, knowing he would make the right call.

Watching from the back of the room, Leticia closed

her eyes and grabbed Coetzee's arm, praying silently that Pedro wouldn't lose his nerve. Coetzee was disinterested; whatever the outcome, he knew he could sort it out.

Pedro Espinoza didn't hesitate for a moment, he didn't know where the bid had come from, but now, winning was everything, losing was not an option. He rose to his feet and called, 'Two million francs.'

'Thank you, sir,' Rupert Jennings looked around the room. 'I have two million Swiss Francs. Do I hear another bid, or are we finished? No?' He paused, 'Once, twice, three times, I'm selling at two million Swiss francs.'

No one heard him announce, 'SOLD'. The noise level in the saleroom had exploded; everyone was on their feet, applauding the outcome of this battle between an elderly Spanish Gentleman and an unseen, unknown usurper. It was clear who they were rooting for. Surprisingly, so was the losing bidder.

'I think you just became a rock star,' Patrice said, putting his arm around Pedro's shoulder and hugging him close. 'Well done. You bought back Jenny and Leticia's diamonds.'

FIFTY

'Good morning, Esther, I hope you slept well.'

'Like a baby, thanks. I suppose you got the good news from René?'

'Not a word since yesterday afternoon, what's happening? How was the last session?'

'Not bad. We sold every single lot, like all the other sessions. How does 4,7,1,0 sound to you?

'We broke the 4 million barrier by 700 grand? Wow! That's the best news I've heard in a while. Kind of puts things into perspective.'

'What do you mean?'

Jolidon told her about the attack on the apartment. 'I didn't want to tell you until after the sale, it might have caused some negative vibrations.'

'Did you get a look at the attacker?'

'No, it was a split-second thing. Same guy as last time, wearing a cap and a scarf around his face. No idea who he is, but I'm betting a client who was pissed-off at never getting an answer to the door. I think he tried to get in, but wasn't able to, I would have heard it from the audio feed, that's still working. I'm going there tonight to see what it's like. Don't worry, I'll get it fixed, but, like you said, we need to think about moving house.'

Esther had a moment of panic. 'You don't think it had anything to do with Jenny Bishop's visit? Maybe a hired hard man to cause us problems?'

'That's not how Ms Bishop would behave. She'd engage a smart lawyer to argue her case, not some berserk maniac with a hammer. Definitely not her style.'

'Yes, you're right, of course, I'm just nervous, after such a great sale, we can't afford any trouble in Zurich.'

'Let me go up there and check things out, worrying doesn't help.'

'OK. I wish I could come with you, but I'm meeting with René in an hour, then I have to get back to London. And Claude, I agree on moving the office, as soon as possible.'

'Definitely, but it's impossible before I get the next sales organised. Call me when you've settled things with Christen. Good luck, and don't forget, he's unfortunately irreplaceable.' He switched off, reflecting on her reaction. *She sounds very nervous, that's not like Esther. It's the thought of all that money; it's getting to her. That's all we need, an alcoholic huissier and a hysterical woman.*

Geneva, Switzerland

'You must all be exhausted. Thanks for keeping the faith; getting 81 lots out of 82, it can't have been easy.'

'82 from 83, actually,' Patrice said. 'We thought you might like this.' He handed her a smart leather case, with a pink ribbon tied around it.

Jenny carefully opened the case, to reveal the pearl and diamond necklace. She removed it and held it up in the light. Tears poured down her face. 'Ellen, my mother-in law had one just like this, you must have known. It's beautiful, I can't thank you enough.'

Leticia fastened it around her neck, and she admired it in the mirror, 'I may never take it off.' She embraced them all. 'How did you get it out of the saleroom by itself?'

'I told them the truth, it's a personal item, for a friend, nothing to do with Durham House, so they let me pay for it and take it right away.'

'Well, I'm very touched and delighted, thanks once more to you all. Now,' her school-teacher persona took over again, 'Let's see where we are.'

Espinoza produced his final summary sheet. 'We wrapped things up within the budget, four million two hundred and seventy thousand Swiss francs. With the buyer's premium, the whole bill is 4.8 million. There was a last-minute panic with the diamonds, someone, we didn't see who, threw in a bid at one point nine. We weren't expecting that.'

'But Pedro held his nerve and we got them for 2 million. Bravo, Señor Espinoza.'

He shook his head. 'I'm a policeman, trained to follow instructions. Jenny wrote the script; I just played my part.'

'The only thing that counts now is that we own almost all of the Private Investment Trust's lots. We bought everything except for about CHF400k, probably not enough to cover their expenses.' Coetzee raised his fist. 'Time to stiff it to them.'

'How is Karen doing?' asked Patrice.

'She's spent three days researching, reading and learning and she's got the syndicated newspaper article lined up, so I guess she'll be typing soon. Don't worry, she'll produce the goods in time.'

'Right, it's over an hour before we have to leave for the airport, why don't we go down to the lounge and celebrate with a glass of champagne. It's after ten in the morning; it must be apéritif time somewhere in the world.'

Carouge, Geneva, Switzerland

There was a ringing sound, but René Christen's befuddled brain couldn't work out where it was coming from. Finally, he realised it was his mobile and he struggled to get up and catch the call. His head was pounding and he felt like throwing up. After calling Esther on Sunday night with the final sales figure, he'd had a couple more glasses of wine to toast the result, then managed to get back to his flat in a taxi, where he'd collapsed, fully clothed on the bed.

'Good morning, René, we fixed our meeting for 10am and it's almost eleven, are you coming?' Esther Bonnard sounded annoyed.

He sorted out his scrambled mind. 'Sorry, Esther, I had to come back to the hotel to certify the final sales report. Just finishing. I'll be at the Richemond in less than an hour.' He staggered into the bathroom, took a paracetamol, threw some cold water on his face, cleaned his teeth, changed his shirt, then rushed out to catch a tram to the hotel. The listing was ready for him at the Drewberrys office and he signed it and affixed his stamp, revelling in the number on the bottom, CHF4,710,000. *A million more than Binghams*, he marvelled, *she can't refuse me with a result like that.*

The 10-minute walk in the cold along to the Richemond cleared his head and he was feeling almost normal when he went up to her suite. In his pocket he had a tube of mints and he popped one in his mouth then rang the bell.

'Well, well, what a fabulous result. Congratulations,

René,' she shook his hand. Unlike the huissier, she had lain awake for hours after his call, counting her money over and over in her mind. Her share of these proceeds was $3 million. She still had $1.5 million in Bahrain and $3 million with Olympic. *Seven and a half million dollars*, she repeated to herself again and again, her head spinning at the thought of her wealth. Finally, she'd fallen asleep, dreaming of sailing down the Adriatic in a beautiful yacht, mooring in tiny ports and lunching on deck in front of the jealous passers-by. Esther had plans and now she had the money to pay for them.

Her mind turned to the problem of Christen's demands, 'Sit down, René. Tell me about that last sale, it must have been incredibly exciting.'

Christen decided to change his tactics. 'I have to say that Claude is good at picking saleable items. Everything sold with great premiums, he did a superb job. Then when the diamonds came up, I managed to play a role myself.'

She waited for the dramatic pause, 'What happened?'

'The bidding was at CHF1.8 million and the under-bidder dropped out.'

'And?'

'I made a bid myself for 1.9 and the remaining bidder went to 2 million.'

'So, you pushed the price up by CHF200k? But you're not allowed to bid on your client's lots.'

'I know, but I was in the crowd and no one knew where the bid came from. Before the auctioneer could take a decision, the buyers panicked and *voilà*, we made 200k more.' He didn't mention his concerns about the buyers, *Durham House Investments*, he had more pressing matters on his mind.

She looked at his self-satisfied smile, unable to work out whether he was embellishing, or telling the truth. 'That's terrific, René, well done, 200k is not to be sneezed at. And it makes it easier for us to talk about your bonus. The other night, you told me what you don't want, but not what you do want. If you want me to change a deal that we shook hands on, I need to know what you're expecting.'

His demeanour changed immediately; the smile replaced by a serious, anxious expression. 'I have a very specific need, Esther; it's urgent and can't be negotiated. If we can agree on the amount, we can continue to work together and, hopefully, make a lot of money. But if we can't, then I'm afraid the party's over. It's a serious problem and if it's not resolved, it will rule out my involvement in future sales and could even affect the sale we've just finished with such a great result.'

A shiver ran down her spine, 'Tell me about it.'

'It's not something I'm proud of, it happened when I was divorcing and being made bankrupt; I was desperate. The short version is that I need an extra half a million Swiss Francs within 30 days, or I'll probably go to prison.' He sat quietly, watching her calculating what this meant to her.

Half a million francs, that's not what I was expecting! Let's think. I'll receive about 3 million after expenses. If I agree and pay him the difference, I get about 2.5M net. Hmm, that's more than I got from the Bingham's sale, which is not a bad result. Plus, if he really did push the diamond bids up by 200k, it's actually only costing me 400k.

'You say you'll probably go to prison if you don't raise the 500k?'

He shrugged nervously. 'Not probably, definitely. It's money that went missing from a trust account. I've got 30 days to pay, if not, they'll call the police to come and arrest me. You'll need a new *huissier*.'

Merde! That's the real problem. We've got three sales lined up in February; just 3 months away and without Christen, we can't enter our merchandise. Aloud, she said, 'That's almost a million francs altogether, more than 20% of the proceeds, I can't pay that for every sale.'

He leaned forward in his chair and she noticed the stale smell of wine on his breath. 'How about 15% going forward? If we keep hitting four million on each sale, I can settle the rest of my debts a lot sooner. That's what matters to me, to clear my name.'

That leaves me with 60%. It's a good deal for everyone. 'Very well, René, I agree. But I don't want to discuss it again, ever, understood?'

Christen stood up, an overwhelming sense of relief flooding over him. 'I won't forget this, Esther.' He put out his hand. 'And I promise I won't bring it up again. Thank you.'

He turned to go, 'By the way, Claude told me about the visitor at the office and the CCTV camera, if there's anything...'

She cut him off, 'We're on it already, Claude's going to look for another solution. Leave it to us, we'll sort it out, just concentrate on getting us ready for February. Three massive sales; with your new deal, you'll be out of the woods.'

He nodded and went to the door, and she said, 'Watch the drinking, René. The mints might fool some people, but not me.'

Lugano, Tessin, Switzerland

'How did it go with René?'

'I've just spent an hour with him; what an incredibly complicated man. I wish to hell I'd never engaged him, but unfortunately you're right, we can't get rid of him. Anyway, it's all settled and it won't cost you a penny, I hope you're happy about that.'

'Great, so we're in good shape for the next sales. That's quite a relief.'

'Maybe, but I'm still worrying about the CCTV incident. I don't think some innocent client, however unhappy he might be, would take a club to the camera. And why would he be hiding his face in the first place? There's something behind this, it could screw up our plans when we're preparing for the big numbers in February.'

'I'll call you when I get there tonight, if there's anything to tell you. And I'll start looking around for another office for the beginning of the year. OK?'

The petrol station café closed at 5pm and Franz Stenmark stood outside until he could hardly feel his freezing limbs or see across the street in the dark. He gave up at 7pm and went across to take the bus home for the night. He waited to climb onto the platform for a man with a suitcase and a heavy shopping bag who was getting off. Too late, he turned and saw him walk into the entrance of no. 819. He hadn't seen the man's face clearly, but he was skinny, had lank hair and was wearing tight jeans under a heavy coat. He switched on Coetzee's mobile and heard the sound of someone opening and closing the apartment door.

Stenmark called Javier, 'I think he's back.'

FIFTY-ONE

'**Morning, Harry, how are you feeling today? Shaken off the bug?**' Tom Newman came into his boss's office, carrying two coffees.

'Thanks Tom. I'm in great shape again, especially after the Atlantic Offshore deal. What a lifesaver that was. And the Eastern markets picked it up this morning, we're up another point and I'm sure the European markets will follow suit.'

'A 5% bonus, totally unexpected, eh? Who are these people, Benelux Mineral Holdings? Do you know them?'

'Never heard of them until Alex Cameron told me about it on Saturday, but I'm going to find out who they are, what they know, why they paid that price. There must be a reason and it has to be valuable to our funds.'

'But you must have given up our right of first refusal in their favour, otherwise…'

'That's not what happened. Atlantic Offshore called me when I was sick in bed and asked me if I'd pay $10 per share. I told them to piss off and they asked me to lift the refusal rights for 3 million shares. At that price I didn't think it was a serious offer. Maybe my brain wasn't functioning 100%. Anyway, that right of first refusal is headed for the dustbin when Brexit gets done, it won't wash with Brussels and the European Court of Justice, so I figured it's not worth making a fuss over and it could earn us some brownie points with Atlantic.'

'OK I get it. I'll need a copy of your renunciation, I suppose you emailed it to them.'

'When I got off my death bed, that's right. I'll send you the file, but it's only for 3 million shares. You never know, if we find out what the Belgians know, the right over future transactions might still be worth something.'

The CFO turned to go, 'Oh, by the way, did you get your personal stuff sorted out, everything OK?'

'Sorry, I forgot to thank you for the quick transfer, it was in good time and everything's just fine. Thanks, Tom, it's appreciated.'

Newman left the room, wondering how his boss had managed to discuss a share deal with Atlantic Offshore, then email a renunciation of Olympic's refusal rights to them, as well as sorting out a $2.5 million personal matter, all while he was lying sick in bed with flu.

Before he forgot, Harry found the PDF letter in his laptop and emailed the file to Tom Newman. *Another problem solved.*

Belgravia, London, England

Esther was having a lazy morning. Her return the previous evening had been passionate and exhausting, Harry relieved by Olympic's last-minute salvation and she buoyed up by the fabulous sales results. He'd gone off to his office early, after seeing TV reports of more upward movement in the Far East markets; she'd never seen him so positive and bullish.

'We could hit six or seven per cent uplift today,' he'd

said as he kissed her goodbye.

Then Claude Jolidon had called her from Zurich. She breathed a sigh of relief when he said there was no sign that anyone had been in the apartment. 'I've switched off the CCTV system completely, I won't get it fixed right away, don't want anyone inside the apartment while I'm busy getting things ready for the February sales,' he told her. 'But I'm getting a third lock installed on the door tomorrow, a different type, just for extra insurance. Next week I'll start looking for a better solution. This place has served its time.'

Esther felt a twinge of apprehension, 'You're right. I never liked that apartment, it made me feel dirty.'

She started thinking about the sales results again and called René Christen. 'Drewberrys payment terms are 10 days, right?'

'10 working days, so it's effectively two weeks, Monday to Monday, but that's the maximum period, most clients like to settle sooner. Don't worry, I'll be chasing them at the end of this week. I'm just as keen to get my money as you are.'

I bet you are, she thought. *A million Swiss franc 'Get Out of Jail' card, that's what it is to Christen, straight out of my pocket into his.*

Marbella, Spain

'I got a call from Franz last night, he thinks Jolidon came back to the apartment about 7pm.' Javier repeated what the Swiss agent had told him.

'He's right, I heard the door being opened and sounds from inside through the audio feed, then it cut out. He must have closed down the system.' Coetzee swore, 'That was a waste of time, going up there to break in and plant that tap. Now he'll get it fixed and they'll find it and he'll be looking out for someone watching him. We'll be no further forward.'

'Not exactly, Marius.' Espinoza was listening on the call. 'Now we know Jenny was right about Jolidon, and probably Christen as well. We know there's a third party trying to get into the apartment, and they know it too, which is good, it takes the pressure off us. And we had a most successful trip to Geneva. All in all, I think we haven't wasted our time. Be patient, and in a week, when we're ready, Karen will step in and we'll start things moving in our direction again.'

'Sorry, Pedro, what I really mean is, do you want me to stay here, or go home?'

'Let's have a talk with Jenny. She's amazingly lucid about all this.'

Edinburgh, Scotland

'Benelux Mineral Holdings isn't a Belgian company. It's South African.'

Alex Cameron looked up from his briefing papers. 'Bugger. Sorry, Moira, but that's not going to make things easier to understand. What did you find out about them?'

'Nothing. It's an SA company, bearer shares, with a corporate director, a Belgian outfit called *Econovest Bruxelloise SA*, also bearer shares. All I could find out about them is that the director's a Luxembourg lawyer called Guillaume Fric.'

'We'll get nothing out of him, professional whores, the lot of them. Even his name, it means 'money' in French slang.' Cameron looked frustrated. 'Nothing further we can do, we'll just have to pray this deal's on the up and up, otherwise it could come back to bite us.'

Marbella, Spain

'Nothing's going to happen until next week, Marius, you'll be happier at home and so will Karen. It was fantastic of you to come up on short notice like that and you've been a rock, as always, but there's no point in kicking your heels here in Marbella for the moment. Javier's going to call Franz Stenmark to shut down the surveillance for the same reason. We'll leave them alone until we're ready to make our move.'

'You might want to think twice about that. With the CCTV system down, an outside pair of eyes is all you've got. It's not the time to get lazy.'

'Hmm, OK, Marius, I'll talk about it again with Pedro. Anyway, it doesn't change your situation, I want you to go home.'

'You'll keep me informed and shout when you need me?'

'You won't miss the finale, don't worry. Now, get back to your business and take care of Karen, she'll be missing you. We don't want any more casualties, not until it's our turn to cause them.'

Coetzee flew out of Malaga at 21:00 that evening with Lufthansa for his 20-hour trip to Johannesburg, via Frankfurt. He was looking forward to it; unlike his flights up to Zurich, paid for with his own money, Jenny had booked him in first-class. Karen was going to be quite jealous when he told her.

City of London, England
Olympic Funds 7% higher after
Atlantic Offshore price reappraisal.

Dr Hugh Middleton read the article in disbelief. At heart, he was a highly sophisticated crook, and it had taken six months as a guest of her Majesty for him to accept and reject this disagreeable fact of life and redirect his considerable intellect toward an honest and useful occupation. *But*, he admitted to himself, *it takes a crook to know a crook, and I know that Harry Fern-Chapman is a crook. What's more, he cohabits with a murderess who most probably killed my dear Ilona. This cannot go on, it must be stopped.*

He pondered on the problem until he remembered something which could be useful, a name, someone who might have a personal motivation to find the truth. He took out the file he kept on Olympic and found the report written by Terry Owen. A couple of contacts later, he had the journalist's mobile number; he called him and arranged to meet the next day at the Crowne Plaza, Kings Cross. He knew there would be a cost attached, but he had a debt to repay that was greater than any amount of money.

FIFTY-TWO

'Morning, Jenny, how's everything? Recovered from the trip?'

'Everything's fine, Patrice. I've had a wonderful couple of days with Ellen, and Chester of course, no problems at all. I'm not bothering you am I?'

'Unfortunately not. I'm really not that busy, it's embarrassing. My staff are so efficient I have to look hard for things to do. What can I do for you?'

'Hang on, I want to get Pedro involved.'

A few moments later, the Spaniard was on the line. 'Buenos días to both of you, what's happening, Jenny?'

'I was thinking about the next sales in February. Do you really think Jolidon's people, whoever they are, will try to sell 100 diamonds at each sale?'

Patrice answered, 'If I was them I would. They've sold 200 already, another 300 in February and they're halfway home. *Wham, Bang, thank you Ma'am.* Get them all sold as quickly as possible and retire to a Caribbean beach. The longer they take, the more chances of being caught.'

'Patrice is right. They've had two sales in a couple of months, they're in a hurry, so the next three sales suit them very well.'

'And I suppose they'll have to deliver everything to the

auction houses quite soon, to get the catalogues printed and distributed. Christmas is just around the corner; they don't have much time.'

'I hadn't thought of that, the auction people will want them done before the end of the year.' Patrice checked the calendar on his laptop. 'They've really only got until next week, so there should be activity soon at the Zurich office?'

'Exactly, and, more than likely, Christen will be going up there to help in the process. Coetzee said we should keep up the surveillance and I think he was right.'

'I agree. We'd better let Franz know there will probably be some action, he'll be delighted to finally see someone. I'll ask Javier to talk to him, he's here with Laura and the baby.' Espinoza hung up and called his son-in-law.

Mayfair, London, England

'Esther my dear, how are you? It seems ages since we've seen you and I've missed our chats. I was just saying to Reggie, we must have you over for dinner; no sooner the thought than the action. Are you and Harry free on Friday evening to come and share our humble repast?'

Esther was unaware of Scarbrough's call to Harry the previous week and a little taken aback at the gushing invitation. 'I'm sure we've no plans for Friday; yes we'd love to come, thank you Nicola.'

'Wonderful. We'll expect you at 7 o'clock.' Lady Scarbrough put the phone down and said to her husband, 'Are you really sure, Reggie? It's one thing to invite them for a party with other friends, but quite different for a tête à tête dinner. I find them quite common, actually, and she has very little intelligent conversation.'

'I have my reasons, Nicola. I've been a bit concerned about our investments with Olympic and I want to get the facts straight from the horse's mouth.'

'Is there a problem?' she asked worriedly. 'I hope we're not going to lose money, I mean after managing to miss that disaster with Flutter, or whatever it's called. It's all so sordid, I don't know why you have all these investments, it's not as if we need to make more money. We just need not to lose any of it.'

'Don't worry, my dear, Harry's funds are coming back well at the moment, he had a very good month. Humour me, please. Let's see what he has to say on Friday.'

London, England

'Friday? That's fine, good to know we're still on their invitation list.'

'Why? Was there a reason we wouldn't be?'

Fern-Chapman swore silently. 'Not really, he called me last week, seemed a bit worried about his investments. I suppose I'm over-reacting to things these days.'

'But there's nothing going wrong?'

'On the contrary, the funds are up more than 7% since that Atlantic Offshore transaction. A lot of good publicity, and the new money's starting to flood in again. Investors are so fickle, the world goes through a difficult period and they start to lose their nerve, it's infectious, like chicken pox. Let's go out for dinner tonight, I'll reserve.'

Esther booked a table at Scott's, the maître d' knew her well by now. Then she called Christen's number. 'Have you heard anything from Drewberrys on the proceeds?'

'I told you I'll check on Friday, I don't want them to think we're desperate. Just relax and let them do their job, it's a lot of money to collect and buyers have to organise their bank payments, like everybody.'

'You're right, I'm just a bit bored, needing to do something. You and Claude have got the February sales to organise, but I'm just twiddling my thumbs.'

'OK, we have to get everything ready for the February sales before the end of the year. With Christmas in the way, we'll need to be organised in the next couple of weeks. That means you need to get three more batches of diamonds ready asap.'

'Very well, I'll come over next week with them. OK?'

He spotted the 'come over with them', throwaway, but ignored it. 'That's perfect. I'll sort out the rest of the goods with Claude, he's almost prepared his list, so we'll be ready in good time. The only obstacle might be that lawyer at Drewberrys; I'm not looking forward to talking to him again, he's a real ball breaker.'

'You think he'll cause trouble?'

'Get me the certification from Appletree and I'll work it out, Esther, same as last time. My incentive is bigger now.'

London, England

Terry Owen was a small man with a permanently disgruntled expression on his long thin face. He took off his duffle coat, revealing an open-necked shirt under a trendy short, tight jacket and tight jeans. His hair was fashionably long and there was an overpowering aroma of aftershave about him. Middleton, a fastidious man, took an immediate dislike to him, but guessed he'd be very good at worming out secrets.

'What makes you so certain?' the journalist asked.

'I've seen scams like this several times in my life and

I know how Fern-Chapman thinks. Believe me, this transaction has only one purpose, to boost Olympic Funds' share prices and save him from disgrace. You were quite right when you compared him with Woodford, he's illiquid and bleeding.'

The journalist sipped his coffee. 'So, what do you want me to do?'

'I want you to find out who's behind Benelux Mineral Holdings. I'll pay a reasonable fee and expenses, plus you'll get the publicity and syndicated news rights, if I'm right. I don't want to be involved or make anything out of it. My name shouldn't be mentioned,' Middleton added.

'I already checked on the OTC announcement, it was made by a guy called Guillaume Fric, he's a Luxembourg lawyer, must be a front man. I won't find out anything by phone, I'll have to go down there and ask around; the sooner the better. There's a flight tonight at 8:15, if you want me take it? It's just a few days since the deal, and Luxembourg's a small place, so if Fern-Chapman was there, I'll find out and that's a good starting point. We can work from there.'

'Agreed. Please send me a modest budget and I'll advance you 50% right away.'

He stood up to leave, 'By the way, do you know his address, Fern-Chapman's I mean?'

'He moved into a posh apartment in Eaton Place six months ago, fabulous situation, must cost a fortune.'

Jealousy is a highly motivating emotion, Middleton observed. 'Do you know the exact address?'

'I'll check it out and text you this evening.'

Dr Hugh Middleton took the bus back to his office. *I hope you're watching, Ilona dear, I'm doing this for you.*

Delmas, Mpumalanga, South Africa

'Welcome home, Marius. You must be dead on your feet, 20 hours is a marathon and you're not as young as you were.'

He gave her a look, mentioning his age was off-limits. 'As you can see, Karen, I'm as fresh as a daisy.'

They walked to the car and she asked, 'So, how was your trip, as successful as you expected?'

'You want to know the best part? Apart from the first-class flights, I mean.'

She gave him a frosty glance, 'What could be better than that?'

'I spent almost a million Swiss Francs at some auction sales, and it didn't hurt a bit. Spending other people's money is a great feeling. And you should have seen the stuff we bought, the jewels and valuables. Beautiful, especially Jenny's diamonds, absolutely fabulous.'

'And it all went according to plan?'

'So far so good. Now we have to be ready for the next stage. How's your tome progressing?'

'Three pages is hardly a tome, but it's taking shape. And I'm really enjoying the research, it's a fascinating topic. Dreadful, but fascinating.'

'Seems the *Sun* likes it too?'

'Not just them, they say they've got over 50 syndications lined up, *London Times, New York Times, FT, Bild, Economist*, maybe even *Time Magazine*, you name it.'

'Wow! You'll be famous, again. I'm really happy for you, I know you miss it a lot.'

She was quiet for a moment. 'I used to, when I first quit, but being with Abby was better and I still kept my hand in once a month. Now, if I can get this right, it might be the last one, we'll see.'

'Go out in a blaze of glory, right?'

'OK, Marius. Thanks for thinking of the idea. If it helps Jenny and does some good, I'll be happy. If it goes viral, I'll be delighted.'

London, England

'I just spoke to one of Fern-Chapman's guys, used to work for me, and he's not overly happy there. He says Harry was sick all last week, didn't come to the office at all.'

'Interesting. I wonder where he really was.'

'I think we've got a pretty good idea.'

'Agreed. Well done, Terry.'

'I got his address as well, 69 Eaton Square, it's a massive penthouse, costs more every month than I make in a year.'

Middleton noted down the address, 'Excellent, thank you. Have a good trip to Luxembourg and call me if you make progress.' He put down his mobile. '*Oh, what a tangled web we weave, when first we practice to deceive.*'

Zurich, Switzerland

'He's definitely back in the apartment. The lights have been on in the office facing the street, I can see it through the blinds. Not all the time, just from time to time, though it's pretty dark all day with this weather. There's no doubt he's there.'

'You haven't seen him come out?'

'Not yet. But he'll need to go shopping for food soon. He had a supermarket bag with him when he arrived, but he'll have to come out eventually. Don't worry, I won't miss him when he does.'

FIFTY-THREE

Wednesday, December 4, 2019

Luxembourg, EU

Terry Owen had managed to get a last-minute room at the Sofitel for less than €100. He was sure Fern-Chapman would have stayed in one of the five-star hotels in the centre of the Principality. Guillaume Fric's office address, in the *Boulevard Grande Duchesse,* was close to two of them, *Le Royale* and *Le Place d'Armes.* It was a cold, bright day; he wrapped a scarf around his neck and pulled his travel bag along to *Le Royale.* In the lobby, he unwrapped his scarf and opened his duffle coat up. He switched on the miniature video recorder in his shirt pocket and walked up to the reception counter. 'Good morning,' he placed a large brown envelope on the counter. 'I have an important document to give to Mr Harry Fern-Chapman, could you call him for me, please?'

The woman examined her screen, 'Can you spell the name for me? I can't seem to find it here.'

She searched for a few moments more. 'I'm sorry, we don't have a guest of that name, are you sure he's staying here?'

Owen walked across to *Le Place d'Armes* and repeated his pantomime. The result was the same, Mr Fern-Chapman hadn't stayed there.

Owen dragged his wheelie bag round for an hour,

moving in an expanding circle, until he got to the *Piemont,* a 3-star establishment on *Route d'Esch*, a 15-minute walk from Fric's office.

This time, the receptionist said, 'I'm sorry, Mr Fern-Chapman's no longer here. He checked out a few days ago.'

Bingo! 'That's strange, he told me he was staying until today.'

'He must have changed his plans,' she looked at the screen. 'He left the hotel last Friday.'

'Do you expect him back, maybe I could leave the document for him to collect?'

'We have no further booking from Mr Fern-Chapman, I'm sorry.'

'I see, thanks.' Owen walked out into the cold and switched off his recorder. *Gotcha!*

He strolled back up to the Municipal Park and along the *Boulevard Grande Duchesse* to no. 77, a smart building about half a kilometre from the British Embassy. Fric's office was on the ground floor, and an attractive young woman sat at a desk in a small reception area.

'Good morning, I'd like to see Maître Fric, if he's available.'

The woman looked at her screen, 'Do you have an appointment, Mr. ...?'

He gave the first name that came into his head. 'Attenborough.' He'd watched *Planet Earth* a couple of nights ago and loved the sound of David Attenborough's voice. 'No, I'm sorry, I came on the off-chance. It's to do with Mr Fern-Chapman's visit last week.'

'I'm sorry, but he isn't coming to the office this morning. I could fix an appointment for you this afternoon, if you like.'

She typed his name on her appointment list at 3pm and he went to the door, then turned towards her again. 'You don't happen to know if Mr Fern-Chapman's still in town?'

'I'm afraid I don't know Mr Fern-Chapman and Maître Fric hasn't mentioned him.'

'I see. Thank you, you've been very helpful. I'll be back at three.' He walked out and switched his video recorder off. *No point in coming back to see Fric, he'll just deny Fern-Chapman was here. Disappointing!*

It was now 10:30 and Owen took a ten-minute taxi ride to the rue Erasme, in Kirchberg, the 'Westminster' of the city. In the Chamber of Commerce, he asked to consult the Luxembourg Business Register. He was already aware that Benelux Mineral Holdings was in reality a South African entity, but he was more interested in knowing who had signed the contract on behalf of the company. He found the filing of the share transaction; Gérard Boillat, the chairman, had signed for Atlantic Offshore Oil & Gas and BMH had been represented by Guillaume Fric, Director of *Econovest Bruxelloise*, a Belgian company.

Owen pulled his bag back into Le Royale and sat in the lounge with a coffee. He searched online but could find nothing about *Econovest Bruxelloise*, except the address, at Fric's office. He gave up this search and called the number he'd saved on his mobile before leaving London, the Atlantic Offshore head office on *Avenue Charles de Gaulle*, a 15-minute walk from the hotel. He introduced himself as a UK financial reporter with the *Financial Times*. 'We're doing a weekend special on the recent drop in oil prices and the impact of the environmental groups on exploration companies like yours. Your recent share sale has caught a lot of attention, and I thought maybe you'd like to build some PR around this?'

He was put through to their 'External Relationships Director', a Frenchman called Auguste Collombe, who spoke better English than he did. Owen fixed an appointment at 15:30, which left him plenty of time to get to the airport for his 19:25 flight back to London City.

Luxembourg, EU

'An English gentleman, Mr Attenborough, was looking for you this morning, Monsieur Fric. I made an appointment for him at three this afternoon, you've got nothing until 4pm. I hope that's alright?'

'That's fine, Marie-Claire. Did he tell you what it's about?'

'He said it was to do with a visit last week by someone called Mr Fern-Chapman.'

A chill ran down Fric's spine. 'He was mistaken, Mr Fern-Chapman wasn't here last week. What kind of man was he?'

'About 35, I'd say. Not very tall, long hair and a bit untidy, wearing a brown duffle coat and pulling a travel bag.'

'Did you tell him anything about Mr Fern-Chapman?'

'I told him I don't know who Mr Fern-Chapman is. I didn't have a discussion of any kind with him, I just booked the appointment.'

Fric worked on the documents for his 4pm appointment. He wasn't surprised when the mysterious Mr Attenborough didn't show at 15:00. He took out the Atlantic Offshore file again and went through every detail. He was certain there was nothing that could incriminate him. At least, he was almost sure he was certain.

Luxembourg, EU

'I'm very impressed with your plans, M. Collombe, you've obviously spent a lot of thought and imagination on this programme. Do you think that's why there's been a sudden interest in your shares?'

'You're referring to the Benelux Mineral Holdings transaction?'

'Exactly. It's caused a lot of noise on the markets, especially in London, because of the Olympic Funds Group connection.'

'I know. Their share prices have jumped, it seems to have been beneficial to everyone involved.'

'You must have been surprised when you got the offer from BMH?'

'I was surprised when Monsieur Boillat told me about it, it wasn't expected.'

Owen's ears pricked up. 'I see. So, the offer was made directly to the company chairman and not through your broker?'

'From what I understand, that's how we received the bid.'

'That's a little unusual, don't you think? And I wouldn't call a 100% increase in the share price a bid. More like a slam dunk, but what about Olympic's right of first refusal? Wasn't that an obstacle to the transaction?'

Collombe moved uncomfortably on his chair and checked the time. He stood up, 'I don't think these details are relevant to our interview, Mr Attenborough. I have another meeting in a moment, so I'm obliged to leave you.'

'Thanks for your time, M. Collombe, please get the FT next weekend. I'm sure you'll enjoy the report.' In the elevator, Terry Owen switched off his video recorder and placed it carefully in his bag. It was too important to lose or get damaged, it was dynamite.

London, England

'Thank you, Terry, that's most interesting.' Dr Hugh Middleton had listened in silence to Owen's edited recordings from Luxembourg. 'So, you think Boillat's 'friend' was the lawyer, Guillaume Fric?'

'Everything points that way. Fric's secretary said she didn't know he'd been down there, but the hotel confirmed he was there, so they must have met somewhere privately. Fric's the signatory for BMH on behalf of a Belgian company that's registered at his office. The next minute there's a personal offer from BMH to the Atlantic Offshore chairman for $30 million of shares at twice the going rate.'

'Bingo! The result saves Olympic Group and Boillat gets rid of the refusal rights, as well as doing the best deal he's ever made. Everyone's happy.'

'And Fern-Chapman left on Friday, the day the OTC transaction was executed by Monsieur Fric.'

'Perfect timing. He was probably back in London when the news came out. The markets moved on Friday afternoon and Olympic's riding high by Monday. I have to admit, it was pretty smart.'

'The problem remains, how do we prove it? We have only a trip to Luxembourg and the name of a lawyer and a Belgian company, no real proof.'

'Leave it to me, Dr Middleton. There's no smoke without fire. I'll start the smoke and the fire will follow.'

'Very well, Terry, I'll follow your eminently sensible advice. Have a safe and enjoyable flight.'

Middleton walked into Ilona's office, still unoccupied. 'Well, well, my dear. They say that vengeance is a dish best served cold. Perhaps we're about to find the recipe.'

FIFTY-FOUR

Thursday-Friday, December 5-6, 2019
Marbella, Spain

'**Good morning, may I speak to M. Tournier, please?** This is Patrice de Moncrieff, from Durham House Investments.'

A moment later, Tournier came on the line. '*Bonjour* Monsieur de Moncrieff, how can I help you?'

'I just wanted to ensure the statement I received after the sale is correct. We intend to settle our account next Friday, within the 10 day period as required and I'd like to transfer the exact amount, to avoid any unnecessary problems.'

'Absolutely, I'll look it up. Right, can you note this down? Four million eight hundred and twenty-three thousand Swiss francs exactly. I hope you managed to acquire most of the items you wanted, the bidding was very lively.'

'We did, thank you, and I'm sure you were satisfied with the overall results. What was the final total, if I may ask?'

'Of course, it's public knowledge, on our website. Before fees, the result was just over CHF400 million. The highest result in the history of our Geneva sales.'

Patrice tried to sound blasé, 'Very well done, Mr Tournier, you must be delighted.'

'Thank you and we look forward to your settlement not later than Friday in a week. Bon weekend, Monsieur de Moncrieff.'

Jenny looked at the two numbers scribbled on the pad. 'Our purchases don't add up to much compared with almost half a billion. There must be far too much money in this world, when an auction sale can raise almost the same as the gross national product of a small country.'

'I remember what you said when we started this plan, *Recycling and laundering, like a Chinese laundry*. I never thought about it that way, but now I see what you mean. Heaven knows how much stolen property is sold through auction houses, there's simply no way to prevent it. I'll be more careful when I'm drumming up business for Drewberrys in future.'

'Well, now they know we're going to pay next Friday, so that should keep everyone happy and patient, including Jolidon. I'll send a text to Marius, just to be sure Karen's fine and on schedule.'

'You worry too much, Jenny. We're in the driver's seat now, just a few more days and we'll be there.'

Delmas, Mpumalanga, South Africa

'There's a text from Jenny Bishop, asking how things are going. What shall I reply?'

'You've read the outline, what do you think?'

'It's bound to be outstanding, like all your articles.'

'No flattery, Marius. There's a lot riding on this, so I want a genuine opinion.'

He put his arms around her. 'Karen, I wouldn't have suggested it if I didn't know what you're capable of. I think you'll win another prize, over 10 years after the last one. And you'll deserve it.'

Zurich, Switzerland

'Nothing new. The office light has been on again and he hasn't been out. He must have bought enough groceries for a month, either that or he never eats.' Franz Stenmark was about to leave for the evening, wearing a scarf, woollen gloves and his heavy army coat, but still feeling the bitter cold.

'OK, thanks, Franz, sorry you're not seeing any action, but at least we know we've got an eye on things after the CCTV disaster.'

'Did you find anything out about that?'

'Nothing yet, but things are going well, a few more days and you'll be back in the warmth.'

'OK, goodnight, I'm out of here.'

As Stenmark's bus pulled away, he looked back and in the light of the entrance to no. 819, he saw a man come out of the building; the same man he'd seen arriving on Sunday. He was carrying a plastic shopping bag. The bus was moving into the traffic and Franz couldn't jump off. He quickly took a snap with his mobile then called Javier back.

Claude Jolidon looked around cautiously as he walked past the car showroom and into the supermarket next door. It was freezing cold and dark outside and he thought nostalgically of his week in the Tessin sunshine. He bought the items on his list, mostly groceries, then returned quickly to no. 819, confident he hadn't been spotted. With what he'd just made at Drewberrys, he was now worth over CHF3 million. This was not the time to be careless.

Malaga, Spain

Javier called his father-in-law. 'Franz just got a shot of

Jolidon coming out of the building. I'm sending it to you now. I think we're on the right track.'

Pedro Espinoza texted the photo to Jenny and Leticia. 'Is this Jolidon?'

The two women were preparing supper with Lily in the kitchen at York House, with their three children and Chester, Jenny's Westie, when their mobiles beeped at the same moment. They looked at the photo, shouted with relief and gave each other a high five. Both sent a one-word reply, 'Yes!'

Geneva, Switzerland

'As of this morning, we've collected CHF440,000, Maître Christen.'

'That means there's over four million still to be received.'

'I'm sure the balance of the funds will be received by next Friday. That's the normal 10-day payment conditions.'

Christen swore under his breath. He knew that more than half of that was due from the Durham House Investments 'syndicate' sitting in seats 47 and 48. He'd seen them win all his lots at the Saturday evening session. He had the numbers in his head, *That's a dozen items plus the diamonds, about CHF2.5 million.*

'Would you like me to transfer the funds we have in hand to the Trust's fiduciary account?'

'No thanks, it's not worth your trouble. Please transfer the full amount as soon as you receive it.' Christen might have answered differently if he'd known that all the remaining *Private Investment Trust* lots had been acquired by the same buyers. But, unfortunately, he hadn't been at the sales and the young woman didn't tell him.

Mayfair, London, England

'Esther, so lovely to see you. It seems an age. And Harry, I hear your business is prospering, congratulations.' Lady Nicola Scarbrough blew kisses in the air and ushered them in from the cold.

'Yes, well done Harry, good to see the funds moving strongly in the right direction again.' Lord Scarbrough poured four glasses of champagne. 'Cheers and welcome back, it's been too long.'

They sat in a small, beautifully decorated reception room, the walls adorned with what looked like original masterpieces. 'Thanks for having faith in me, Reggie. I think that Atlantic Offshore transaction proves my stock-picking abilities haven't diminished.'

'Do you know why they made such a generous offer?'

'You mean the Benelux people? They've obviously been doing their homework and I intend to find out what they know. I've got a man on it now. Atlantic have been picking up drilling options at very good prices lately, with the oil price being under pressure. There must be a diamond amongst those acquisitions that we didn't spot, but maybe BMH did.'

'That's why you didn't block the deal with your right of refusal?'

'To tell you the truth, I wasn't feeling 100% when they called, and they wanted a quick answer. At that price, I couldn't see the upside, but I didn't want to sabotage their transaction. After all, everybody benefits; they get a chunk of cash to invest in more acquisitions at good prices and Olympic's holdings benefit from the share price and future deals.'

'Well done, it certainly worked, and if Boris gets in with a good majority, the turnaround should continue.'

Fern-Chapman breathed a sigh of relief, it sounded like Reggie wouldn't be bailing out yet. If the election went badly and the markets crashed, it wouldn't be his fault. 'Let's drink to that, Boris's majority.' They clinked glasses.

Over dinner, the conversation continued around the markets, politics and Brexit, until Nicola said, 'You men can talk all night about shares and investments and politics if you like, but I want to tell Esther about our cruise. My dear, the Silver Horizon is the most beautiful ship we've ever been on and the Owner's Suite was superb. You must look at their itineraries, perhaps we could go together sometime.'

Wandsworth, London, England

Terry Owen sat back and re-read the first few paragraphs of his partly-written article, provisionally titled, *The anonymous investor who doubled the value of Atlantic Offshore Oil & Gas*. He was really enjoying this assignment; someone had to teach Harry-Fucking-Fern-Chapman a lesson. He attacked the keyboard again, eager to get the piece finished.

Belgravia, London, England

In the cab, on the way home to Eaton Square, Esther said, '*Mon Dieu*, I can't think of anything worse than being stuck on a ship with Nicola Scarbrough. I'd be tempted to jump overboard.'

'Don't worry, that was just flattery, there's no way she'd go anywhere with the likes of us, we're just hired help as far as she's concerned.'

'And I didn't know you'd been off colour last week.

You didn't say anything to me.'

'Oh, that. I didn't want to worry you. It was no big deal, just a sniffle, but I think I'll get a flu jab, just in case.'

She didn't seem to notice his hesitation. 'By the way, I forgot to tell you, I've got to take a quick trip on Tuesday, so let's be sure to make the most of the weekend.'

'Don't tell me. I know, you've found another million-dollar deal.'

FIFTY-FIVE

'*Salud*, Esther, thanks for breaking the weekend boredom. What's new?'

'I'm flying over on Tuesday morning, to deliver the next batches of stones, so you can get the February lots to Christen in good time.'

'Perfect, that's 300 stones?'

'Right. I'll make three envelopes, same as usual; as near as I can guess, 100 carats each.'

'I'll have everything else ready. Christen can come up for them right away.'

'Wait, Claude. I was thinking about the CCTV attack and what you said about moving offices.'

'I'm listening.'

'That's a few times that maniac has tried to get in, and I don't believe he was an unhappy client. Normal people don't smash things up because no one answers the door. I'm sure there's something we don't know about. You absolutely need to find a new office as soon as possible.'

'OK, you could be right about that, but I can't find a place, fix it up and move in anytime soon. When I've got everything prepared for Christen, I'll look seriously for new premises, I promise.' She heard him suck on his cheroot. 'Why are you suddenly so nervous?'

'I just have a bad feeling. It's something about that apartment, I don't trust it. I can't explain, but I don't want to go there again.'

He searched for a reason. 'You think someone might be watching it?'

'*Quoi*? You think it's possible?' Esther suddenly felt afraid, she couldn't afford to be recognised. *Someone watching the building? The man with the cap and scarf, maybe. But who was he?*

Jolidon went to the window, opened the blinds and looked across the street. It was a Saturday morning, there were several cars at the petrol station and a lot of people walking past. He searched for a man in a cap and scarf, but no one fitted the description and he could see nothing unusual.

'It looks perfectly normal out there, just people shopping and drivers filling their cars up.'

'Perhaps, but I really don't want to come up there on Tuesday.'

'So, you want me to come to Geneva to meet you?'

'I'd feel safer if you do.'

'No problem, what time do you get in?'

Franz Stenmark was standing outside the petrol station café when he saw the blinds open. He quickly turned, walked behind a fuel pump, zoomed his camera up and saw the man from the bus. He snapped a long-range shot and sent it to Javier.

Malaga, Spain

'*Bueno*. We've got confirmation that Jolidon's still in that apartment.' Espinoza looked at the photograph more closely. 'Jenny and Leticia's description was good, he hasn't changed much, still looks greasy and untrustworthy. Thanks, Javier and well done to Franz. I'll let Patrice and Marius know we're on the right track.'

'And Jenny?'

'It's her first weekend with Ellen since she got back and she already knows it's probably him, no need to disturb her. Nothing's going to change by Monday, we'll call her then. Have a good weekend and give my love to Laura and little Pedro.'

Espinoza went into the living room, where Soledad was playing the piano, a soft Chopin nocturne. 'That's very nice, *querida*.' He kissed her on the forehead, 'I'm going to the market for some fresh fish for lunch. What would you like?'

Marbella, Spain

Jenny enjoyed a peaceful weekend at York House, with Ellen, Chester and the indefatigable Lily, who mostly left her to quiet and private times with her daughter. She spent a lot of time thinking about her husband, Ron, her father and mother-in law, Charlie and Ellen, and how she'd lost them too soon. She wasn't sure if her quest to find the truth about the diamonds and to foil Claude Jolidon and his accomplices, whoever they were, was an attempt to right some wrongs and help to solve the mystery of the fire and the death of Giles, or was it simply a personal mission, motivated by revenge for the deaths of her loved ones?

In typical Jenny Bishop fashion, she snapped out of these reveries, remembering how her friends had prepared and executed their plan so successfully, hardly believing that they were now on the cusp of success in revealing who were the brains behind these criminal acts; ensuring that they would be exposed and punished, as they should be.

She went out onto the terrace, 'Come on, Ellen, Chester, we're going up to the pond to feed the fish.'

Zurich, Switzerland

On Sunday, late afternoon, Claude Jolidon was watching the recording of a match between Marseilles and Paris Saint-German. He'd spent the day preparing the last of the valuables and recorded the game so he could enjoy it with a glass of wine when he'd finished his task. The living room in the apartment was as bare as the office; just a dining table, a couple of chairs, a settee and a coffee table with a small TV set on it. The room was at the back of the apartment and the only window looked onto the alley at the side of the building. He could put on a lamp and relax in front of the TV, without fear of it being seen from the street; it was his one luxury in the prison he'd created.

At half-time, he went into the kitchen to pour himself another glass of chardonnay, which reminded him of Christen's problem; hoping he'd be able to get through the future sales without crashing out in a drunken haze. The sudden sound of the doorbell ringing caused him to pour most of the wine onto the benchtop.

Who in hell is that? How did they get up here? It's a Sunday, people don't come visiting offices on a Sunday. He sat down quietly on the kitchen chair, looking at the door, hardly daring to breathe, cursing himself for leaving the strongbox open, ready to finish the packaging of the valuables in the morning.

The bell rang again, twice, then again continuously for what seemed like minutes. It stopped, and he heard the sound of scraping and realised the intruder was picking one of the locks. It clicked open and he felt a shudder of fear. By the time he heard the second Yale click back, Jolidon was terrified, unable to move. He sat immobile in the kitchen, praying that the new lock he'd had installed would prove impossible to crack, as he'd been promised by the locksmith. The sounds from the door continued for a while, then changed; unable to pick it, the intruder had started to hit the lock with something. *Maybe the hammer he broke the camera with*, the Frenchman imagined. The sound of the blows echoed around the apartment as he hit the lock with more and more force. Splinter cracks appeared on the door jamb around the lock. Jolidon was frozen with fear as the noise increased until he thought the door would burst open.

He heard a voice shout, '*Was ist dort oben los? Es ist ein Sonntag!*' What's happening up there? It's a Sunday.' '*Ich rufe die Polizei an.*' I'm calling the police.'

The hammering ceased and Jolidon heard no further sound. After fifteen minutes trying to compose himself, he ventured to the door, opened the new *SMART* lock with a signal from his phone, and peered outside. There was no one there. He relocked the two Yale locks, then closed the *SMART* lock again, it had suffered superficial damage from the blows and there were visible cracks on the upright, but it had kept the door closed. He thanked the Lord that the locksmith had been a good salesman, he was certain it had saved his life. *Esther's right, I have to find a new office, asap.*

Malaga, Spain

'That guy was back, the one with the cap and scarf, he was carrying a small bag. I followed him in and heard him upstairs trying to get into the apartment. With what sounded like a fucking hammer!'

Javier felt a jolt of excitement, something was going on, at last. 'What happened?'

'He must have been smashing at the door and one of the residents heard him and started yelling blue murder. He did a runner, went sprinting past me in the lobby, almost knocked me over. I got a shot as he was coming down the stairs, still not perfect but a bit better than the others.'

'And Jolidon is still in there?'

'He sure is, he must be having a heart attack, it was pretty frightening stuff. I thought the guy was going to break the door down and ransack the place.'

'OK, Franz, I don't know what it means, but I guess we'll find out soon. Please send me the photo and get yourself home, it's Sunday and you should be with your family. Thanks again and we'll talk tomorrow.'

Marbella, Spain

'It's infuriating, I'm sure I know this man, but I can't think from where.' The latest shot taken by Franz Stenmark was again unclear. This time Jenny had a better impression of the jaw and lower face, but she couldn't see the eyes, she knew Franz had taken it almost by instinct, when the man was rushing towards him, and it was slightly out of focus.

'Don't worry, Jenny, everything will fall into place soon. We're very close to resolving this business.'

'I hope so, Pedro. But I just don't understand why there's some apparently random third party trying to get into that apartment. Who is it, what do they want? Is it just another customer like me, looking to recover their possessions, or something quite different?'

'Time will tell. Goodnight, Jenny, my dear, sleep well.'

FIFTY-SIX

'I have a call for you from a Mr Owen, in London, Maître Fric.'

'I don't recognise the name, did he say what it's about?'

'Something to do with Olympic Funds.'

Fric's heart rate went up. He was about to say, 'Tell him I'm busy,' but thought again. *Better to take the call and find out what he wants, or he'll just keep calling and Marie-Claire will start to wonder what's going on.* 'Put him through, please.'

He took a deep breath. 'What can I do for you, Mr Owen?'

'I'm writing an article about the Atlantic Offshore share purchase by BMH and I just wanted to confirm a couple of facts.'

'You're a journalist, I see. Well then you'll be aware that I'm unable to discuss lawyer-client relations, so I'm afraid there's nothing I can tell you that you don't already know.'

'But you're the signatory to the transaction on behalf of *Econovest Bruxelloise*, the corporate director of BMH. That's not a lawyer-client relationship.'

Fric was startled, but he kept his nerve. *He knows more than I expected, but he's still fishing.* 'Since you know nothing about the ownership of *Econovest Bruxelloise,* you're not in a position to judge that, Mr Owen.'

'I see, *Econovest Bruxelloise* is a client? Then I assume it belongs to Harry Fern-Chapman and that's why he came to see you last week, to instruct you to buy the Atlantic Offshore shares on his behalf.'

'I have no idea why you would assume that and I'm afraid I have no more time to discuss this. Goodbye, Mr Owen.'

Fric was shaken. *How did he know Fern-Chapman was here last week?* He went to the reception desk. 'You remember that Englishman, Mr Attenborough, who came last week, Marie-Claire? Did you discuss Mr Fern-Chapman with him at all?'

'Absolutely not, M. Fric, I told you that after his visit.'

He saw from her face that she had said nothing and went back into his office, thinking back to his meeting with Harry. He looked up the *Piemont Hotel,* and called the number, asking in English for the reception desk. 'I'm looking for M. Harry Fern-Chapman, is he still staying with you?'

'Is this the same person who came looking for him the other day? I told you he's no longer here and he isn't booked to come back. Please stop bothering me, I'm very busy. *Au revoir, Monsieur.*'

Fric put the phone down and took out the Atlantic Offshore file again. The ownership of *Econovest Bruxelloise* was impenetrable, but a good journalist would get around that. Thanks to the Internet, fake news and innuendo were the order of the day, the truth was just an inconvenience. Fric knew he had a problem and he was a worried man.

Marbella, Spain

'Hello, Marius. I was thinking about calling, but I didn't want to sound like a nag. I hope all's well in Delmas and Karen's piece is progressing?'

'That's why I phoned, I'll put her on to update you herself.'

'Hello Jenny, just to let you know, the final draft is in at *The Sun* for publication on Saturday, and they have 60 syndications confirmed!'

'Wow. That's marvellous, Karen, you'll help us win our battle and get the Pulitzer Prize into the bargain.'

'Maybe not, but it's convinced me to keep writing, I loved the material, reminded me of the research I did when I was working full-time. Thanks for the opportunity.'

'Am I allowed a preview?'

'I'll send it now, but please keep it to yourself until it's published. And let me know if I've hit the right nerves.'

Marius came back on the line, 'OK, thanks to my wonderful wife, we're ready at this end, how about you?'

'You know about the man who tried to get into Jolidon's apartment?'

'Pedro called me; the guy with the hammer. He's obviously an amateur, but it's another ripple in the pond, I wonder how many more there'll be.'

'I hope that's the last ripple, we're making good progress. Patrice has agreed the payment date with Drewberrys for Friday, so Jolidon won't be worrying until then, and he'll have to wait over the weekend. After Karen's article on Saturday, we expect a lot of noise and Patrice will be onto them again on Monday, so next week should be busy.'

'I was thinking about this week, actually, Jolidon getting the goods ready for the next sales.'

'That's why we kept Franz on guard, there's likely to be some activity in Zurich.'

'And Christen will probably be involved, I suppose he handles the arrangements with the auction houses. I know where he lives, maybe we should keep an eye on him too.'

'I forgot that, Patrice told me you'd followed him home. You want to hire another spy?'

'A low-level guy, just for this week?'

'Can you set it up?'

'I'll call Javier, don't want to tread on his toes.'

Three hours later, Luca Dragavei, a young Romanian employee of *Privatdetektei Huntzer's* Geneva branch was sitting in the window of a café, watching René Christen's apartment building. He had a photograph, provided by Coetzee, and instructions to follow the man wherever he went. He was determined to match the face when his target came out.

London, England

'I've called Fric and put the wind up him. He'll be looking for ways to extricate himself from this deal. He's a lawyer, he won't hang around to carry the can. And my article is finished, I can get it in on Wednesday. '

'That's good work, Terry, but I recommend delaying publication for a few days, ideally, until Saturday.'

'I don't agree, we should strike while the iron's hot, get these bastards on the defensive.'

'I understand, Terry, but please consider my reflections.' Hugh Middleton paused, collecting his thoughts. 'As we know, lawyer Fric is a friend of Gérard Boillat, both prominent businessmen in Luxembourg, a small, but very corrupt country. I imagine he has already spoken with him, in order to protect their relationship. They will both be hurt if this news comes out, so it's probable that they'll be taking precautions to protect themselves which could negate the achievement of our objective.'

'I know what you mean; burying the evidence. What else?'

'A second point. The General Election is in three days. The newspapers are full of that subject to the exclusion of all else, your article will be swamped and relegated to the Business Section and will have limited exposure and even less effect. In addition, if the election goes in favour of the Conservatives, as I believe it will, Olympic Funds will presumably benefit from the optimism with higher share prices. With any luck, by Saturday, you will have a larger balloon to burst.'

'That's smart thinking, Dr Middleton, but I'm still not sure it's a good idea to give Fric more time to think and act.'

'Thank you, Terry, I will come to my final point. There is another potential victim of this fraud, someone who is not involved, directly or indirectly, but who will be greatly affected by the collateral damage which will ensue.'

Owen thought through the imagined scenario in his mind, identifying all the players, unable to work out who Middleton was referring to. 'OK, you win. Who have I forgotten about?'

When Middleton spoke the name, he said, 'Shit! I never even thought of him. How do you think we should handle that?'

'Let's discuss that aspect in more detail. It is potentially the key to providing the kind of publicity we both desire.'

Geneva, Switzerland

'It's definitely him, I saw him clearly when I followed him onto the tram. No doubt he's our guy.'

'He hasn't clocked you?' Javier had picked up a few useful phrases from Franz Stenmark.

'No, he looks like he's had a few drinks, a bit unsteady on his feet.'

'Sounds like Christen alright. Where is he now?'

'In a gay bar in the old town. I'm standing outside and I've never been so cold.'

Javier looked at the time, it was 9pm. 'He's not going anywhere important tonight. Go home and get warm. Tomorrow will probably be just as cold.'

'Franz warned me, I'm wearing just about all the clothes I've got. I'll be back in Carouge at 8am. *Bonne nuit.*'

Marbella, Spain

Jenny was dreaming; she was on an inflatable lilo, floating in the middle of a lake, so large that she couldn't see the shores. She'd swum alongside it for a while, then climbed on top to lie in the warm sunshine. The water had been perfectly flat and calm when she'd started sunbathing, but now the mattress began to rock. Ripples were moving towards her, pushing against the plastic sides, harder and harder, until she had to hold on with all her strength. She couldn't see what was causing the ripples, which were fast becoming small waves, threatening to submerge the flimsy raft and her with it. The waves increased in size until a massive surge of water overturned the lilo and threw her off into the lake, leaving her floundering in the middle of the vast expanse of water. There was nothing in sight, no swimmers, no boats, only the overturned plastic raft, drifting away on the waves.

Jenny sat up in bed, trembling from the memory of the dream and remembering what Coetzee had said that morning; *'another ripple in the pond, I wonder how many more there'll be.'*

She got up and quietly went to her office, found Franz Stenmark's three photographs of the Zurich intruder on her mobile and printed them out. She placed the prints on top of each other on her desk, moving them around and snipping away at them with scissors to try to piece together a complete picture.

That's it, that's the jaw, the nose and the eyes, I knew I'd seen him before. But it's not possible, it can't be him. It doesn't make any sense.

FIFTY-SEVEN

Tuesday, December 10, 2019
Zurich, Switzerland

'I just saw Jolidon leave the building. He came out and ran to the bus stop just as it was arriving, must have been watching for it. It was the city centre bus, goes to the station.'

'He's getting careless.' Javier and Espinoza were both on the line.

'Maybe, or he's not so worried about being seen.'

'Was he carrying anything?'

'That same shopping bag he came with.'

'Did it look empty or full?'

'It looked empty, why?'

'We're expecting him to be carrying something, either going out or coming in.'

'OK, I'll look more closely next time.' Stenmark put his mobile away. *What's this all about?* he wondered.

Luxembourg, EU
Guillaume Fric had spent a lot of time worrying after Owen's call, looking for an escape route, one that covered his and if possible, Harry's backside. And more importantly, guaranteed, or possibly improved his fees from the transaction. Finally, he realised there was only one option that might work in everyone's favour. He

made a call and arranged a luncheon appointment at his club the next day.

Marbella, Spain

'Karen sent me a preview of her report last night.'

'That's great, can you send it to me?'

'I promised to keep it to myself, Leticia, and I don't want to spoil the effect of your reading the published article, but I can tell you now it's absolutely amazing. She's learned more about Angola in a couple of weeks than I have in over 10 years. Just wait, I think it'll be a very emotional experience for you, and I'm sure it will have just the effect we're looking for.'

Geneva, Switzerland

'Be careful with these, they're worth six million Swiss Francs. Esther placed three padded envelopes on the coffee table in front of Claude Jolidon. They were in her second home, suite 520 at the Richemond.

'Do I need to look at them?'

'If you like, they're identical to the previous two batches, 100 stones, just over 100 carats, as close as I could estimate.'

'Then I'll leave them be, ready for René.' He placed them in the grocery bag he'd brought with him.

'You're sure they're safe like that?'

'Safe as houses. Nobody steals a shopping bag.'

'You'd better be right. How are you progressing with the rest of the goods?'

'Finished.' He showed her a photograph of three cartons, the size of shoe boxes, wrapped up in strong paper and sealed with tape. 'All done, about 300 items; I told you I'd get them ready in good time. You want to see the inventories?'

She shook her head, knowing it would be pointless; impossible to tell if he was stealing from her, and he probably was. 'When is René coming for them?'

'Thursday, I've told him to come by car, so he can take everything safely. He'll deliver them to the auction houses on Friday, so they've got plenty of time to catalogue them before the end of the year. February's going to be a big month for us, between 10 and 12 million.'

She almost fainted with delight but managed to hold herself together. 'You've done a great job, Claude. We're proving to be quite a team.'

'*Merci*,' he paused, bracing himself, 'but you were right about the apartment.'

Her mood changed immediately. 'What do you mean, more problems with visitors?'

Jolidon hadn't yet told her about Sunday's attack, he knew she didn't like the office and wanted to explain it quietly, face to face, without drama. 'There was an intruder on Sunday afternoon, I'm pretty sure it was the same guy as before.'

'What happened?' She sat up, nervously squeezing her hands together.

'I think he figured the place was still empty and he tried to get in, picked the two old locks, but couldn't get past the new *SMART* one I had fitted. It operates from my phone, and he couldn't open it, so he pissed off. That's all there was to it.' He kept his hands under the desk so she couldn't see them trembling at the memory of the attack.

'We were right, he must have been watching the building. Thank God you had that lock fitted, I hate to think what might have happened if he'd got the door open. Claude, you must find a new place right away, we can't risk him coming back. We've got three sales coming up, there's too much to lose.'

'I don't think he's been watching, because he would have seen me, I've been out a couple of times. But you're right. As soon as Christen takes everything to Geneva I'll have time to look for another place, even harder for clients to find. I'll let you know when I've found something and you can come and look at it.

'And the good news is that Christen's back on track. This morning he's visiting the auction houses at all three hotels to sign us up for the February sales. Everything will be ready for him to deliver the goods to them on Friday.

'It cost me an arm and a leg, but he'll be happy for a while, at least until after the sales. But if he continues to drink like that, we'll have to look for another solution, he's not dependable and I'm afraid he'll get plastered and shout his mouth off about our business.'

'Let me have a word with him on Thursday, I doubt he'd like hearing that from a woman; you know what I mean? And I won't tell him about the attempted break-in, it won't help and it could affect his mind.'

'Agreed, he's screwed up quite enough already.'

Esther watched Jolidon go off in a taxi to Cornavin Station for his train back to Zurich, conflicting emotions running through her mind. The business was incredibly successful, better than she could ever have imagined, but there were two serious threats: Christen's drinking and the madman with the hammer. She didn't know which was the most dangerous and she hoped she wouldn't have to find out.

At 6pm she called Harry; her flight back to London was not until noon the following day. He had good news, her Olympic Funds had moved up another 1%, now she was making a decent profit.

'Just wait until Boris gets in this week, then you'll see some solid upward movement,' he told her, ebullient with the success of his strategy.

For a moment Esther thought of increasing her investment again, from the $2 million plus she'd receive from Drewberrys at the end of the week, but she said nothing. *Let's wait and see what happens, there's no rush.* 'That's great, Harry. I'm happy for you, see you tomorrow.'

'Call me when you get on the Paddington train and I'll pick you up at the station.'

'Will do, thanks. Love you.'

After the call, she showered and changed and at 19:00hr she went down in the elevator. She'd made a dinner booking at *Chez Mario*, the Italian restaurant Christen had introduced her to. What little food she'd eaten had been superb and she'd enjoyed it, until she'd walked out. She was looking forward to taking up where she'd left off.

Zurich, Switzerland

'Jolidon just came back on the bus and went into the building. This time there's something in the bag, something light, it swings but it's not heavy.'

'Did you get a shot?'

'It's too dark, but the light went on in the office. That's all for tonight, he's back and I'm iced up. Talk tomorrow.' Stenmark rang off.

Malaga, Spain

'He must have been collecting something, something very light, maybe the diamonds?' Javier was reporting to Pedro Espinoza.

'He was gone the whole day, most probably out of town. If it was the diamonds, I wonder where he picked them up? And why would he be taking them to Zurich, when they'll be sold in Geneva?'

'It's an ownership thing? He likes to be in charge. He puts everything together in his office in Zurich, then Christen, or whoever, takes them to Geneva and signs them up in the sales. I've got another call, it looks like Luca, I'll ring you back.'

Geneva, Switzerland

'This morning Christen went to three hotels in town, the Fairmont, Hotel des Bergues and the Mandarin Oriental.'

'Was he there long?'

'Half an hour each time. He had a document case with him and was fiddling about with papers when he came out.'

'That's good news, well done, Luca. Anything else?'

'He went shopping this afternoon and now he's in that gay bar again. I've got two pairs of socks on and I'm not quite so cold.'

Malaga, Spain

'Sounds like he's setting up the arrangements for all three February sales.' This time, Patrice was on the call with Javier and Pedro.

'Yes, your instinct was right, they're definitely going full speed ahead to cash in while they can.'

'I'll text Marius, he'll be happy to know his suggestion paid off.'

'Now we have to watch for Jolidon. He'll be handing over the valuables.'

'Time will tell. Goodnight, Patrice, Javier, give your families a kiss for me.' Espinoza sat for a while, wondering how the pieces of the jigsaw fitted together, he was good at jigsaw puzzles, but this one was becoming quite difficult.

FIFTY-EIGHT

'Who's this, please?'

'Good morning, Mr Cameron. My name is Terry Owen, I'm a financial journalist in London and I'm calling you about the Benelux Mineral Holdings Over-The-Counter purchase of Atlantic Offshore shares.'

Cameron switched on the recorder on his phone. 'Why would that be of interest to me, Mr Owen?'

'Because you're the CEO of Cameron Overview, the corporate Managing Director of Olympic Funds Group.'

'I'm not sure I see the reason for making such an obvious statement?'

'Olympic Fund share prices have risen by 7% in the last few days. They were in very bad shape and since that transaction, they're suddenly the flavour of the month. Don't you think there might be a connection?'

'What are you suggesting?'

'I'm just wondering if it might have to do with the Olympic Group Investment Advisor, Mr Fern-Chapman, being in Luxembourg last Friday, the day the OTC share transaction was announced.'

There was silence on the phone.

'Are you there, Mr Cameron?'

'What makes you think Mr Fern-Chapman was in

Luxembourg? I understand he was ill at home all week.'

'Please listen to these recordings which I made when I was there last Thursday.'

Before Cameron could refuse, he switched on the tape he'd edited, introducing the voices of the Piemont Hotel receptionist and Auguste Collombe, External Relationships Director, at Atlantic Offshore Oil & Gas.

There was silence again, then, 'Thank you, Mr Owen. I'm not sure why you're playing those recordings. Assuming of course, that you can validate them?'

'I certainly can. They're from video recordings I made myself in Luxembourg and they prove Fern-Chapman was there on Thursday and Friday, probably to meet Guillaume Fric, the signatory for BMH. Also, that the Atlantic Offshore offer from BMH was introduced to Mr Boillat by a private source, almost certainly by him, or by M. Fric.'

'I'm struggling to follow your reasoning. Why exactly are you contacting me with this information?'

'Because I believe it constitutes 'Insider Trading'. I'm writing an article about the share purchase and its consequences and I wouldn't want you to be an innocent victim of such a revelation.'

'Be careful what you say, Mr Owen. Accusations like that are slanderous and as far as I can tell from the recordings, there is no evidence whatsoever that if Mr Fern-Chapman was in Luxembourg, it was for that reason.'

'He told his staff he was sick at home, but we know from the hotel receptionist he was in Luxembourg on the day the transaction was done. So, why was he there? Come on, Mr Cameron, we're not kids, we know that deal saved his bacon at Olympic.'

'I'm sorry, I don't think you can extrapolate these few facts in that fashion, and I advise you to take great care in anything you publish; you may come to regret it. Goodbye, Mr Owen.' He slammed the phone down. 'Damn. What the hell's going on with Fern-Chapman?'

Cameron listened to the recordings again, noting the exact words of the speakers. He called in his assistant. 'Moira, I want you to find out everything you can about Gérard Boillat, the chairman of Atlantic Oil & Gas. I think we may have a problem with Olympic Funds.'

London, England

'I'm sure he's got the wind up, he warned me about slander and libel, but he wasn't very convincing.'

'Indeed? If that's the case, Mr Cameron may very well unknowingly prepare the ground for your article. Have you confirmed the publication date for Saturday?'

'I've told them I'll file it on Friday, Dr Middleton.'

'Excellent. Perhaps tomorrow will provide us with good news on two fronts, a Conservative majority and further revelations about Olympic Funds.'

Paddington Station, London, England

'Hi, Guillaume, good to hear from you. Are you calling to congratulate me on Olympic Fund's share prices?' Harry Fern-Chapman was in a great mood, his funds had picked up another 2% on the week, wiping out their recent losses. He was now showing a 5% return for the year. Moreover, the election was in two days. If it went well, he could end 2019 with a 10% performance, if it didn't, he wouldn't be the only fund manager to be hurting. Either way, now, he couldn't be harmed by whatever happened, his strategy had worked perfectly.

Fric's reply caused his mood to change drastically. 'Are you on your own, no one around?'

'I'm at the station, so there's a crowd of people around. Hang on, I'll find a quiet corner. OK, go ahead. What's wrong?'

Fern-Chapman listened in silence as the lawyer told him of the journalist's call, his heart sinking when he heard the name Terry Owen. 'Damn! That useless little piece of shit, Owen. He could bring Olympic down if he publishes this kind of speculation. Can he prove I was there?'

'I'm pretty sure he's been down here and checked the hotels. The *Piemont* told me someone was asking for you last week. Anyway, listen, Harry, the only thing to do is to admit it. The Atlantic Offshore transaction was set up by me, directly with my friend, Gérard Boillat, on behalf of BMH, nothing to do with you. At the last minute, I needed the letter from Olympic Funds and you kindly flew down with it on Thursday evening and returned Friday lunchtime. I already told Boillat about this, to pre-empt any contact Owen might make to get him onside. He got really worked up at the thought of a journalist trying to rob him of the best deal he's done in a lifetime. He's got $10 million in the bank, a share price twice what it was and a break in the first refusal clause. He won't let anybody take that away from him.'

'You're sure of that?'

'I just had lunch with him. He almost threw up when I told him the deal might be in danger. He'll swear black is white to protect it.'

Harry started to relax, 'I'll have to work out a way to explain to Alex Cameron and the people in the office, I told them I did it by email, because I had the flu.'

'Just tell them we needed the original letter and you knew it would look dodgy if you said you'd been down here, so you told a little white lie. I've told you, nobody can prove any different, Boillat and I will swear to it.'

'Thanks, Guillaume, I really appreciate your advice.' Harry realised this was going to cost him dear, Luxembourg lawyers didn't do favours for free. 'Is there anything else Owen can come up with? He's a sneaky guy.'

'That's it; BMH is impenetrable, Atlantic Offshore is on board and your only involvement was to deliver the letter I needed.'

Fern-Chapman saw Esther coming through along the platform. 'OK, I've got to go. Let me sleep on it and I'll get back to you in the morning.'

'Harry, you look very thoughtful. Is anything wrong?'

He forced a laugh, 'How could anything be wrong? I'm in great shape, so is Olympic and you're home again. The world is a wonderful place.'

Malaga, Spain
'Nothing special today. Both Franz and Luca had a cold, uneventful day. Let's hope for more action tomorrow. Good night, Pedro.' Javier went in for dinner with Laura, his favourite time of the day.

FIFTY-NINE

Thursday, December 12, 2019
Edinburgh, Scotland

'Good morning, Monsieur Boillat. Thanks for taking my call.' Alex Cameron didn't try his schoolboy French on the millionaire businessman, he assumed his English would be better than his own and he was right.

'Not at all, Mr Cameron, what can I do for you?'

'As you know, my firm is the corporate Managing Director of Olympic Funds Group.'

'I'm aware of that and that Olympic owns a total of 25% of my company, Atlantic Offshore. I imagine that's what this call is about?'

'Exactly. Firstly, I'd like to congratulate you on your recent transaction with BMH, at $10, per share. You must be delighted to achieve a 100% increase in your market cap.'

'Thanks, I am, our shares have been undervalued for a long time. I hope the market takes note of this and the trend continues.'

'I hope so too. My other reason is one of normal corporate governance, since we are still your second largest shareholder. I have a couple of questions, if you don't mind. I understand that the bid was made personally to you and not through your market maker?'

'That's correct, the director of BMH is Guillaume Fric,

a personal friend here in Luxembourg, and he approached me directly. I was happy to negotiate the transaction with him, it was done very rapidly, which saved everyone a lot of time, stress, and, of course, cost.'

'As did Mr Fern-Chapman's cooperation, I imagine.'

'You mean by putting aside your right of first refusal? Yes, that was most helpful, to both parties, since as you say, Olympic also benefits from the new valuation. You must be pleased at the result.'

'On that subject, how did Mr Fern-Chapman deliver the letter to you?'

'He didn't, I've never met him, only spoken on the phone. I received it from Guillaume on the morning we closed the deal, Friday. I assume he got it from Fern-Chapman, but I don't know when or how.'

Cameron didn't reveal that he knew Harry had been in Luxembourg that Friday. 'Do you know much about BMH, I mean who's behind it, what they do, where they're based?'

'Apart from the fact that it is a South African investment company, I know very little. What I do know is that Monsieur Fric is a first-class lawyer, whom I trust absolutely and who is very well connected. He brought me a terrific deal and I seized the chance to do it.'

Cameron realised that he would get nowhere with this line of questioning, Boillat was obviously a skilled operator who could talk his way out of any situation. 'Very well, M. Boillat, I look forward to further improvements in your share price. Thank you for your time.'

'A pleasure, Mr Cameron and good luck with your election today.'

Cameron thought back on his conversation with Fern-

Chapman on the Saturday after the transaction. *Harry said he'd received a call from Atlantic Offshore on the Wednesday and Boillat says he's only spoken to him on the phone, so that ties in. But Boillat also said he received the letter from Fric and Harry says he doesn't know BMH, so Fric must have called him at Boillat's request. I just don't see this clearly.* He called Moira. 'Have we received a copy of the first refusal renunciation letter sent by Fern-Chapman to Atlantic Offshore? If not, please get it asap, I want to take a look at it.'

Geneva, Switzerland

'Christen took the tram to the *Europcar* hire firm, it's just two stops along from his flat. Then I saw him drive out in a white Opel. The number is AG 687623.' It was 9:30 am and Luca was talking to Javier. 'He went onto the Route des Jeunes, in the direction of town, but he could have been going anywhere.'

'Was he carrying anything?'

'Sorry, I should have said, he was pulling a travel bag.'

'Did it seem heavy, or light?'

'It was light, he lifted it on and off the tram with no effort.'

'Great! I think he's probably going to Zurich. How long does the drive take?'

'About three and a half hours, but I'd be surprised if he is. Most people prefer to take the train to Zurich if they don't have a car. Renting one for that trip is unusual.'

'It depends on what's in the bag, Luca. Has Franz got his photo?'

'Marius sent it to him as well.'

'OK, call Franz to watch out for him.'

Javier updated Patrice and Pedro. Things were starting to move.

Edinburgh, Scotland

'Here's the printout of the renunciation letter file we got from Tom Newman.' Moira Mackenzie placed the one-page document on her boss's desk.

Cameron read it through, it was short and to the point. Olympic Funds renounced their right of first refusal to acquire 3,000,000 shares of Atlantic Offshore Oil & Gas SA, at a price per share of $10, total transaction value, $30 million. The letter was signed with Harry's electronic signature, as Investment Manager. He reread it a second time, but it told him nothing, except what he already knew.

He handed it back to her. 'Better just file this, please. It's of no help.'

'What exactly is the problem, Alex?'

He decided to confide in her, he knew how discreet she was. 'Apparently, Harry was in Luxembourg on the day of the Atlantic Alliance transaction. There's a journalist who's insinuating that he set the sale up at that price to save Olympic from suspension. He intends to write about it. And Harry's recollections of what happened don't seem to pan out.'

'Oh, I see. That's quite an accusation, insider trading and all that. You have to ask Harry if that's the case, you've no other option.'

'You're right, of course. I've got to sort out the mess around the Lindsey Premier Bond issue first. I'll call him this afternoon, see what he has to say.'

Moira put the letter in her filing tray, she also had a lot to do.

Cameron's problem with Lindsey Premier Bonds still wasn't resolved by the end of the day. He was tired and late for a family celebration, so decided to postpone his call to Harry until the morning.

Geneva, Switzerland

Luca was in a pizzeria near the apartment when Franz Stenmark called from Zurich. 'Christen's here. He just came around the corner from the back of the building and he's disappeared from the lobby. Jolidon must have been expecting him and let him in.'

'Did he have his bag with him?'

'Yes, he carried it in.'

'You've never seen him, did you get a shot to be sure?'

'I'm sending it right away, but it has to be him. I'll call you when he leaves.'

Malaga, Spain

'I'm sending you a picture of Christen going into Jolidon's building. He's got the travel bag with him.'

'Tell Franz to follow him when he comes out. See if that bag looks heavier.' Javier transmitted the news to Pedro Espinoza.

Zurich, Switzerland

'*Bonjour René*, how are you?' Claude Jolidon looked quickly around the landing and ushered the notary inside, locking the door behind him.

Christen took off his heavy winter coat. 'That's a new lock you've got on the door?'

As he'd agreed with Esther, Jolidon hadn't told the *huissier* about the attack. He answered, 'I figured we needed to look after our assets a little more carefully. It's virtually burglar-proof and I'm sleeping better.'

'Glad to hear it, Claude, but I'd kill for a coffee, it's like Siberia out there.'

He went to switch on the machine, 'Where did you leave the car?'

'Just behind the building, it's a 30-minute spot, so we'll have to be quick.'

'No problem, everything's ready.'

He put the coffee on the desk for the notary and opened up the strongbox. 'These are three envelopes of diamonds from Esther, same as always, 100 stones, approximately 100 carats.'

'Still no idea where they come from, Claude?'

He ignored the sarcasm and put the cartons on the desk. 'Three boxes of valuables, I estimate each one worth about CHF2 million. The list of reserve prices is inside each box.'

'It doesn't matter which goes into which sale?'

Jolidon laughed, 'As long as they all sell, who gives a shit?'

'Good point. We're looking at 10 to 12 million from the three sales. Not to be sneezed at.' *With that Fribourg problem off my back, I'm going to make some real money.*

He took several towels from his travel bag and wrapped everything carefully, then packed them inside, zipped it up and fastened a small padlock to tie the two zippers.

'Did you see that Drewsberrys' lawyer who gave you a tough time before the last sale?'

'Not yet, something to look forward to. That reminds me, I need the three letters from the Trust, signed by Appletree.'

'No sooner said...' Jolidon placed three envelopes on the desk, addressed to each of the auction houses. 'I just hope they don't talk to each other and wonder what's going on.'

Christen put them in the inside pocket of his overcoat. 'They're more interested in their buyer's premium than in what's being sold. Don't forget, it's Geneva.'

'That's what Esther said, I just hope you're right.'

Christen finished his coffee. 'Right, I'm off, another 3 ½ hours back home. I'll be knackered, I should have come by train.'

'Too dangerous, with boxes of jewellery worth millions of francs in a wheelie bag. You'll be fine, just don't have a drink until you get back.'

'What's that supposed to mean?'

'Esther's worried you're drinking too much, that you might do something foolish.'

'Claude, the last foolish thing I did was to get CHF200k more for the diamonds at the last sale. Don't worry about me, I know my limits, I won't screw up, I need that money; there's a lot at stake.'

'Whatever you say, René, but be careful.'

He let Christen out and called Esther. 'René just left with the goods for Geneva. He'll deliver everything tomorrow, so we're in good shape. And he promised to control his drinking, let's wait and see.'

Geneva, Switzerland

It was 2pm when Javier got the next call from Luca. 'Franz just called. Christen came out pulling the case, he followed him to the Opel and said it looked heavier when he lifted it into the car.'

'So, he's picked something up at the apartment. That's great news, Luca. Can you hang around his place and catch him arriving?'

'He'll be here about 5 o'clock if he doesn't hit much traffic. I'll be waiting.'

At 6 pm, he called back. 'He's home, with the case. I'm sending you a shot of him getting off the tram. It looks heavier.'

'I agree. Looks like he collected something from Jolidon. I don't think anything else is going to happen tonight, but tomorrow will be busy.'

'OK, I'm out of here, I'll be back in the morning.'

Javier texted the photo to everyone, including Coetzee and Jenny.

She called Leticia. 'You've seen Javier's message?'

'Patrice just showed it to me. It looks like more of Charlie's diamonds are going to auction.'

'I'm afraid so. We're getting to the end of this now. No regrets?'

'Sure I have regrets, especially for Charlie, I think we all have.' She sighed, 'But it's the only way.'

'I know. I'll arrange a call tomorrow, make sure everyone is in agreement.'

'Goodnight, Jenny dear, give Ellen a big kiss from me.'

Zurich, Switzerland

Claude Jolidon finished the spreadsheet calculating what he was now worth and closed his laptop. *More than $3 million, not bad*, he decided. He went to switch off the desk lamp and a pen fell to the floor. Jolidon stooped down to retrieve it and noticed something fastened under the desk. He ripped it away.

Merde, merde, merde! The transmitting device was tiny, but he knew it could be lethal. *That can't be from the guy who tried to break in last Sunday. It must have been set up before I got the new lock. Who the fuck has been in here? What have they found, or heard?*

SIXTY

'**Good morning, Monsieur de Moncrieff, what can I do for you?**'

'Hello, Mr Tournier, sorry to trouble you, but we're processing your payment today, as promised, and I just want to confirm the IBAN, if you don't mind.'

'Not at all.' He read out the letters and digits slowly and distinctly. 'Is that what you have?'

'Exactly, thanks very much and I'll give the necessary instructions. *Bon weekend*, Monsieur Tournier.'

Patrice called Jenny. 'That should keep everyone quiet until Monday.'

Edinburgh, Scotland

'Harry. You must be a very happy man.'

'You mean the Boris bounce? It's great news for all of us, our investors most of all. We've picked up another percentage point already this morning. But that's not why I'm calling.'

Cameron's ears pricked up. 'So, to what do I owe the honour?'

'I have an apology to make. I told you something that wasn't true, and I want to put it right.'

'Go ahead, I'm listening.' He switched on his recorder,

wondering if his decision not to call Fern-Chapman the previous evening might have avoided an unnecessary disagreement.

'It's about the BMH transaction. I told you I sent down our letter of renunciation to Atlantic Offshore by email. That's not what happened.'

'So, what did happen?'

'OK,' Harry paused, concentrating on his storyline. 'On Wednesday, I was home sick, and Gérard Boillat, their chairman, called to say they'd had an offer of $10 per share; he didn't say who. I said I'd think about it. No way I'd pay that price, but it's true I knew it would be a great deal for Olympic, since we hold 25% of the capital. I called Boillat back and asked him who was the bidder. He told me BMH, never heard of them, but what the hell, if they wanted to double the share price, who was I to get in their way?

'Before you say it, I agree, it was marginally contentious, but I said we'd step aside and let Atlantic Offshore do the deal with BMH, it would clearly be beneficial to everyone concerned.'

'But you didn't send a confirmation?'

'No, I didn't confirm it in writing, they didn't ask for it and I was knackered with the flu and I never thought of it. That's what caused this whole screw-up. On the Thursday afternoon, a lawyer called Guillaume Fric called me on behalf of BMH. He told me Atlantic needed an original, signed renunciation from Olympic, in case of future EU considerations, or the deal would fall through.'

'So you flew down to Luxembourg with it?'

'I was feeling a lot better, so I wrote the letter, printed it out, and went down Thursday night. I signed it and gave it to Fric on Friday morning and flew back at midday.'

'Why didn't you just tell me the truth?'

'I knew it would look like a put-up job, like I was involved somehow with BMH. I made a mistake; I was too cautious and I behaved stupidly.'

'Where did you stay in Luxembourg?'

'That's a funny question, why do you ask that?'

'I got a call the other day from a columnist, Terry Owen, do you know him?'

Fern-Chapman had been half-expecting this and tried to take in his stride. 'I know him, he's a second-rate broker who writes newspaper articles. He used to work for me at Selchurch Peak and he hates my guts because he got fired for incompetence.'

'He knows you were at the *Piemont Hotel* in Luxembourg and he says he's writing a piece about the Atlantic Alliance transaction.'

'I've told you exactly what happened, Alex. He can write what the hell he likes, but it won't change anything. I have no idea why those BMH people did that deal at $10 and I'm delighted that it pushed our valuations up. I'm going to look closely into the whys and wherefores and if I find a compelling reason, something we've overlooked, I might decide to increase our own stake.'

Harry held his breath; would Cameron buy his story?

'Did you know that BMH is a South African company?'

'I told you, I never heard of them, why is that important?'

He ignored the question. 'I don't see what Owen can prove, that's what counts. Your version confirms what Gérard Boillat told me and I doubt he'd lie about such an important matter. We need to be ready to deny any accusations or insinuations by this journalist. Let me think about it and I'll get back to you. And Harry, never

ever lie to me again, whatever the circumstances, or we're finished. Understood?' The phone went dead.

London, England

So, he's spoken to Boillat and our stories are in sync. Harry suddenly felt an overwhelming feeling of relief. He'd saved Olympic Funds Group, saved his career and friends and saved his relationship with Esther.

He checked the time, it was just after 10am; he called her at the apartment.

'Good morning, Harry. You were off early this morning, what was the emergency?'

'The markets are going crazy after Boris's victory. He's going to get a majority of 70 or 80, by the looks of it.'

'How are my funds doing?'

'They've all picked up another percentage point and when the US markets open, it'll continue. The pound is strengthening too, up over 1%.'

'So, it could be a good time to buy?'

'If you can get in before lunchtime, I think you'll be in great shape.'

'I'll call you back.'

Esther called René Christen. 'Any news from Drewberrys on the payments?'

'I'm with them now, delivering the valuables for February. I'll ask.'

A moment later he came back on the line. 'They've just received confirmation that the remaining payments will be made today.'

'Great news, René, I'm sure you're as pleased as I am. Your problem just disappeared.'

She rang off and scribbled the numbers on a slip of paper. Apart from the $3 million with Olympic, in her Guadeloupe and Bahrain accounts she had almost $3 million in cash. Her share of the Drewberrys sale proceeds was $2.4 million. *That means I'll have more than $5 million sitting there doing nothing, while the markets are promising great returns.*

She took her decision and called Harry back. 'I can get $2 million to you by midday, can you guarantee me the best current prices?'

'Bloody hell, that's quite a shock. Are you sure you want to do it?'

'Are you sure the markets are going to continue their recovery?'

'There's no doubt about it, everybody's buying, I've never seen anything like it in 20 years.'

'And you can get me the best prices?'

'I'll block them for you as soon as I hang up.'

'Right, I'm calling my bank now. It'll come from *Almeida Enterprises* as usual. Thanks, darling, I won't forget it.'

The manager at the First Credit Bank of Bahrain was most disappointed to see her reduce the balance on the *Almeida Enterprises* account to just over $900k, but she promised to replace the $2 million within a few days and he guaranteed he'd get the funds to London before midday.

Esther sat back on the comfortable settee in her magnificent penthouse apartment in Eaton Square, Belgravia, thinking about her rise from total poverty after Ray d'Almeida's death to where she was today. *I just sent $2 million from Bahrein to London with a telephone call. Ray would be very proud of me, very proud indeed.*

Geneva, Switzerland

'I'm sitting in the lobby of the Mandarin Oriental and Christen's still in there somewhere with his travel bag. He's been there for almost an hour. Do you want me to keep waiting?'

Javier checked the time, it was 11:30 am. 'He should be going to the other two hotels today as well, we'd just like to make sure of it. At least you're inside in the warm. Keep it up and I promise you a bonus.'

Marbella, Spain

It was late afternoon when Jenny called Coetzee. 'Hi, Marius, tomorrow's the big day, you must be excited at the thought of your wife becoming even more famous.'

'Don't start giving her big ideas, she may decide to get rid of me again.'

'Chance would be a fine thing,' she laughed. 'You heard the news from Javier? Christen delivered the valuables to all three hotels today, they're going for broke in February.'

'Unless they get stopped in their tracks.'

'Exactly why I'm calling. Hang on a moment, I'm getting the others on the call, so we can confirm we're happy with our decision, before we press the destruct button.'

When everyone was listening, in her matter-of-fact way, Jenny summarised the agenda of Monday's actions. No one spoke and she said, 'We all know the consequences of this plan and in one way or another, we're all affected by it. Can we each please confirm that we should go ahead, no doubts, no tears?'

One by one, Espinoza, Patrice, Javier and Coetzee agreed, without comment, then Leticia said, 'Charlie would want us to. We have to do it for him.'

'You're right, we owe it to his memory to do this. Good, that's settled. Now we can relax and have a calm, quiet weekend with our families, before the storm breaks on Monday.'

Edinburgh, Scotland

Alex Cameron had left for an evening meeting and Moira Mackenzie was clearing her desk for the weekend. Her boss had played the recording of his conversation with Fern-Chapman for her that afternoon and she'd listened carefully to every word, in her punctilious fashion.

Cameron sighed. 'It seems like an honest mistake, but we're going to have to fight the flack whenever that article comes out. It'll be suppositions and insinuations and whatever we do or say, people will always believe there's no smoke without fire.'

'I suppose we have to give Harry the benefit of the doubt, compared to a newspaper hack,' she'd replied.

Moira reread Harry's renunciation letter again before putting it in the Atlantic Offshore file. She was a very conscientious woman and checked the calendar on her laptop. *That ties in, he signed it on Friday 29th, the morning of the transaction.* She filed the letter away and locked up for the weekend.

SIXTY-ONE

Saturday, December 14, 2019
Johannesburg, South Africa

Karen's report covered pages 6 and 7 of the *Johannesburg Sun* and was the lead article in the Life & Arts section of the *FT Weekend*. It carried the headline:

Are we Seeing the Return of Conflict Diamonds?
An appeal by **Karen Spellman,** Prize-winning **Sun** investigative journalist.

Prior to the Portuguese 'Revolution of the Carnations' in April 1974, the three rebel groups fighting to liberate Angola from 500 years of Portuguese possession were united in their war against this last remaining European colonial power. The aim of the MPLA, supported by Russia and Cuba, the FNLA, backed by US funding, and UNITA, a Chinese protégée, was specific and identical, **Independence for Angola**. After the revolution, Portugal began withdrawing its troops, ready to hand over the country to a tripartite government formed by these three factions. However, immediately after independence was proclaimed, in November 1975, these once united groups turned against each other. The FNLA was quickly defeated and forced into exile by Agostinho Neto's MPLA, with on-the-ground assistance from Russian and Cuban troops, whereupon Neto became Angola's first post-colonial Prime

Minister and the first communist-backed leader in Africa.

However, UNITA was not the same pushover. For almost three decades, from 1975 – 2002, civil war raged in Angola as Jonas Savimbi's UNITA anti-communist rebels attempted to bring down the soviet-backed MPLA government. In reality, this was a proxy war between a determined Soviet Union and a lukewarm United States; communism against democracy. The human cost of this tragedy, thousands of kilometres away from its sponsors, was a million displaced citizens and an undetermined number of deaths, possibly just as many.

This was not the only cost, however. Wars must be paid for, and despite their political differences, these opposing forces still shared one common concern; how to finance the endless conflict. Not surprisingly, they found the same solution as did other African ex-colonies, like Guinea, Liberia and Sierra Leone. Angola's natural resources are legend. This immense, majestic country sits on vast deposits of oil and gas, rare metals, minerals and precious stones. However, whereas the government could continue to finance its army through oil and mineral production from their inherited infrastructure, supported by legal international cartels and markets, the rebels had no infrastructure, no ownership of resources, no organised, recognised distribution or marketing channels. They needed a commodity that was comparatively easy to extract, requiring little infrastructure, small and light to transport and hugely valuable to sell. The precious resource that ticked all these boxes was obvious: Angolan Diamonds, among the most beautiful precious stones in existence. Thus, the nature of the Angolan Civil War was transformed into **Government Oil** against **Rebel Diamonds**. This is how

CONFLICT, or **BLOOD** diamonds became the rebel forces' common currency in 20th century Africa.

Official statistics and related reports estimate that during the '80s and '90s, more than 20% of Angolan diamond production was under rebel control, and for some time, UNITA became the largest producer of natural, or rough diamonds, in the country. These diamonds were mined and recovered by slave labourers, conscripted by Jonas Savimbi's rebel forces; workers who died in the volcanic basins, lakes, mines and rivers, searching through the Kimberlites that held the highly compressed carbon atoms in their grasp. For most ordinary Angolans, men, women and children, the choice was simple, die searching for diamonds to buy arms or die fighting with the arms bought by the diamonds. After Savimbi was killed, in 2002, UNITA fell apart and the civil war came to an end. Statistics from 2004 estimated that by that time, only 1% of the international diamond trade was illegal, or conflict based.

In 2003, United Nations General Assembly Resolution 55/56 led to the introduction of the Kimberley Process Certification Scheme, which requires certification of all rough diamonds moving between countries. In theory, this should have put an end to the deaths, slavery and misery caused by what had been a mainstream means of financing rebel activities. But it seems that wherever there's a will there's a way. When illicit rough diamonds are cut and polished, it's impossible to trace their source and distinguish them from legitimate diamonds. By smuggling the rough diamonds out and processing them in neighbouring countries they can be sold in the legitimate market at top prices. After the civil war ended, other motives financed the industry: **CORRUPTION AND GREED**.

In 2011, Rafael Marques de Morais, an Angolan investigative journalist and human rights advocate, published ***Blood Diamonds: Corruption and Torture in Angola.*** The book describes human rights abuses and violations committed by security guards and soldiers in the diamond fields of northern Angola, near the border with the Republic of the Congo. Marques de Morais alleged that army generals and government-related businessmen, shareholders in the mines and the security companies, were criminally responsible for abuses against minors, conscripted as 'diamond fodder'. He filed a criminal complaint against these wealthy and influential people. Lawsuits and countersuits continued for years, and finally, Marques de Morais was given a suspended prison sentence. During all this time, the Angolan MPLA government, under **José Eduardo dos Santos,** President and Commander-in-Chief of the Armed Forces since 1979, **DID NOTHING TO INTERVENE** in the illegal diamond mining activity.

Dos Santos, who was educated in the Soviet Union, stepped down in 2017, and quickly shipped off to Barcelona, Spain, having accumulated a vast fortune for his family during his 38 years in power. His successor, João Lourenço, soon discovered the immense problems he was faced with. Despite sitting on the richest deposits of Africa's precious minerals and natural resources, Angola's economy was fatally weak after four decades of the dos Santos Presidency. Lourenço instituted a tough economic restructuring programme focused on the sale of state-owned oil and diamond assets and reform of the national budget. He also launched a battle to investigate the dos Santos family and try to recoup the estimated **$100 billion** embezzled from the state during the presidency of José Eduardo dos Santos.

He was assisted in this by the publication of the **Luanda Leaks**, which exposed two decades of unscrupulous deals that made **Isabel dos Santos**, the ex-president's daughter, Africa's wealthiest woman and first billionairess; and left oil and diamond-rich Angola one of the poorest countries on Earth. This dossier exposes a vast network of more than 400 banks, companies and consultants engaged in money-laundering for the dos Santos family's business empire, comprising more than 400 companies and subsidiaries in 41 countries, including almost 100 in havens such as Malta, Mauritius and Hong Kong. In one singular investigation, the International Monetary Fund reported that **£32 billion** in oil revenue went missing from the government's ledger before being tracked to having been used on 'quasi-fiscal activities'; better described as **'stolen'**.

Dos Santos has been accused of leading one of the most corrupt regimes in Africa by accumulating incredible wealth for his family and silencing his opposition, while nearly 70% of the population lived on less than $2 a day.

At the time of writing, almost the whole dos Santos family is in Spain and all have been removed from their positions as heads of major Angolan companies and institutions, including his son José Filomeno, and daughter, Isabel. They are both now being investigated for fraud and money laundering.

What has this to do with Blood Diamonds?

In September, at a public auction sale in Geneva, Switzerland, 100 Angolan cut diamonds were sold for $1.75 million. Then, just a few days ago, at another Geneva auction, a further 100

Angolan diamonds were sold for $2 million. In both cases, the seller was described as a *'Private Investment Trust'* and the accompanying photographs were virtually identical.

The diamonds were described in the auction catalogues as; *'from the pre-independence period; known provenance, guaranteed not blood diamonds'.*

Angolan independence was declared in November 1975, 44 years ago! Yet, within a few weeks of each other, identical lots of 100 diamonds worth almost $4 million, supposedly mined more than 4 decades ago, suddenly reappear, to be sold anonymously at public auctions, by a *'Private Investment Trust'*.

There are two possible explanations of the truth here. Which of them is more likely?

1. These two batches of identical, supposedly legitimate diamonds, have lain undisturbed for almost a half century, in the midst of civil war, illicit diamond mining and government corruption that caused hundreds of thousands of deaths, only to reappear and be sold at public auctions in Switzerland as *'known provenance, guaranteed not blood diamonds'.*

2. These are Conflict/Blood Diamonds mined illegally by slave labourers; including starving, suffering children, smuggled out of Angola, cut and polished in a neighbouring country and now offered for sale by illicit diamond dealers posing as a *'Private Investment Trust'*, with a so-called guarantee as to their origin.

This writer thinks the truth is inescapable. Whether by companies run by army generals, corrupt governments or powerful businessmen or women, illicit diamonds are still being mined, processed and sold throughout the world. And innocent people, men, women and children, are still suffering, starving and dying to make these wealthy diamond mine owners, smugglers and dealers even richer.

I am a South African, the Angolans are my neighbours, and I feel for these innocent victims of the bloodthirsty, despoliation of their country. I cannot believe that a half-century after throwing off the yoke of colonialism, this rancid corruption still continues to line the pockets of those who pretended to be 'Fighters for Independence'. We ordinary bystanders can do nothing to change venal governments and corrupt businesspeople, but we can raise our voices against this blatant insult to our intelligence and try to prevent more suffering and abuse of innocent citizens.

If, like me, you believe it is finally time to do something, anything, to put a stop to this corruption, slave labour and murder, please send a message of support and sign the online petition at:

change.org/- stopconflictblooddiamonds

On behalf of the oppressed African victims of illicit diamond mining, Thank You.

Karen Spellman <u>karenspellman@truthmatters.com</u>

Over the weekend the article appeared or was reported in 62 syndicated international newspapers, magazines and other media outlets in over 100 countries. It was liked, shared, tweeted and retweeted by millions and achieved international prime time TV coverage. By Monday, the number of signatures on the petition was more than a million and rising rapidly. Karen's phone and email account were inundated with requests for comments, interviews, invitations to speak at events and conferences; and, many times, just thanks from grateful citizens around the world who were happy to see that someone cared about them and was taking a stand against corruption.

London, England
Terry Owen's article was shorter and restricted to the third page of the FT; it wasn't picked up by any other outlet. It started out:

Last-minute race to Luxembourg to save Olympic Funds Group
By **Terry Owen**, financial correspondent

Just a few days ago, several of Olympic Funds Group's investment vehicles were on the brink of suspension. Today, thanks to a last-minute share deal in Luxembourg last week, the group's fund valuations are riding high again. This improvement was boosted yesterday by the 'Boris Bounce', but the real reason behind the change in Olympic's fortunes was an OTC purchase of shares in Atlantic Offshore Oil & Gas SA, on the Luxembourg exchange, by an unknown South African investment company, Benelux Mineral Holdings SA. This purchase doubled the value of the 12.5 million Atlantic Offshore shares held by Olympic. An FT investigation reveals that Mr Harry Fern-Chapman, the Investment Advisor of Olympic Group, was in Luxembourg on the day of the transaction. The question is, WHY?

SIXTY-TWO

Saturday, December 14th, 2019
Marbella, Spain

Leticia called Jenny. 'I've just read Karen's article in the *Financial Times*, it's incredible. My mam and dad came over and I read it to them in Portuguese. It brought back all the memories of the terrible times when they had to escape from those Russian and Cuban murderers. I was too young to remember, but it didn't matter, we've been crying for an hour since I read it to them. They couldn't believe that someone who wasn't Angolan could have such a knowledge of our beautiful country and the civil war that forced them to leave, and now the crime and corruption that is destroying it. Patrice read it and even he was crying with us.

'I'm going to call Karen. I have to thank her for what she wrote, and you too, Jenny, for making it happen. Even if our plan doesn't work, you've both done a wonderful thing, we'll never forget it.'

London, England

Dr Hugh Middleton was under the cosh again, this time for the most important assignment the Institute for Global Internet Security had received since he and Ilona had set it up, eight years ago. The report had been commissioned by the UN Technology Bank, a newly created entity, whose mission, in their own words, was: *'To help least developed countries build science, technology and innovation capacities, ecosystems and regulatory frameworks.'*

The institute's substantial treatise, representing two months of work by a team of thirty researchers, analysts and writers, was entitled, *'Social Media, Cybercrime and the Big Four Tech Threats to Developing Nations'*. Middleton considered that the institute's vocation was not to instruct clients how to execute projects, but to warn them of the dangers of executing them wrongly. The report was due at the end of the coming week, and his problem was, as usual, that Ilona was no longer there to make it happen.

He was ploughing his way through the second volume of the five-part marathon when his mobile rang, 'Have you seen the article yet, Dr Middleton?'

As usual, that morning, he had walked along to his local bakery and newsagent to purchase croissants and the Weekend edition of the FT. He had discovered Terry Owen's article on page 3, reading it several times over breakfast. He skimmed through the other articles in the main section of the paper and then reluctantly returned to his day-time job, putting the supplement sections aside for later enjoyment.

'Indeed I have, Terry,' he answered. 'An apposite concoction; just enough fact and not too much fiction. Well done, I believe this exposé could be the first of the several straws required to break the camel's back. Let's be patient for a day or two to assess the damage before deciding on our next manoeuvre.'

Middleton rang off and checked the time. *An appropriate moment to rattle Sir Reginald's cage, as it were*, he decided. He opened up his laptop and chose the *enough@stopfraud.com* email account and typed a short message. As he pressed *send*, he smiled to himself. *Strange how much I'm enjoying this.* He picked up volume II again, with much less enthusiasm.

Edinburgh, Scotland

Alex Cameron also studied Terry Owen's full article several times. As he had expected, it was long on innuendo and supposition and short on facts, but it worried him. The rumour mill would love to ruin Harry's reputation, that's what they were there for. *I'll have to get Harry up here and talk to our lawyers about damage limitation, make sure this doesn't spiral out of control. Why the hell didn't he just tell me the truth right away? I just hope there's nothing he's holding back, or we're all in deep shit!*

Belgravia, London, England

Esther didn't read much of the Saturday FT, she wasn't very interested in property and fashion articles, nor world news for that matter. If she had, she'd have seen Karen's report in pride of place on the first page of the Life & Arts section. She looked immediately for her fund prices in the Companies & Markets section of the paper, they were up another 2% since her last-minute purchase. *That's $100k I've made in a single day!* 'You were right, darling, the timing couldn't have been better.'

Harry had been watching her from across the room and walked over as she turned back to read the front-page headlines. He took the paper from her before she could get to Terry Owen's article and threw it onto the coffee table. 'We've both done well, that's worth celebrating.

Let's go into town for lunch and choose something for your Christmas present. It won't cost anything, courtesy of Olympic Funds.'

When they returned that afternoon, she couldn't find the newspaper, but didn't bother looking for it, Harry was feeling amorous and they continued to celebrate in the bedroom. He was convinced the story would die a death after a few days, no one could prove anything, and people have short memories.

Mayfair, London, England

Sir Reginald Scarbrough read the article on page 3 with apprehension. As Terry Owen and Alex Cameron had assumed, like most readers, he thought, *There's no smoke without fire.* He'd received a second message from the mysterious *enough@stopfraud.com* email account, *'Why would BMH pay $30 million for $15 million of shares? For the answer, ask Fern-Chapman'.*

Someone was trying to tell him something and he wished he knew exactly who, what and why. He decided to call Harry on Monday and have it out with him.

Geneva, Switzerland

'Sorry about your Saturday, but this report is dynamite. I need to know if we're exposed and what action we should take?' Stéphane Tournier asked anxiously.

'Let me read it again and think for a moment.' Bernard Villeneuve, the Drewberrys' Swiss lawyer was studying Karen's article in the FT. He hadn't known about it until Tournier's call asking him to come over to his office immediately.

He put the newspaper aside. 'This is about that *African*

Benevolent Trust, they had about 100 lots in the November sale. It's been syndicated all over the world.'

'I know that, Bernard, but what's Drewberrys risk?'

'They were represented by a *huissier*, M. René Christen, a second-rate notary from Fribourg. I gave him a tough time and he produced a letter of confirmation of provenance from the trustee, Benjamin Appletree, in Angola.'

'I know that too, but what does it mean?'

'We have no liability of any kind; our due diligence obligation doesn't require any further investigation if we receive satisfactory paperwork from the sellers or their representative.'

Tournier felt a flood of relief, 'You're absolutely certain of that?'

'Of course. It's not our job to make sure the notary does his work. If there's anything dubious about the provenance of the goods, he's on the hook, not us.'

'In the case of the diamonds, it looks like that's highly probable. And it's big news. I've had several messages from colleagues; the article's going viral on Facebook and Twitter.'

'So, thank God I insisted on the letter from Appletree.'

'Of course, thanks, that's the first worry out of the way.'

'There's something else?'

'I just checked, and the buyers haven't paid yet.'

'It's been more than 10 days, who are they?'

'A Bahamas company called Durham House Investments. The MD's a Frenchman called Patrice de Moncrieff, I liked him, well presented. They bought just about all the items from that trust, almost $5 million, with the premium.'

'What? They bought all the lots then didn't pay?'

'Moncrieff called me twice to say they'd pay yesterday,

but they didn't. They've got the funds, a $5 million LOC from the *Banque de Commerce de Genève*, so I'm getting worried.'

'You think it's a set up job? Someone wants to screw up that African Trust?'

'No idea, but something like that, no?'

Villeneuve said, 'You still look as worried as hell. What else is there?'

'Sandra told me Christen brought in 100 lots on Friday, for the February sales.'

'Including more diamonds?'

'Same, another batch of 100.'

'With another provenance letter from Mr Appletree, in Angola?' When Tournier just nodded, he said, 'This is definitely dodgy. A spat between whoever wrote, or paid for, that article, and the people behind the trust. They're probably smuggling and selling illicit diamonds and that article was timed to wreck their plans. We need to get out of the way, the collateral damage to our reputation could be massive.'

'How do we do that?'

'On Monday, we ask these Durham House people to pay. If they don't, we can be pretty sure it's them behind the report.'

'And then?'

'We ask them to confirm their reasons in writing and we send a copy to Christen, see what he says. Second, we refuse the new lots until this is cleared up. Do you have an address for Durham House Investments? I'll try to check them out.'

SIXTY-THREE

'I hope you celebrated last night? Can I speak to your amazing wife?'

'Fat chance! Karen never had a quiet moment all day and night, endless interviews and now she's exhausted. She's fast asleep and I don't want to disturb her. By the way, don't tell her, but I agree; she's amazing.'

'That's the price of success, it was a fabulous piece, she deserves whatever prize they give for investigations like that. And of course, it was especially nostalgic for Leticia and her parents. When she wakes up, please tell her we're all in awe of her research and writing.'

'I'll be pleased to do that, she'll appreciate it, she really loved the chance to investigate it, kind of one last blast before retirement. I was also thinking it should get some reaction from the Zurich people. It'll be interesting to see what they do tomorrow.'

'That's actually why I'm calling, to ask you a favour.'

'Ask away, Jenny, your wish is my command.'

'Can you come back up here for a couple of days?'

'Has something happened?'

'Not yet, but you're right, things will probably get difficult tomorrow and it's always a comfort to know you're by our side.'

'I promised Pedro I wouldn't hurt anyone, you remember?'

She laughed, 'I doubt it'll be necessary, one look from you and you don't need to hurt them. But I'd feel safer with a backstop, unless Karen needs you more down there?'

'On the contrary, she'll be happy to get me out of the way of reporters and celebrities crowding round to be seen talking to her.'

'So, you'll come? You're a treasure, Marius. You can stay here in my house. I'll take care of the flights, I know you're getting used to first class, don't want you to slum it.'

Zurich, Switzerland

Claude Jolidon had a subscription to the Swiss, French language newspaper, *Le Temps*. It cost him CHF29 a month and he read it online every morning, it helped relieve the boredom of his self-imposed imprisonment in the apartment. Karen's article wasn't published until the Sunday edition and because he was busy searching property agents' sites for another office location, he didn't get around to reading it until that afternoon.

The sight of the photographs of the diamonds was like a physical blow to his chest and he struggled to breathe. He thought of the attack on the apartment, the transmitter he'd found taped under his desk. *What the fuck is going on?* At that moment, Claude Jolidon knew the game was up. He called René Christen. 'Have we been paid by Drewberrys yet?'

'I haven't looked at the fiduciary account this weekend, but they were expecting everything to be paid on Friday. Why, what's wrong?'

'Check it now, it's urgent.'

He waited impatiently while Christen checked the account at the *Banco de Credito de Luanda* online. 'No, it hasn't come in yet.'

'Fuck, *putain de merde*, shit!'

Christen started to feel nervous, *A million francs of that money is mine.* 'I asked you, what's wrong?'

'Can you get *Le Temps* online?'

'You mean the newspaper? No, but I can get today's edition, they have a free trial deal, I can sign up and get it right away.'

'Do that now René, and look for an article on pages 4 and 5, by someone called Karen Spellman, then call me back. We have to find a way to get that money.'

Geneva, Switzerland

'That's odd.' Bernard Villeneuve was checking the Bahamas Company Register, trying to learn what he could about Durham House Investments Ltd. The only director listed was Patrice de Moncrieff, whose address was given as Puente Romano, Marbella, Spain. What Villeneuve had spotted was that his occupation was given as, 'Banker'. He'd also noticed that the address of DHI was the same as the Nassau headquarters of *BIP, the Banque Internationale de Paris*, one of the biggest banks in the world.

He looked up BIP management executives and found 'Patrice de Moncrieff, General Manager, Spain'. Villeneuve asked himself why a Bahamas company, whose MD was a senior executive with the BIP, would go to the *Banque de Commerce de Genève* for a Letter of Credit for $5 million? Drewberrys banked with the BIP's branch in Geneva and their main UK banker was the BIP in London.

And why would this company, with the people and resources it has in Spain, Nassau and Geneva, buy almost all the valuables put up by a dodgy 'African Trust' and then not pay for them, even though they have a $5 million LOC? It makes no sense. This whole thing stinks. We have to extricate ourselves as quickly as possible, before we get burned when something goes wrong.

He called Tournier and brought him up to date.

'This is a nightmare. So what do we do?'

'Same as I said yesterday, but a lot faster. Have you got an email address for them?'

'It's on the card Moncrieff gave me.'

'OK. I'll draft a mail for Sandra to send tomorrow first thing, asking for immediate payment. If we don't receive it by Tuesday, we've got to return those goods to that notary, Christen. If that article is true and these are conflict diamonds, we can't be seen to be holding them for one minute longer than necessary.'

Geneva, Switzerland

Claude Jolidon had looked up Karen's *change.org* appeal. He knew it had been promoted by newspapers and social media throughout the world, but his stomach lurched when he saw it had already gathered over a million signatures. He was frantically wondering whether he should pack his bags and run when René Christen called back.

'You think that's why they haven't paid?' The notary had read Karen's report in the online Le Temps. He'd also drunk almost a bottle of white wine and Jolidon could hear it in his voice.

'It's just a coincidence, is that what you think?'

'But they have to pay, they were accredited buyers, so

they must have had a bank guarantee or letter of credit. Drewberrys can sue them if they don't pay.' Christen was grasping at straws, desperate to get his million francs, to stay out of prison; the combination of stress and wine made him slur every other word.

'You're pissed and your brain's not functioning, you idiot. Whoever the buyers are, they have a legitimate right to refuse to buy anything without satisfactory proof of provenance. You're the fucking notary, you should be explaining that to me!'

'But what about the letters from Appletree, the trustee?'

Jolidon couldn't risk admitting anything further to the *huissier*, they might end up on opposite sides of a court room. 'I'll call Esther, see what she thinks. Sober up before I call back, René, so we can have a sensible conversation.'

Belgravia, London, England

After Jolidon told her it was a reprint of an article from Saturday's FT, Esther found the paper in the recycling bin. She didn't know why Harry had thrown it away and he'd gone out for a run in the park, so she couldn't ask. She flicked through to the Life & Arts section, the headline taking her breath away. *'Are we Seeing the Return of Conflict Diamonds?'* Then, she saw the name of the writer and thought she'd be physically sick.

Karen Spellman, wife of that vicious, two-timing bastard, Marius Coetzee, close friends of Jenny Bishop. They screwed up my plans in South Africa and Dubai and now they're trying to do the same again.

She forced herself to read the article, thinking at first that Karen had got hold of the wrong end of the stick, *Charlie Bishop's diamonds are definitely not blood diamonds.* Then, as she read on, she realised this was a report directly aimed at the sellers of the diamonds. *She wants the auction house to cancel the sale, so Jenny Bishop can get her diamonds back. It's been printed in dozens of papers all over the world, there's no safe place to sell those diamonds.*

Esther threw the newspaper back into the rubbish bin and called Jolidon back. 'The Bishop bitch has somehow found out her box 72 has been emptied and her diamonds are being sold. She's trying to stir up trouble for us, this is personal.'

So, I was right, that's where the diamonds were. 'How do you know that?'

'Because Karen Spellman's husband is Marius Coetzee, a cyber-security spook and their daughter is married to Jenny Fucking Bishop's nephew!'

SIXTY-FOUR

Monday, December 16th, 2019

Marbella, Spain

The message read:

Durham House Investments Ltd
Nassau Bahamas,
By email, attention M. Patrice de Moncrieff, Managing Director

Dear Sirs,
We note that you have not respected the payment terms for the lots acquired by your company at our November sale in Geneva. According to our accounts, as of today, the amount of CHF4,823,000 (Four million eight hundred and twenty-three thousand Swiss Francs), remains unpaid. Kindly note that if this amount has not been received in full in our account no. CH84076638007802441 at the Banque Internationale de Paris, Geneva, by close of business tomorrow, Dec 17th, the sales will be cancelled and the items bid for will be returned to the owners immediately. In this case, legal action may be instigated against you by Drewberrys or by the sellers, and you will be responsible for any costs involved in such a procedure. Please note that such costs will include the buyer's premium due on all successful bids.
Yours sincerely,
Drewberrys Auctions International Ltd
Stephan Tournier, Managing Director, Suisse.

'Right, pretty much what we thought. Do you want me to call now?'

'If you can, Patrice, he seems to be in a hurry to get rid of the goods. We need to get some information on this trust if we can.'

'OK, I'll call now and get back to you.'

Tournier took his call right away. 'I imagine this is about my email, Mr de Moncrieff?'

'That's right, I'm sorry I was a day late, but I was inundated on Friday, then about to order your payment on Saturday when I read the article about conflict diamonds in the FT. I suppose you've seen it?'

'I certainly have, but how does that explain your non-payment for lots that you bought two weeks ago?'

'As I said, I apologise for being late with our payment. However, in the circumstances, after Ms Spellman's article, I'm concerned about the provenance of these diamonds. Frankly, I agree with her appeal and I have signed the petition.'

'So, exactly what is it that you want, Mr de Moncrief?'

'You mean before I sign the payment order? It's very simple. I'd like to know the identity of the seller, this *'Private Investment Trust'*, and to confirm the provenance of the diamonds.'

'That's not possible, Monsieur. We never divulge the identity of a seller until the ownership of the goods has changed hands.'

'I see, that's most unfortunate. It means, in the present case, I would have to pay CHF2 million plus fees for a parcel of diamonds, only to then perhaps discover that they are conflict diamonds. In which event my company would be in breach of the Kimberley Process Agreement. Is that what you seek?'

'The only thing I seek, M. de Moncrieff, is to avoid any possible breach of any kind, for you, or for me.'

Smart guy, Patrice thought. 'I'm sorry, M. Tournier, in the circumstances, I'm not prepared to take the risk, unless I know where these diamonds came from.'

'And what about the rest of the lots you bought? I assume you'll fulfil your purchase obligation?'

'A close friend of mine said to me recently, *Recycling and laundering, like a Chinese laundry*. She was talking about the auction business. At the time, I didn't understand what she meant, but now, I do. All of the valuables purchased by us carried the same description of the seller, *'Private Investment Trust'*, an unfortunate coincidence, perhaps. In any event, as things stand, I'm afraid Durham House Investments won't be acquiring anything at all from your sale. Naturally, Drewberrys or the sellers are entitled to instigate any legal procedure they think fit, but in the circumstances, I doubt whether they would have much success. *Au revoir, M. Tournier.*'

Edinburgh, Scotland

Moira Mackenzie had been worried over the weekend. She'd also read Terry Owen's article and realised how much trouble Alex would be in if it turned out later to be true. Arriving at the office on Monday morning, she had an idea that should settle her mind. Moira took out the Olympic renunciation letter from the file and opened up the PDF version she'd received from Tom Newman. She compared the text on her screen with the printed version, it was identical. Alex wasn't in yet and she listened again to the recorded conversation in his office. *No mistake, that's what he said.* Back at her laptop, she opened up the *'Properties'* of the PDF file to make one more check.

She sat back in her chair. *Thank heavens I checked, but Alex is not going to be happy with this.*

'Couldn't it simply be a mistake when he delivered the letter? He got the date wrong. He'd been sick with the flu, it can happen.' Cameron was desperate to avoid a scandal; he'd never been on the wrong side of the FCA, the Financial Conduct Authority, and it could ruin his career.

'It's not possible, Alex. Here, I'll show you.' Moira Mackenzie pulled up the PDF file on her laptop and, without comment, showed him the details listed under *Properties*.

'Oh shit! Sorry, Moira. If you're right, this whole Atlantic Offshore deal is a fake and it definitely breaks the Insider Trading rules. I'll have to suspend trading and instigate an investigation.' He thought for a moment. 'Listen, I don't want to discuss this on the phone with Harry, I want him to look me in the eye and tell me why your theory is wrong. Please call him now and tell him I want him here this afternoon.'

She turned to go out and he said, 'Well done, Moira, you've probably saved us from a serious breach, though there'll be a lot of fallout if you're right.'

London, England
'What's the problem, Moira? Why the great rush?'

'I don't know, Harry, but Alex insisted on your coming up immediately. I checked the flights and if you leave right away you could catch the 11:30am and be at the office by 2pm. Alex said you don't need to stay over, it shouldn't be a long meeting and there's a return flight at 7pm.'

He checked the time, it was 9:30am. 'Right. I'm leaving now for Heathrow, tell Alex this better be important.' He put his mobile away and went to the door, 'I've got to rush off to a meeting, Mandy, I don't think I'll be back today. Call me only if there's a major disaster.'

Fern-Chapman thought of telling Esther he'd be late home but decided against it. She had seemed preoccupied since the previous evening, he didn't know why. It was better to give her the day to shake it off. In the taxi to Paddington Station, he called to book the flights, desperately trying to work out what could be so important that he had to fly to Edinburgh on a moment's notice. His fund prices were up another 1% that morning and business was booming; what could be wrong? Harry was a worried man.

Belgravia, London, England
'What did he say?'

'They still haven't received payment for 81 lots. They've given the buyers until tomorrow evening to pay, and if they don't receive the funds, I have to go to pick up the valuables on Wednesday.' Christen's voice was shaking, it was 9:30am and he hadn't had a drink, he was shaking with fear.

Esther swore. 'Including the diamonds, that's over 4 million francs?'

'Only the first two dozen items have been paid for, they've got the same 440k as last week.'

'Did you get the name of the buyers?'

'He wouldn't tell me, it's against the rules, they're not allowed to.'

'*Merde, merde, merde*! I don't fucking believe this. I know who the buyer is, it's a bitch called Jenny Bishop and she's not going to pay. She's done this to screw me!'

'Who's Jenny Bishop?'

'Never mind, did he say anything else?'

Christen's voice broke completely. 'They're returning the new lots as well, everything. There'll be no more sales of our goods at Drewberrys!'

Heathrow Airport, London, England

Marius Coetzee was, unusually for him, a little tired. He was in Terminal 5, transiting before his flight to Malaga. Even in his first-class bed-seat from Joburg, he hadn't slept well and the stifling lack of fresh air for so long made him feel dull and listless, and he didn't like it. He needed to get out of the terminal for a while; the stop-over was almost 4 hours, he had plenty of time. He went through immigration and out of the arrivals door on the ground floor, took the elevator up to level 3 and walked outside. It was a bright, breezy day and he immediately felt better, pulling his travel bag along, stretching his muscles and breathing in the fresh air. After a while, the cold got to him, and he decided to check in and go to the business lounge for something to eat.

Coetzee was walking back into the departures hall when his mobile rang. 'Hi, Marius, how are you holding up?'

'Not too badly, Jenny, thanks for making it as comfortable as possible, but it's still a hell of a long trip.'

'I'm sorry, are you feeling OK?'

'I've just had some fresh air, so I'm fine, no worries.

What can I do for you?'

'Did you check in any luggage?'

'No, I've just got my wheelie bag. Why?'

'Marius, I know I have no right, but I have another favour to ask.'

'I'm listening.'

'Patrice tried to find the name of the seller at Drewberrys, but they wouldn't tell him, it's not permitted until they receive payment.'

'So he told them to stuff their valuables?'

'I wouldn't put it exactly like that, but you're right.'

'And we need to know who it is, or we can do nothing and the whole plan goes down the toilet. OK, what do we do?'

Coetzee was pulling his bag through the domestic check-in area, listening to Jenny's suggestion when he bumped into a passenger rushing across the hall for his flight. 'Sorry, I'm terribly sorry,' the man said, 'I'm a bit late, you OK?'

'No problem, I hope you catch it.'

'Thanks,' said Harry Fern-Chapman and sprinted off towards the security control scanners.

Belgravia, London, England

After screaming, crying and cursing Jenny Bishop's name for a while, Esther was attempting to calm herself down and consider Christen's news pragmatically. She'd immediately realised if Drewberrys wouldn't accept their valuables for future sales, they'd make sure no one else did either; the net result would be no CHF12 million sales in February. So, if the game was up, she had to minimise the damage, think about what she could salvage from the aborted plan.

I don't care about the other valuables, but there are 400 diamonds with the auction houses, worth 2 or 3 million dollars at a knock-down price and I've got another 500 in the vault in Geneva. That's just a briefcase to carry, nothing big or heavy. I've got $5 million with Olympic Funds. There must be a way for me to get out of this with at least $10-$15 million. Christen's a broken man, I can't rely on him. The first thing to do is to get Jolidon on my side. He's not dumb, if he thinks he can get something out of it, he'll work with me.

Esther called him in Zurich. 'I've been waiting all morning, what's going on?' he asked impatiently.

She repeated what Christen had told him. 'It's like I said, that bitch Jenny Bishop has set this up to get her diamonds back, but she's not going to get away with it, not this time.'

Jolidon played his cards carefully. 'Why didn't you tell me they were in the briefcase, maybe I could have helped. You said you've got more, are they safe?'

'Don't worry about that, Claude. Think about how we can get the valuables back from the auction houses.'

'René will do that, they'll all want to get rid of them when this story gets around.'

'I don't trust him to do it, he's in bad shape.' She shared the story about the *huissier*'s impending imprisonment.

'Christ, no wonder he's drinking too much, the poor guy must be on the edge. You didn't know about this when you hired him?'

'Of course not! It's not the kind of thing you tell a prospective employer, but now, he knows he's going to prison and he'll be thinking of nothing else and he'll screw things up. If he stays sober long enough, that is.'

'OK. I'll go to Geneva tomorrow and hold his hand, take him into the auction houses on Wednesday to pick up the merchandise. One question; what's in it for me?'

'I'll make a deal with you, you keep all the valuables, I get my diamonds back. How about it?'

SIXTY-FIVE

'What's all the urgency, Alex? Our funds are in great shape, we've taken in twice as much new money than we lost in November and we're set for a terrific end of year with mega-bonuses for everyone.'

Cameron placed a printout of the renunciation letter on the desk in front of him. 'See the date? It's Friday's date when you say you signed it and gave it to Fric in Luxembourg, right?'

A chill ran down Fern-Chapman's spine. *What's he found? I corrected that date, why question it?* 'That's right, what's the problem?'

'Hang on, Harry. You told me you'd written it and printed it out on Thursday night, before going down to Luxembourg?'

'Of course. I wrote it after the lawyer called and I printed it out, took it down and signed it in front of him.'

'Right. And you sent the file to Tom Newman on Monday morning?'

'As soon as I got back to the office, that's right.'

'So you're absolutely sure you wrote and printed that letter on Thursday, 28th, signed it on Friday, 29th, then forwarded it to Tom on Monday, 2nd; no doubt at all?'

'Yes! How many times do I have to tell you, Alex.

What's the fucking problem?'

Cameron placed another printout on the desk, a screenshot of the details of the 'Properties' attached to the PDF file sent to Moira by Tom Newman. It read:

Created:	26 November 2019 10:49:27
Modified:	29 November 2019 07:47:33
Accessed:	02 December 2019 09:24:15

Fern-Chapman sat back in his chair, his eyes closed. He felt exhausted, as if he'd just run a mile. He hardly registered Alex Cameron's voice as he called in Moira Mackenzie and said, 'I'm announcing the suspension of trading in all Olympic Funds, effective close of business today. I'll contact the Financial Conduct Authority and advise them that we're resigning as corporate Managing Director. I'll also recommend an investigation into Mr Fern-Chapman's probable involvement in Insider Trading with intent to influence Olympics' fund prices in the acquisition of 3 million shares of Atlantic Offshore Oil & Gas by Benelux Mineral Holdings on 29th November at a price of $10 per share.'

'Do you want me to advise the Olympic office in London?'

'Not yet, we don't know if there's anyone else involved. Get everything ready for the announcements to go out at 5pm and I'll order Tom Newman to close the office down then. Thank you, Moira.'

'You'd better leave now, Harry, before I get really annoyed,' he said, without looking at him.

Fern-Chapman pulled himself to his feet. 'You'll regret this, Alex,' he said, then stumbled out of the office.

Cameron sat quietly for a moment, considering the

situation, then called a number. 'Mr Owen, I think you should be the first to know. I apologise, you were right, thank you.'

Carouge, Geneva, Switzerland

Coetzee's flight landed at 3:30pm and he took a taxi directly to Carouge. He called Luca from the cab and met him in the café pizzeria on the corner. 'Hi, I'm Marius Coetzee, you're Franz's colleague?'

'That's right, I'm Luca. Great to meet you, Marius, Franz told me I can learn a lot from you.'

Coetzee laughed, 'You should meet my wife, she taught me everything I know. Is Christen in his flat?'

'I suppose so, he hasn't been out all day.'

'Right, I'm going to talk to him. If you hear gunshots, call the cops.'

He walked across the street to Christen's flat, the Romanian wondering if he was serious.

Belgravia, London, England

'Come on, Harry, answer. Where the hell are you?' Esther Bonnard was shouting at her mobile, she'd been calling Fern-Chapman every 5 minutes for the last hour and he wasn't answering. She was desperate to tell him to liquidate her investments immediately, now, today. From experience she knew that bad news seldom came singly; if Jenny Bishop knew about her 'business', it wouldn't be long before she'd know all about Esther and she couldn't take that risk. She was a wanted woman and if her name was circulated again, she knew her luck would finally run out. It was time to save what she could and move on.

She'd booked a flight to Geneva at 11:00 the next

morning to retrieve the briefcase with the 500 remaining diamonds from the *Banque d'Epargne Vaudoise* and run for cover. But she needed to get the $5 million from Olympic Funds to Bahrain. Then, even if Jolidon and Christen screwed her somehow and kept the diamonds from the auctions, she'd survive very well. *I can live a good life, no yacht, but comfortable.*

But Harry wasn't at his office; Mandy had told her he'd left that morning for a meeting and hadn't been back; she didn't know where he'd gone. Esther checked the time, it was coming up to four o'clock and he'd have to give instructions before the markets closed at 4:30. No one else at Olympic knew who was behind *Almeida Enterprises* and she didn't want to share any information or take any more risks. Esther Bonnard/Rousseau was at her wits' end.

Carouge, Geneva, Switzerland

There was no reply when Coetzee rang Christen's doorbell. He opened the Yale lock in a few seconds and walked quietly into the flat. The notary was lying on a settee, a half-empty bottle of white wine on the coffee table; he seemed to be in a very deep, peaceful sleep. Marius fetched a glass of water from the kitchen and threw it over his face.

'*Quoi? Qu'est-ce qui se passe?* What's happening?' Christen tried to sit up and ended up on the floor. Coetzee picked him up as if he was a child and dumped him back on the couch. He rubbed his eyes, saw the South African and put out his hands as if to defend himself. 'Who are you? What are you doing here?' He squeezed himself into the corner of the settee, as far away as he could get from the man.

'I'm Coetzee, just visiting.' He sat down beside him, staring into his frightened eyes.

After a moment, the *huissier*'s mind started to clear. He squinted closely at the intruder and said, 'I know you. You were buying our lots at the Drewberrys auction.'

'Well done, Maître Christen. Whose valuables were they?'

'You should know, you bought them.'

'OK, I'll make it easy for you. Who's behind the Private Investment Trust?'

'I need a coffee, my head's hurting.'

'If you think it's hurting now, just think how it'll feel if you don't answer my question.'

'Why are you so interested? You're not even going to pay for them, so why do you give a shit?'

'Because I'd like to know who stole them from my friends.'

'I don't know anything about that. They just asked me to act as *huissier* and enter them into the sales.'

'I'm not accusing you of anything, just asking for information.'

Christen's head began to clear. 'How much is it worth?'

'Maybe I should just beat you up, ransack the apartment and find the papers. What do you think?'

He put up his hands again. 'No! Listen, I was desperate, I needed money and they had all these valuables to sell. I was just providing a service. She told me there was no risk, and when I found out, it was too late, I was involved.'

'She? Who's she?' *Now we're getting somewhere.*

'I don't know. I don't think it's her real name. You have to give me something, I'm broke and I've got debts. I'll go to prison if I don't find some money from somewhere.'

Christen started weeping, tears pouring down his face.

'OK. Let's start at the beginning. When did she contact you?'

Over Birmingham, England

Harry was on a Loganair flight from Edinburgh to Southampton, due in at 18:30. He was going to visit his mother in Poole, near Bournemouth. A divorced woman in her 60s, she lived alone, and he hadn't seen her for several weeks. He expected to be arrested fairly soon, and knew he'd have to post bail to avoid being imprisoned until the investigation and trial were over. It was a $30 million crime, so the bail would be substantial. He had virtually nothing left, *probably not enough to pay Guillaume Fric's fees*, he thought with a smile. He knew he couldn't count on Esther; her funds would be blocked and she'd want to murder him, not help him out. His mother had negotiated a tidy settlement from his father a few years ago, in the millions, and she was a frugal woman. It was time to show her how much he loved her.

London, England

Esther had resigned herself to waiting for Harry to liquidate her investments the next morning. She still hadn't heard from him, but assumed he'd been tied up in a meeting and couldn't talk, *or maybe his mobile battery has run down*. In between bouts of screaming and cursing, she thought of every reason to rationalise his lack of contact, then finally gave up and poured herself a glass of wine, switched on the TV and caught the end of the 6 o'clock news.

The presenter announced, 'And now the latest market update from our business correspondent, Clive Frazer.'

'Good evening, stock markets here and in Europe are in turmoil this evening after a leading UK fund group suspended trading today. We have a special report from Terry Owen, an independent financial journalist, who uncovered what seems to be an insider trading transaction at Harry Fern-Chapman's Olympic Funds Group.'

Esther sat in silence, hardly believing her eyes and ears, as Owen described in detail what he had discovered, finishing with, 'We've been unable to contact Mr Fern-Chapman for his comments, but we'll be reporting on developments as and when we discover further details.'

She sat on the oversize settee in her magnificent penthouse apartment in Eaton Square, Belgravia, her mind spinning. *He said all the funds were suspended today. Five million dollars of my money is stuck there for God knows how long. What in hell do I do now? Where is that fucking bastard? I want to kill him!*

London, England

Hugh Middleton switched off his TV, he had taken a break from volume IV of the UN Tech Bank report to watch Terry Owen's newscast. *Vastly more enjoyable than the tedious prose which has consumed my weekend and the whole of today,* he considered. His mobile rang, 'Did you see the news, Dr Middleton?'

'A fine report,' he said, 'Well done, Terry, you've become a TV pundit.'

'Thanks to you, Dr Middleton. I don't know how you sniffed it, but you were on the button. And if Cameron hadn't spotted the error on the date, he would have been clean away, still making a fortune with his high-risk stocks.'

'Indeed, as you say, *There, but for the grace...* Please send me your bill, Terry, I like to keep my accounts up to date.'

'There'll be no need, it's on the house. I've just been offered a job as a financial reporter with Sky News. You wouldn't believe the salaries these TV companies pay.'

Middleton put his mobile away and went to pour himself a glass of Bordeaux. He'd called into the wine store on his way home and bought a bottle of Château Latour Pauillac. He doubted that Sir Reginald Scarbrough had done the same. He picked up volume IV again, *A few more days and we'll be famous for another fleeting moment, but my dear Ilona won't be with me to make it a special occasion.*

Marbella, Spain

'How's Geneva, Marius?'

'Bloody cold, I feel sorry for our snoops, but they'll be finished pretty soon, we're on the home track.'

'You've got news for us? Hang on, Patrice and Leticia are here, I'll get Pedro and Javier on and put you on speaker.' A few moments later, she asked, 'Right, everyone's listening, what do you know?'

'Something we should have guessed a while ago. The name of the ringleader, an old friend.'

'It's Esther Rousseau, isn't it?'

There was silence on the line as the others registered her unexpected interruption. Then Coetzee replied, 'Jenny, why did you send me to Geneva to beat up a drunken gay when you knew all along?'

'Sorry, everyone. I wasn't sure, it was just one of my dreams, and of course, she and Jolidon have worked together before. But now we know for certain?'

'She's calling herself Esther Bonnard, but it's her, alright. Jolidon's managing things from Zurich and she's pulling the strings from the UK. Christen's in a bad way, he's bankrupt, been embezzling clients' money and he's looking at a prison sentence. And he's an alcoholic. I feel sorry for him actually, he's a sad case.'

'I can't believe that woman's back again. After all these years she's still determined to steal our money and diamonds.' Leticia sounded tired and dejected. 'Thanks, Marius, but where is she, how do we catch her and stop her for once and all?'

'He says she lives in London, but he doesn't know where. But he's pretty sure he knows the whereabouts of the rest of the diamonds. A bank in Geneva's old town.'

'She'll be going to get them,' Jenny answered immediately. 'She's clever, she must know it's us who've destroyed her auction business and she's worried about what else we might know. She'll want to get them to safety; nothing is more important to her than Charlie's diamonds.' Jenny wasn't aware of Esther's problems with Olympic Group, but as usual, her logic was correct.

Patrice was trying to understand the structure of her network, 'Did he tell you what's behind this Private Investment Trust?'

'It's apparently called the *African Benevolent Trust* and the trustee's a guy called Benjamin Appletree, in Angola. That's who's supposed to have signed the certificates of provenance.'

Espinoza laughed out loud. 'Benjamin Appletree? I think I could invent a better name than that. You can check it out, Marius?'

'It shouldn't take long, even Angola has got a primitive form of registries for most things. I'll ask Karen to take a look, she's really enjoying all the research.'

'Last question, Marius, what's happening to the valuables from the sales?'

'He told me Jolidon's coming down tomorrow and they're going together on Wednesday to collect them.'

'I suppose you've got a plan to spoil the party?'

'I was just about to discuss it with you guys.'

'Did you really have to beat him up to tell you all this?'

He laughed, 'I never touched him Jenny, except to pick him up off the floor. You were right, he didn't like the way I looked at him.'

SIXTY-SIX

Tuesday, December 17th, 2019

Mayfair, London, England

'**How are our investments in Harry's funds doing?** You said you were a little worried and you'd have a chat with him.'

Lord Reginald Scarbrough thanked the Lord that his wife read nothing in the newspapers apart from the headlines, fashion pages and gossip columns. 'Not the time to change, Nicola, dear,' he replied. 'The markets are still sorting themselves out. We'll leave things as they are for a while and keep a watching brief. There's no hurry to do anything.' He knew from the Woodford scandal this would be a long and painful experience, in lost money and lost friends. *I wonder if that fellow Middleton invested after our talk. I hope so, can't stand the dreadful bore, never uses one word where three will do.* 'Why don't I book lunch at Scott's, it's a miserable day, that'll cheer us up.'

Luxembourg, EU

'How in hell's name did that happen?' Gérard Boillat sounded apoplectic with rage.

'From what I understand, it was the date on the renunciation letter, he got it wrong and none of us noticed it.'

'I don't believe it, the man's a complete cretin.'

'Listen, Gérard, it makes no difference to me or to you, in fact it's the best thing that could have happened. We've done nothing wrong; you sold some shares at a price you were offered and I made the offer on behalf of a company I represent, instructed by the owner, whom I believed was acting in good faith. Naturally, now that I've discovered there was a fraudulent objective behind his instructions, I'll resign and bring a lawsuit against him for reputational damage. You should do the same, to keep your nose clean.'

'What about the shares purchased by BMH?'

'It'll take some time and good legal work, but the transaction will almost certainly be annulled, you'll get your shares back and keep the $10 million as damages.'

'Hmm. Am I allowed to retain your services to sort out this mess?'

'Absolutely, Gérard, and I'd be delighted to accept. I'll send you a form of mandate and get started right away. *A bientôt.*'

Guillaume Fric put his mobile down and rubbed his hands together. *Excellent work Guillaume, and merci beaucoup, Harry. The Boillat family has a lot more money than you.*

Geneva, Switzerland

'*Bonjour*, Madame Bonnard, welcome back to the Richemond.' The receptionist at the Hotel Richemond was most gushing in her welcome. She knew the client was very generous, and Christmas was just around the corner, a large tip would be most timely.

After watching Terry Owen's report on TV the previous evening, Esther had cursed in several languages; first, Fern-Chapman's name and character, then her own greed and avarice in naively trusting almost all of her cash with him. She knew she couldn't recoup her money; the funds were closed for business and, judging from the Woodford suspension that was already six months old, they wouldn't be open any time soon. She couldn't wait around in England and be involved in a scandal that might expose her. If she could have found Harry, she'd have happily killed him, but she had no idea where he was, he seemed to have disappeared off the face of the planet.

Finally, she'd reconciled herself to the catastrophic reality. He had cost her $5 million and change. Somehow, Esther forced herself to be pragmatic and realistic about her situation, she'd had a lot of practice through the years. Knowing she had to restrict the damage as quickly as possible, she'd booked a flight to Geneva for the next morning and reserved her suite at the Richemond for that day. Then she'd drunk a half-bottle of champagne and gone to bed, determined to negotiate her way out of the mess caused, as usual, by other interfering people; especially Harry Fern-Chapman and Jenny Bishop.

Esther had only one suitcase with her, into which she'd packed a few favourite items of clothing and the jewellery and gifts that Harry had showered on her in the last 18 months. She didn't intend to return to London, he was on the hook for the lease on the apartment and she imagined it would cost him a fortune to cancel it. From the reports on the morning TV news, where Olympic Funds Group was now a headline topic, it looked like he'd end up in prison and she hoped he'd spend a long time there. *He won't need an apartment*, she said to herself, *the government will look after him. What a shame!*

Her suite was ready, as always, with champagne and flowers, and she sank back onto the settee, feeling a little better about things. *I'll miss coming here*, she reflected, *but Europe will be too dangerous for me, it's just a matter of time before I run out of luck at an immigration control.* Esther wasn't intending to stay more than one night at the hotel, she'd already booked her Emirates flight to Dubai for the next afternoon. *Thank God I have my life-saver, 500 of Charlie Bishop's diamonds, still safe at the bank. If I handle things well with Jolidon, I can get to Dubai in relatively good shape.* She had lived in the UAE for a while during the aborted Russian cyber-attack and loved the city. The weather was always beautiful, and it was a great place to meet good looking, wealthy guys, even princes. More importantly, it was a good place to hide.

Zurich, Switzerland

'Jolidon just left the apartment with a suitcase. I followed him to an overnight garage and he came out in a blue Peugeot 308, licence plate ZH 957298. Nice car, about two years old.' It was midday and Franz Stenmark was reporting in to Javier.

'We expected that. We think he might be going to Geneva.'

'No idea. What do you want me to do? Is it worth waiting here?'

Javier looked at Espinoza, 'What do you think?'

'One more day?'

'Can you manage another freezing day, Franz?'

'At the rate we're charging you? You must be joking.'

'OK. Last day on the job. Can you update Luca to watch out for him?'

Delmas, Mpumalanga, South Africa
'*African Benevolent Trust*? That's a paradox in three words. Who are they supposed to be?'

'That's what we'd like to know, Karen. Can you do a bit of digging? Don't laugh, but the trustee's name is Benjamin Appletree.'

'And he's supposed to be Angolan?'

'I know, there's room for speculation, but it's a starting point.'

'When are you coming home? I'm missing you.'

'It shouldn't take long to wrap this business up, a couple of days, I guess.'

'Be careful, and I'll get digging.'

Carouge, Geneva, Switzerland
'Jolidon just arrived at Christen's apartment. Walking and pulling a case. He must have left his car in a garage somewhere, there's not a lot of overnight parking around Carouge.'

'Excellent, Luca, as we expected. They'll either be leaving together to meet someone, a woman, or she'll be coming to the apartment, I guess. Has Marius turned up yet?'

'No, he called earlier. Apparently, he slept for 12 hours and was ravenous, but he's coming over now, so we're on top of things.'

Geneva, Switzerland
'*Bonsoir*, Claude, where are you?'

'In Carouge with René, how about you?'

'I'm at the Richemond. How is he? I mean is he compos mentis and sober?'

Jolidon chose his words carefully, 'Everyone's fine here, Esther, no problems. When are we getting together?'

'This evening, I'm not taking the risk of coming over there. After what's happened, I wouldn't be surprised if his place is being watched.'

He went to the window and looked out, it was almost dark and he could see nothing. 'Thanks for the suggestion, you certainly know how to make people feel safe. Where do you want to meet?'

'Did you think about my proposal?'

'We can talk about it later.'

'When Christen's there, why involve him?'

'I'll tell you when we meet. Where do you have in mind?'

'The more public the better. I've booked a table here, downstairs in *Le Jardin*. We'll meet there at 7.30 pm for dinner. If the Bishop woman has got anyone watching, she won't want to make a fuss in a smart hotel.'

'I didn't bring my dinner jacket, but I'll do my best. See you later.'

Christen looked enquiringly at him and he said, 'Dinner at 7:30 with the ex-boss in *Le Jardin*. OK with you?'

'Fine, I'll choose the wine.' Christen had said nothing about Coetzee's visit. He was hoping against hope that the South African would fulfil his promise to go easy on him. Besides which, he was desperate; either way, he risked going to prison.

Zurich, Switzerland

'It's him again!' It had started snowing and Franz Stenmark was about to leave for the evening when he saw the man enter no. 819 Badenerstrasse. As usual, he was wearing a mackintosh, cap and a scarf against the cold. And he was carrying an umbrella and a small bag. A moment later, a resident came out and Franz ran across the street, assuming the intruder had gone through into the elevator. He was wrong, he was still waiting and turned when he heard the door open. Stenmark pointed his camera at him, pressed the trigger then sprinted out of the building, across the road and behind the petrol pumps. He saw the man come out and look around for a moment, then he put his umbrella up and walked off down the street towards the bus stop.

Geneva, Switzerland

Le Jardin restaurant was busy, as was the hotel. *Plenty of wealthy visitors to Geneva for luxury Christmas shopping,* Esther thought as she admired the expensive clothes and accessories worn by the guests.

'This looks delicious, *bon appétit.*' She cut into her rare steak with relish, hiding the sense of disappointment and anger she felt inside. She couldn't let either of the men see her with her defences down, it was time to show strength and leadership.

'When are you going to pick up the valuables?'

'They called me this afternoon and I fixed it up for between 9am and 11am tomorrow.'

'That's just Drewberrys?'

'No, they all called. I think they had a meeting and agreed to kick us out of the auction business for good.' Christen took a sip of his wine, he was sober, but looked exhausted and desperate.

'It's what we expected,' Jolidon grimaced. 'Geneva's a small place and that article made a lot of noise. I looked this afternoon and it's got over 2 million signatures now.'

'Don't forget that they can't actually prove anything, it's all just speculation, no facts to support any claims.'

'How does that change anything?' Christen asked despondently, thinking of Coetzee's instructions.

'It means they can't confiscate our goods. We pick them up and split them between us and we can market them quietly over the next few months or years. We can still make good money, it's not a total catastrophe.'

He pretended to brighten up. 'I can keep my share?'

'Of course. We're not going to screw you, are we Claude?'

Jolidon hid his surprise, he'd been ready to defend Christen's position, but it seemed it wasn't necessary. 'I'm happy to hear it, Esther. I'll go round with René to pick them up. I expect we'll have to sign all kinds of disclaimers, so it'll take a couple of hours.'

'*Bien*, I'll meet you here at midday and we'll organise the split, OK?' Her flight to Dubai left at three-fifteen. *That's enough time if they accept my deal.* She raised her glass, 'To the phoenix, rising from the ashes.'

They left the table at 9pm and she walked with them to the exit. The lobby was crowded and only Christen observed Coetzee sitting reading a newspaper on a settee, watching them leave. Esther and Jolidon had never seen the South African before and the *huissier* gave no sign.

'*Bonne nuit*, Esther,' he said, shaking hands. Thanks for your offer, I think I'll be able to sort things out now.'

Well done, René, you're learning fast. Coetzee watched Esther cross the hall to take the elevator to her suite. *She's a good-looking woman, no wonder she's caused such a lot of trouble. What a waste.* He went out to get a taxi across the bridge to the Hotel Métropole. In the cab, he looked again at the text he'd received earlier from Franz Stenmark, with a good image of the Zurich intruder. He had no idea who it might be.

Marbella, Spain

Jenny had received the text at the same time via Javier. She'd recognised the photo and was still puzzling over it, *I was right, but it makes no sense.* She stroked Chester and put some water in his bowl. Lily and Ellen were already in bed and she was tired. She climbed the stairs, her legs feeling heavy. *Let's see what tomorrow brings.*

Delmas, Mpumalanga, South Africa

'Marius, I didn't wake you, did I?'

'Great minds. I was just going to call to say goodnight. How are you?'

'Exhausted! With the retransmissions of the diamond revelations, the phone hasn't stopped ringing and my inboxes are overflowing in every direction. We have more than 3 million signatures on the petition and people in other countries don't seem to know what time it is here, so I'm getting woken up at all hours. I'm not sure I want to be this popular.'

'Enjoy it while you can, my love, you deserve it.'

'But I did find the time to do your research.'

'Thanks, that's great. And?'

'*The African Benevolent Trust* does exist. It was set up in Luanda in June, by a lawyer called Jonathon Appletree, honestly! The address is at his office.'

'That's a couple of months after the Ramseyer, Haldeman fire, in April.'

'I don't know what you're talking about and I haven't got time for a long explanation. Is it helpful?'

'Very. What else?' He knew there'd be more, his wife was a perfectionist.

'Appletree's father is Benjamin, the Trustee, and he lives in Rio de Janeiro, has done since fleeing Angola when the civil war broke out.'

He waited silently, knowing she was saving the best for last, as she always did.

'Benjamin Appletree's wife is called Alicia Beatriz.' Another pause. 'Her maiden name was Melo d'Almeida.'

This time, Coetzee's silence was caused by astonishment. 'You mean?'

'Her younger brother was Raymundo Jesus Melo d'Almeida, Esther Rousseau's psychotic lover.'

SIXTY-SEVEN

'I don't believe it. It can't be true, there has to be a mistake.'

'You know as well as I do, Jenny, Karen doesn't make mistakes.'

'But after all these years. I remember she had health problems, she must be over fifty now, it's incredible. José Luis, the lawyer that d'Almeida worked for told Leticia and I that he used to send part of his salary to her in Rio. We couldn't understand how a sadistic killer could show such compassion. After his death, we sent her a little money, just enough to help her get on her feet, and she's obviously survived and made a good marriage.'

'And Esther must have kept in contact with her, then found out she could be useful to her plans.'

'They can't have known what was going on?'

'I doubt it, they were just providing a service and I'm sure she paid them something. Clever, really, keeping it in the family, as it were.'

'We'll have to tell the others, it all ties together. Esther, d'Almeida, the diamonds; it's like a merry-go-round that never stops.'

Coetzee checked the time, 'I'll leave it to you, I'm off to the Richemond to keep tabs on her. Today's the big day.'

London, England

Hugh Middleton was in his apartment, reading the previous Saturday's FT Supplement section with a glass of sherry, before his lunch. Last night, he'd finished up the last revisions of the UN Technology Bank report with Peter Findlay, Ilona's replacement. Nothing they wrote was ever as good as their previous combined creations, but the five volumes had been couriered off on time and their substantial fee would soon be in the bank, so he had to be grateful for small mercies. One of them was that he could catch up on his newspaper reading.

Turning to the Life & Arts section, he saw that the lead article was published in coordination with over 60 other national newspapers; his attention was immediately riveted. The story covered the main page and he devoured it greedily, hardly drawing breath. When he came to the last part, '*Two hundred Angolan diamonds sold in Geneva auctions, supposedly pre-independence, guaranteed not blood diamonds*', his mind jumped back to 2010, the aborted kidnapping of Leo Stewart involving Esther Rousseau and a hoard of Angolan diamonds, destined, fortunately, never to become a ransom. The author's name, Karen Spellman, was also familiar to him and he finally placed it, Marius Coetzee's wife, now the mother-in-law of Leo Stewart.

He sat back, assessing what all of this could mean. *It can't possibly be a coincidence*, he told himself. *Why would Coetzee's wife be writing about blood diamonds being sold in Geneva auctions, if it didn't have to do with the treasure Charlie Bishop smuggled from Angola after the Revolution of the Carnations. But Madame Bishop has no need to sell those diamonds, she's a very wealthy woman; moreover, Karen Spellman wouldn't write a damaging report which could destroy her reputation, they're virtually related by marriage. There's only one possible solution; someone has taken possession of the diamonds, is selling them and this is a very subtle attempt to put a spoke in their wheel.*

He looked up the *change.org* appeal, there were almost 4 million signatures on the petition. *Quite a large spoke, I imagine.*

Dr Hugh Middleton considered the situation. Harry Fern-Chapman was no longer in the picture and would very probably be restricted in his movements for quite some time. Thus, Esther Rousseau/Bonnard no longer had a wealthy sponsor and was less likely to present a threat to his wellbeing. Esther would also most likely be aware of the article, since she was obsessed by those diamonds and always had been. *It could even be she who has stolen or discovered them,* he suddenly realised. *Although it seems improbable, even fanciful. Nevertheless, she will most probably be preoccupied in trying to discover what has happened to them.* Middleton took his decision. It was time to employ the knowledge he had, to abrogate any possible future action on her part.

He called in his assistant, Peter Findlay. 'I wish to send a message to a very senior member of the constabulary, Assistant Commissioner Callum Dewar, at New Scotland Yard. Can you kindly obtain his email address for me? Thank you, Peter.'

Middleton opened his *enough@stopfraud.com* email account and began typing the message.

Geneva, Switzerland

It was 11:30 am when Esther Bonnard/Rousseau walked out of the Banque d'Epargne Vaudoise with Charlie Bishop's briefcase containing 500 pre-independence Angolan diamonds, weighing approximately 520 carats, valued in the region of $10 million. It was a cold, misty day and she wrapped her cashmere coat around herself and took a cab back to the Richemond, carrying the case to her suite. She wanted it close at hand.

Marius Coetzee had followed her since she left the hotel, he was now sitting in the lobby with a newspaper and watched her go up to her suite. He called Luca. 'What's happening?'

'They've just come out of the Mandarin-Oriental, with the case, it looks heavier.'

'OK, that's the first call done, and it looks like they haven't had any problems. They'll be going to the Hôtel des Bergues next, then the Fairmont. Christen said they're meeting here at midday. Just keep an eye on them and call when they're finished or if anything changes.'

New Scotland Yard, London, England

'Excuse me, Assistant Commissioner, I just received a message on your official account, it could be important.'

'How in hell did anyone get that address?' AC Callum Dewar snapped. 'It's supposed to be totally confidential, is nothing safe from hacking around here, Charlotte?'

'I don't know, sir, but I cleared it with security before opening it.' Sergeant Charlotte Robson handed him a printout of the message and left the office.

Dewar saw the sender's address, _enough@stopfraud.com_ and was immediately suspicious, He called his Internet security advisor, 'Check out this email address, right away.'

The message read:

'A French woman named Esther Rousseau, aka Esther Bonnard, aka Elodie Delacroix, has been sought by Interpol since 2008. She has been involved in several murders and robberies in Spain, in 2008, Australia and South Africa, in 2010, a kidnapping in South Africa in 2010 and an aborted cyber-attack in Dubai in 2017.

This woman is living under the name of Esther Bonnard at 69 Eaton Square, Belgravia, with the disgraced investment fund manager, Harry Fern-Chapman.'

Esther, I've heard that name before. Somewhere in the distant past, what was it? Dewar shook his head, failing to bring the memory to mind. He called the head of the UK Interpol National Central Bureau, in Manchester, Billy Cooper. 'I'm sending you a message about a French woman called Esther Rousseau, she's supposed to be on your wanted list. Can you check it out, Billy, it's urgent?'

'Hang on, I'll look it up now.'

AC Dewar called his subordinate, 'Arthur, get someone round to 69 Eaton Square, looking for a woman called Esther Rousseau or Bonnard, or a man, Harry Fern-Chapman.'

'Are you there, sir?'

'Go ahead, Billy, find anything?'

'She's here, Esther Rousseau, French citizen. Spanish police put her on the wanted list in 2008, then the French in 2010. I'm sending you a photograph.'

'So how come you've never found her?'

'You'll have to ask the Frogs about that, she doesn't live in England. We can't control what happens on the other side of the Channel.'

'I've just been informed that she's living here in London. What about the other names? Bonnard seems to be the latest.'

'I have no record of that. I'll have to check with Paris. I'll get back asap.'

Malaga, Spain

'How are things going, Marius?'

'Hi, Pedro, good to hear from you. Everything's on schedule. Jolidon and Christen are picking up the valuables and Esther just took the briefcase from the bank and took it to her room. You heard about Appletree being d'Almeida's brother-in-law, I suppose?'

'I was speechless, I remember the conversation with José Luis at the time. That was 12 years ago; whatever happened to those years? And I'm annoyed at my failing memory. Jenny just reminded me that Esther Rousseau has been on the Interpol wanted list since 2010. She has quite a record and I'm astonished they have never caught up with her.'

'I didn't know that. She's a clever woman, keeping out of sight all those years. But it confirms my theory about the efficiency of the cops.'

'International cooperation isn't always what it's intended to be, Marius. If she's been in the UK for a while using the name of Bonnard, she'd get lost under a lot of radars. But it's an important point and we must exploit it.'

'What do you have in mind?'

'Thanks to your observation this week, we now know for certain that she, Jolidon and Christen are all involved in robbery and money laundering, and possibly arson and murder too. We have photographs of them, and we know that all three are presently in Geneva.'

'So, you think it's time to hand it over to the professionals?'

'That's been on my mind. It so happens that I know someone who will listen to us. I could make a call and see what the reaction is. Do you agree with my assessment?'

'Almost, Pedro, but not completely.'

'On what points?'

'OK. Esther is certainly a hardened criminal and she's probably guilty on all counts. She must have been well trained by d'Almeida and she's driven by a desperate desire to make up for his death by hurting everyone involved and recapturing the diamonds.'

'Agreed, and Jolidon?'

'Yes, he's a crook, but I don't think he's a murderer, he doesn't have the backbone, or the brains. I've seen him, just a common or garden parasite, living off other people's ideas. It's obvious this operation wasn't his plan, he was offered an easy option to make a lot of money and he grabbed it.'

'What about René Christen?'

'He's not a bandit, not even near, he was trained as a notary and he's proud of it. Like I told you, he's in deep shit and he thought he'd found a way to dig himself out. He's definitely no murderer, too soft by half, and he wasn't involved in the robberies, except to inventory everything as a *huissier*. So he's turned a blind eye on the origin of the auction goods; is that a hanging offence?'

'It sounds like you have a soft spot for him?'

'Pedro, you know my story. I've been there. I've been in that place when nothing goes right, and your life seems to fall apart. You take bad decisions, I took bad decisions, and I could have died in that crappy place if I hadn't suddenly been surrounded by people who became my friends, good people who were prepared to forgive and forget, and help me to do the same.'

'It wasn't only the work of others, Marius. You worked at it too and your dedication saved Leo's life, at the risk of your own.' Espinoza sighed. 'Maybe I was a policeman for too long. I still see things in black and white, but it's true that there are many shades. In fact, what happened to my cousin, Ricardo, is another example where I can't see a clear line between what's right and wrong. I accept your argument, you're the proof that it's correct. What do you suggest?'

'We have to stop Esther Rousseau getting away and finding a new way to attack Jenny and Leticia. But those other guys, they don't deserve to be thrown under the same bus as her. Let's try to give them a chance to get out of this rat race.'

'So, you want me to make my call, but not to talk about Jolidon and Christen?'

'Please, Pedro. We can be sure that she'll blame anything and everything on them to drag them down with her and plead a lesser sentence, but I don't want us to help her do it.'

'Agreed. When should I call?'

'They're due to come here at midday. I'll text you as soon as they arrive, then give them a half hour, Pedro. If it's not enough, there's nothing more we can do.'

'OK, Marius, I'll wait for your text.'

New Scotland Yard, London, England
'There's no one there, sir, the place is empty.'

'You're sure, Arthur?'

'The constable's standing outside the door, a nosy neighbour on the ground floor let him into the building. She doesn't know their names, they're been renting the place for a few months, apparently. She hasn't seen the man for a couple of days and the woman left yesterday morning in a taxi. She had a suitcase with her. She's certain there's nobody in the apartment.'

AC Dewar cursed. 'I just got a call from Cooper at Interpol in Manchester. The Paris people told him her maiden name is Bonnard, but they somehow forgot to circulate it to the rest of Europe, so they've all been looking for Esther Rousseau for ten years or so, and she's probably been travelling as Esther Bonnard. I'll send you a photograph of the woman, keep someone watching the flat for the rest of the day, we might get lucky.'

He called Charlotte Robson, 'Find out about this fellow, Fern-Chapman, I saw something about him on TV this weekend, a fraud of some kind. This looks like a serious tip-off; I don't want to read about it afterwards in the papers. And send this photograph to Arthur Bell and get it circulated to all the immigration control units and border points, with the choice of names.'

His phone rang. 'That email address was set up by someone who knows what they're doing. I can't get past it to the originator. Sorry sir, but I've tried everything and it's a brick wall.'

He looked again at the photograph on his screen. 'Hmm, bloody good-looking woman. Where the hell is she?'

SIXTY-EIGHT

Wednesday, December 18th, 2019
Geneva, Switzerland

'I assume everything went smoothly?'

'We've got everything. The diamonds, all 400 of them and all the valuables except the 28 that were sold to other buyers.'

Esther felt a flood of relief. *That's 900 diamonds in all, they must be worth more than $10 million on the black market.* Charlie Bishop's briefcase with the remaining diamonds was in her wardrobe. 'So, what's your answer to my proposal, 'My diamonds, your valuables'.'

'It could work, except we agreed that René has to have his share, that makes 60-40. I reckon the diamonds are worth probably twice the other stuff we picked up, so the numbers aren't quite right.' Jolidon was gambling that she wouldn't realise he also had a box of valuables he'd brought from Zurich in his case.

He was right, Esther was distracted. She looked at her mobile, they had been late in getting to the hotel and it was now almost 1pm. She needed to be at the airport no later than 2pm for her 3:15 flight. Although she was travelling in first-class, the timing was tight. *I've got half an hour to get the best deal I can.* Jolidon was holding on tight to his suitcase full of diamonds and valuables and she didn't want to end up in a fist fight. *I'll have to be flexible, just a little.* 'OK, what do you want?'

Downstairs, Marius Coetzee had moved into the lounge, from where he could see the elevators and the main entrance. He'd texted Espinoza when Christen and Jolidon came in and took the lift. He ordered another coffee and picked up the *New York Times*, it would soon be over.

New Scotland Yard, London, England

'There is a Spanish gentleman asking for you, sir. He says you might remember him from South Africa in 2010, Detective Chief Inspector Espinoza.'

Dewar racked his memory; the name was familiar. *Yes! The business with that fake Lord Dudley. It must be ten years ago. We could only get him on undeclared foreign bank accounts, but at least we pinned something on him.* 'Please put him through, Charlotte.'

'To what do I owe the pleasure after all this time, Chief Inspector?'

'First of all, congratulations on your impressive progress, Assistant Commissioner, I'm sure it's greatly deserved, and you must be very proud. Secondly, I present my apologies. I am no longer a policeman, merely a sometimes-occupied private detective. But in that connection, I have some information which may be useful to you.'

'Thank you, and no apology needed, Señor Espinoza. I'm looking forward to that ex-Commissioner day myself. The world, crime and criminals are becoming too complicated for me. What is it you have to tell me?'

'It's a long story, but I'll cut it down to the essentials. Several years ago, I was involved in a very nasty crime in Spain, a pathological killer called d'Almeida, multiple murders and robbery. He was killed, by my own gun, as a matter of fact, but he had an accomplice who escaped. The accomplice has been involved in many other crimes over the subsequent years, kidnapping, murder, money-laundering and cyber-crime.'

Dewar reached for the email lying on his desk from *enough@stopfraud.com.* 'Was the accomplice a woman, wanted by Interpol since 2008?' he asked.

Espinoza was nonplussed. 'How did you know?'

'Esther Rousseau, née Bonnard, is that her?'

'*Mis complidos*, my compliments,' he said. 'I assume you've had dealings with Mademoiselle Bonnard, may I ask how?'

'We haven't, Sr Espinoza, but I had a vague memory of the name from that business in South Africa and then this morning, we received an email about her, with pretty much the same information as you just gave me. There's no mistake, it's the same woman. My problem is, apparently she was in London, but she's disappeared, and we have no idea where to.'

'Then the timing is extremely appropriate, because I know exactly where she is.'

Geneva, Switzerland

Marius Coetzee saw the two men come out of the elevator. *So they've done their deal with Esther.* They walked across the crowded lobby and out of the revolving doors, Jolidon pulling his suitcase and Christen his travel bag. Coetzee was happy to follow the strict instructions from AC Dewar, via Pedro Espinoza, to observe and not intervene, 'Don't contaminate the arrest scene,' were his orders, so he was watching and waiting. *So far, so good*, he said to himself. *I wish them bon voyage and hope they've learned a lesson they'll never forget. Now, where's the ringleader?*

Geneva, Switzerland

It had cost Esther 50 diamonds to seal the deal with her ex-partners. 350 stones were back with the others in Charlie Bishop's briefcase, which was now inside her suitcase. *850 carats of Angolan diamonds, worth at least $10 million, plus almost $1 million in my Bahrain account. Not a bad start to my new life in Dubai. It could have been a lot worse.* There had been a few fake kisses and good wishes between them when they parted, but she knew they were happy to see the back of her, as she was them. It was now after 1:30pm, just an hour before her flight would be called; she put on her coat and pushed her suitcase out of the suite. She had settled her account earlier that morning and didn't need to stop by the cashier's desk. *I'll be back some time*, she promised herself, as she pressed the button to call the elevator.

There was a large number of clients around the reception desk when Esther emerged from the lift and she could see two uniformed policemen speaking to the receptionist; the people in the crowd eavesdropping while waiting for attention. She walked between them and alongside the reception desk to overhear what was being discussed. Her heart began to pound when she heard, '*Madame ou Mademoiselle Bonnard.*'

She looked straight ahead and kept walking. *Those bastards Jolidon and Christen must have shopped me*, was her immediate reaction. The police officers went towards the elevators and some of the clients walked away to the exit; she could hear the gossip, 'What's happening? They must be after criminals. How exciting!'

Esther pushed her $10 million suitcase slowly through the crowd towards the revolving doors. A group of people were coming into the hotel and she mingled with them then strode quickly across to a door on the other side of the lobby marked, 'Personnel'. She had reconnoitred the ground floor on previous visits and knew her way around. A passageway led past the staff quarters to an emergency exit with a push-bar release. A moment later she exited at the side of the hotel. The mist had now turned to fog; it was bitter cold. She walked cautiously forward and looked along the front façade, where two police cars were parked, with their beacons flashing.

Merde, I don't like this. Esther crossed the road, went along beyond the empty taxi rank, and into the middle of the Brunswick Garden, where she found a bench out of sight of the hotel entrance. *The airport's out of the question now. If they're looking for me, that's their first port of call.*

After a few minutes shivering in the cold, she heard the police sirens start up and saw the cars drive past and turn up the *Rue de Chantepoulet*, towards the station and the airport. She forced herself to stay calm and think carefully, it wasn't the time to panic. She pulled her coat tight around her against the freezing fog, then keeping one hand on her case, she checked her mobile for departure times; Esther always had an escape plan in case it was necessary, and this time it was.

There was another taxi rank by the bus station, just 500 metres away and she walked quickly across, there was one cab waiting. She said to the driver, 'The *Hôtel le Rive*, in Nyon, please. And put the heating up.'

Geneva, Switzerland

The two policemen had caused a crowd to form at the reception desk and Marius Coetzee strolled across the lobby to hear what was going on. A moment later, Esther Rousseau was less than a metre away as she walked behind him through the throng of people to the personnel door. For once, the South African's surveillance was less than perfect, but he wasn't aware of it until later.

The police officers were speaking in French and he couldn't follow the discussion until he heard the name 'Bonnard'. *Got her*, he shouted silently. *Well done, Pedro. Now, I just have to wait until I see her in handcuffs.*

But Coetzee never did.

Geneva, Switzerland

Maître René Christen entered the *Luanda Banco de Credito, (Suisse) SA* and asked for Alberto Cortola, who looked after the *African Benevolent Trust* fiduciary account. They'd met on several occasions and Cortola was most friendly, he knew how much money had flowed through the account; from or to where, was not his business.

Christen gave him the transfer request he'd prepared the previous evening, with the perfectly forged signature of Mme Esther Bonnard alongside his own. 'We won't be requiring this account any longer, so I'd be obliged if you'd close it and transfer the balance, minus your charges of course, as indicated.'

After agreeing charges of $10,000, Christen thanked the banker and wished him a Merry Christmas. He walked happily back to Jolidon's car, waiting around the corner. *Right, that's $530,000 in the Comina's account* *in Fribourg. What I owe them, plus a little bonus. I'm beginning to feel a lot better.*

'Thanks, Claude,' he patted him on the shoulder. 'A great idea to persuade Drewberrys to transfer the funds they had in hand. You've helped to salve my conscience.'

'My pleasure, René. And, between you and me, I much prefer to have as few of those Angolan diamonds as possible, they're too conspicuous. I only gave Esther a hard time so she could feel she'd won. She'll have tough work getting a decent price for them. But I reckon we've got maybe 10 million dollars of unidentified valuables that we can get rid of through my Italian fence over the next few years. Nobody knows where they came from and we're not about to tell them. OK with you?'

'Absolutely fine!'

'Right, time to take the tourist route.' He switched on his fog lights and drove off into the mist in the direction of Annemasse and the Italian border.

'How long do you reckon to Genoa?'

'It's about 300 kms, so we should be there by dinnertime, barring avalanches or blizzards en route.'

'And the boat to Tunis leaves on Friday, *fantastique.*' Christen put his hand on the Frenchman's knee. 'I won't forget this, Claude, you've been a great friend. I'll make sure you don't regret it.'

Silently, he gave a prayer for his unlikely saviour. *Thank God. Whoever he is, that tough guy Coetzee saved my life. Who would have thought it?*

SIXTY-NINE

'**Did you check the taxis around the hotel?** She was seen leaving just as we were asking for her and was gone when we came out. She must have jumped into a cab immediately.'

The gendarme was certain, 'There weren't any taxis outside the hotel. It's foggy and freezing cold, they're all busy.'

Caporal Nicollet thought for a moment. The trip to the station and the airport had been fruitless, no one resembling the photograph he'd received from the top brass had been seen and there had been no response to the Tannoy announcements, though that didn't surprise him at all. He knew the background, a French woman with a long history of murder and thuggery, sought by Interpol for years without success. He wanted to be the one to catch her, for all the obvious reasons, including his candidature for promotion.

'And on the other side of the square,' he asked, '*François Bonivard*, beside the bus station?'

'*Pardon, Caporal*, I didn't think of it. I'll get over there now.'

After dropping off his passenger at the Hotel le Rive in

Nyon port, Raoul Deschamps had driven back on the lake road, so he could spend his ten-franc tip on a sandwich at his favourite bakery in Versoix. It was 2:45pm when he pulled up for business again alongside the English Church in *Rue François Bonivard*, there were no other cabs there.

An elderly couple were waiting, and he got out and opened the door for them. '*Temps glacial, eh*? Bloody cold weather,' the man said to him as they stepped into the warm interior. Deschamp put the heating up a little, '*Où allons nous?* Where are we going?'

He was about to pull away when a police car, with the siren blaring, pulled in front of him. '*Un instant*,' he said to his passengers and climbed out into the cold.

15:05, Nyon, Vaud, Switzerland
The diesel ferryboat, '*Valais*', was moored in front of the Hotel le Rive. It was a smaller vessel, which ran a ferry service during the winter months between Nyon and Yvoire, on the French side of the *Lac Léman*. It was mostly used by *Frontaliers*, French residents who worked in Switzerland. Esther had missed the 13:55 service. There was no one at the ferry company's kiosk by the landing-stage and by the time she'd bought her ticket at the tobacconist/newsstand opposite, the boat had sounded its hooter and pulled away. It was now just after 3pm, foggy and cold. She was sitting in a café on the square in front of the pier, nursing a coffee after her meal, pretending to read the local newspaper and waiting impatiently for the next departure at 15:55.

She struggled to keep calm, thinking about her escape route. Switzerland and France were both in the Schengen zone and she needed no ID to take the ferry across the lake to Yvoire. From there, she'd take a 50-minute taxi ride across the border, back into Switzerland, at St Gingolph, which had a direct train service to Milan, still in Schengen, about a four and a half hour ride. She'd spend the night in Italy, where no one would be looking for her, and she'd already booked a flight from Milan to Dubai tomorrow at 15:00.

In her handbag, along with her travel documents for Esther Bonnard and Rousseau, was a Belgian passport, in the name of Elodie Delacroix, given to her in 2016 by her Russian paymasters. She hadn't used it for a few years, worried that it might have been circulated, but she figured it would be a less risky ID in Milan airport than the others. She was confident that she could make her way to Dubai safely, after so many false starts, finally able to enjoy the fruits of her labour, all these years since Ray d'Almeida's murder. She checked the time again, just three quarters of an hour and she was safe.

Marbella, Spain

'I have an update, Jenny, Marius. AC Dewar has been informed by Geneva that they've tracked Esther Rousseau to a town called Nyon, just outside of Geneva. They don't have her yet, but they're getting very close.'

'That's my fault!' Coetzee swore. 'She must have left the hotel when the police were causing a riot at the reception desk.'

'Marius, I have bad news for you. **YOU'RE NOT PERFECT.**'

Both he and Espinoza burst into laughter at this most uncharacteristic jibe from Jenny.

'OK, fair comment. But who is?' he replied.

'What are we going to do about Jolidon and Christen?' she asked.

'We had a talk and decided they were more victims than villains. That woman has corrupted a lot of people, they were just the latest to fall for her charms.'

'And you decided to give them a second chance?'

Pedro said, 'Jenny, Christen told Marius that Esther was insisting on keeping the diamonds, so he and Jolidon have ended up with some valuables that no one can possibly identify or return to the rightful owners. Remember what happened to Ricardo's security box and to yours? There's no proof of who those items belonged to and no records available to even start looking for the owners. It would be a pointless exercise to try to bring them to justice, since there's nothing to prove that they have ever done anything illegal.

'Esther, on the other hand, is already wanted by Interpol, because she's a killer, a kidnapper, a thief and accomplice to a cyber-attack. She's the brains behind this whole conspiracy and she is the one who should pay the price of her villainy.'

'It's about time, Jenny,' Coetzee added.

'We have to consult Leticia and Patrice, maybe Javier too. This is too important to be decided by just us three. I'll get everyone on a call now.'

15:30pm, Near Morges, Vaud, Switzerland

The speed camera flashed as Brigadier Bruno Forestière of the *Lausanne Gendarmerie* drove past at 140km per hour near the turn-off for Aubonne. The traffic was fairly heavy, going more slowly than he liked in the misty light, and he swore regularly when cars in the outside lane were slow to get out of the way of his blaring siren.

With him was *Officier* Ernst Charles, a special interventions gendarme, and in the car following behind them were two more policemen. All of them were heavily armed and wearing flack jackets. Forestière looked at the dashboard clock, it was 15:30. 'We have to get a move on, it's been over an hour since that woman got to Nyon. Fucking red tape.'

He was referring to the argument about jurisdiction that had taken a half-hour to resolve. Although Esther Bonnard hadn't realised it, going to Nyon was the best thing she could have done. The town is in the canton of Vaud, not Geneva, and like everything in Switzerland, the police forces are organised on a cantonal level. When the Geneva Gendarmerie learned her whereabouts, they asked for permission to follow up their search and, hopefully, her apprehension. It was refused; Lausanne insisted on their cantonal priority and asked for the documentation leading to their intervention and her flight. It was only 15 minutes earlier that Forestière had been given the assignment and he'd grabbed his friend, Ernst, conscripted two gendarmes and two cars and set off in the foggy dusk for Nyon, normally a 30-minute drive.

Marbella, Spain

After Coetzee and Espinoza explained their reasoning for giving Esther's accomplices another chance, Patrice asked, 'You don't think either of them was involved in the fire at Ramseyer, Haldeman? Remember, Gilles Simenon was killed in that fire. It may not be murder, but it's definitely manslaughter.'

Coetzee said, 'For what it's worth, Patrice, Christen told me he was in Zurich when the fire occurred and I believe him, he's a lousy liar, especially when he's drunk. He also told me that when he got back the next day, Jolidon was in a state of shock. He was desperately trying to justify badgering Simenon to finish the audit and had no idea he'd decided to do it at night. Christen said he'd never seen him so upset.'

'I don't think Jolidon is clever enough to make an explosion and a fire like that. He'd probably blow himself up. It must have been some kind of a technical specialist, probably Esther hired him, and the others didn't know.'

'Good point, Leticia. There's also the possibility that it was simply an accident. That's what the inquest decided, so maybe we shouldn't try to second guess it.'

'Listen guys. I don't know these people like you do, so I'll go with whatever you decide,' Javier said. 'But it's now fairly irrelevant. Jolidon and Christen are gone and we don't know where, so it's pointless wasting time on something we can do nothing about. Marius says Esther's kept the diamonds, so they've got some unclaimed valuables belonging to nobody knows who, and we can't do anything about that either; even if we had them, we couldn't. And that's Edificio's fault, not theirs. The moment they agreed to hand over those boxes, the whole possibility of repatriation of the valuables was lost. My opinion is we've done everything we could to bust up their plan and it's worked. It's Interpol's job now to catch Esther Bonnard for good and all and I think we should just turn the page.'

'And what about Charlie's diamonds?'

Jenny intervened, 'Marius, the day we came up with this plan, Leticia and I knew that it was most likely that the diamonds would be lost, and we accepted that. She talked to Patrice and he agreed, it would be a bad omen for Emilio to ever inherit them. Those diamonds have cost more lives and misery than we could have thought possible. As for me, I would be happy if I never heard those words again, *African Diamonds*. Is that right, Leticia?'

'Jenny's right, Patrice and I never want to hear about them again. Now, the only thing that counts is to find Esther Bonnard and get her put in jail for a very long time.'

'*Bueno*, I think it's agreed, *gracias* everyone.' Pedro Espinoza breathed a sigh of relief. 'Now, we know that the police have placed her in Nyon, near Geneva. As soon as I have more news, I'll update everyone.'

15:52pm, Nyon, Vaud, Switzerland

'Have you seen this woman?' Brigadier Forestière showed Esther Bonnard's photograph to the receptionist at the Hotel le Rive. She looked at it closely and shook her head, '*Non.*'

He and *Officier* Charles were walking back to their car in the parking next to the hotel, when one of the gendarmes called to him from the doorway of a café in the square. They ran across the road, 'What is it?'

'This waiter says she was here for over an hour. Had a meal and sat with a coffee for a while. She left five minutes ago.'

Just then, they heard the hoot of the steamer as it pulled away from the pier. Charles looked around at the ferry departing into the mist. '*Merde*, maybe that's her plan. Hang on.' He went into the newsstand next door, showed the photo to the proprietor and came running out. 'She bought a ticket two hours ago. She's on that fucking ferryboat for Yvoire!'

SEVENTY

Esther had been waiting in the freezing fog at the end of the ferry pier when she saw the police cars arriving in the car park next to the hotel, their sirens blaring. There was only a half-dozen passengers and she showed her ticket and pulled her case quickly onto the vessel, into the main cabin, in the warm. She sat on the starboard side, facing away from the landing. *How the hell did they find me?* She had shared her plan with no one; even if it had been Jolidon and Christen who had ratted on her, they had no idea where she was headed. And it was a one in a million chance that they could have found the cab driver who'd driven her, he'd have been busy picking up passengers all over Geneva on such a freezing day.

It doesn't matter anyway, she told herself. *They've found me and now I have to work out what to do about it.* Esther knew this was the narrowest point of the lake, only 4 km separated the two countries and the border was at 2km from each shore. The transit time was just 20 minutes, so she would exit Switzerland and enter French territory after 10 minutes. She checked the time, 5 minutes gone, five to go, then they would be arguing about who had jurisdiction. She didn't know it, but that was the only reason she was on the ferry.

4:00pm, Nyon, Vaud, Switzerland

'*Oui, mon Commandant*, she's heading to Yvoire and they're about a kilometre out.'

'She's a French citizen, so we can't let her get into their territorial waters, it'll be a slanging match and she'll be the only winner. I know one of the CGN Directors here in Lausanne, Pierre Longireau, my golfing partner. I'll call him now.'

Forestière waited impatiently at the landing, watching the clock tick away the minutes. It was 16:04 when his mobile rang, '*Oui, mon Commandant?*'

'Longireau called the captain and told him to stay in Swiss waters. He explained about this Bonnard woman and that he's not to intervene, she's obviously a dangerous criminal and we don't know if she's armed. He's going to circle until we can get a boat alongside, there's a patrol boat arriving for you any minute. You'll have to board the *Valais* and apprehend her, you've got *Officier Charles* and a couple of men, plus there's another sailor on the ferry.'

'What about the other passengers?'

'We don't want to start a panic, so the captain will say they have engine trouble and the mechanic is looking at it to avoid a problem when they go into port. I've sent the photograph of the woman so the captain can discreetly identify her and keep an eye out for any dangerous moves she might make. It's up to you now.'

4:04pm, Lac Léman, Switzerland, en route for Yvoire, France

Esther Bonnard felt the vessel lose speed when the captain turned to port to start his circling. On the misty horizon she saw the faint lights of the French shore move round to the starboard side, then slip gradually behind her.

An announcement came over the tannoy: 'Ladies and gentlemen, we have encountered a minor problem with our engines. This is not serious, but to avoid any complications when we arrive at our destination, Yvoire, our engineers are resolving it immediately. This will take only a few minutes. Thank you for your understanding.'

Esther knew exactly what was happening. She wheeled her case out onto the port deck to see at first hand; in the foggy dusk, Nyon seemed so far away. The headlights of a motorboat were heading towards the ferry, it was going quite slowly. The air from the lake was intensely cold and the mist exacerbated the chill factor. Pulling her coat tightly to her, she walked around the deck to the starboard side of the ship; there was no one there, she was alone outside the cabin. She could hear no sounds of work from the engine room, but she didn't expect to. *It's just an excuse to stay in Swiss waters, another excuse to take Ray's diamonds away from me.* She looked again towards the lights of Yvoire, it seemed closer than Nyon. *Just a few minutes more, that's all I needed. I could swim there if the water wasn't freezing.*

She remembered her last trip on the lake, when she had sold Claude Jolidon on her brilliant scheme. *That was just over a year ago, and I made over $10 million in that time. Who said Esther Bonnard was a failure? And I got Ray's diamonds back for him. If he's watching, he must be proud of me.*

Now she could hear the sound of the motorboat on the port side of the ferry, becoming louder until it died to a murmur. Then she heard voices, several of them. *They've come on board the ferry. All this pantomime, is it for*

Esther Bonnard; or is it just for Ray's diamonds?

A voice called out, 'Mme Bonnard, please come around the deck slowly and quietly. There are innocent passengers on board and we want to avoid any trouble.'

She heaved her case up and held it on the barrier above the deck. *Jenny Bishop will never get Raymundo's diamonds. He promised them to me and that's where they'll stay, with me. They're not her diamonds. They're mine.*

Esther Bonnard/Rousseau climbed onto the barrier, wrapped her arms around her case and fell overboard into the icy water.

At over 300m, *Lac Léman* is one of the deepest freshwater lakes in Europe; the River Rhône runs through it from east to west. Esther's body was found several days later, near the *Pont de la Machine*, the Machine Bridge, in Geneva, just a few hundred metres from the *Banque de Crédit Vaudoise*, where the diamonds had been stored in her security box. Her suitcase was never recovered. Not that anyone was looking for it; although Jenny and her friends assumed that the diamonds had disappeared with her, they made no mention of them when they were questioned. As Jenny had said, '*I would be happy if I never heard those words again, AFRICAN DIAMONDS.*'

SEVENTY-ONE

Tuesday, December 24th, 2019
Marbella, Spain

'**Did you receive the cutting from Franz?**' Jenny was speaking on WhatsApp to her 'team'.

'I thought it was him, from the photographs, but I said nothing, because it didn't make any sense to me.'

'It certainly explains a lot of things, and maybe we judged Esther Bonnard too harshly.'

'In this particular instance, I agree, Patrice,' Espinoza said, 'but she was a killer, just the same; believe me, I'm speaking from experience.'

'I still can't understand why he did it, and how he disguised it as an accident.'

'Sounds like he was a brilliant, very mixed-up guy. I wonder what will happen to him,' Coetzee said.

'Manslaughter, I'd imagine. But there's nothing we can do, he's confessed and that's all there is to it.'

'OK, enough of that,' Jenny said. 'We've all been through a tough time and it's Christmas tomorrow, so let's forget all these horrible events and think of our families and friends. Leticia, Patrice and I've got a glass of champagne in our hands and we send our love and best wishes to you all for a peaceful and happy holiday season. Merry Christmas everyone.'

When Leticia, Patrice and their children had left, Jenny checked that Ellen and Lily were asleep and sat with her champagne in front of the fire. Chester came to put his head on her knee and she stroked him absent-mindedly. She picked up the printout of Franz Stenmark's cutting from the *Tages-Anzeiger* to which he'd appended a translation in English. It read:

Son of Swiss Benefactor arrested for breaking and entering confesses to arson.

A spokesman for Zurich police force announced today that Patrick Haldeman, son of Dr Dietrich Haldeman, the late Geneva businessman and philanthropist, has been arrested on charges of breaking into an apartment in Badenerstrasse, Zurich. He was apprehended after a neighbour alerted the police. During his interrogation, Haldeman confessed to causing the explosion and fire which destroyed the Ramseyer, Haldeman security building in Pâquis, Geneva, in April this year, resulting in the death of a Swiss employee, Gilles Simenon.

Haldeman pleaded guilty to arson and manslaughter, but not murder. According to the police report, he stated that, 'He wanted to get rid of the monument to his father's success and achievements and his own incompetence and failure. He had no knowledge of Simenon's presence in the building at night and greatly regretted his death.'

The reasons for the break-in at Badenerstrasse are not known at this time. However, the police also disclosed that a large number of valuable items were found on the premises. Further information will be released as the investigation continues.

This won't bring Gilles back, she thought sadly, *but I hope it might give Marie some closure. I must call her after the holidays, see how she is.*

Wednesday, December 25th, 2019
Djerba, Tunisia

'*Santé et Joyeux Noël*, Claude.' René Christen, one-time Swiss *huissier juridique*, now unemployed beach bum, clinked his glass against the Frenchman's.

'Happy Christmas, René. First time I've ever celebrated it on a beach in 20 degree heat.'

'Better get used to it, we could be here for quite a while.'

'Suits me. I spent enough time freezing to death in Zurich.'

January, 2020
Delmas, Mpumalanga

'I received some news today, Marius.'

'Something good, I hope?'

'I've been nominated for the *Taco Kuiper* award for investigative journalism again.'

He kissed her. 'That's fantastic, Karen, congratulations. Thirteen years since your last nomination. Older but wiser, you're sure to win it this time around.'

Marbella, Spain

Jenny had cried a lot over the last few days. Thinking of the loss of her husband, Ron, his mother, Ellen, and father, Charlie, the genius who had created the Angolan Clan, only to lose his partners, Laurent, Nick and Alberto, then his own life at the hands of Ray d'Almeida. More deaths had followed, Adam, Gloria and other unknown victims of his and Esther Rousseau's manic obsession to steal the fortune created by the aftermath of the Portuguese revolution.

Ellen was in bed and Jenny was sitting in her favourite chair with Chester at her feet. She suddenly found herself shedding tears for Esther, who had wasted her life in her never-ending quest to avenge Ray d'Almeida's death, only to suffer her dreadful fate in the *Lac Léman*.

Needing to hear a friendly voice, she called Pedro Espinoza. 'What was that all about, Pedro?'

He was quiet for a moment. 'Can I answer you as a friend, not an ex-policeman?'

'You're not just a friend, you've become a part of my family. Be as honest as you like.'

Espinoza said, 'You know, I've never had money. Even when I was a high-flying DI, Soledad and I struggled and then my work took over and it was a while before we found a better solution. The solution was not to have more money, because after my retirement, I had less work, which was good, but we had less money, which could have been bad. But you know what, Jenny? It wasn't and it isn't; we are poorer, but happier than we have ever been.

'So, I think the answer to your question is that money doesn't always help your life or relationships, but it can hurt or destroy them, like it did Patrick Haldeman's. Just think, Jenny; you became a target, more than once, because you are wealthy. My cousin, Ricardo was destroyed because he had saved enough for a modest retirement, and Esther and d'Almeida lost their lives because they shared the same all-consuming passions; vengeance and money. I think it speaks for itself.'

Jenny remembered her first meeting in Malaga with

Chief Inspector Espinoza, as he was then, after the deaths of her husband and father-in-law. He had been convinced there was a common motive, and she didn't want to believe it. Later, when she discovered the size of her inheritance from Charlie, her reaction had been; *It can't be right to come into all that money without earning it. Something is sure to go wrong. There's just too much involved.* Within two weeks, both of them were proven correct. Her newly acquired wealth was a magnet, and murderers and thieves were drawn to it like moths to a flame.

'You're right, Pedro,' she said. 'It's time I did something about it, then I won't need to teach it to Ellen when she's older. You've given me a wonderful idea, thank you. Please give my love to Soledad and all your family. Goodnight, dear friend.'

The next morning, Jenny called Patrice at the bank. 'I've decided to set up a Bishop Family Charitable Foundation. I'm going to endow it with half of my wealth. I'd like you to become a Trustee with me and help in getting the structure organised. There'll be a lot to do, setting it up, finding other prominent trustees and skilled employees and, of course, compiling a list of needy and worthy causes and charities we can help to support. Will you help me?'

'Jenny, that's a wonderful idea. I'm flattered that you've asked me and of course I'd be proud to help in such a generous, humanitarian act of kindness. I'm sure that Leticia will, also. What kind of causes do you have in mind?'

'Let's start the list with: Less fortunate people who don't take up a career in murder and robbery for a living.'

THE END

Christopher Lowery is a 'Geordie', born in the northeast of England, who graduated in finance and economics after reluctantly giving up career choices in professional golf and rock & roll. He is a real estate and telecoms entrepreneur and inventor and has created several successful companies around the world, including Interoute and Wyless Group. Triple Jeopardy is the follow-up to the African Diamonds Trilogy, answering many readers' question; 'What happened to the diamonds?'

The story draws on his wife, Marjorie's, experience in the Geneva auction business and his own knowledge of banking and international financial markets. Chris also writes poetry, children's books and songs. He and Marjorie live between London, Geneva and Marbella. Their daughter, Kerry-Jane, a writer/photographer, lives in London.

CHRISTOPHER LOWERY

THE
ANGOLAN
CLAN

CHRISTOPHER LOWERY

THE
RWANDAN
HOSTAGE

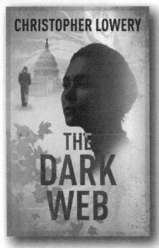

CHRISTOPHER LOWERY

THE
DARK
WEB

Have you discovered the thrilling African Diamonds trilogy from author Christopher Lowery?

The Angolan Clan takes the reader on a heart-stopping roller coaster ride, from past to present and back again. It is a deadly intercontinental treasure hunt laced with secrets, deceit and murder. The prize is a fortune in Angolan diamonds...or death at the hands of a pathological killer. The perfect read for fans of Frederick Forsyth, Wilbur Smith, Gerald Seymour and Clive Cussler.

Set against a European-African backdrop, the fast-paced plot twists and turns in a gripping series of events and action. The Rwandan Hostage is a compelling international mystery that will enthral all thriller fans, in the best traditions of Gerald Seymour, Frederick Forsyth and Richard North Patterson.

Christopher Lowery delivers a gripping final chapter in the bestselling African Diamonds trilogy, with a thriller that is powerfully resonant of today's global dangers, hidden behind the ever-changing technological landscape.

AVAILABLE FROM AMAZON AND ALL GOOD BOOKSHOPS

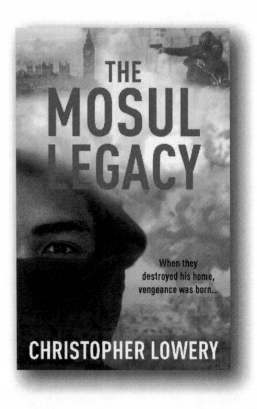

'The Mosul Legacy is a poignant read that takes you behind today's headlines about terrorism and the refugee crisis and gives them a human face like you've never seen before. Although fiction based around facts, Lowery's novel is as emotionally moving as it is thrilling. You will not be able to put it down.'

Louise Fligman, CUB Magazine

ACKNOWLEDGMENTS:

My wife, Marjorie, daughter, Kerry-Jane Lowery and nephew Nick Street, for their usual dedication in reading, correcting, rejecting and influencing the final versions of my stories. Also to my publisher, Matthew Smith, who somehow still manages to sell my books.

Urbane Publications is dedicated to developing
new author voices, and publishing fiction and non-fiction
that challenges, thrills and fascinates.

From page-turning novels to innovative reference books,
our goal is to publish what
YOU want to read.

Find out more at

urbanepublications.com